THE WEST WIND

The Four Winds

ALEXANDRIA WARWICK

SAGA PRESS

LONDON SYDNEY **NEW YORK** TORONTO NEW DELHI

SAGA PRESS
AN IMPRINT OF SIMON & SCHUSTER, LLC

1230 AVENUE OF THE AMERICAS, NEW YORK, NEW YORK 10020

First Saga Press trade paperback edition November 2024

SAGA PRESS and colophon are trademarks of Simon & Schuster, LLC

Simon & Schuster: Celebrating 100 Years of Publishing in 2024

For information about special discounts for bulk purchases, please contact Simon & Schuster Special Sales at 1-866-506-1949 or business@simonandschuster.com.

The Simon & Schuster Speakers Bureau can bring authors to your live event. For more information or to book an event, contact the Simon & Schuster Speakers Bureau at 1-866-248-3049 or visit our website at www.simonspeakers.com.

Map by Robert Lazzaretti

Manufactured in the United States of America

1   3   5   7   9   10   8   6   4   2

Library of Congress Cataloging-in-Publication Data is available.

ISBN 978-1-6680-6520-4
ISBN 978-1-6680-6521-1 (ebook)

For the frightened and the fearless

PART 1

THE PIOUS

1

A MAN LIES PRONE ON THE GROUND AT MY FEET, AND IF I AM NOT mistaken, he is dead.

Dead, or close to it. His back is still. There is no rise and fall, no air moving within the lungs. A mess of filthy, gold-streaked hair encrusts the curve of his skull, insects slithering among the tightly coiled curls.

Setting aside my basket of foraged pearl blossom, I step closer. A gust rattles the ancient wood where the mountain stands alone. Carterhaugh, this forested expanse of moss and fern, is so dense that as soon as the wind dies, the world quiets. Sound does not travel far here. No birdsong. Not even screams.

I nudge his leg with the toe of my boot. No response. He has obviously strayed from the trail—his last mistake. If he is dead, the abbey must be informed. At the very least, he will receive a proper burial.

I kneel. The earth, moist and spongy from frequent rain, softens beneath my weight. Quickly, I don my thin leather gloves, and only then do I reach forward to touch his face.

Warm. Despite the leather barrier, the heat of his skin bleeds through.

With a great heave, I roll the man onto his back. My gasp slips free as he twitches once, then falls limp. I was mistaken. The man is not dead.

Two blackened eyes bulge grotesquely above a horribly broken nose. Chapped lips surround a glint of white teeth. Then there is his sun-kissed skin, barely discernible beneath the bruising. Dried blood clots along his hairline.

I perch on my heels with a frown. The reek of smoke clings to my dress, reminding me of the blades awaiting tempering in the forge.

His attire, similar to his battered face, has clearly seen better days. A heavy green cloak fans out beneath his mud-spattered tunic. Trousers, torn at the knee, encase a pair of strong legs ending in worn, knee-high boots.

"Judge what you know," I murmur to myself. "Not what you perceive."

I do not know this man's story. He could be a traveler. Maybe the darkness of Carterhaugh disoriented him and he lost his way to Thornbrook? Kilkare lies only nine miles southwest of here—half a day's journey by wagon. But his injuries suggest that someone dumped his body and left him for dead. Where does this man hail from? More importantly, who hurt him, and why?

The air shimmers with golden sound. Bells, echoing off the mountain peak. Seven tolls mark the sacred hour, and I am already late, having wandered too far to collect the medicinal herb.

Another glance at the man's motionless form. My hands curl into fists as the echoes falter, then fade. Who can say whether this man encountered the fair folk? It is not uncommon to hear of mortals dragged beneath the earth, held captive by those who dwell in Under. Indeed, the Abbess of Thornbrook herself was once trapped in the realm below, if the stories are true. But even if I wanted to help him, I cannot. No matter how often Mother Mabel insists that Thornbrook's doors remain open for those in need, only women may enter the abbey.

I rise, belly cold with the understanding that my departure will leave this man alone, vulnerable. But it must be done.

Snatching my basket, I fly across the sloped earth, navigating the winding footpath north. A break in the trees ahead reveals the impressive church spire overlooking the abbey's moss-eaten walls, which enclose its sprawling grounds.

Thornbrook is a climbing triumph of pale stone. According to the Text, the Father's most devout acolytes built this structure themselves, dragging the massive stone up the mountain, stacking it three stories high. Ferns cloak its base and crawl through cracks in the edifice.

The gatehouse offers two methods of entry: a wide archway for carts and horses, and a narrow doorway for those traveling on foot, both barricaded as a precaution against the fair folk. I wave to the porter, and she promptly lifts the iron gate.

The open-aired cloister comes into view as I dash across the grassy yard toward the dormitory, climbing the staircase to the third floor. Once inside my bedroom, I exchange my gray, everyday dress for my alb—the long white robe worn during Mass—and the cincture, which wraps my thick waist, secured by a single knot. Those who have taken their final vows tie the slender white cord into three knots. My time, however, has not yet come.

Sweat coats my skin by the time I reach the church, where the Daughters of Thornbrook have congregated, a sea of white interrupted by the acolytes' ruby stoles.

Before entering the worship space, I wash my hands in the lavabo near the doorway. Once purified, I insert myself at the back of the church, sliding into a pew next to a fellow novitiate. She does not acknowledge me. Her attention remains fixated on the altar, white marble shrouded in scarlet cloth. Three everlasting candles—Father, Son, and Holy Ghost—burn atop it.

At the front of the room, Mother Mabel climbs the steps to the chancel, where the choir sits. She continues to the presbytery before turning to face us, hands lifted, palms up. Directly behind the altar, a window of green glass pours verdant light onto the draped marble and its fixings.

As one, we bow our heads.

"Eternal Father, our hearts are open. Guide us in these coming months as we navigate the approaching tithe." Palms pressed together, I lift my hands to my forehead, as does the rest of the congregation. Mother Mabel's prayer slides into a lull. My thoughts begin to drift.

It would make perfect sense for the man to have been attacked. Indeed, the fair folk have their reasons. Confined to those cramped tunnels and lightless caves, barred from entering any mortal town, they are prohibited from governing or holding council, despite having settled in Carterhaugh centuries before we mortals drove them belowground. But the wood, with its blanketing shadows and concealing nature, still draws many of the fair folk out into the open.

As for the man … I should not be thinking of him. This is the Father's house, its walls and doors a rare sanctuary. What would He think, knowing I held space for a man other than Him? With some effort, I shove my treacherous thoughts aside, lift my face toward the heavenly Eternal Lands. Our Father, the maker of two realms. Carterhaugh: idyllic, abundant, unspoiled. And Under: a rotting seed beneath the earth.

"Let us recite the Seven Decrees," Mother Mabel says, her voice succumbing to its own echo.

Dutifully, we repeat what is spoken.

"Thou shalt not kill. Thou shalt not steal. Thou shalt not covet, nor disrespect thy mother or thy father. Thou shalt not forsake thy God. Thou shalt remember the Holy Day." And the last: "Thou shalt not lie."

"In weaving these decrees through the very fabric of our lives, may we uphold our vows," Mother Mabel continues. "May we act, always, with honor and rectitude."

I clench my sweaty hands. *Honor.* What honor is there in abandoning a man to the forest, prey for whatever insidious creatures pass?

"May we abide devotedly by the faith. May we keep no secrets from the Father."

My eyes snap open as the congregation stirs.

"And," Mother Mabel intones, her gaze holding mine, "may we never lust for man's flesh."

2

LIFTING MY ARM, I SLAM THE HAMMER ONTO THE SMOLDERING metal. The discordant ring expands, then expires, crushed into silence beneath the sweltering heat of the forge.

Another strike. Back and shoulders tighten against the rising sting of exertion, but this, too, is familiar. Molten iron, shaped and cooled. The dagger, once complete, will be added to the rest awaiting transfer into Under. Though the tithe is months away, preparations have already begun.

Down falls the hammer. The work is never done. Sweat plasters long, red strands of hair to my neck and forehead. My cheeks flame scarlet—an unfortunate side effect of milk-pale skin.

While I work, I think of Carterhaugh. I think of the fair folk and their penchant for violence. An entire day has passed since I stumbled across that man in the wood. I told myself I would forget him, yet my thoughts reach for his battered face, the questions that plague me.

When the blade loses color, I return to the great slab of stone where the fire burns and shove the weapon into the smoking coals. I work the bellows surely. The contraption contracts, air punching outward, the coals flaring in response.

Hammer, reheat, hammer, reheat. The pattern will repeat itself until the dagger is properly profiled. Gripping the tang with my heavy tongs, I beat the metal against the face of the anvil. A chip flakes off the blade's edge, singeing the front of my cowhide apron. After another hour of hammering, I quench the dagger in a bucket of water. A spitting hiss seethes the air as the iron hardens, its structure stabilizing. I examine the blade from all angles. Its silvery sheen brightens like a star, and satisfaction warms me.

While the weapon cools on the table, I refocus on my surroundings. Night has fallen beyond the small, darkened doorway.

Dampness springs to my palms, though the heat has nothing to do with it. Evening Mass finished an hour ago, but I often return to the forge following service to work in the more favorable temperatures, with Mother Mabel's permission. It's silly, this fear of the darkness. My lantern provides more than enough light. I tell myself it is enough.

After untying my apron, I hang it on a hook near the doorway, then toss my leather toolbelt onto the table with a clatter. Lastly, extinguishing the fire. I stir the coals, watch the cooler air lick their searing edges until they begin to darken. Within minutes, the fire is out.

Outside, I set my lantern on the ground and plant my feet. In the shadow of the forge, I draw my dagger and begin to practice a short round of exercises. I stab and duck, striking high, driving low. Although my old swordsmithing mentor taught me the basics, it is Mother Mabel who demands that I whet my knife-fighting skills as I would a blade. Not many know she is an accomplished swordswoman.

Drenched in sweat, blood humming eagerly, I sheath my dagger and return to the main complex, hurrying toward its distant glow. The bathing chamber is empty at this hour, allowing me the rare opportunity to bathe in peace, without any snide comments about how I take up too much room.

I soak in the tub, sloughing the soot and grit from my body, before returning to the dormitory, my wet hair plaited, cool cotton whispering against my skin. The bell tolls the ninth hour—curfew.

The moment I enter my bedroom, I light the candle on my bedside table. Amber light warms the plaster walls. Like every dormitory in Thornbrook, mine is sparse. Very few personal possessions. The Text lies open on my desk, along with my journal.

All novitiates must share a room, but because I'm the bladesmith, coming and going at odd hours, I sleep alone in the eastern tower at the end of the hall. My window offers a view of the highlands to the north, and the strait—a dark line ruffled by white waves, twenty miles eastward—which separates Carterhaugh from a realm known as the Gray.

Text and journal in hand, I climb into bed and open my journal to the most recent entry, an entire page inked with last night's musings.

I do not know where this man has come from, but I wonder.

I thumb the corner of the page pensively, then close the slim, leatherbound book. I've nothing more to add. The man remains a mystery.

Setting aside my journal, I complete my nightly prayers, ending with a mumbled, "Amen." That leaves the Text. Seven sections comprise the complete liturgy: the Book of Fate, the Book of Night, the Book of Grief, the Book of Truth, the Book of Origin, the Book of Change, the Book of Power. These chapters are both history and moral compass, penned by the first of the Father's followers: the bedrock upon which our faith is built.

Turning to the Book of Fate, I pick up where I left off yesterday. But the script may as well be freshly inked for how it blurs before me. I shut my eyes, think of the man lying in the wood, so still. His horribly disfigured face stamped into my mind.

My nature is not impulsive in the slightest. I am not the river's current, cutting pathways into earth. I am the rock within the stream. The man is likely gone, dragged off by the beasts of Under, where only the truly insidious dare dwell, and yet—

My eyes snap open. The dark cuts shapes into the ceiling.

Easing onto my side, I stare at the flutter of candle flame. Here, safety. A small brightness. Yet sweat stings beneath my arms, as though my body has already sensed my mind's intention. Night curtains Carterhaugh. These woods are not safe. But if I were to carry my lantern, surely that would be enough to guide me?

Cursing my soft heart, I toss off the blankets and throw on my cloak, my lantern gripped tightly in hand. As long as I return before dawn, Mother Mabel will be none the wiser.

I move with haste, tucking myself into the shadows along the pillar-lined cloister. By some miracle, I manage to navigate the corridors unseen, slipping wraith-like onto the outer grounds.

Darkness coats the cobblestoned courtyard and its ring of trees. The herbarium sits on the other side of an open gate to my left; tucked inside is a small shed whose door swings open to reveal pails, gardening tools, and a cart to carry heavy burdens. To muffle the creak of the wheels, I oil the axles of the cart, then toss a blanket into the back. Thankfully, I reach the gatehouse without incident.

Since Thornbrook hasn't the funds to hire a night watch, I lift the gate with painstaking slowness. The crank shrieks so loudly I'm certain the townsfolk of Kilkare will hear it. I glance over my shoulder as a wave of cold pebbles my skin.

Nothing. Neither movement nor sound. Fear of discovery hastens me. As soon as the opening is large enough, I haul the cart through and lower the gate behind me. The iron barricade is all that stands between Thornbrook and the fair folk.

It's a slow journey through the dark. Moonlight brightens the earth's swells in silver, for which I'm grateful. The cart bounces and clatters onward, four wheels rolling sloppily over the uneven terrain.

I tread cautiously, for the fair folk revel in their nightly schemes. Not much farther. I lift my lantern high, let its orange light brighten the surrounding area. If memory serves me correctly, it is here I ventured off the path to collect pearl blossom—

And there lies the man.

He is exactly where I left him, spread-eagled in the dirt. It is strange. He seems to blend in with the soil, the ferns curling over his torso in a disconcerting impression of affection. I'm relieved by the rise and fall of his chest.

After setting down my lantern, I tug on my gloves and arrange his arms against his sides. My waist is thrice the size of his, my arms broad, heavy with muscle. Thus, it takes little effort to lift him into the cart. I cover him with the blanket for warmth.

The return trip takes an age. With a misaligned wheel, the cart veers crookedly over the ground, and the burn of exertion hooks talons into my upper thighs. Yet I push onward up the mountain, up and up and up. The ground levels off, then climbs once more as the east lightens. Soon, color will run cracks through the world.

By the time I reach the crumbling abbey walls, sweat pools beneath my arms. With dawn so near, it would be foolish to haul the cart back onto the grounds. I discard it outside the entrance, along with the lantern, heave the man across my shoulders, and enter Thornbrook via the gatehouse.

A worn footpath rounds the back of the forge where the smoky air lingers. After a few paces, I stop to adjust the man's weight. Despite the filth coating his garb, a sweet scent, like moss and sunshine, drifts from his skin. I cannot hide him here, for Mother Mabel often drops by unannounced. My options are limited: the infirmary, or my dormitory. Ideally, I would take him to the infirmary, but with men barred from the abbey, I fear the physician would cast him out to the elements despite his injuries. And I cannot abandon him. This I know. Only my room will provide sanctuary.

My ears strain for sound as I pass through the herbarium, skirting the raised beds of vegetables and medicinal herbs before entering the cloister. Voices drift like a muffled fog through the pillars of stone. Who would be up this late? Curfew was hours ago.

I slow as I turn a corner. A dark, quiet passage, brightened by islands of flickering light. Moments later, a silhouette, tall and rigid, materializes at the end of the hall.

My blood turns to ice.

I dare not stir, though my muscles strain beneath the man's weight. The distance is too great to determine if Mother Mabel looks this way, but something has caught her eye. As the twinge in my lower back lights to a brushfire, a whimper slips out, cracking the silence of the warm evening.

Her head swings in my direction. Shadow engulfs her form save the sheen of her eyes, the glint of her gold, serpentine necklace.

"Mother Mabel," someone calls.

She startles, whirls toward dark-eyed Fiona, one of the novitiates. "My dear. What are you doing up at this hour?" Together, they stride in the opposite direction, vanishing through the doors leading to the church.

Silent as the dead, I climb the narrow dormitory staircase. I'm panting by the time I reach my bedroom. The door opens soundlessly, then shuts, a muffled click as I engage the lock.

My knees immediately liquify, and the man slides face down onto my cot seconds before I sink to the floor.

That was far too close.

To touch a man's flesh is a grave sin. To house a man, unchaperoned, in one's room? The thought of repercussions tightens my airway. We've all heard the gossip: women who had given themselves to faith, suddenly banished out into the cold, their vows broken.

No home.

No warmth.

No purpose.

No god.

But—the man.

Pushing to my feet, I turn to inspect my guest by the glow of the still-burning lamp. The rip in his tunic reveals a smooth, muscled chest covered in sparse brown hair. I push the fabric aside, revealing yet more wounds. A beating? If so, this is not the work of the fair folk. Those who dwell in Under enjoy their violence. It is a game to them. The objective is never to end, but to prolong, always. Why snap when you can bend and tear and wrench?

I straighten the man's legs, which are so long they hang off the edge of my cot. Then I rummage through the chest at the foot of my bed, searching among my few worldly possessions. For I had another life before this one, long ago.

A small, woven basket holds a plethora of poultices and balms— the work of my mother. Unscrewing the top off a glass bottle, I pour a small amount of ointment into my gloved palm, coating the leather to a high shine.

I begin with the worst of the bruising—the underside of his jaw. As the swelling on the man's face begins to recede, I pluck leaves and twigs from his hair, brush the curls from his face. Fringed lashes rest upon lightly freckled cheekbones. The color of his eyes remains hidden from me.

And then, inevitably, the tolling of the bell: dawn.

Followed by a knock at the door.

3

THE DOORKNOB RATTLES. "BRIELLE!" A BARKED COMMAND.
My pulse scatters, and I leap halfway across the room before remembering the door is securely fastened.

"Mother Mabel wants to speak with you." Another rattle. The door-frame groans in protest. "Why is the door locked?"

I look to the door, the bed, the window. Blood throbs in my ears. It branches down my limbs in a paralyzing cold. Two, three, four heart-beats later, I'm still rooted to the spot.

All Daughters of Thornbrook receive keys to their bedrooms when admitted as novitiates, though most rarely utilize them. Only twice in ten years have I used mine. This is the second occurrence.

"I'm changing," I croak. Footsteps echo through the corridors as everyone heads to the church.

A scoff through the door. "I suppose you *would* need a locked door for that. Kind of you to consider others."

The insult is but a distant nuisance. What am I supposed to do with the man on my bed? And why have I been summoned prior to service? Is it possible Mother Mabel spotted me last night in the cloister?

My hands shake as I peel the sweaty cotton from my body and don a clean dress, fumbling with the buttons stamped down its front. Through my window, the sleeping world has warmed to violet, and gold rims the curve of the earth.

"While I'm still young, Brielle."

I flinch despite the barrier separating us. But she cannot hurt me if I keep it hidden. As for my unexpected guest, I toss a blanket over him—the best I can do for now. Whatever follows, I leave it in the Father's hands.

I unlock the door to reveal a small-boned woman outfitted in the same gray, long-sleeved dress that all Daughters of Thornbrook wear, a clean alb tossed over one arm. Her name is Harper, and she is a woman of three temperaments: cross, irate, and hellish.

The first two, she reserves for her closest friend, Isobel. The last, she reserves only for me.

Her lip curls. "You look like a cow."

"At least I don't have the brains of one."

Harper blinks at the unexpected rebuttal. "Excuse me?" She draws herself higher, though the top of her head barely reaches my nose.

Before Harper can peer into my room, I grab my robe from its hook, snap the door shut, and lock it.

Two eyes the color of lake water narrow at the sight. "Something to hide?" she murmurs, blocking my way forward.

"I have the right to privacy," I mutter. "Please excuse me."

She doesn't move.

It takes a heroic effort not to give ground. I glance around the corridor. The novitiates have gone, and we stand alone.

"Did Mother Mabel request my presence or not?" If so, then I must not delay. Tardiness is grounds for punishment.

Harper's mouth curls in a half-smile. Her long, shining black hair is secured in a plait down her back. "You are a mindless dog, Brielle. It is not becoming of you." She shakes her head in vicious amusement. "Worry not. Mother Mabel isn't expecting you. Why, she wouldn't care to call on you anyway."

Shame flushes my pale skin. If I am not a cow, then I am a dog, or a pig, or a rat, or some other useless creature. Unsurprisingly, this is merely a visit to antagonize me.

I stand there, quietly seething, until Harper flounces down the hall. With her disappearance, my heart slows its pace. The bell clangs thrice: once for the Father, once for the Son, once for the Holy Ghost. And I am officially late for service.

Thornbrook is a vast complex anchored by a cloister, each open-aired passage facing one of the four cardinal directions. The church, the largest of the buildings, sits north of the cloister—the heartbeat of a devout life. Tucked against the cloister's eastern edge is the dormitory, with the lavatory and bathhouse attached to the end of the oblong edifice. The refectory sits south of the cloister. It is there the Daughters of Thornbrook gather for meals.

Following Mass, we head for breakfast. The cool darkness of the refectory welcomes me as I sidle through the entrance behind my peers. Simple wooden tables and long benches line the stone hall, enough to comfortably seat one hundred. Open windows line the eastern wall, welcoming the heavy, loam-scented breeze.

The hall is so quiet nothing can be heard beyond the padding of slippered feet. Grabbing a bowl, I plop a spoonful of porridge from the pot. My stomach cramps unpleasantly. Most mornings I'm not hungry, but I force myself to eat, knowing the next meal won't be until noon, after an entire morning of hard labor.

Meals are a simple affair. There is always bread, always wine, always vegetables and fruits, rarely meat, and only if one is sick. Since I know better than to drink the water—who knows whether the fair folk have tampered with the well—I pour a cup of wine from the barrel, then choose an empty table near the back. Moments later, the doors open. I snap to attention, as do the rest of my peers.

Mother Mabel arrives draped in heavy folds of white. A gold stole warms her shoulders and hangs in equal lengths down her chest, the trinity knot embroidered at both ends. Acolytes wear the diaconal red stole to represent service. The gold stole, however, represents authority of the faith.

The Abbess of Thornbrook is an ancient woman, though she appears no older than middle-aged. No lines carve her face. Nothing droops below her chin. She stands as the tallest of pines, and glides toward her dining area atop the dais.

Stepping onto the platform, she surveys the room, her white-blond hair pulled into a bun. Snapping black eyes sit beneath pale, slashing eyebrows. Many claim her eyes used to be blue.

According to some of the older acolytes, Mother Mabel was stolen away into Under decades ago, having sacrificed herself to save three novitiates abducted by Under's overlord, yet somehow she managed to escape. No one knows what occurred during her time there. She returned to Carterhaugh with an undying appearance—the mark of everlasting life.

"All rise for the morning prayer."

Benches scrape as the women push to their feet. Heads bowed, hands clasped at our fronts, we speak as one.

"Eternal Father, bless this food to nourish our bodies, and strengthen the bonds that bind us to you."

I lift my head. Mother Mabel's gaze captures mine, its intensity burrowing straight through me.

With a softly uttered "amen," I drop onto the bench, weak in the knees. Does she know of my disobedience? The man in my bed? It is too early to say. Following prayers, we dine in silence, using the opportunity to reflect upon our relationship with the Father. I focus on eating, the spoon scraping the bottom of my clay bowl. Eventually, her attention moves elsewhere, and I'm able to breathe freely.

At the table diagonal to me, raven-haired Harper settles next to silver-tongued Isobel, chin haughty, a queen before her subjects. When I close my eyes, I remember all that I have weathered: lashing insults, barbed words hurled down with stinging force. Cruelty, every shade of it.

Of course, no reign would be complete without a band of slavering followers. Today, three novitiates have joined Harper and Isobel, thrilled to finally be included in their circle. It pains me to remember that I once desired to sit in their place.

Breakfast ends just as it begins: in silence. Everyone carries their dishware to the kitchen before heading off to complete morning chores.

The abbey itself shelters fourteen acres within its fortified wall. In addition to the main complex, there is the herbarium, the stables, a few storehouses, the winery, fields of varying crops, and the forge. The remaining grounds contain plenty of benches and shade trees for prayer or meditation. Like all abbeys, Thornbrook is self-sustaining. There is always something to be done.

Those of us assigned to harvest barley congregate at the garden shed. On the eve of the tithe, when another seven-year cycle comes to a close, we will place milk and barley on the sills of our open windows, the thresholds of our doorways. A shield against the fair folk on the night when the veil between realms grows thin.

One woman grabs the twine. Another snatches the sickles and hurries toward the fields in the distance. Two more swipe the pails. What is left? The cart.

I am built for such labor, I suppose.

The wheels of the cart clatter over the trail, and I'm relieved to have had the foresight to return it to its proper place late last night. A sweet-smelling wind grazes the bottle-brush stalks, bending them in ebbing waves.

I cut barley until sweat drenches my clothes, back bent, neck crisping in the sun. Again and again, my thoughts drift toward my unconscious visitor. Each time, I recenter my focus. At noon, we break for lunch and individual prayer, then return to harvesting, tying the barley into bundles for drying until the bell tolls the third hour.

Lessons occur for two hours daily, except on the Holy Days. Reading, writing, astronomy, arithmetic, geometry. I've enough time to wipe myself clean within the privacy of the bathhouse before hurrying toward the library. After lessons, there is dinner in the refectory, followed by an hour of service. As I trail the women slogging up the dormitory stairs, the wall sconces flicker, though the abbey's passageways contain no windows to provide a breeze. I'm halfway down the hall when I spot Harper hovering in her doorway, regarding me with suspicion.

The pit in my stomach pinches uncomfortably. Behind those frigid eyes, I can almost see her thoughts churning, slotting into place like a metal trap. Harper is cunning. She understands the subtleties of human behavior.

My gaze drops, and I shuffle toward my bedroom. Her attention follows me until I'm locked safely inside.

Moonlight slides over the vague, blanketed form lying on the cot. The man hasn't moved since this morning. That worries me. Is it possible he is more grievously injured than I originally suspected? Still, I cannot risk bringing him to the attention of Thornbrook's in-house physician. The question remains: What am I to do with a man who will not wake?

After slipping on my gloves, I move to his bedside and remove the blanket, prodding the base of his skull beneath the gold-tipped curls. No evident swelling. That is good. At least his breathing has evened into a slow, peaceful cadence.

"Who are you?" I whisper. "Where do you come from?"

The man does not answer.

4

Ten miles southwest of Thornbrook lies Kilkare, a collection of mud-brick homes tucked in a shallow valley where the River Mur and River Twee converge. As with all towns in Carterhaugh, it is surrounded by a stone wall spiked with iron teeth. Kilkare adheres to some of the older beliefs about combating the fair folk, so a thick piling of salt rings the wall as an additional layer of protection.

We're stopped at the gates prior to entering town. The chestnut mare drawing our wagon paws the dirt as the gatekeeper searches our cargo, the boxes of wares. Ten novitiates wait beside Mother Mabel, myself included.

The gatekeeper lifts a hand. "Clear."

Fiona draws the mare forward by the reins, and the cart lurches onward. Aligned in single file, we trudge down the wide dirt lane. Every tree has been cleared, every blade of grass crushed underfoot, Kilkare a dark scar in the center of green-flushed Carterhaugh.

The air smells of smelted metal, and the sun peels away from the mountain's crown to flood the valley in mid-morning light. Market Day—the first of the month. Although Thornbrook is self-sufficient, we sell much of what we produce—herbs, wine, fresh bread—to supplement the resources the abbey provides to the surrounding community.

Chaos overwhelms the main thoroughfare. Cart wheels dig trenches in the mud. Half-dressed children, all knees and elbows, dart beneath horses, dirt flinging from their bare feet. Tables, stalls, and storefronts clutter the road, merchants swinging their wares, artisans belting out prices as if they're moments away from going out of business. The forge where I once apprenticed belches smoke from the next lane over. In the distance, the white spire of a cathedral interrupts Kilkare's earthen tones.

"You know the drill, ladies." Mother Mabel gestures to an empty lot squeezed between two storefronts, where we unhitch the wagon. "I will return shortly with sweets. Any requests?"

Harper pushes to the front of the group. "Sugar cookies, if you please." She scans the group expectantly, as if anticipating a challenge. A few women drop their eyes to the ground.

Mother Mabel nods, somewhat distracted. As soon as her attention moves elsewhere, Harper's expression presses into disappointment.

"I will see if they're available," The abbess says. "Anyone else? Brielle?"

Though I'm partial to the raspberry tarts, I merely say, "No, thank you." I've little inclination to stir Harper's ire, and my preference feels too trivial to voice anyway.

"Very well. Fiona, if you will accompany me?" She gestures to the fair-skinned youth, and off they go to the bakery.

Harper's eyes narrow on Fiona's back. The loathing twisting her features needles my spine, for I have seen that expression directed at me before.

The novitiates talk. They claim Fiona will be next in line to undertake the calling of a vowed life. I sincerely hope otherwise. Ten years I have studied and prayed, all to one day accept my appointment as an acolyte—a shepherd of the Father. Due to the exhaustive instruction required to train new acolytes, only one novitiate may ascend each year. Yet again, I worry I will fall short in the abbess' eyes. Does Mother Mabel not see how deeply I desire to serve the Father? It must be me. It *must*.

My back twinges as I haul the crate of knives from the wagon to my table. Prying open the lid, I remove a bolt of white fabric and begin to unfold it.

"Give that to me."

I glance up. Isobel looms over the table, her hand outstretched.

The cotton crinkles in my fist, and I frown. "I need it for my knives."

"And we need it for the wine." Harper appears at Isobel's side. Both wear their trinity knot pendants, which we must never take off. Mine rests beneath the collar of my dress.

"You already have a tablecloth," I say. Two, in fact.

Isobel grins rapaciously. Her teeth gleam like rows of pearls against her dark skin. "We want this one." Striding forward, she snatches the fabric from my hand, pivoting so fast the cotton whips my legs and her numerous coiled braids nearly whack my cheek. Together, she and Harper drape it over the table where they'll sell jugs of wine.

My chest tightens with a feeling I know well. How easily they rile me. Today of all days, I seek clarity. Without a clear mind, I cannot safely move forward in handling my predicament, the mysterious stranger in my room.

Business is steady throughout the morning. The sun climbs, and my skin grows sticky in the heat. I sell four daggers and two kitchen knives before noon. When the crowds begin to thin hours later, a cloaked figure strolls our way, parting the lingering chaos like a river cutting through limestone.

My gaze tracks the limber motion. Beneath the raised hood, two dark eyes swallow the woman's ashen face. They sit dull as rocks, as though someone plucked out her eyes and shoved smooth black stones into the sagging hollows instead.

I straighten, a hand drifting to the iron dagger hanging from my waist. Fair folk. How did one manage to slip through the iron gates?

As the woman halts at my table, Fiona darts off, hopefully to find the abbess, or at least to alert the authorities. I'm afraid of what will happen if I move too suddenly.

"I do not see a touchmark stamp," she mentions in a low rasp, gesturing toward one of the daggers lining the table. Those stony eyes lift to mine. "Are you the bladesmith?"

"They were forged in Thornbrook," I whisper. She is small, this woman, her body underdeveloped, bony beneath her long, sheep-skin cloak. Her papery lips peel apart over oozing gums. Seeing this unsightly creature, it is hard to believe the fair folk once shared Carter-haugh with us mortals long ago.

"By your hand?"

I glance around to find that the market has all but cleared, aware-ness of Kilkare's undesired visitor having spread. It is true: I coaxed the fire to life, commanded the hammer, yet the blade bears no signature identifying its maker. I've never had the courage to create a touchmark stamp of my own.

She purses her mouth. Beneath the cowl of her hood, shadows swirl, even in brightest sunlight. "I am in the market for a blade. One can never underestimate the tithe. I'm sure you understand."

My palms dampen, the leather-wrapped hilt fusing to my skin. She dares speak of the tithe? Here?

"May I?" She reaches for one of the blades encased in its protective sheath, and I nod, watching her slide the weapon free of its casing, fitting the hilt to her palm.

"Ah!" A bark of pain, and the dagger slips through her grotesquely elongated fingers. It clatters against the table. I recoil from the sound.

The woman whimpers, clutching her hand to her chest, teeth gritted. Horror bleeds like a killing cold through me. "I'm so sorry." I glance around in a panic. Harper hunches behind Isobel, who clings to another novitiate as the group cowers behind the wagon. "I can fetch you a healer—"

"It's not your fault." Her hand unfolds, revealing large white growths swelling on her streaked gray skin. "A mortal-forged blade would contain iron." She closes her wounded hand, smiling tightly, and slips it into her pocket. "I should have known better."

"You should not be here." Mother Mabel speaks softly, stepping in front of the woman with her chin erect, dark eyes ablaze with the fury of a thousand suns. She presses forward, forcing the visitor into the center of the lane. "I will give you the opportunity to leave

Kilkare freely. Otherwise, I will call the sheriff, and he will not be so merciful. Choose wisely."

The woman looks to me. I flinch, yet hold my ground. Is that fear, or do I only imagine the emotion crossing her expression? Pulling her cloak tightly around her body, she hurries off, glancing over her shoulder once before slipping down an alley.

Mother Mabel turns to me, her mouth pinched with suppressed rage. "She did not harm you, did she?"

"No, Mother Mabel." My voice wobbles. It must be shock, for my limbs buzz with a numbing cold.

Relief softens her face, eases those lines of worry. "Good." She scans the area. "I do not know how that creature was able to enter Kilkare, but if one managed to slip through the gates, there might be more. It is best if we return to Thornbrook immediately."

We have barely finished unloading the wagon before I'm hurrying to the dormitory, taking the stairs two at a time. I've ten minutes before the dinner bell rings.

My boots slap the icy flagstones. The wall sconces dance, teased by the moving air snaking through the vacant hall. I've nearly reached my bedroom when a shape snags the edge of my vision, and I falter.

Harper stands in a shadowed alcove, watching me.

The surge of fear is so overpowering I momentarily cease to breathe. How did she arrive here before me? When I left the court-yard, she and Isobel were deep in discussion, likely plotting how best to humiliate me, and at the soonest hour possible. It matters not that we are women grown. In their eyes, I am Mother Mabel's pet. My very existence is a threat to their ambitions, for they, too, desire the acolyte's red stole.

"Are you following me?" I ask, chin lifted despite my thundering heart.

Harper slinks into the light, no better than a fox in the brush. "What are you hiding, Brielle? What is it you wish to keep hidden from prying eyes?"

She suspects, but she does not know. It makes no difference. My door is locked. Only Mother Mabel and I have a key.

"I'm going to change for dinner," I state with impressive calm.

She cuts into my path, blocking my way forward. "Do you think I'm blind? The others are oblivious, to be certain. Perfect Brielle, who can do no wrong. But I see beyond that." One step closer and we stand nose to nose. She is so slight in comparison to me. "I see the truth."

I'm shaking. The fury and the fear. "I do not answer to you."

"No, you don't." Looking over my shoulder, she croons, "Good evening, Mother Mabel."

"Good evening, Harper."

My heart skips a beat. Harper's smile reveals bone-white teeth.

Slowly, I pivot to face Mother Mabel. Hands clasped at her front, she strides forward, boots scuffing the ground. That heavy gold necklace hangs like a yoke around her neck. "You claimed the matter was urgent," she says with thinly veiled irritation. "Well? What is so urgent that you would have me delay supper?"

Harper's mouth pulls in obvious discontent. "I'm afraid one of our own has made a grievous error." She gestures to me. "It is my belief Brielle has brought an outsider into the abbey."

I cannot speak. If I open my mouth, I fear I will vomit.

Mother Mabel's face grows pointed with displeasure. "That is a harsh accusation. Do you have evidence to support this?"

"I do," she replies, head bowed, the image of pious humility. "I'd hoped it was untrue, but I heard something yesterday. A man's voice." She swallows. "*Groaning*."

There is a pause. All is still. "A man, you say?"

"Yes, Mother Mabel."

No matter how hard I fight the blush, it rages red across my cheeks. Has the man awakened at last, then?

"Brielle," Mother Mabel says, her black gaze drilling into mine. "Is this true?"

I think of our Seven Decrees, the bedrock of our faith. The seventh, the most inviolable.

Thou shalt not lie.

But I made my choice days ago. I chose this man's life over Thornbrook's safety. I hadn't thought of what perils I might invite. I'd thought only of the unanswered questions, and above all, helping a person in need.

"Well, my dear?" The abbess stares at me, waiting.

My leaden legs shamble toward the door, which I unlock before stepping aside.

She crosses the threshold. I fist the fabric of my dress in my clammy palms. It is entirely possible I will be banished from Thornbrook. That is a decision I must live with, and yet, an overwhelming dread depletes my lungs, for I have risked all that I hold dear to *save* this man, who means nothing to me.

"Harper, can you help me with something?"

The younger woman saunters forward. "Yes, Mother Mabel."

"Can you please point out this mysterious visitor?"

There is a pause. "A man was here! I am certain."

"Then where is this man now?"

My heart lifts with tentative hope as I enter behind them. Torchlight from the corridor illuminates the bed where the man had lain this morning. But the cot is empty. The rumpled blankets have been smoothed. The spots of blood staining the floor have been scrubbed clean. It takes every effort not to gape in bewilderment.

My attention cuts to the window. Closed shutters, latch secured. The door to my room was locked as well. How, then, did the man manage to escape without notice?

"I heard someone, Mother Mabel, I *swear* it." Harper's blue gaze scours the room. "Brielle was acting oddly. I knew something was amiss."

Mother Mabel turns, straightening to her impressive height. "The next time you decide to waste my time with petty games, you will know the sting of the lash. Am I clear?"

Harper's dumbfounded silence is perhaps the most beautiful thing I have ever experienced.

"You will have latrine duty for a week. Think deeply on your actions and whether your values align with those of Thornbrook." With that, she takes her leave, heels clicking down the corridor.

Quiet engulfs us. Harper's stillness pricks at me, yet I remain motionless, a hind caught in an open field.

Slowly, I begin to retreat into the hall.

Harper snags my arm, fingernails gouging so deeply into my skin I'm surprised she does not draw blood. "I don't know what you're hiding," she snarls, "but I'm going to find out." Before I can shake her off, she storms past me, slamming the door behind her.

My hands tremble as I light my lamp. Then I sink onto the lip of my mattress, the bed frame groaning beneath my weight. I do not understand. A man cannot walk through walls. Neither can a man lock a window from the outside. Though the bloodstains are gone, my pillow bears the imprint of his head, and a springtime aroma saturates the room.

"Well, that was quite the scene."

I whirl around, freeing my blade from its sheath and leveling it at the man's sternum. He slouches next to the now-open window, a shoulder propped against the wall, completely unperturbed.

A pair of clover eyes take me in.

We stare at each other, neither of us moving. Red-edged panic recedes from my vision, and my pulse eventually returns to rest. It is the man from the wood. Strange, indeed, but not a stranger.

Somehow, he has managed to procure a set of clean clothes. A green tunic hits mid-thigh over a pair of form-fitting trousers tucked into boots of dark, supple leather. His shoulders are broad, though his physique, on the whole, is on the leaner side. He does not wear his cloak. My fingers twitch around the dagger.

"Do you agree?" the man asks, canting his head. An errant curl falls across his forehead.

"Excuse me?"

"Quite the scene, wouldn't you say?"

Perhaps, if his countenance were not so distracting, I could focus on the conversation rather than his appearance. Though the swelling is somewhat reduced, he is still a sorry sight to behold.

There is no natural flow to his features. His nose appears broken, bent horribly out of shape. His skin stretches in uneven patches across a jaw far too wide and sharp to be natural. Only his eyes are striking, slightly translucent in color, a certain curiosity darkening his gaze as he scans me from head to toe.

"Is it you I have to thank for my swift recovery?" he asks in a low, musical tone. The weightless timbre of his voice seems content to drift until the end of time. It is too pretty for his mien.

"It is," I reply.

"Then I thank you." He dips his chin, and gazes at me with a forwardness that draws heat to my face. "This is a kindness I must repay."

After some consideration, I lower the dagger from his chest. I sense no ill-will from him. "No repayment necessary, but in the future, I would think twice before startling a woman in her bedroom. I could have hurt you beyond repair."

"I do not think that is likely," he says, eyes bright with amusement, "but I appreciate the forewarning."

My mouth twitches in irritation, and I retreat toward my cot to put additional space between us. If the shutters were locked, how could he have gained access from outside the window, and on the third story no less?

"It seems that I am in your debt."

"As I said, repayment is unnecessary. You were hurt. Anyone would have helped."

"So you claim." I cannot read the intention behind his response. "Even so, debts must be repaid."

The intensity of his focus briefly forces my attention back to the window. Darkness lies thickly over Carterhaugh. It is not my business, the why or how or what of his predicament.

"I can sense your curiosity." He lifts a hand, studies it front to back, before sliding it into his pocket. "What is it you wish to know?"

My eyes drop. I take a breath, then another for good measure.

"What manner of creature gave you those wounds?" Peeking through my eyelashes, I catch an emotion tightening his facial muscles, too fleeting to read. Doubt maybe, or pain.

"The manner of creature would be my brother, unfortunately." A shrug. "What's done is done. I insist on repaying your kindness."

"It was nothing."

"A life is not nothing. Isn't that what your teachings preach?" He gestures to the contents of my desk, the heavy tome that is the Text.

"You keep the faith?" Intrigue colors my inquiry.

He pushes off the wall, and I am taken aback twice in the span of a few minutes. Buoyant. It is the only way to describe his gait. A seamless floating of limbs, nothing but ebb and flow.

"You could say I was once quite devoted to faith. Now I am merely faithless."

The bell tower tolls the sixth hour, signaling dinner. At the man's approach, I retreat further, lifting my dagger in warning. Was I naive to think him harmless?

He studies my weapon yet does not come within striking distance. Perhaps he recognizes I will not hesitate to use the blade if I must. "That's a fine knife," he says. "Where did you procure it?"

"I am a bladesmith, sir. It was fashioned by my own hand."

He merely blinks. "Well, that's not something you encounter every day."

Insult, or compliment? I cannot discern his intention. "Is the dagger your weapon of choice?" I ask, unable to stop myself.

He laughs, and my heart skips a beat. "No. I favor the bow. I have found knives to be an inconvenience. They force you into an enemy's space, which I find disadvantageous."

So he considers the dagger an inferior weapon? "Perhaps practice is needed. Maybe then you would not feel unprepared."

He inclines his head, regarding me with those bright, bright eyes. If I am not mistaken, he accepts the challenge with an eagerness that borders on desire. "Perhaps."

Distant footsteps inform me that the women are heading downstairs for dinner. Meals cannot begin until everyone has arrived. Someone will notice my absence. They will question my delay.

"I would ask for the name of the woman who cared for me," he says. "Surely you would not deny me that?"

I look to the door. I should go, yet my feet remain in place. "You are fair folk." Though he does not look like one of their kind, his insistence on repaying debts makes perfect sense. The fair folk will do anything to gain leverage over another.

"No," he says harshly, his tone suddenly acrimonious. "I am not one of the fair folk. But much of my time is spent in Under. Now will you tell me your name, or do you insist on remaining a mystery?"

I consider this man, the information given. The fair folk cannot tell a lie. It is good enough for me. "Brielle," I concede. Just a name. So why does it feel as if I am granting this man more than he asked for?

"Brielle." My name unfolds in a single wave of warm curiosity. "A lovely name for a lovely woman. I thank you, Brielle." He touches a hand to his chest. "I am Zephyrus."

Lovely? He hardly knows me. But I keep the thought to myself.

The man—Zephyrus—glides to my desk, scans the various liturgical manuscripts. He flips open the Text, idly shifting aside documents as though he has every right to. My fingers tighten around the hilt of my dagger. *Don't touch that.* But the words will not come.

"What is your station at the abbey?" He glances over his shoulder at me, green eyes keen.

"Novitiate." I've dedicated every spare moment to the consecrated life: deepening my relationship with the Father, examining the faith, expanding my self-awareness, understanding the importance of community. It has been no small task.

Leaning back against the desk, Zephyrus folds his arms over his chest, one ankle tossed lazily over the other. Candlelight gilds the curling tips of his hair. "How old are you?"

This, too, I am reluctant to announce, though it shouldn't matter. "Twenty-one."

His eyebrows wing upward in surprise. "How long ago did you enter the abbey?"

"When I was eleven."

"You have been a novitiate for ten years? Shouldn't you have taken your vows?"

"I have. My first vows, at least." I will take my final vows once I'm appointed an acolyte, my commitment to the faith set in stone.

Generally, a novitiate studies for five years, although there are always exceptions to the rule. Following the novitiate phase, a Daughter of Thornbrook is appointed an acolyte, a station she will maintain for the rest of her life, as long as her final vows remain intact. It is possible to climb higher in station, as Mother Mabel has done, solidifying her religious leadership over the region, but a woman may climb no higher than abbess.

"Why haven't you taken your final vows then?"

"It is not up to me," I say, more tersely than I intend. "Mother Mabel decides who is ready to graduate. Considering there is only one slot available per year, it is understandably a difficult decision. My time as an acolyte will come."

There is a silence. The longer we regard each other across the room, the stranger the man's eyes seem. He cannot be human. The green fires too brightly. "You're certain of that?"

"I have worked toward this for a long time," I state. "Mother Mabel recognizes my efforts. She will choose whoever is best fit for the position."

"And if that person is not you?"

Steel snaps my spine straight. What is the purpose of his animus? To prove a point? To draw the red to my skin?

I've considered the possibility. I've seen it come to pass too many times. Still, I hope.

"That woman with the black hair? She is hungry for the opportunity as well." A lazy, pointed remark. The corner of his mouth tucks into his cheek. "What will you do if she is chosen over you?"

"Your antagonism is unnecessary."

"Is it?" he croons, sidling closer. "I merely speak the truth."

His scent hits: moss and rain. My throat opens; my heartbeat spikes. I'm so blindsided by my body's response I fail to gather an appropriate retort. Instead, I glare at him, and Zephyrus winces, a hand going to his temple, as though his head pains him. "I must leave you now," he mutters. "But first, there is something I would ask of you."

"No."

Zephyrus merely arches an eyebrow. "No?" He appears intrigued by this, amused even, though I do not understand why. *No* is a complete sentence. "But you have not heard my request."

Something about his presence fuels increasing alarm in me. His own brother wanted him dead. Why?

"You have been here too long," I manage. "I must ask you to leave at once."

The hallway echoes from another wave of departing novitiates. My eyes dart to the door. Zephyrus slides into my path, blocking my view of the exit. "You saved my life. I only ask that you hear my request and then decide."

"Whatever it is, I'm not interested."

"Oh, I think you'll want to hear my offer." He returns to the window. I have half a mind to yank him out of sight. Anyone peering up at the tower could spot him. "Haven't you wondered why your abbess continually overlooks your accomplishments? Have you not questioned what might *guarantee* your ascension?" Lowly, silkily, he murmurs, "Come with me, learn what it is you wish to know, and my debt to you will be repaid."

Whatever I wish to say—*No, Leave, Go away*—the declaration fails to emerge. For I know this feeling. The unholy desire to reach and grasp, and catch something solid within one's hand.

A decade I have studied. How many seasons will pass before I'm selected to take my final vows, if at all?

"How?" I whisper. "If I am to learn this information, what must I do?"

"We will pay a visit to Willow," he says with burgeoning delight, "and you will have your answers."

I lower my dagger slightly. Willow. I've never heard of this person. "Why do you want to help me? Why can't you accept that I want no repayment and be done with it?"

A little notch crinkles his brow. "There is no such thing as goodness of heart. There's always a catch."

Not from me.

"Is there somewhere we can meet tomorrow evening?" Zephyrus asks.

"Tomorrow is the Holy Day. Our day of rest."

"Then the day after."

I am likely going to regret this, but any advantage will outweigh the risks. Serving the Father is all I have ever wanted in life. To be known, embraced, revered? Only my final vows will grant me such privilege. But more than this, I wish to be proven worthy of them. "There's a forge south of the main complex. It is empty in the evenings."

"Excellent." Zephyrus braces a palm on the wooden sill. "Light a lamp in your window two nights hence. When you see an answering glow, head to the forge. I'll meet you there."

Leaping through the window, he vanishes into the night.

5

I ARRIVE AT THE FORGE WHEN THE NIGHT IS DARKEST, FOR THE abbey sleeps, and I must return before the rising sun.

When I enter the shrouded, still-warm workshop, however, I find it deserted. Had I misunderstood Zephyrus' instructions? The lamp hangs in my window, a mellow glow likely visible across the strait to the east, a small sun atop the tower to lead those at sea home.

Lingering smoke stings my nostrils as I pace the area, tugging on the cord cinching my waist. Zephyrus said he would be here. Yet I am alone.

As I consider my options, I spot a note nailed to the front door.

Brielle, meet me where the River Twee splits. I will await your arrival.

Irritation washes through me. Of course he informs me to meet him at the most inopportune time, and at the most inconvenient location. I consider returning to my room, forgetting this fool's bargain. But the promise he'd given me: Willow. Whoever this person is, they hold the answer to my prayers.

With my dagger secured at my waist, I cross the outer grounds to the deserted gatehouse and make the treacherous journey down the mountain. My pulse thunders as I navigate the rocky trail on shaky legs. The moon is not as bright as I had hoped. It hides from me, and forces me through the dark. *Do not stray from the path.* Mother Mabel has hammered this warning into our very beings.

Last year, tragedy struck Thornbrook. Curious Madeline, a novitiate in her second year, went missing while roaming Carterhaugh after dark. Seven days later, we found her in a nearby glen, wandering in circles around a ring of mushrooms sprouting from the moist soil. The girl rambled about a strange man smelling of roses, whose face she could not remember.

The pregnancy progressed at an inhuman speed. Within a few short weeks, Madeline could no longer hide the enormous swell of her stomach. The transgression resulted in her dismissal from Thornbrook. We never heard from her again.

"I suppose they do not teach you to step lightly at this abbey of yours," a musical voice drawls from somewhere in the dim.

I'm panting, dripping sweat, and in no mood for barbed conversation. Moreover, I cannot determine if that was an underhanded insult about my size.

"I'm here, aren't I?" Ahead, the river glitters through the trees.

"Indeed." Zephyrus materializes between two towering oaks, a heavy green cloak warming his shoulders. Moonlight silvers the tips of his eyelashes and softens the awkward planes of his face. "Most do not brave the forest after dark."

Apparently, I am more foolish than most. Desperate, certainly. For only desperation would send me into utter blackness, no lamp to light my way.

"I am to return before dawn," I state, falling into step behind him as he gestures me across a shallow section of the river.

"And you will." He leaps from stone to flattened stone. "This should not take long." Another effortless bound and he reaches the opposite bank.

"You will not leave me?"

His eyes catch the light, the small black pupils narrowing. He studies me for a time, and if I am not mistaken, there is some semblance of understanding in his gaze, though it may be a trick of the light. "As long as you follow my instruction," he assures me, "you will have nothing to worry about."

We delve deeper into the innards of Carterhaugh, surging through the vein-like openings between the long-standing trees. The tangle of leaves shutters the stars, yet Zephyrus glides over every dip and knoll as if our path were marked by sunlight. My tread is not as light, nor as quick. This man denies he is one of the fair folk, but how else could he navigate so well in the dark?

We arrive at a clearing as perfectly round as a plum ripe for plucking. A spring interrupts the spread of softened grass, a deep pool of icy clarity.

Without turning around, Zephyrus whispers, "We're here."

"Where is *here*?" My voice drops, for the night sounds have hushed. And the wind? That, too, has died.

He approaches the edge of the water, painted in white moonlight. "Under."

My toe catches on a root, and I stumble. "What?" When I manage to regain my footing, I stare at Zephyrus' back, the strong line of his shoulders beneath the heavy cloak. "You said you weren't one of the fair folk," I manage faintly. Am I truly so naïve as to have accepted his word?

He glances over his shoulder at me, expression cold. "I'm not. The fair folk and I have an understanding. I am allowed to come and go from their realm as I please."

Only on the tithe, when the veil between realms is at its thinnest, may the Daughters of Thornbrook venture into Under, and only accompanied by Mother Mabel. Without her guiding hand, one might lose oneself.

We all understand the tithe's importance. The contract between Thornbrook and Under is clear. The land upon which the abbey was built belongs to Under. The abbey may only continue to lease the land if we participate in the tithe. Too many towns depend on Thornbrook to risk its closure, Kilkare and Aranglen especially. Even Veraness, my hometown.

"You didn't mention Willow would be in Under," I say, hesitating by the edge of the pool. Then again, I never asked. "I'm forbidden to enter."

Zephyrus hums in acknowledgment. "That is quite the predicament."

A moment of silence passes.

"Well," he says casually, "the way I see it, there's a simple solution." He pins me in place with that evergreen gaze. "Do it anyway."

It is no jest. That concerns me. "You understand there are rules I must abide by. I am not free to go where I want."

"So it would seem." He laughs, and the sound is almost too pleasant to be scornful, despite the tension behind it. "You are free to choose your own path, yet you choose to live your life within the boundaries Thornbrook has set for you. But please, correct me if I am wrong."

I've half a mind to shove him into the spring for dismissing my faith, but I would not disappoint the Father with my actions.

Zephyrus sighs and rocks back on his heels. "Let me explain. Beyond your abbey walls"—he sweeps an arm eastward, toward the distant realm of the Gray—"there exists an entire world you have never touched. If you are truly committed to your faith, then consider this: once you take your final vows, you will be forever bound to the church. Why not take the opportunity to explore while you still can? It may be the last thing you ever do for yourself."

I wish I were not so easily swayed. Obedience: the first of my vows. But might breaking it be worth the guarantee of my appointment?

"Be that as it may, I am still mortal. The fair folk do not look kindly on us." I tug the ends of my cincture with both hands, twisting the rope around and around.

"Never fear. As my guest, you will be granted amnesty." At my hesitation, he says, "Do you want to become an acolyte or not?"

I have worked too hard and for too long to allow this opportunity to pass me by. To watch someone like Harper, of all people, obtain the honor before me. It's hard enough believing I belong in Thornbrook most days. Forsaken, motherless, fatherless but for my god. Maybe I'm tired of being stepped on. Is there room enough for change in me?

I take the deepest breath I can manage, and when I release it, my fear ebbs with it. "I don't know if I'm capable of completing the journey, but I will try. What must I do?"

Zephyrus offers me one long-fingered hand, which I accept. Even through the leather, the heat of his skin seeps into mine.

"Do your gloves serve a purpose?" he asks. "I noticed you wore them in your bedroom as well."

I step to his side, toeing the edge of the spring. The wall of trees edging the clearing hoards shadows. "It is against our moral law to touch a man."

"Why?"

"Because it is," I snap. "Why is the sky blue? Why does water flow downhill? It is fact. It is known. There is nothing to understand beyond that."

"Isn't there?" How piercing that gaze is when resting wholly on me. "Tell me, Brielle," he continues softly. "Have you ever wondered what a man's touch feels like?"

An unexpected heat flutters through my stomach. This conversation has begun to slide into uncharted territory. I am not ignorant. The Text explains what occurs when a woman lies with a man. Purity—our second vow. To live a consecrated life, one cannot be impure of body. The Father would know. *I* would know.

"I have not," I state. "Only a virgin may become an acolyte." Despite the unnerving focus of his stare, my tone permits no argument.

When he speaks, his voice comes throaty and low. "Who said anything about losing your virginity?"

A sweep of chill bumps pebbles my skin. What he insinuates ... No. I refuse to respond to such a ridiculous comment.

Zephyrus smirks and faces forward. "Originally," he says, still fighting a smile, "Under had four entrances, each aligned to the cardinal directions. All cut into the mountain's heart."

I'm so relieved by the subject change I do not retreat when he edges closer to me.

"Over time, however, Under came alive and shaped new entrances. Today, only two of the four doorways remain."

"This is one of them?" Knowledge. I encase myself in its armor, for I will need it.

"Indeed it is. The original doorways can only be accessed by the fair folk and those whom they have granted the right of passage. But they are not the only means of entering Under. You might wander a path and cross into the realm without realizing it, or an entrance might one day decide to seal itself off, never again to open. There is no rhyme or reason to it. Trees, springs, doors, caves, holes in the ground—all might lead to Under with the right conditions."

"And what are the right conditions?"

Zephyrus shrugs. "That is for Under to decide."

He turns to me then. A strange man standing in an even stranger place. "Can you swim?"

"Yes." My attention flits to the water. I cannot see the bottom.

A cunning little grin ghosts across his mouth. Beautiful teeth for a face that is anything but. "Here." Zephyrus offers me a small white shell. "Place it between your teeth and breathe through your mouth. It will prevent you from drowning." He pulls me closer as I follow his instructions. Our shoulders brush, and even that brief touch brings a dryness to my mouth. He smells of the mountain. "Don't let go of my hand."

What awaits me beneath the surface? Salvation, perhaps. Or the ruination of everything I hold dear.

"Trust me," he murmurs, slow and mesmeric.

I do not.

A sharp tug drags me forward, and we free fall into the spring.

Frigid water engulfs me. Then—panic.

A wave of heat branches down my limbs, and I begin to flail. My shoulder rams into hard substrate; the rush of bubbles blinds me.

I will die here. I will die in this watery grave, alone, without a proper burial, forever denied the Father's divine gates of respite. As my lungs seize, I kick in the direction I believe is up, only to slam my face into stone, its edge slicing my cheek open.

Someone grabs my arm, halting my frenzy. Zephyrus. He is close, overwhelmingly so. Short tresses float from his scalp like brown river grass. The clarity of his crystalline eyes in the murk has an odd, calming effect on me.

Recalling his instructions, I inhale through my mouth, salt bristling on my tongue from the hard, spiral shell clamped between my teeth. Water tickles my nostrils, and when my throat opens, air rushes in.

By the Father, he was right. What is this sorcery?

Darkness yawns beneath, and the underground current tugs us farther from the surface. My fingers twitch, deepening the contact with Zephyrus' hand—the only warmth in this airless, lightless place.

As we drift, the gloom thickens, the enclosed tunnel that surrounds us narrowing, like a long throat swallowing us whole. Down we sink into the obscured depths. I fight the climbing panic in my chest, the instinct to claw my way back toward the light. I am breathing. I am alive. The water will not take me.

As we hit the bottom of the spring, pressure shoves against my feet. With Zephyrus' guidance, we float upward toward a separate branching tunnel, bubbles streaming from our open mouths.

My head breaks the surface. Releasing Zephyrus' hand, I tread water, peering at our surroundings. We've reached the heart of a prodigious cave, all dark rock against which the echoing splash bounces. My teeth chatter around the shell, and I promptly spit it out, swimming to the edge of the pool and dragging myself from its icy clasp. Water pours from my dress onto the smooth, stony ground. The drenched fabric adheres to every generous curve, so my body feels more exposed than if I were wearing nothing at all.

Zephyrus, meanwhile, hauls himself from the spring with ease, lean muscle displayed beneath the clinging cotton of his clothes. A glimpse is all I allow myself, no less and no more, before I push to my feet and look elsewhere. I have seen a man's form before, but never one so revealed.

I brush the thought away as if it were an errant cobweb and focus on the chamber. Tunnels branch from the main cavity. Its ceiling is supported by multiple arches glowing with faint pink light. "This is Under?" I assumed it would be more fearsome.

"Not quite." Zephyrus squeezes droplets from the hem of his tunic. "The mountain is a neutral zone between Under and Carterhaugh. See that archway? Passing beneath it will lead you into Under."

The path ahead vanishes into the murk. I release a slow, shaky breath. I have come this far. I cannot stop now.

"There are three things you must know if you wish to leave Under alive."

My throat dips with a nervous swallow, but I nod in understanding. After all, I have heard the sordid tales.

"The first thing to remember," he says, lifting a finger, "is that you must not eat or drink anything offered to you." His expression, pressed into solemnity, holds a curious allure. "The wine tastes sweeter, the fruits brighter, the meat is impossibly rich with flavor. Once you begin to eat, you will lose your sense of self."

Decades before, one of the novitiates failed to resurface following the tithe, or so the story goes. Mother Mabel returned to Under, only to find the woman dead, having gorged herself for so long her stomach split clean in half.

"The second," he says, "is that you must not stray from the path."

"The path?"

"The path," Zephyrus emphasizes, and gestures to the ground.

Indeed, an uprise of grass sprouts from the bedrock a stone's throw ahead, which passes beneath the carved archway. A chilled gust belches from the passage, reeking of decomposed plant matter. I choke on the taste.

"The path will keep you safe," he says. "Do not stray."

This is Under, an unfamiliar current, and Zephyrus is my anchor. I will follow his instructions without complaint. "And the third?"

"If you must remember one thing, let it be this: never speak your name aloud. Ever. Should any of the fair folk learn your name, they will have power over you, more power than you can ever imagine. Keep it safe. Trust no one."

"What of your name?"

His mouth curves too sharply to be pleasant. "My name has already been claimed by another, so you may use it freely. It will make no difference."

"What do you mean your name has been claimed?" As I fall into step beside him, we pass into the dense gloom of the tunnel. Quiet like a void, like a tomb.

Nothing. I see nothing.

"Once your name is known," says Zephyrus, "the sound is captured and stored in a glass bottle. It may be sold, or bartered with, or given to another, or set free, though rarely are the fair folk amiable enough to do the latter. Whoever among their kind possesses your name may dictate your every movement, the where and when and how of your life."

Is it the darkness that makes his reply slither and spit like a viper? I wrap my arms around my front as we shamble onward. Beneath the chilly air, a warmer, tamer breeze skims my ankles. "There's nothing you can do?"

"When your name is called, it is impossible to ignore. Only death can break the bond."

Then I must keep my wits about me.

One moment, we shuffle in utter blackness, a low pulse of sound building in my eardrums, and the next, the walls fall away, the ceiling climbs, the space before us bleeds red. It is not natural, this light.

We stand on the bank of a wide, underground lake. It expands so far into the distance that I cannot see the opposite shore. At my feet: grass. Safe to tread, though I do not know if I am willing.

In the center of the lake floats an extensive wooden platform the size of a barley field, on which a crowd of creatures has amassed, writhing to the blood-pounding rhythm of thundering drums. Large glass orbs bob like lanterns in the water, flushed pink, occasionally a richer scarlet. It's obvious we have intruded on a celebration of sorts.

I peer upward, startling in surprise. There hangs the moon, only I do not recognize it. The globular shape reminds me of a yellowing growth attached to the ceiling, except it is not a ceiling, but the sky. A few stars throb dully in the darkened fabric.

"Under's enchantments reflect what occurs aboveground but, as you can see, there are some differences." Zephyrus points to the feeble glowing orb above. "The realm's sun and moon do not always cycle reliably. Sometimes, the moon gets stuck. A rudimentary design, but it does the job most days."

"I see." One last glance upward before my attention returns to the lake.

"Stay close," he murmurs. A boardwalk extends from the grassy bank to the platform, and it rocks gently beneath our combined weight as we make our way across. When we reach the raft, the crowd parts around us, then sutures into a neat seam at our backs. I press nearer to Zephyrus, trying to avoid touching anyone or anything.

The fair folk do not share any specific traits, no single skin tone, no general shape, really, except for their eyes—black stones, like that woman from the market. Some possess tails. Others, beaks or antlers. Their skin is a collection of browns, ochres, olives, whites, grays.

Bare shoulders.

Bare arms.

Bare stomachs.

Bare legs.

They slink and they fondle. Their hands stroke and slither across torsos, down arms, over backs, up spines.

I look away, but there is always another person of interest amongst the loose-limbed dancers, the undulating hips. They wear waist-coats and elaborate gowns, top hats and long, ragged tunics. When I spot a man's hand slipping between the thighs of another, I drop my gaze.

"The fair folk enjoy their merrymaking," Zephyrus drawls beside me, having no qualms about studying their half-naked forms, male and female both.

"It is unholy," I state stiffly.

"To you, perhaps."

As we push through the festivities, I notice a woman draped in gauzy silks, one arm bared, and one breast. A pair of antlers protrudes from her skull. We then pass a trio of men whose skin resembles the texture of tree bark. The tallest man brings a glass of pale, sparkling liquid to his mouth. A forked tongue slithers out, curling slightly to capture the fluid, before retracting behind his teeth.

"Dryads," Zephyrus murmurs, tracking my dumbfounded gaze. "They prefer the taste of flesh."

I hasten my steps. This place is like nothing I've imagined. There appears to be no purpose to the gathering. They drink and laugh and dance as if it's a compulsion.

"Excuse me," I mutter, trying to squeeze between two owl-eyed girls while attempting to avoid the downy wings folded across their backs. I dodge a woman lying spread-eagled across the listing platform, a scaly tail wrapped around one leg. As I shrink from the sight, Zephyrus catches my eye and smirks.

"You have lived a sheltered life," he says. "It is nothing to be ashamed of." And yet, he cannot quite conceal the condescension.

"Maybe I have seen less of the world than you," I snip, "but I have the Father. I need nothing else."

A shrill, raptor cry soars over the gathering, followed by raucous laughter. "Is that so?" Intrigue colors his voice. "You are comforted by your god. I understand that. Indeed, there was a time when I myself was a symbol of good tidings."

The last bit of information snags my attention, but Zephyrus continues before I have a chance to question him.

"Your world is not the same as mine. You sleep and you read and you eat and you pray. Every hour of every day is spent safely within the boundaries of your faith. My world?" He bares his teeth, and for a moment, I could have sworn they had developed points. "It is a treacherous place, unfit for the pure." The warm, heavy weight of his palm braces my lower back, and I startle, my eyes flying to his face. "But we are attracted to things that lie outside of our lived experience," he says lowly. "We crave something deeper."

I do not agree. Why would I be attracted to *this*? What is the purpose of exploring something so depraved? Under lacks morals, it lacks faith. It is walls with no foundation, nothing to build upon. His claims are ridiculous. The abbey is my home and my heart. I want for nothing there.

The deeper we tread into the frenzy, the greater my awareness of the unwanted attention I am attracting becomes. For this reason alone, I remain close to Zephyrus.

"They stare," I whisper.

He smiles, a small, contemplative thing. "They smell the innocence on you."

A few paces later, someone slips a chalice into his hand, which he lifts to his mouth. I catch his arm. "Don't drink the wine, remember?"

His eyes dance over the rim of his goblet. "*You* cannot drink the wine, my darling novitiate. You are mortal. I am not." And he downs the red liquid, a bright sheen staining his laughing mouth.

At last, we step onto the boardwalk leading to the opposite shore. I thought the crowd would have cleared out, but if anything, it has multiplied. Something pinches my rear, and I whirl, my breath shortening. Look at these fair folk with their dark, oil-slick eyes, wildness clinging to all their wretched points. What has possessed me to accompany a man I know nothing about to a place that will readily eat me alive if given the chance? A moment of weakness, apparently.

"I want to go back," I tell Zephyrus. But the crowd is so dense I cannot see the cavern walls.

He slows, cants his head in my direction. A single curl tumbles across his forehead. "You can't go back."

"Why not?" I fiddle with the cord around my waist, tightening my grip to strangulation.

"It's not that I won't take you back. It's that I *can't*. The only way to return is to go forward. Should you attempt to backtrack, you will find yourself helplessly ensnared in Under."

"That makes absolutely no sense."

"Doesn't it?" He regards me for an uncomfortably long moment, and my cheeks heat. I do not think I imagine his eyes lingering on my dress, the damp fabric clinging to curves of skin. "Consider this: you are a mortal who has wandered into Under. The fair folk will do whatever it takes to prevent your escape. Why? Because they are bound to the shadows while mortals are gifted the sun."

His claim rings with authority, and I dare not challenge it. Turning, I take in the scene. The black lake shines like oil beneath the scarlet glare. If I cannot go back, my only choice is to trust Zephyrus to lead me forward.

"Fine," I manage, though my chest twinges. "We continue. But hurry, please."

The crowd parts, and the grassy path unfolds as we veer from the shore toward a grove of trees draped in twinkling blue lights. They float in long strings, these lights, catching the air on the upswing, briefly suspended before drifting back into place. It is strange, yes, but any light is better than none.

Zephyrus strides ahead, limber and sure-footed. I am not certain how long we walk. An hour? An age? My clothes are nearly dry by the time he lifts a hand, signaling us to slow. I peer around him, and my jaw drops.

It is without a doubt the most beautiful tree I have ever seen. It sprawls in a field of darkness, its smooth, twisting trunk the color of fresh snow, innumerable branches clothed in strands of blue lights.

"It's lovely," I say, though *lovely* seems an inadequate description of something so *other*.

"According to the fair folk, Willow is the heart of Under." Ducking beneath the hanging lights, he calls back, "Ask, and you shall receive."

Willow is not a person, but a tree. It makes sense, I suppose.

"So I just ... speak?" When I push through the strands, a pale chime brightens the air.

Zephyrus lounges against the trunk, mouth quirked in mischief. "You may ask Willow anything you wish, but she will only answer the questions she believes to come from your true self."

That, I can do. "Do you mind if I have a little privacy?"

His eyebrows lift. "You're sure?" When I merely glare, he says, "I'll be over there if you need me." Pushing off the tree, he melts into the darkness beyond.

With Zephyrus gone, the burden eases from my chest. I want him far away when I make my request. I'm ashamed of my voice's tendency to wobble under pressure, how easily it breaks beneath the great weight of the unknown.

"My face is here, child."

The throaty command draws my gaze upward. What I had believed to be knots in the bark have cracked open to reveal lidded eyes, the curving seam of a mouth.

"There you are." The bark creaks as the eyelids sink low. "It has been a long time," Willow intones, "since a mortal woman has graced my presence. But tell me, child. What do you desire?"

This answer, at least, is easy.

"I would like to know what I must do to become the next acolyte." And then, hushed: "How can I be seen as worthy?"

The tree's mouth pinches into a dark whorl. "I can see your whole history in your eyes. Ten long years you have toiled. You wonder why your efforts have failed to bring about the opportunity you seek. You wonder why it has not been enough."

My throat aches fiercely. Tears well, and the blue lights burn into brightest stars.

"What must I do?" I whisper. Shall I kneel? Shall I close my eyes and lift my hands to the Eternal Lands?

"My dear." Willow sighs. "Your path is not an easy one. It is lonely, and long, and marked by conflicting desires." The great tree pauses, her wooden mouth crimped in what I believe to be sympathy. "You ask whether there is anything you can do to bring about the change in station you so desperately desire? Unfortunately, there is not."

I clasp my trembling hands at my front. "I see."

"One cannot control another's actions, but do not despair. This path is yours alone, and a time will come when you gain your heart's desire."

"When? Am I to work diligently for another five, ten, fifteen years before I'm granted the opportunity to become one of the Father's most loyal shepherds?" A novitiate's duty is to build a foundation upon which faith can rest, but an acolyte acts as the Father's own messenger, traveling to far-reaching towns and communities to spread His word, the good of all that is holy. It is a privilege many never experience. The truest representation of belonging to the faith.

A branch drifts down with an aged creak to skim my back, the way a mother might console a disappointed child. "Do not fret," soothes Willow. "Trust that what will be, will be."

What did I expect, exactly? Comfort, perhaps. Reassurance of the Father's warmth, proof of Mother Mabel's investment in my future. But all I feel is the hollowness where my heart once beat, cotton stuffed in its place.

"Very well. Thank you for your guidance." It's silly to have believed I could change something beyond my control. I had hoped—too much, I think.

Soft grass muffles my footsteps as I turn to go. Pushing aside the strands of blue lights, I step into the clearing. Darkness rests as a veil over my vision, a relief after the piercing brightness. Zephyrus, however, is gone.

6

I WHIP AROUND, SQUINTING THROUGH THE CERULEAN GLOW AS MY pulse begins to climb. Only minutes have passed since I felt Zephyrus' solidity beside me. Now? I cannot pick out his head of oaken curls, nor his fluid, slim-hipped gait among the trees.

"Zephyrus?"

The blue strands sway, bright beads nestled in translucent casings. There is a distinct lack of wind.

I'm moving before I realize it, my pace surging to match my racing heart. I'm running, *sprinting*, feet pounding the grass in a furious rhythm. By the time I return to the lake I feel ill, ensnared once more by the red glare flooding the massive cavern. The fair folk, with their horns and claws and teeth, continue to slink across the floating platform, gulping wine with abandon.

My dagger is all that grounds me. What are the odds that, were I to draw my weapon, I could fight my way out of here alive? The fair folk are incredibly swift, impossibly strong. I may be experienced with a blade, but I am mortal. I cannot fight my way forward, for I do not know the way.

Something brushes my neck. I whirl, blade extended, to face a rotund creature with white skin the texture of parchment.

"Red," coos the creature—a girl. The tips of one clawed hand tangle in my copper hair. I recoil, imagining the lash of those talons across my throat, a scarlet line that swells, then bursts with blood.

The girl smiles, twisting one of my curls around her knobby finger. She is tiny, with a face made of points. She wears a loose white dress beneath a fraying waistcoat. Her hair, the same snowy shade as her eyebrows, has been lopped at the chin.

Thankfully, she steps away, tilting back her head to look at me. "Do I frighten you?"

It seems too innocent a question. The fair folk cannot lie, though I've heard they're able to sense untruths regardless.

"Yes," I whisper hoarsely. I fear Zephyrus has abandoned me to this place.

Her lips part to reveal a mass of rotting gums. "Wonderful," she sings. "Absolutely wonderful." Slipping her small hand into mine, she tugs me through the crowd. We skirt the edge of the rocky shore, pushing through a group of creatures with necks encircled by rings of thorns. Their pierced skin weeps blood.

"How are you enjoying Under, sweet?" The girl appears unaffected by the incessant drumbeat and wild cries.

"It is . . . unusual," I say.

She pats my arm in comfort. "And this is only the beginning. Soon, we will have our tithe. But you know this, coming from the abbey."

"How do you know I'm from the abbey?"

"Your dress. It is quite drab—no offense intended." A pause. "What is this?" She lifts the ends of the white cord around my waist.

"It's called a cincture," I reply stiffly. There must be something I can do, a way to escape this place. "I mean no insult, but what manner of creature are you?"

"I am what they call a sprite." She does not appear offended. Pleased, rather. Practically gleeful from the attention. "My mother was a nymph. She taught me everything there is to know of the healing arts. Unfortunately, I never knew my father. I was hatched from an egg along the lakeshore." She rubs the crown of her head against my shoulder like a cat. "What about your parents? What manner of creature are they?"

I do not know who my father is. As for my mother, I try not to think of her. Most days, I'm successful. "They are human."

"How quaint." She hums as a drink appears in her hand, though I did not see anyone place it there. Her white fingers curl around the glass, which contains a dark, viscous liquid.

We've stalled near the fringe of the celebration, where the shore has climbed to a natural outcropping jutting from the wall. From this vantage point, I'm given an unobstructed view of the chamber. Its hollow holds fast to echoes. The lake appears still despite the activity rocking the platform, and the reddish lights swirling inside the spheres that dot the lake's surface appear restless, seeking escape.

The sprite turns to me. "You must be thirsty." A harmless smile, meant to reassure.

I accept the glass with a nod of gratitude and make a show of taking a sip. My lips, however, remain pressed firmly shut. Lowering the drink, I search for a man dressed in a green cloak, but Zephyrus is well and truly gone.

"Good?" the sprite wonders. I nod vaguely and abandon the glass on the ledge, then begin to wander back toward the boardwalk. Every so often I glance down to make sure I keep to the grass.

"You seem melancholy, sweet." She presses her nose to my shoulder and inhales. "What is your name?"

The answer materializes fully formed in my mouth. I only need to let it unfurl.

What was it Zephyrus told me? Does it even matter?

"Lissi?" A hulking creature with ram horns curling from its skull pushes through the throng. Its chest is round as a barrel, agleam with sweat. Upon catching sight of me, its eyes narrow. "Who is this?"

"Don't even think about it," the sprite snaps. "I found her first."

The horned beast takes me in suspiciously. "A mortal. But the tithe is still two months away." Its voice is so deeply resonant I feel its reverberation down to the soles of my feet.

"I'm looking for Zephyrus," I say.

"Zephyrus?" The sprite wrinkles her nose. "You'd be better off without him. He is not one to trust."

Neither are they. "Why is he untrustworthy?"

The sprite—Lissi—takes a delicate sip, then proceeds to chomp through the glass with satisfaction. I watch, in horror and fascination, as a black, worm-like tongue slithers out to lick the blood from her lips. "Oh, sweet! Haven't you wondered why one of the Anemoi has found himself bound to Under?"

"The Anemoi?" I do not understand.

"Leave it, Lissi." The ram-horned creature slaps its meaty hand upon her shoulder. I'm surprised her knees don't buckle. "The girl is the abbess' property. Do not meddle."

What a strange thing to say. I am no one's property.

Lissi scowls. "Hush, Balfer. A little information never hurt anyone." She angles toward me. "You have heard the tales, haven't you?"

As a matter of fact, I have not. There is no mention of this strange word in the Text.

"The Anemoi," she says, "are four brothers who were banished to this world millennia ago. You might have heard them called the Four Winds? Zephyrus is known as the West Wind."

The Four Winds. Why does that sound familiar? "Why were these men banished?"

"Not men, sweet. *Gods*."

Zephyrus, a god? Of all the absurd claims I have heard, this tops it. "You must be mistaken."

"But I am not. You know him as Zephyrus. We know him as the Messenger, or the Bringer of Spring."

"That's enough, Lissi. Let the girl be." He grasps the child's slim arm. "This is between her abbess and our king. We do not want to be caught in the middle of it."

The sprite hesitates. Fear is an emotion I know most intimately. I sense it in the taut line of her back. Eventually, however, she nods. "Very well. Luck to you, sweet. Try not to wander too far."

Turning on her heel, the sprite saunters off with her burly companion, leaving me with so many questions my head begins to pound.

Zephyrus is a god. From another realm.

If he is not from Under, where does he hail from? Lissi mentioned that he is bound to this world. As punishment, or as a precaution?

I'm so lost in thought I pay little attention to my wanderings. I've returned to the woods. The strands of blue lights brush my shoulders, and a strange sound intrudes, giving me pause. Movement in my periphery draws my eye.

Beneath the draping branches there sits an ornate, four-poster bed swathed in a panoply of blankets. Atop the bed, two figures lie intertwined.

The woman is bare: dark skin, silver hair, voluptuous curves. She lies spread over the white blankets, chest heaving. Her nipples peak—large areolas, rosy tips. She turns her face toward me, eyes pinched shut.

A man, equally bare, kneels between her parted thighs. His wheaten skin ripples across a muscled back, and beneath his round, soft stomach hangs his erection, a flushed protrusion that juts from a coarse thatch of brown hair. Two short antlers sprout from a head of tight sable curls.

From this angle, I watch a serpentine tongue slither from his mouth. As soon as the forked end skims the wet glisten of her flesh, her hips drive upward, a hoarse cry cracking the air.

A warm flush suffuses my skin, and I take a small step closer, parting the willow branches further. Again, the man angles his head, tongue fluttering. The woman whimpers, tosses her head from side to side, eyes still closed. An involuntary pulse throbs between my legs.

"Don't move." A hot expulsion of air steams the side of my neck, the order drenched in a honeyed tone. Then the long, lean shape of a body warms the length of my spine.

I practically vibrate with the urge to pull away. I cannot stay here. To watch—

"Closing your eyes will make no difference," Zephyrus whispers. "You have already seen."

It is true. How I hate that it is true.

In the dark behind my eyelids, there lingers the imprint of two people coupling. The man's groan sends a dart of heat through my core. The bed squeaks. There is the slap of skin colliding, wet and immediate.

"Tell me your thoughts, darling novitiate."

I squeeze my eyes shut tighter. "Why do they do this here?" My voice wobbles. "Anyone could stumble across them."

"I believe that is the point."

The woman moans wantonly, and I flinch. A weight sinks onto my hip—his hand?—then is removed. "Why does she allow him to do this?"

"He brings her pleasure," murmurs Zephyrus.

"He touches her inappropriately."

"Does he?"

Their breathing spikes, audible over the squeaking bed frame, the man emitting low grunts, the woman's gasps climbing to higher frequencies.

"Have you ever touched yourself?" Rich and throaty, his voice reminds me of every temptation. "Look again," he says.

I must be under some charm. It is the only explanation as to why I follow his instruction. There is the couple on the bed, their languorous movements and flushed, open mouths. The man mounts the woman from behind. An uncomfortable warmth spreads through my lower belly.

"Why did you abandon me?" I demand, voice low. "You left me alone, among all those creatures."

Zephyrus leans closer, and the smell of rain washes over me. "I wanted to see what kind of woman you are. Do you close your eyes, or do you face the uncomfortable truths of the world?"

"What does this prove," I mutter, "except to make me feel small and afraid?" Whirling around, I brush past him. "If that was your goal, then congratulations, you have accomplished it."

Zephyrus catches the sleeve of my dress. "Don't you want to see how it ends?"

The couple, he means. I am ashamed to have been caught staring. More so, I am ashamed by my inexplicable fascination with the display. Why should I care how it ends? It has nothing to do with me.

"No." I yank my arm free. "I want to return to Thornbrook."

Zephyrus sobers then, stepping back to give me space. "About that." He brushes aside a curl falling into his eyes. "There is something I must do first."

I'm quickly realizing the depth of my stupidity. Trusting a man I know nothing about. I feel helpless, for Zephyrus is my only way out of Under. I must follow him whether I want to or not.

We depart the woods in silence, trees exchanged for a soaring, pillar-lined hall located at the far boundary of the grove, the chaos of the lake muffled by growing distance. Eventually, mist clouds the air, its cooling touch dampening my dress. The walls narrow into a small chamber where a waterfall pounds white foam into a pool below. Pink lights flicker from crannies in the walls.

Partially submerged rocks provide a crossing over the water. Zephyrus leaps across with ease. I pick my way across slowly, following him into an even narrower tunnel behind the waterfall.

"From this point forward," Zephyrus says, "I will go alone."

My stomach bottoms out. "You're leaving me again?"

He glances sidelong at me. "Not for long. The person I'm meeting would take an interest in you. For your own safety, it is best to remain out of sight."

A nice sentiment, but rather pointless considering how many of the fair folk noticed my presence at the festivities. Then again, why take unnecessary risks?

"Stay here." He moves off without bothering to wait for my reply. The arrogance of him.

Crouching down, I press against the wall, grateful for its solidity. Darkness stamps the space before my eyes. I fight the shudder that runs through me. *I am safe*, I think, but am I, truly? I imagine a candle, a fire, lamplight, the sun. A floral aroma teases my senses, reminding me of Thornbrook's lush, manicured grounds.

"Zephyrus." An unfamiliar male voice drags through the dark in a low, faint rasp. "I did not expect you so soon."

"Ever the obedient servant," he drawls. "You call, I answer. Is that not how this relationship works?"

There is a pause. "Zephyrus," says the man. "I called for you three months ago. I do not appreciate being kept waiting."

My mouth parts soundlessly. This must be the keeper of Zephyrus' name. He who holds power over the Bringer of Spring.

"Not that it's any of your concern," he responds insouciantly, "but I was visiting my brother."

Whoever he speaks to laughs. It is a sound made of fragments, spewed forth. "I'm surprised your brother wanted to see you. But how is Boreas?"

"He is well. He and his wife are aptly suited." The hesitation is so slight I nearly miss it. "I have not seen him this happy in a long time."

"Do I detect jealousy?" I hear the smile in his voice, and its oily quality slips beneath my skin. "You had your chance at happiness. You do not deserve another."

"Do you not grow tired of this?" Zephyrus snaps out. "I am here. Let that be enough."

A scuffling sound in the darkness: something massive being dragged across stone.

"It will never be enough." Ice coats the clipped response. "I had hoped you would have realized that."

It is heavy, this quiet, all the world a void.

A heavy *whump* interrupts the silence, as though something wallops the ground. In a conversational tone, the man adds, "Who is the mortal woman you have brought to Under? I daresay I would like to meet her."

My heart stutters in my chest, and I press deeper into the crevice. How? I've made absolutely no sound.

"I do not believe the lady would be comfortable in your presence. This is her first visit to Under, and she is already overwhelmed."

"Do you imply I will frighten her?"

"No implication necessary. I know it to be true."

Another hoarse cackle. "You have always entertained me, Zephyrus. Bring the girl. I wish to exchange words with her."

The jagged wall jabs into my spine so severely the vertebrae will likely bruise by morning. I cannot flee, lest I lose myself and remain trapped here forevermore. Before me, the grassy path extends toward whoever speaks with that abrasive tone.

A shrill cry of pain cuts through the passage, and my heart shrivels as a wave of cold sweeps through me. It sounded like Zephyrus.

"You continue to test me, Bringer of Spring. Bring the girl, and make haste. I have waited long enough."

Crouched within the recess, I stare unblinkingly at the lightless passage, willing something to take shape. No footsteps reach my ears. But I am not surprised when, moments later, Zephyrus emerges from the inky mouth of the tunnel, a small pink orb aglow in his palm.

Something in his face has changed, the warped angles cut into new severity. Then it comes to me. His mouth no longer holds the shape of laughter.

"I don't want to go," I whisper.

"You are wise to feel this way." He scrubs a hand over his jaw, up into his hair. The glass sphere trembles in his grip. "Come. We do not want to anger him."

One, two, three heartbeats later, I still haven't moved. "Will he kill me?"

Zephyrus strides forward, grass hissing beneath his boots. He is frighteningly grave. "No. He is curious as to why I've brought you here. He's likely contemplating how best to use this to his advantage—use you as a tool to control me."

I swallow to bring moisture to my mouth. What manner of creature awaits me on the other side of this gloom? "What's his name?"

"Pierus. He was once a sovereign of distant lands. Now he has asserted his rule here, under the name of the Orchid King."

My legs wobble as I push to my feet and adjust the dried, crusted fabric around my legs. No matter how hard I try, I am unable to smooth my ragged breathing.

"Heavenly Father," I whisper. "Guide me through the darkest waters. Lead me to your house of worship."

Zephyrus peers at me. All emotion has been wiped clean from his features. "Your god cannot help you here."

The light he holds goes dark.

The tautness in my chest fuses into a cold, hard diamond, an ache of sharp points. "Can you turn the light back on?" I feel lightheaded. "Please?"

"Pierus has temporarily blocked its ability to glow. He knows I have it and would prefer to make me as uncomfortable as possible. We will have to walk in the dark."

I fall mute. My tongue, slack with rising terror, will not take shape.

A warm hand cups my elbow, and he murmurs, low enough that I'm certain the sound does not carry, "Do not fret. The darkness is not forever." Gently, Zephyrus draws me forward. "Put your hand on the wall," he says. "Let it be your guide."

Damp rock whispers against my glove. If I close my eyes, I can almost convince myself this darkness is one I have chosen.

"I heard a scream earlier," I murmur, oddly reassured by Zephyrus' presence. "Did he hurt you?"

"Pierus enjoys his punishments." As the passageway narrows, the air turns to frost in my mouth. "Remember not to speak your name. Of all those in Under to be bound to, Pierus is the worst."

He does not have to worry about that. I am as tight-lipped as they come. "How did he capture your name?"

A touch guides me to the left. Zephyrus steps so lightly I cannot hear his boots making contact with the grass. "Pierus and I have long been acquainted, unfortunately. Although he possesses my name, that is not what binds me to him."

Since venturing into Under, my questions have multiplied, and here is another tossed onto the pile, this mystery surrounding the Bringer of Spring. If he is not bound to the Orchid King by name, then what?

"When you see him, try not to stare, and do your best to make polite conversation. Pierus appreciates the effort." His hand spasms around my arm, and we slow. "You can open your eyes."

We stand inside a shining, moonlit cavern, its walls dripping silver. Pink blooms capped in tiny, curling petals carpet the earth, interspersed among the grass. Roses. It explains the honeyed aroma. But what awaits us against the opposite wall strikes me with numbing cold.

The man's lower body appears to have been consumed by the nightshade plant—enormous, carnivorous flowers flushed scarlet and shaped like open mouths. Roots, pale and lumpy as spoiled milk, slither from beneath the leaves and vines shielding his lower half from view. His torso is humanoid, though a few blossoms have erupted through the naked skin of his muscled shoulders, their stems heavily spined, pricked red, red, red.

"Hello, young novitiate." The man cannot be fair folk, for his eyes do not resemble stone. They are like mine, like those of the Bringer of Spring, though this man's are blue. "You smell of the incense they burn in the church."

Remembering Zephyrus' advice, I nod politely. "We burn it every Holy Day."

He lifts a clawed hand. A ropy vine slinks toward me along the ground, gently parting the overgrown grass. I recoil, slamming into Zephyrus' chest as Pierus coaxes, "Let me have a closer look at you."

The vine locks around my wrist. It tugs, forcing me to step forward or be dragged. And there the vine remains, a heavy bracelet, faintly spined.

Pierus gives me a thorough once-over. My cheeks grow warm from the attention. "May I ask what they call you?" he inquires.

I thought I was prepared for this question, but truthfully, my mind blanked the moment the light vanished in the tunnel. "You may call me novitiate."

A small, secret smile graces the man's mouth. Were his body not so hideously unnatural, I might consider him handsome. "Zephyrus has taught you well." Pierus turns his attention to the Bringer of Spring, who stands isolated in a corner. "Though I wonder why he has brought you here. Mortals are forbidden to visit Under except on the eve of the tithe."

I look from Zephyrus to the Orchid King. "He claimed I would be granted amnesty. I don't want to cause trouble."

"Nonsense." Strands of silver hair slide across his smooth, hairless chest, that chiseled abdomen. "The ritual will not take long. If you have a weak stomach, I suggest you avert your gaze."

A low buzz begins to vibrate my eardrums. *Run*, a voice hisses, but my feet are rooted. "Ritual?"

The Orchid King lifts his eyebrows. They veer sharply together, forming a severe mountain peak. "He did not tell you? But I should not be surprised."

"She doesn't need to see this," Zephyrus growls, the first words he has uttered since entering the cavern. "Allow her to wait in the tunnel until the ritual is completed."

"Zephyrus." His chuckle skates across my shivering flesh. "You are the one who invited her into Under." The Orchid King's gaze returns to me. "Do not be frightened, young novitiate. Zephyrus and I have an understanding."

"I implore you again," Zephyrus says. "Let her leave."

A second vine lifts to curl beneath the Orchid King's chin. Lips pursed, he considers me, and I quake from the intrusion of his pervasive gaze. I imagine those curved talons pricking the ripeness of my flesh, their possessive hold.

"No." He shakes his head. "Lessons must be learned, and I want this woman to know what happens when my orders are disobeyed. You have kept me waiting long enough. Let the ritual proceed."

The Bringer of Spring goes still. Truly, I did not realize how expressive he was until the brightness was extinguished from his face.

He moves in pieces—shoulders, arms, wrists, fingers. Grasping the hem of his tunic, he peels it over his head, tosses it aside. My attention flicks to his naked torso before skittering elsewhere.

"This will not take long," the Orchid King assures.

One of the flowers uncoils, latching its spined mouth against Zephyrus' neck.

I trip backward with a horrified yelp and land hard on my rear. A second flower extends from a slender vine, affixing itself to his cheek, a third to his forearm. Zephyrus twitches, face rigid with pain, and falls to his knees.

Scuttling backward, I ram into the wall, paralyzed by the atrocity unfolding before my eyes. Five flowers fuse to Zephyrus' naked torso, then seven, now ten.

Another twitch renders his arms useless, yet he emits not a sound. When a blossom sinks into the pectoral muscle above his heart, his back arches, taut abdomen flexing in shallow pulsations. His mouth yawns in a muted scream.

The petals' pink hue darkens to carmine. They grow engorged, inflamed, the drink too bountiful to contain. Red seeps from their suckling mouths.

By the Father. My gaze lifts to the Orchid King, who watches me with avid fascination. I flinch, pressing harder against the rock.

Under is a poison. This I knew. I should never have agreed to this fool's errand.

When the blooms finally detach with wet sounds of suction, Zephyrus slumps forward, panting through his teeth. The spines have punctured his skin, leaving half-moon markings. Across his ribs, there appears to be a tattoo—flowers colored white, pink, and violet. Strange. But the sight is quickly masked as he replaces his tunic and climbs to his feet. He will not look at me. For whatever reason, I wish he would.

"Refuse my call again," Pierus intones, "and I will drain every last drop from your body. This is your final warning." A wave of his clawed hand. "Dismissed."

Zephyrus' dull, distant eyes stare straight through Pierus. There is no sign of the charismatic man from earlier. Turning on his heel, he strides from the room.

The Orchid King shifts his focus onto me. At his back, the entire field of roses has hemorrhaged, pink replaced with a dense red. "You would do well to heed my warning, young novitiate. Do not trust Zephyrus. He will use you for his own gain." One of the flowers curling from his back unfurls, then clamps shut. "Should you need aid, you may seek me out. Under is a treacherous place, after all."

7

"ZEPHYRUS!"

He pushes onward, walking so swiftly I'm forced to run. By the time we emerge behind the waterfall, sweat and mist drench my skin.

Zephyrus leaps across the slick rocks, landing lightly on the opposite bank. I scramble after him, but I should know better than to think I can outrun the West Wind. He lengthens his gait, driving continuously forward. It does not take long before we return to the underground lake with its pulsating drums and shattering noise. Grass sprouts before me, Zephyrus only two strides ahead.

"Wait." I reach for him without thought as he stops, stiff in the frame, and angles his face away from me.

"The Orchid King," I gasp. "Why did he . . .?"

My gaze drops to Zephyrus' chest, but his tunic shields the aftermath of that gruesome feeding. The image marks my vision, set to scar. A dark cavern. A blanket of pink blossoms, the scent of honey in the air.

"Drink my blood?" he offers.

I nod slowly. We may as well be standing alone in the vaulted cavern, for the fair folk, every shape and every shade, seem to diminish in light of what has just occurred, veiled behind the red brightness dousing the walls.

The West Wind sighs. "There are forces at work you will not understand. Old blood. Old debts. For your safety, it is best to remain in the dark." He speaks all this without looking at me. His voice, however, trembles.

"But why does he treat you so poorly?" No, *poorly* is not the right word. That display of power? Absolutely disgusting. "If Pierus—"

"Please." Zephyrus lifts a hand. The long, tapered fingers curl slightly, as if grasping for something to hold. "Do not speak his name." Quickly, he searches the crowd. It has somewhat dispersed, though I spot a number of the smaller sprites, identified by their rotund figures and twig-like limbs. "If you must, refer to him as the Orchid King. It is disrespectful to do otherwise, and many fair folk are employed in his service."

I take a few breaths, trying to process this new information, arrange it beside all I have learned this evening. The effort fatigues me. It is too complex, too overwhelming. "What I don't understand is why you had to complete that—" My stomach turns at the recollection. "*Ritual.*"

Only now does Zephyrus turn. His eyes are darkened moss with little light to brighten them.

"The only thing I can tell you is that the past is always present. As such, this is the life I must live."

"But you're his captive," I press. "Why? For how long?"

He rests a hand against the wall. Beneath his touch, the stone shimmers into a bright opening that reveals a familiar bend of water singing over rocks. There is no mistaking it. Carterhaugh lies on the other side of the doorway.

"This is where I leave you," Zephyrus says.

A gentle push sends me stumbling through the quiet wood. When I turn around, there is no sign of the entrance, nor the Bringer of Spring, only the smooth, leaden face of a boulder.

I blink, a bit dazed. Daylight streams through the broken canopy. Noon, judging by the sun's position, which means I have missed not only service, but breakfast and morning chores. Zephyrus failed to maintain his end of the bargain. My absence has no doubt been noticed.

Lifting my dress, I hurry back up the mountain, trying to think of an adequate excuse for my absence. I could claim I was gathering pearl blossom, which only blooms under moonlight, and which the infirmary is dangerously low on. Soon enough, the church spire breaches Carterhaugh's leafy crown. Once the porter admits me through the gatehouse, I fly across the grounds toward the cloister. As I turn a corner, I run into Isobel and Fiona, both of whom I was supposed to harvest barley with this morning.

Isobel shrieks and recoils against Fiona, whose face drains of color so quickly she teeters. "Brielle?"

I offer my most apologetic smile. Perhaps it is not too late to fix the damage I've wrought. "Sorry for missing chores earlier. I lost track of time and . . ." And nothing. The lie is so pathetic it doesn't seem to be worth voicing.

They stare at me, slack-jawed, eyes wide.

Isobel recovers first. "What are you going on about?" she cries, and the strength of her ire sends me back a step, my shoulder knocking one of the pillars. "Mother Mabel has been worried *sick* about you. Is this some kind of joke?"

Joke? I look to Fiona in confusion. The younger novitiate approaches me, slow and watchful. Never before has she regarded me this way: as though I have risen from the dead. "Brielle," she says hoarsely. "What happened to you?"

Too much, I nearly say, but I must remain tight-lipped. "The infirmary is low on pearl blossom, so I went to gather some at the riverbank. I'm sorry I lost track of time." It has happened before, so it isn't completely out of the realm of possibility.

Fiona's expression grows troubled. She knows, as I do, that traveling from Thornbrook to the River Twee, where pearl blossom thrives, takes less than an hour on foot. "Did you get lost?"

"No."

"Then what happened?" Isobel demands. "We looked everywhere for you. Mother Mabel sent for the sheriff."

THE WEST WIND • 65

"The sheriff?" My voice crests sharply. Through the open doors at the end of the corridor, a group of novitiates startles at the disturbance. Shade obscures their features, but someone gasps, "Brielle?"

I do not understand. Only once before has our abbess sent for the sheriff. It took seven days of searching to find Madeline, whose mysterious pregnancy led to her eventual dismissal from the abbey. "Why would she send for him? I was only gone for an hour."

"An hour?" Fiona is incredulous. "Brielle," she whispers. "It's been seven *days*."

The words do not immediately process. "What?"

"You've been gone for a week."

"Stop." My voice cracks. "Do not toy with me. I went down to the river, but I am here now." Have they fashioned this hoax as a punishment for my tardiness? If so, I do not appreciate the distress it causes me.

I begin to brush past them, but Fiona snags my arm, her expression grim. She is stronger than I had anticipated. "It is no act. We've been searching for you for many days. We believed you to be dead."

My blood pounds so forcefully my skin throbs with each heaving beat. In the far doorway, the novitiates have multiplied, their mystified whispers seeping out into the open air. Any attempt to neutralize my features crumbles as my mind falls quiet.

It cannot be. Because if what they claim is true, then somehow, over the course of a single night in Under, an entire week has passed in my absence.

"Mother Mabel truly sent for the sheriff?" I croak.

Fiona nods. Isobel shuffles backward as if I carry a pox.

"I will speak with her." I nod to myself, for it is a good plan. We will speak, and I will explain my mysterious absence. "What time is it?"

"The midday bell rang a short while ago." Isobel and Fiona stand as a single unit against me, wariness in their eyes. "She is at the church."

The weight of their suspicion trails me as I head for the church, hurrying as quickly as my weary soles will allow. My dress has dried into a crusty mess, and my red curls have become so snarled it will take the entire evening to separate them. Mother Mabel will know something is amiss.

The sanctuary doors stand open. It feels silly to wash my hands when the rest of me is so filthy, but I stop to use the lavabo prior to entering, watching the clouded water settle into the basin. The air cools as I step onto hallowed ground: gray stone walls, jeweled glass. The rug that runs between the rows of pews mutes my footsteps as I pad toward the altar, atop which the trio of candles burn. Father, Son, Holy Ghost. Never to be extinguished.

Mother Mabel kneels at the railing surrounding the sanctuary, her back to me. She wears the ornate, sleeveless chasuble, which she dons during Mass and other ceremonial events, a symbol of her unselfish service. Beneath it, the billowing white sleeves of her alb frame her clasped hands.

Joining her at the railing, I kneel on the cushion and bow my head. What are the ways in which I've strayed?

I have taken a man into my room.

I have watched a private, sexual act and did not shut my eyes to it.

I have entered a place that is forbidden to me.

Shame rises to clot my airway. It hardens, becomes stone. *Forgive me, Father.* For He will know where I have been and with whom.

Mother Mabel stirs at my side. A long exhalation streams from her beaked nose. "I have questions for you," she murmurs.

My eyes open, and I turn to meet her gaze. My stomach twists. Disapproval or disappointment? I'm not sure which is worse. "Yes, Mother Mabel."

"Come." Pushing to her feet, she gestures for me to follow.

A short aisle branching from the main altar flows into the sacristy. The tiny room is barred by a heavy oaken door, which thuds shut upon our entrance, the wood thick enough to muffle any sounds from within.

I have visited the sacristy countless times over the past decade. Here, the abbess vests and prepares for service. It also houses the sacred vessels used during Mass—the altar linings, the chalice and paten, and the Text itself.

Tapestries depicting particularly violent scenes from our literature line the walls: the story of Byron, from the Book of Fate, who was beheaded after admitting to incestuous relations with his daughter; the story of Bram—Carterhaugh's last true king before northern barbarians slaughtered his clan—from the Book of Night.

"Sit," Mother Mabel says.

I obey. It is for the best, since my knees have begun to tremble. The abbess' features are never more severe than when cast in the shadow-dark flicker of candlelight.

She strides past me with a scuff of silk slippers. "You were missed this week, Brielle. When you did not show up for service, your fellow novitiates believed you to have fallen ill." She stalls, pivots, and slowly paces the opposite direction, sweet incense wafting in her wake. "But when Fiona checked your room, she found it empty, your bed unmade."

Nothing I might say could explain my absence. I cannot stop a stone rolling downhill.

Sometimes it is easier to say nothing.

"When you did not show up for breakfast, I grew worried. It is unlike you to miss meals, which is why, when evening fell, I decided something terrible must have befallen you and called on the sheriff."

The hair on my body stiffens. Then it is true. Someone must have trekked all the way to Kilkare to alert him to my disappearance.

"He lost your trail at the River Twee. We feared you had drowned."

My eyes widen at this. When a person drowns, their soul is denied the opportunity to pass into the Eternal Lands. Water, which touches the earth, rather than the heavens, is believed to store the sins of all who have come before us.

"No, Mother Mabel." My sweating palms stick to the inside of my gloves as I rub my hands over my thighs. "I am well, as you can see."

"I'm glad," she replies, but the terseness of her response reveals her distaste for my frazzled appearance. "It is a miracle you have returned healthy and whole." There is a pause. "I would like an explanation."

She demands something I am unable to divulge. By entering Under prior to the tithe, I have broken the abbey's oldest rule, set in place to secure our safety in the wilds of Carterhaugh.

"I'm sorry," I manage, and bow deeper. "I left because I wanted to help gather supplies for the physician, but it is no excuse."

"And what, exactly, did Maria ask you to gather?"

"Pearl blossom," I stutter.

She hums, a flat, shapeless sound that offers no indication of her thoughts. "That's interesting, because when we questioned Maria about your absence, she claimed not to have spoken to you in days."

And I have officially said too much.

"Did anyone else know where you were going?" she demands.

"Fiona." It is the first name that comes to mind. "I informed her I might be late for morning chores, but I grew disoriented in the darkness. I must have lost the trail."

Her eyebrows climb high. "You, lose the trail? But you have been exploring those footpaths for a decade." A moment of silence passes. "Look at me."

My throat contracts with the force of my swallow, and I lift my head. Mother Mabel's facial muscles have frozen in an expression of polite interest.

"What are the Seven Decrees?" she demands.

I have not had to state the Decrees since I was a child. It is the worst form of humiliation, that the abbess believes I need reminding of the Decrees when I carry them in my heart all days of the week. "Please, Mother Mabel."

"The Decrees, Brielle."

I take a shaky breath as the flush climbs my throat and singes red across my face. "Thou shalt not kill. Thou shalt not steal. Thou shalt not covet. Thou shalt not disrespect thy mother or thy father. Thou shalt not forsake thy God." My voice grows hoarse the longer I speak without pause, each rule a dead weight I must cast aside. I swallow and finish with, "Thou shalt remember the Holy Day."

"You missed one."

I had hoped she wouldn't notice.

Once I complete the set, it will become real. The last vestiges of this dream-like state will peel away. I am not ready.

"What is the Seventh Decree?" she snaps.

"Thou shalt not lie."

Mother Mabel links her fingers together, studying me. Cold radiates through my dress, and my knees begin to ache from pressing into the hard stone. "You vanished for a week. Where did you go? What was so important that you thought it necessary to leave without informing anyone where you were going? And I want the truth."

Sweat slithers down the column of my spine. Once this information comes to light, I might be dismissed from Thornbrook. I do not think I could survive the world untethered. "As I said, I was seeking pearl blossom."

"Then why did your trail lead northwest as opposed to southwest, where the plant grows?"

The lies spin webs, but I cannot keep track of their sticky threads. Whatever the consequence, I will accept it, however sharp the barbs. Do I deserve to bleed, then?

"Mother Mabel—"

"Enough. I have heard enough." Presenting her back, she shrugs off the impressive chasuble, hangs it on a wall hook. Beneath, she wears her alb, the gold stole, the cincture with its trio of knots.

She unties each knot deliberately. Her long nails pick at the rope and slide it free. Setting aside the cord, she then removes the stole, hanging it with the chasuble. Lastly, her alb.

Mother Mabel now wears only a flimsy white tunic. I stare at the pasty skin of her exposed calves.

She crosses the room to remove something from a box that sits on a low shelf. After a moment, she returns to my side. "Knowing the Decrees that guide us, is there anything you would like to add? Anything at all?" She regards me with much knowing. I think I have fallen far in her eyes.

Nothing I say would change my fate, so I do what I have been taught to do since I was eleven years old, hunched on the abbey stoop beneath the pouring rain, watching a dark figure descend the mountain out of sight.

I keep my mouth shut.

Mother Mabel strides for the door. Its lock thunks into place. "Please remove your dress."

My eyes drop, fingers twitching into loose fists. A wave of cold drags at me. "I do not understand."

"I will not repeat myself."

The punishing edge of that statement sends me to my feet. Presenting her my back, I remove my dress so I'm left in only my chemise and breastband. I shiver in the cool air.

"Kneel."

My knees crack against the flagstones. There is a faint snap of leather—the lash. A metallic taste coats my tongue.

Mother Mabel rounds my back. The church's incense has always comforted me, but now it turns my stomach, its sweetness curdling to rot. "I am sorry to do this to you, Brielle. I hope you understand."

The air keens seconds before pain ruptures across my spine.

I scream, lurching forward as the searing line burns with increasing agony. My fingernails bite into the rough stone. My head hangs, and I pant through the shock, the wounded girl within me whimpering.

"A lash for every day you were missing," the abbess whispers from behind. "A lash for every lie that spoils your tongue."

The lash comes down. Then—fire across my back.

Seven lashes for seven days.

Seven lashes for seven decrees.

Seven lashes for the stark cruelty of a realm beneath the earth, and rivers, rivers, rivers of blood.

8

"BRIELLE."

The waspish tone slaps me into wakefulness. Harper stands before me, hands on hips, mouth pinched as though having recently sucked on a lemon.

I straighten from where I dozed off at my table, wincing from the twinge across my back. The refectory clamors with scraping utensils, clattering bowls. It smells of boiled greens and the hot, bubbling sweetness of fresh porridge.

Harper continues to glare at me expectantly. "What?" I hiss. Conversation is prohibited during meals.

"What is it Mother Mabel ever saw in you?" A cant of her head. "After that embarrassment with your disappearance, she must regret trusting one so pitiful."

Harper spews so much vitriol it's a wonder plants don't wither in her presence. And here I sit, receiving blows like a pelting rain.

Disappointment and shame hit me all over again. I have worked tirelessly for this opportunity, and within a day, my hopes were dashed. Mother Mabel will not select me as an acolyte this year. Perhaps never. I am not worthy. I cannot be trusted.

"Well?" Her toe taps with irritating calm. "Will you answer me, or will you stand there like a dolt?"

Meals are a time to reflect on ourselves, deepen our faith, strengthen our principles. But Harper will not cave. She will pry every desired emotion free. She will hammer blows until I sunder.

"I have nothing to say to you." My voice rings with surprising strength. "The fact that you insist on belittling me when I am already brought low reveals just how weak your character is." Indeed, in all the years I've known Harper, I have seen no growth from her, only stagnation.

Her eyes flare. She seems to grow four inches in the next breath. "Weak character. How ironic. According to Isobel, your lies got you into this mess. Your deceptions will only make it easier for Mother Mabel to choose me to become the next acolyte."

"No matter who Mother Mabel chooses to ascend, it won't stop me from continuing my studies," I press. "Acolyte or not, I will deepen my relationship with the Father."

Thankfully, the bell peals, signaling the end of breakfast. Everyone files out the doors to begin their morning chores. Since I'm assigned clean-up duty, I remain in the hall, where the smell of boiled vegetables lingers. A single novitiate to clean the mess of one hundred women, normally a task shared by four. But I will not complain, just as I did not complain yesterday. Stacks of bowls coated in food fill three large buckets. One by one, I drag them to the kitchen, where I fill a massive tub with water from the well and begin to scrub each dish and utensil clean.

I move slowly, for that is the only way I can move lately. Three sundowns, three sunrises, yet my back still aches fiercely. Any slight shift drags my dress across the bruised flesh. I expected the pain to subside, but it has worsened over the passing days.

It takes two hours to wash the dishes, clean the tables, sweep the floor. That done, I head upstairs to exchange my slippers for boots, shuffling slowly to combat the lightheadedness. I've an hour before I'm needed in the fields.

Once inside my room, I move to the mirror. My hands shake as I unbutton the front of my dress, then my chemise, peeling both from my clammy skin and exposing my back to the looking glass.

Deep violet curdles the surface of my skin. The bruises' outer rings have cooled to a mealy gray, but the centers rage a livid red, nearly the same shade as my hair. I flinch in remembrance of the lash, seven painful welts received.

With an unsteady breath, I rebutton my undergarment and adjust my dress. Mother Mabel has barred me from the infirmary. In the Book of Grief, Arran traveled across the highlands for twelve days enduring the pain of a festering sword wound, and lived. According to our Abbess on High, I, too, will withstand this suffering.

I've revealed nothing of what transpired in the sacristy. I spend my evenings in the forge, away from prying eyes, but my smithing comes at a cost. I can only shape the metal for so long before my back spasms and the tools slip from my grasp. Before my disgrace, the abbess had trained me after evening Mass each week, but she did not show up for our knife-fighting lesson yesterday. Another punishment?

As I depart my bedroom, something creaks behind me, and I glance over my shoulder. The window shutters swing open, revealing the ferocious black waters of the strait in the distance, a line of soot ground into the space between the cliffs and the Gray's rocky shore. A scented breeze drifts inside: spring.

My slow, drudging pulse begins to climb. Something flashes in my periphery, and it is a wonder I'm able to rein in my ire as I spin around to face Zephyrus.

"Get out."

The West Wind arches a brow. He practically glows with health, curls ashine, skin kissed by a rosy hue. His face, however, maintains its strange, angular appearance, even without the swelling and gore. "Is that any way to greet a guest?"

"You are not welcome here," I snap.

His lips curve. A dangerous thing, that mouth, able to snarl and croon in equal measure. "So there *is* fire within you. I was wondering when it would manifest."

That he treats my anger like a performance to witness prods my fury from its doze. Even my red curls spring from their confinement.

Moving to the door, I engage the lock. I cannot risk anyone discovering him here. Then I whirl around to face him again. "I will not repeat myself. I wish never to see or speak to you again. Leave."

Closer he sidles, padding with all the quiet of a barn cat. White tunic, rough trousers, weathered boots. I am remembering the way his garb, drenched from the water of the spring, clung to his frame. I promptly shut the door on such thoughts.

"I admit, your anger confuses me," he muses, with a softness that borders on uncertainty. "I thought you would be pleased. After all, I gave you the opportunity to learn the answer to the question closest to your heart."

"You assumed incorrectly." I never should have agreed to accompany him, but I allowed myself to dream.

He stops at my desk, skimming a hand over my copy of the Text, open to the Book of Truth—last night's reading. The West Wind, standing in my room, stealing the air. A god. I cannot believe it.

"What has changed?" A calm inquiry, yet tension simmers underneath.

Nothing, and everything. I have glimpsed things—terrible, lovely, yearning things—in a world that is not for me.

"It is simple," I state. "I will not be returning to Under, nor will I associate with you in the future."

"You have not answered the question."

"Because it is none of your business."

"Is it not?" His hands slide into his pockets. If only I could read him better. "Tell me why."

I consider it—saying *no*. "Should Mother Mabel learn of my visit to Under, I could be cast from the abbey. Should she learn of our association, I absolutely would be. Thornbrook is my home. I will not risk it."

Strangely enough, this last statement seems to weaken whatever barrier exists between us. It lessens the intensity rolling off his shoulders, the stiffness of his posture. It quiets him momentarily.

"Did you know that time passes differently in Under?" I ask.

He ambles to the window, plucks the sprig of dried lavender from the sill and twirls it between his fingers. Sunlight marks a pale bloom across his cheekbone. It smooths the patchy quality to his tanned skin. "I was aware," he remarks. "Under decides what length of time passes below, whether it is slower or faster compared to above-ground. But I did not take it into consideration. I am used to working alone."

Yet I told him how important it was to return to Thornbrook before dawn. What is the truth—these words, or his actions?

"You promised I would be back in a timely manner."

He sighs, as though this conversation is an inconvenience, and returns the lavender to its spot on the sill. "What can I say? I lost track of time. What is a few more hours, really?" This next pause is decidedly more bitter. "Even if I wanted to leave, I could not have in that moment. Pierus called for me, and the power he exerts over my name dictates that I must submit. If he demands I sit submerged in a river for seven hours, unclothed, then I am helpless to resist. The closer in proximity I am to him, the stronger the compulsion to obey. I am, in all ways, his puppet."

I cannot quite hide my distaste. It sounds like an excuse to me. "Maybe it didn't matter to you, but it mattered to me." Then, quieter: "You lack much care, Bringer of Spring, when it comes to thought for others."

A silence descends. He appears as though he wishes to speak, yet remains oddly mute, his posture hunched. Very well. I will waste no more breath on someone so lacking in humility. "You have overstayed your welcome," I inform him, though he was never welcome to begin with. "I insist you leave at once."

"There are things I wish to say to you, Brielle. I had hoped you would at least allow me that opportunity."

Enough of these games. If Zephyrus will not leave, then I will.

I'm nearly to the door when he catches my shoulder and unknowingly places pressure on my bruising. A cry of pain cracks out of me as I recoil.

Zephyrus drops his hand, startled.

A hiss punches past my clenched teeth. The throb migrates up my spine, digging deep into muscle, bone. I shuffle sideways to put more distance between us. His gaze drops to where my hand curves around my shoulder, sheltering it from his touch.

"You are injured?" Too quiet.

I do not respond.

He steps forward.

I step back.

Zephyrus' eyes darken, and a discomfiting thrum of energy courses through me. He smiles so readily and weaves such pretty lies, but something lurks beneath that facade, and it is not as mild as I had assumed.

"What happened?" he demands.

"That's my business," I state. He will take nothing more from me. I will not give him the satisfaction.

A rough hand drags through his curls with leashed patience. He tucks his tongue into his cheek, the look of a man considering a situation from all angles, examining responses and discarding them, all but one. "Be that as it may," he continues with willful obstinacy, "I have a responsibility to you. A debt."

The West Wind will never be satisfied. He will tear into flesh until he hits bone. "You have no such thing. Let me be clear. I aided you in your time of need, and you repaid that debt. We have no further business with each other."

He eyes me doubtfully. "But was the debt repaid?" Seeing my confusion, he elaborates, "You're saying you gained the knowledge you sought? If I recall, you did not appear particularly enthused after your meeting with Willow. Why, you didn't mention it at all."

I hate how I begin to cave despite my intentions. He knows so much more than me. Thus, he must know best.

"You want to know what happened?" I manage, voice hoarse with shame. "By the time I returned to the abbey, an entire *week* had passed." My throat strains as the tears well. "Everyone thought I was dead!"

His expression has frozen into something borderline inhuman. Zephyrus is not mortal, I remind myself. He is something far beyond my comprehension.

"You were punished because you did not confess where you had been. Is that it?"

"I told you I was forbidden to enter Under." A single tear tracks down my cheek. I wipe it away.

A gust snaps at the shutters, startling me.

"What punishment did you receive?" Zephyrus demands.

"It doesn't matter." The penalty was deserved. I strayed. I trusted the wrong person, someone blind to my discomfort. I am beginning to think the Orchid King was correct in his assessment of Zephyrus.

"Brielle." And now his voice mollifies, stretching slow and languorous as a cat. "I cannot help you unless you tell me what happened." His mouth tugs, his eyes sparkling. It would be easy to fall into them.

Yet I take another step back. "I did not ask for your help, and I do not want it."

He hesitates, as if coming to a decision. Then his shoulders slump, and he finally takes his leave via the open window, using the dense ferns clambering up the tower for footholds. "You are right," he says, pausing in his descent. "I should have kept track of the passing time, but there was much on my mind. If I could explain—"

"You have taught me a valuable lesson, Zephyrus." Leaning forward, I grip the windowsill, fingers digging into the warped timber. "Never trust a man."

I slam the shutters in his face.

Later that evening, I sit in bed, journal propped open on my lap. Since Zephyrus' departure, I've struggled to pacify the creature pacing inside my chest. Rather than retreating to the forge, I pick up my quill, my jar of charcoal ink, and scratch at the parchment until the tightness within me eases, my mind quieting. I reflect on Zephyrus'

unexpected arrival, the shock and fury and dismay I'd felt. I parse out the moments of shame. I list all that I wished I'd said to him but did not. I speak to the paper as I would to a dear friend, though I have none.

I write until my hand cramps, until my eyes sting with fatigue and the words blur, until ink smears the parchment, until my spine cracks from hunching over the journal. But alas, I still do not understand why this series of events occurred, why I have received this misfortune. Poised at the bottom of the page, my quill hovers, awaiting direction.

I write, *Who am I to question the Father's plan?* and leave it at that.

A sound startles me awake.

It is brief—too brief to know what, exactly, woke me. My room does not harbor its usual amber glow. The candle I light nightly has burned to its wick, and the far wall reflects only the brightness of moonlight on white plaster. The shutters, when I prepared for bed, were closed. They currently hang open, a frame for the forested hills, the darkness of Carterhaugh in slumber.

I lie frozen on my stomach, blankets tangled around my legs. Snagging my dagger from beneath the pillow, I suck in air, preparing to scream.

"I would not recommend that if I were you."

The scream finds a premature death. It is an age before the strength to reply returns. "I told you not to show your face again."

"Is my face displeasing to you?"

Conscious of my bruising, I sit up gingerly. "This has nothing to do with your appearance," I say, scanning the veiled room, "and everything to do with your character."

"Can they not be one and the same?"

Zephyrus sounds close, but that can't be possible. I would have seen him move. As it is, I see nothing in the mottled light and shade, no bodily figure or silhouette.

"I'm aware," he says solemnly, "that I am unwelcome. But I have come to pay yet another debt."

I'm so taken aback I wonder if this is a dream. "Another?" My fingers twitch around the hilt of my dagger. In the chilly air, my sweat-pricked skin tingles, my nipples drawn to points beneath my thin nightgown.

The West Wind clears his throat. A floorboard creaks to my right. "You were punished and the fault was mine. I can ease your pain if you will allow it. I can right the wrong I have done."

Cool air floats across my face. In the darkness, I need not be afraid, not on hallowed ground. "The last time you offered to right a wrong, I was punished. Why should I trust this will be any different?"

The shape of a hand imprints itself on my nape, but when I reach back, nothing is there. "Would you believe that I wish to heal the wounds marring your back?"

My ability to respond fails me. I am frozen, a sculpture crafted from bone.

"You are unsettled," he says. "You need not be."

There—something moved in my periphery. I spot a shadowed figure detaching itself from the wall near my dresser. Moonlight transforms his eyes into wells of light.

"Lie down, Brielle."

A new depth enters his tone, a strange, assertive quality, enthrallingly grounded. I feel a compulsion to obey. My limbs twitch in conflict, to stand and put distance between us, or to rest, ease the pain. *Lie down*, the West Wind orders. Setting aside my blade, I sink into the mattress with a grateful sigh.

A cork springs free of a glass vial. Moments later, a stringent aroma stings my nostrils.

"What is that?" I whisper into the dark.

"A salve made from pearl blossom." His voice flows along my skin in pacifying strokes. "Highly effective." He glides across the room, halting an arm span away.

No wonder it smelled familiar. My fingers curl into the sheet. "My nightgown—"

"You will need to remove it so I can access your back."

I stiffen. "Who said anything about accessing my back?"

"Can *you* reach your wounds?"

His gaze snags mine, bright with intensity. It is easy to overlook the displeasing countenance, the misshapen nose and awkward features, in the presence of those brilliant, crystalline eyes.

And yet, the daring in him. What he asks violates everything I've been taught. Purity: our second vow. "The welts will heal, in time."

"They will scar without the proper treatment."

"Then I will live with it."

The West Wind tosses the vial from hand to hand as he gazes out the window. The starlight is so plentiful it appears to have been poured from urns by the Father himself. "You are awfully quick to accept this punishment. Do you know what I see? Lack of sleep. Exhaustion." He points to my face, tracing the lines of weariness in the air with contempt. "Though I am not surprised, considering how sterile this room is."

There is nothing wrong with my room. It holds a cot, a desk, a chair, a trunk at the foot of the bed, and a dresser. Why would I need useless trinkets and finery when the Father fills my life?

"I'm not sure I understand," I say.

Moving to the bed, he rests a palm flat against the mattress and sinks his weight onto it. The wooden slats squeak beneath the pressure. "Your mattress is filled with old straw. It offers no support. You sleep little because you are uncomfortable."

"I sleep little," I counter, "because you have entered my room unwelcome and unannounced."

"No personal touches," he continues, motioning toward the plain plaster walls. "You possess not even a book."

"I have a book." The Text rests on my desk.

"Not a book to read for pleasure or comfort."

"The Text comforts me." It is steadfast, it is true.

"But nothing else in this room does."

I do not need comfort. I need only the Father. But I do not expect Zephyrus to understand.

"You are denied pleasure," he says.

I clear my throat and shift to a more comfortable position on my side. "Pleasure is temptation," I whisper.

"Mm." A low, curious sound, neither agreement nor disagreement. "Is this what you believe, or what you are told to believe?"

"I do not see a distinction between the two."

For a moment, I'm positive his gaze has fallen to my chest, where my arm conceals the shape of my breasts, but it is too dark to be certain. "How can you judge pleasure when you have not experienced it yourself? You are not curious?"

This again. "No, I am not."

He purses his lips, then relents. "Very well." This near, I smell the rain on him. "If your wounds are not treated, you might always live with this pain."

My fingers dig into the mattress. It is agony, my injury, though I do not want to admit it. "Give me the salve, then. I will apply it myself."

"You cannot reach, and you have no one to assist you. Allow me to do this for you."

My pulse leaps. "Absolutely not."

"You truly want to punish yourself in this way?"

The question gives me pause. Mother Mabel might consider my sentence just, and I agree, to an extent, but we are armored differently, she and I. The West Wind offers me relief. I question whether I deserve it. "I can't," I whisper.

"You can," he says gently, "if only you say yes."

I cannot read his expression. "I don't know."

"Let me help you."

My tongue is rendered useless, naught but an awkward chunk of flesh behind my teeth. "No man may touch a Daughter of Thornbrook."

"You are in pain," he says. "Pain I have directly caused." Another step forward, boots quiet. When I walk the room, the wooden floorboards buckle and groan, but Zephyrus—it is as though he weighs nothing at all. "Let me heal you. Let me ease your burden."

My eyes burn, yet no tears fall. I have been unable to properly sleep these past few nights. Exhaustion has threaded through my skin, piercing every muscle and tendon and bone.

If I were to guide another in this situation, what would I say? *Accept the healing for what it is—grace.* But I have never taken my own advice.

"What must I do?" I say.

Zephyrus pulls a pair of gloves from his back pocket, slides them on. I blink in surprise, having not thought him capable of such a courtesy. Once again, he's left me unbalanced. "Unbutton your gown to the waist and lie on your stomach."

My cheeks sting so hotly I fear I will melt. It is a difficulty I did not anticipate, dragging my focus from his face. "Turn around while I undress."

He follows my instruction without complaint.

I am but a body in motion. As my mind detaches itself from my limbs, I loosen the buttons running down my nightgown and lie across my bed, the fabric parting over my back, ruined skin exposed to the chilly air.

"You can look," I whisper.

A soundless step brings Zephyrus to my bedside. My skin tingles from the proximity.

"How bad is it?" I ask.

In my periphery, I watch the hand dangling near his thigh form a fist. "There's an infection near the base of your spine." He exhales through his nostrils. "My brother received a similar lashing . . . a long time ago."

"A switch to the back?"

"A whip."

The word stings—*whip*. With a deep breath, I force down the curdling sensation in my stomach. Discipline is expected in the church, but it has never sat right with me. "How many brothers do you have?" A test, to see if his information aligns with what Lissi told me.

"Three." A curt response. "My eldest brother once took responsibility for a punishment I should have received, just as you have done."

Five fingers skim my spine. I flinch, my muscles clenched. Zephyrus wears his gloves, I remind myself. His flesh will not touch mine, though I cannot deny my curiosity of his skin's texture, its unexpected heat.

"Why should you have received the punishment?" I stare at my desk, the blocky Text, my leather-wrapped journal.

"What does it matter?" he says. "What's done cannot be undone."

The sheets sigh beneath my shifting legs. I curl my hand into a fist, tuck it against my cheek. "You sound sad," I whisper. The sadness must be something he carries, just as my loneliness is something I carry. I understand its weight: a stone around one's neck.

"Many would argue I don't deserve the privilege of sadness."

It is curiously vague, his response. "In times of trial," I offer, "I turn to the Father. Through my faith in him—"

"Do not speak to me about faith." He practically spits the words, and I feel the trembling of his hand, pressed to my shoulder. It is so silent I hear the tolling of Kilkare's town bell ten miles away.

"Do you believe in faith?" I ask softly.

"No," Zephyrus says. "I do not."

I'm suddenly cold. Frighteningly cold.

I shove myself upright. "Stop." The motion tugs on my inflamed skin, and I hiss out a breath.

Shadow eats half of Zephyrus' face. "I cannot heal your back if you do not allow me to touch you," he says. Gone is the mischievous, cunning creature I saved from the woods. This version of the West Wind is decidedly haunted.

Pushing to my feet, I snatch the cloak hanging from its hook on the wall and wrap it around my curves. I should have sent him away the moment he entered my room. What was I thinking? Does this faithless immortal hold sway over me, my will? Have I allowed his power to skew my own devotion? But no, I made the decision, however poor, on my own.

"You have overstayed your welcome. Please go."

Wordlessly, the West Wind places the salve on my desk before taking his leave. "Smooth it onto your wounds, if you can," he murmurs. "It should nullify the pain by morning."

The shutters clap shut following his departure. I pluck the glass vial from where it lies beside my journal, lift the substance to my nose. Its harsh odor clears my head. Silly, foolish girl. Never again will I trust a man. Never again will I place my well-being into the hands of one so careless. Let this balm be a reminder. With these scars, I will never forget.

9

I T TAKES TIME, BUT EVENTUALLY, LIFE RETURNS TO ITS PREVIOUS rhythm. Meals, chores, service, the forge, all in an unending blur. Unfortunately, a gulf separates me from the other novitiates. With no explanation for my disappearance, they resort to gossip. They do not ask me about my day. They do not greet me in the halls. They assume that I have lied, and they are correct.

What do they give me? Silence.

I scrawl these words with tear-stained cheeks in my journal late one evening. My hand cramps from the hours of furious inscription. Only when I am purged of the hurt does my pulse slow, easing me into a calmer state, though never calm enough to truly feel at peace.

Setting the journal aside, I move to the window and peer below. Tucked in the shadow of the towering complex, a woman brandishes a blade of solid steel. Its silvery arc catches the torchlight as she moves slowly through various exercises with painstaking intention.

Many nights I watch Mother Mabel train in secret. How many know of her skill? Who has she informed other than me? I am in awe of her grace, yet trailing that emotion comes the inevitable shame. We haven't revisited our evening training sessions. I wonder if the break is permanent.

Returning to my bedside, I kneel, place my linked hands atop the mattress, and bow my head in the low candlelight. "Eternal Father.

Hear me, for I am struggling. I do not always know the answers to life's questions. I do not know why it was *I* who found the West Wind, or why I allowed him to lead me into Under."

I squeeze my eyes tighter, blow out a breath. I wish I had never stumbled across Zephyrus. Since my return, I feel more alone than ever.

Recentering myself, I reach into the farthest depths of my heart and pull the last traces of this confession free. "Despite these obstacles, I know you have a plan for me. I eagerly await its revelation. In Your name, I pray. Amen."

Early one morning, weeks after my lashing, Mother Mabel directs us to the refectory following Mass. Watery light leaks through the cloister, and beyond the manicured yard, low clouds gather, dragging the scent of rain inland.

One by one, we file through the doors, solemn, for the change in routine is unusual. A pair of novitiates heaves shut the oaken doors. The thud lingers in the rafters, then ebbs, the quietest death.

"Please take your seats." Mother Mabel strides up the center aisle, toward the dais where she takes her meals.

Someone gasps.

One heartbeat is all it takes. I do not imagine the scent tingeing the air—something ensnared in soil, long buried, now unearthed. My pulse spikes as the crowd presses in. What disturbs them so?

"Calm, ladies," Mother Mabel soothes. "You are not in danger. Please take your seats and I will explain."

I crane my head over the crowd, seeking the reason for the disturbance. Someone's elbow drives into my back.

"Quickly." Our abbess' command snaps out, and a moment before the crowd lurches forward, I spot him.

The Orchid King squats like an overgrown weed atop the dais. His bare chest, indecently exposed, draws my focus, the round, disked nipples flushed a healthy pink. His lower torso transitions into a heavy stalk fringed by broad leaves, from which thick vines slither out in place of legs. Lastly, the small, red, open mouths of the nightshade blossoms, their vines curled around his wide shoulders like docile serpents.

My gaze swings wildly across the room. With an impending storm shrouding Carterhaugh in a dreary pall, the candlelight breeds shadows. Zephyrus is nowhere in sight, not that I expected his presence. I have not seen him in weeks.

Everyone vies for the tables farthest from the dais. Harper and Isobel rush toward the back corner, the latter reaching the last remaining bench steps ahead of everyone else. Harper claws at her friend's arm, yanking her back. "I don't think so."

The shorter woman sneers. "I arrived here first." Her nails gouge into Harper's wrist, drawing blood. "Let go."

Harper's blue eyes glitter, but when she notices the Orchid King's attention, her confidence falters, and she releases Isobel. "I'll remember this," she hisses.

"I'm sure you will."

"Ladies." Mother Mabel glares at them across the hall. "If you please."

Three tables at the front remain. I shuffle forward with the rest, yet veer toward the kitchen, using the throng as a cover while I slip into a shadowed corner. Everyone is too stricken to notice. For once, I appreciate being overlooked.

Mother Mabel lifts a hand, and the noise cuts out.

"Please join me in welcoming the Orchid King." She gestures to Pierus, whose shifting weight bows the platform beneath a heap of swollen, milk-white roots. Due to his bulk, there isn't enough room for both of them on the dais. Thus, Mother Mabel stands to his right a healthy distance away. "As he is my guest, you will treat him with the same formality and respect you would show any visiting official."

"Thank you for your hospitality, Mother Mabel. I will not take up much of your time."

Mother Mabel offers him a bland smile. She stands as the stone pillars do, with rising majesty, blond hair darkened to gold as the refectory dims further and candlelight winks into distant islands. With everyone focused on the Orchid King, no one else seems to notice her clasped hands, the catch of tightening skin over rigid knuckles. If she is uncomfortable, why offer Pierus this invitation?

Arms extended, the Orchid King takes in his audience. "Daughters of Thornbrook, you have my respect. The tithe draws near. I want to extend my deepest gratitude for what you will provide my people. Please know your contribution will not be overlooked."

As he scans the room, I press my back against the cool stone, grateful for my quick thinking. The brightness of my hair would surely have attracted his attention.

"Your participation is vital to the success of Under. As such, all requirements must be carried out with the utmost precision. Mother Mabel"—he turns to our abbess, all smiles—"have you secured the girls who will participate in the tithe?"

"That has yet to be determined," she replies stiffly. "And they are women, Pierus." Her gaze flicks to a wayward root, which eases through the legs of a bench, startling the group of acolytes sitting on it. The women flinch, though manners dictate that they remain seated.

Mother Mabel frowns at her wards.

"My apologies." Pierus rests a hand on his chest. Cracked, sooty talons interrupt the silver strands of his long, unbound hair. "When you live forever, every woman appears as a child. I only meant to inquire as to the number."

The tithe requires the blood of twenty-one Daughters of Thornbrook. There has never been a lack of volunteers. Most are curious about Under, and the cost is little: one drop of blood, pricked from the finger with the point of an iron blade. Mother Mabel claims Under's survival depends on the strength of our faith, expressed through the willing donation of our blood. Following the tithe, the fair folk assist Mother Mabel in wiping participants' memories, to shield them from the horrors of what occurs. But the process is not foolproof. Some women have been known to recall certain memories or visuals years later.

"Rest assured there will be exactly twenty-one women." She steps into a pool of shifting candlelight. I believe the movement is intentional, for her chasuble, with its gold threads, comes alight. Even the Orchid King stares. "We will meet you at Miles Cross, as is tradition."

"I am glad to hear it," he says, "and I am grateful for our continued allyship. If you have any questions or concerns, you are welcome to voice them. I will linger for a time, but I must return before noon."

With that, we are dismissed. A few of the more courageous acolytes approach Pierus with questions. I slink toward the doors with the rest, though I swear I sense the Orchid King's gaze on the back of my neck as I leave.

I spend the morning carting bins of laundry down to the wash. The dresses and albs will soak in lye overnight, followed by any necessary mending. I'm on my way to the refectory for lunch, fingers sore from stitching thread, when someone calls my name.

With a sinking stomach, I turn toward Mother Mabel. She stares at me for an indeterminate length of time. "Please join me in my office."

She knows. It is my only thought as I shuffle after her retreating back.

The abbess' house, tucked snugly against the cloister's western edge, contains a small dining room, a chapel, an office, and additional bedchambers for any prestigious visiting authorities. Tapestries hang from the plaster walls. A side table contains multiple copies of the Text in various shades of brown leather.

She settles at her office desk, a massive slab framed by the arched window overlooking the western grounds. Her chair is all angles. Her spine reaches, straight as a pole. The Abbess on High still wears her chasuble. Perhaps she needs the Father's reassurance after the Orchid King's visit.

She gestures to the empty chair before me. "You are welcome to sit."

It does not sound like a request.

I sit.

"How are you healing?" she asks with unexpected compassion.

I blink stupidly, then relax into the chair. I'm not here to discuss my foray into Under. Hopefully my absence in the refectory was not noticed. "Well enough."

"Good." Mother Mabel drags the Text toward herself. For a time, she stares at the cover, and I wring my hands, wondering if I should speak.

"I have been thinking lately." She pinches her gold necklace and looks to me. Two serpents shape the metal, a clasp formed by their open mouths. "You accepted your punishment without complaint and have displayed true devotion to Thornbrook these past few weeks. In light of your good conduct, you are welcome to visit the infirmary and have your wounds checked."

I stiffen at the suggestion. Zephyrus' pearl blossom salve has hastened my healing, and I would not have the physician question my lack of scarring. "I appreciate the sentiment," I say carefully, not wanting to appear ungrateful, "but my back has healed well enough."

"I'm glad to hear it." She flips to a bookmarked page. "We all have our scars, our lessons learned. They are paramount to our growth." Frail parchment whispers between her fingertips. "However, I would like to extend my apologies. I did not enjoy dispensing your punishment."

I remember the scream of the lash seconds before my skin split. Sweat dampens my underarms.

"No apology needed," I whisper. "I understand why it was necessary."

That watchful stare scans me from head to toe. As always, I fear she finds me lacking. "Is there anything you wish to discuss with me, Brielle? Anything at all?"

Mother Mabel is not warm, exactly, but she has provided me a home and a purpose when I feared my life had ended. Eleven years old, abandoned on a rain-drenched doorstep, three words to usher me into a new life: *Be good, Brielle.*

"No, Mother Mabel," I reply, head bowed. "There is not."

"I see." The disappointment in her voice catches my attention. "You can always come to me in times of need. There is nothing we cannot navigate together."

Guilt is the hound dogging my heels. Higher the secrets pile: Under, Zephyrus, lies upon lies. "I understand."

"May I ask you a question?"

She has the right to ask. She also has the right to demand answers of me. "You may."

"What is it you want from this life?"

Her question gives me pause. No one has ever asked this of me, but I thought the answer was obvious. "I wish to bring myself closer to the Father," I say. "I wish to be His servant in all ways."

"You do not wish for something different? A family, or your own home to tend? There is no shame in it."

"I do not." My response does not waver. Only the Father may claim my wounded heart.

Mother Mabel closes the Text with a snap. "I wonder if the abbey is enough for you."

The pit that has steadily amassed in my stomach opens wide and engulfing. Am I no longer welcome here? If so, what purpose will I serve? *Who* will I serve, if not the Father? Another moment ticks by before I'm able to collect myself. "It is enough, I promise you. I do not wish to leave." My voice fractures.

She sighs. Fabric shifts as she rounds the desk in a few short strides and gently cups my cheek with one hand. "I do not wish that either. I have never met anyone so focused on their studies. But with your behavior of late, I have begun to question your place here."

The coolness of her touch only serves to remind me how feverish I have become. Turning my head away, I fight to regulate my increasingly chaotic emotions. "I never want to disappoint you, Mother Mabel. I've worked hard to prove I belong here."

"You are dedicated," she assures me. "Of that, I have no doubt."

I should find satisfaction in Mother Mabel's words. Rarely does she bestow praise. Yet this conversation stirs up many long-lived insecurities.

"If I am worthy," I dare to say, "why have you continued to pass me over?" My hands ball into fists. "A decade I have been at Thornbrook. Why choose novitiates less driven, less experienced, than I?"

She drops her hand, pulls away. I cannot read her expression. "I admit I have been unfair to you. When one becomes an acolyte, one gives everything to the Father. Your studies become more intense, your cause calls you away to the outer reaches of the realm." Finest lines feather her mouth, its subtle upward curve. "But I need you here, in the forge. You are the only one who can do what you do."

"So you will keep me a novitiate forever?"

She shakes her head. "Truthfully, I was going to select you as a candidate this year, until I learned of recent occurrences."

We stare at one another, but she has always been obdurate, uncowed. I drop my gaze to the floor.

Mother Mabel says, "I know you have visited Under."

Calmly, I lift my eyes. Sadness and grief bring years to one's face, but this has never been more evident than it is now. Between one blink and the next, folds sink into the soft flesh of her visage, the skin sagging beneath the chin, but in the next blink, the vision vanishes. She remains unaged.

"Mother Mabel." The words crumble to a dry wheeze, and I fall to my knees. "I'm sorry. I admit, I have visited Under, just once." The trembling in my limbs intensifies, for I fear. Oh, how I fear. "When you asked me if there was anything I wished to tell you, I was afraid. I thought that if you learned I had broken the rules, you would send me away. The truth is, I stumbled across a wounded man in the forest, and he manipulated me into trusting him. He took me into Under."

"Who did? I want a name."

"Zephyrus." Curiously, the air changes shape around his name, but I fear witnessing the abbess' reaction and keep my focus on the floor. "I do not know how to explain it, Mother Mabel. It was . . ."

"Terrifying?" she inquires softly.

Closing my eyes, I let the warmth of her compassion wash over me.

"Yes." That inky lake, those scarlet glass orbs, the field of roses sheltered within the cave. "There is much I do not understand about the realm."

Mother Mabel rounds my other side. "My dear, we have all been tempted by Under one way or another. However, as Daughters of Thornbrook, we must remember our purpose. We must stay the course."

"I know, and I'm sorry," I whisper. "It was a brief upset. I promise it will not happen again. I will work hard to regain your trust."

"It is not my trust you need to regain. It is His."

The comment lands with painful precision, as intended. I stay quiet.

She touches my shoulder in comfort, a fleeting warmth. "I wish you would have come to me. I would have been able to guide you through this mess. It hurts me to know you have been suffering."

She's right. I *have* been suffering. But wasn't that the point of my punishment? What else did she expect me to do?

"Do you know why you're asked to forge the iron daggers for the tithe?"

"I assumed it was for the ceremony, for the participants' protection, since iron is fatal to the fair folk."

"You are correct, but they also serve a greater purpose." Fingertips steepled against her mouth, she paces the length of the room in a cloud of sweet incense, the myrrh having fully infused the office. "They act as an anchor and help ward off any enchantments that might touch us. Without them, we would lose ourselves to that which tempts us."

"I understand."

"Promise me you will do everything in your power to resist Under's allure." She halts, angles toward me. "I would hate for your disobedience to be cause for dismissal."

Every horror, every sadness, every tatter of grief I have carried these weeks freezes to ice inside my chest. If I do not have the abbey, if I do not have my god, then I have nothing. I *am* nothing. "I promise."

Gently, she pats my arm. "You are a sweet girl, Brielle. You try your best. I cannot fault you for that."

I am not a girl though. Twenty-one years I have walked this green earth. Body, mind, and soul, I am wholly a woman.

Mother Mabel returns to her desk, and I'm surprised when she offers me a genuine smile. It smooths the harshness from her features.

"It takes a woman of great character to admit her wrongdoings. I would like to offer you the opportunity to ascend, if you are interested."

No matter how many times I dissect that statement, it does not seem real. "Truly?"

"Should you begin the process of transition, your heart will belong to the Father. Once you speak your final vows, He becomes your life."

"I understand." By all that is holy, I never thought this day would come. My chest swells in elation, and the world radiates color.

"Good." Her smile softens. "You understand, then, that before a novitiate can ascend to an acolyte, she must prove her dedication by completing a task that tests her devotion. Normally, the task is granted to a single candidate, but in your case, there is another who seeks the same opportunity."

Just as quickly, I deflate. I had hoped, prayed, but there is yet another obstacle to overcome. "Who?"

10

RAISING MY FIST TO THE OLD, CREAKING DOOR, I GIRD MYSELF FOR what will occur the moment my knuckles touch wood.

I can do this.

A hard *rat-tat-tat*, a sharp crack of sound. Then I wait.

It doesn't take long before the door swings open, Harper's unpleasant features fixed into a scowl. Her blue eyes thin, a scouring glare that rips me open from boot soles to scalp. "What do you want?"

As if she cares about such a thing. "Did Mother Mabel speak with you about the appointment?"

Her beautifully groomed eyebrows snap inward above her nose. "Why do you care to know? Is it not enough that I'm forced to interact with you daily? Must you spy on me as well?"

"There are many ways I would rather spend my time, Harper." Like shoveling dung.

Her foot taps out her irritation. It is not unexpected. She has always moved in fits and bursts, propelled by the tightly coiled energy stuffed beneath her skin. "What is it then? I don't appreciate having my time wasted."

"If Mother Mabel spoke to you, then she likely mentioned you are not the only one vying for the position of acolyte."

At this, she straightens, and I watch her slide the bits of information into place with satisfaction: my unforeseen visit, this topic of conversation, the odd lack of fear as my gaze meets hers.

"You're joking." A small, spiteful laugh descends into a sound of utter bewilderment. "Who knew you had the capacity for humor. What's the real reason for this disturbance?"

It took all morning to gather the courage to knock. Now I fight the urge to vomit, or pass out, or both. The tightness in my chest is never more severe than when I'm forced to face my oldest adversary. "I've been offered the opportunity to earn the position."

"Excuse me?" Her shrill cry is as hair-raising as an outright shriek. "After the stunt you pulled? You can't be serious."

"It is the truth."

For once in her life, Harper is speechless. No insults, no scathing remarks. Blessed silence.

Her attention whips up and down the deserted corridor. Lunch ended an hour ago, but Mother Mabel freed me from obligations so I would have time to pack. I assume she granted Harper the same respite.

"Get inside." She yanks me across the threshold, slamming the door behind me. "It's embarrassing enough learning this without someone overhearing it."

I jerk my arm from her grasp. "What, exactly, is embarrassing? That I'm worthy enough to be offered the spot, or that you have to compete with me for the title?"

A little snarl punches past her clenched teeth. Harper wants to become the next acolyte as much as I do, but in the end, only one of us may claim the spot. I vow it will be me.

Keeping her within my sight, I angle myself away from her, scanning the cramped space, which she shares with Isobel. Zephyrus called my bedroom sparse. I suppose that makes Harper's sparse, too. The Text rests on her bookshelf, coated in months' worth of dust.

"What did Mother Mabel tell you?" she demands. "Leave nothing out."

Harper's outrage is total. It breaks upon me like ferocious waves. They will suck me under if I do not hold my ground.

"I assume the same things she told you," I reply, crossing the room to put space between us. "She mentioned the quest."

When I do not elaborate, she spits, "No one believes the story surrounding your disappearance. You would never be that irresponsible. Yet here you are, acting like we've all done you a disservice in ostracizing you. Do you think me a fool?"

If I say *yes*, Harper will readily rip my head from my body. So I say nothing. Sometimes no response is best.

"I can't believe she's giving you a chance," she mutters, beginning to pace. "You are the last person to deserve the appointment."

I've learned a thing or two about Harper over the past decade. She seeks attention. She places importance on image. She cares a great deal about Mother Mabel's opinion, despite her failure to excel, her poor study habits. As long as there is an ear to absorb her complaints, Harper wants for nothing.

"You understand it will be a long journey, yes?" she goes on, too self-centered to realize my eyes have glazed over. "I will not wait for you. With your bulk, you will likely fall behind. Do not blame me when that happens."

My cheeks warm. Years I have weathered her atrocious insults, and still I struggle to fortify my defenses.

It is true I'm larger than most. Tall, wide, muscular. An ample chest and soft hips. Most days, it doesn't bother me. Beneath my white robe, I am no different than any other Daughter of Thornbrook.

Stomping over to her cot, Harper plops onto the edge of the mattress. Leather slippers peek beneath the hem of her gray dress. "Did she mention the task to you?"

"She did." Am I thrilled about this quest? Not exactly. If, however, Mother Mabel demands I load stones into my pockets and plunge into the deepest river, I would do so without question. "We must seek out the blade called Meirlach."

Harper frowns. "She told me the same." For a time, she stares out the window, across the rain-damp forest, unusually ponderous. "The name is familiar," she admits. "I can't remember where I've heard it before."

My attention wanders to her bookshelf. If she bothered to open the Text, she would know that name.

Harper tracks my gaze, and frowns. Leaning back on her elbows, she eyes me as one would a particularly loathsome creature. "Spare me your false piety. Are you going to tell me or not?"

The story can be found in the Book of Change. There are but a handful of sentences mentioning the remarkable sword. Only those deemed worthy could wield it. I know the words by heart, so I recite them to Harper:

Encased within the stone of destiny, a god-forged blade awaited its master. And on that seventh day, a king heard his name whispered by the fabled sword, and pulled free the shining steel.

When I'm finished, Harper drawls, "Sounds like an ordinary blade to me."

Unbelievable. "Did you not hear the part where it whispers to its bearer?"

She snorts at the ridiculousness of the notion.

I do not share the sentiment. The Text must be considered truth, always. "May I see your Text, please?"

She waves her fingers in dismissal, as though my asking is an inconvenience, but I wouldn't want anyone handling my personal copy without permission.

Plucking it from her bookshelf, I flip to the Book of Change, scan the story of Meirlach, seeking additional details while Harper watches from the bed. Her right leg, tossed over her left, bobs a rhythm as it hangs.

"According to the Book of Change," I say, "Meirlach can cut through any shield, pierce any armor, even hack through walls. Those held at bladepoint will be unable to tell a lie." Bumps pebble my flesh as I read further. "It is even said to command the winds."

Harper's eyebrows climb all the way to her hairline. "I'm sure," she drawls.

I snap the book closed. "Why do you question the words on the page? To doubt the Text is to doubt the Father and His teachings."

Does Mother Mabel know of Harper's skepticism? She must not, otherwise she would never have given this woman the opportunity to transcend her current station.

Harper glowers at me. "You're saying you believe a sword can *cut through stone*? You believe it can *command the winds*?"

"Yes."

"Without proof?"

"Harper." A huff of exasperation escapes me. "That's the entire point of faith. It only exists in the absence of proof."

Her face pinches in contemplation. Then she nods, perhaps conceding to the idea that there exists such a blade despite the lack of evidence. "All right. Let's pretend this blade is real. How are we to find it?"

Setting aside the Text, I pull a square of folded parchment from my pocket. "With this map."

She bolts upright. "Where did you get that?"

"Mother Mabel."

"Why would she give you the map and not me?"

If I were to guess, it's because I'm the more responsible one.

Mother Mabel has marked an entrance into Under on the map. Relatively unknown, it requires an offering to pass through. Apparently, the nymph guarding the doorway is easily bribed.

"We're looking for someone called the Stallion," I say, ignoring her question and slipping the map back into my pocket. "If we find the Stallion, we find Meirlach."

"Who is the Stallion?"

"I don't know." Mother Mabel told me nothing about who or what the Stallion is. She offered me only three things: a name, a command, and a warning.

You must kill the beast. It is the only way to obtain Meirlach. And whatever happens, do not climb onto its back.

The order sits queasily in my stomach. Mother Mabel has always been forthright with us. The lack of information is concerning. "All I know is that he lives in a place called the Grotto."

"Sounds wonderful," Harper mutters.

I refuse to feed her sour mood. "Navigating Under will present unique challenges. We must remain alert."

Harper goes still. Her hands, planted on the edge of her cot, curl over the straw mattress. "You mean to tell me I am to travel into Under? With *you*? Into some horrible beast's lair for a sword that may not even exist?"

It appears Mother Mabel told Harper very little about the details of this task. Not for the first time, I wonder why.

Harper shakes her head. "No. No, this is absolutely ridiculous. Sending two mortal women into Under without a guide?" Strands of black hair hang in her face, and she bats them aside with a growl.

Despite our differences, Harper and I do share a similarity. We fear the unknown. Perhaps all of us at Thornbrook do. I'm not particularly thrilled about the quest either, but I recall Mother Mabel's expression when she informed me of this task, her eyes reduced to furrows of skin, a rare sign of distress. It is clear that this task is necessary, just as our participation in the tithe is necessary. There is little enjoyment in it, but it must be done.

"I'm not going," Harper clips. "She can't make me."

Then my success is all but guaranteed. "Very well. I will inform Mother Mabel that you will be remaining behind."

I'm nearly to the door when she calls, "Wait."

Slowly, I turn. Harper appears torn, furious at the idea of being painted a coward, yet refusing to hand over the opportunity without a fight. It is to be expected.

"Seems like a lot of effort for something that may as well be hearsay." Pushing off the bed, she reaches the window in four steps. Fog shrouds the vineyards in the distance, the air sweet with rain. "There is a high chance we will not return."

I am well aware.

"Why does Mother Mabel want this sword anyway?" she demands.

"I don't know." The abbess has access to plenty of iron blades, enough to keep the entirety of Under at a distance, if necessary. It bears the question of why *this* blade is so special. What need does she have of its powers?

Harper stares at me until I grow uncomfortable. "What?"

"Aren't you afraid to go into Under?"

"No." *Yes.* "Are you?"

She sniffs delicately. "Not in the slightest. But it matters not." She brushes past me. "I am not traveling with the likes of you."

This, too, is expected. She thinks me a pawn to be positioned at the point of greatest advantage. But my future at Thornbrook depends on the outcome of this quest. I will not go quietly.

"How do you expect to enter Under without a map? Is your plan to wander Carterhaugh until you stumble across an entrance by happenstance?"

"Obviously not." She holds out a hand. "You will give me the map."

Too easily, the noose tightens in the face of confrontation. I swallow to draw moisture to my mouth. "No."

Harper stares at me. "No?"

I force out the rest. "I'm not giving you the map. Traveling on this journey alone is your choice, but eventually you'll realize how little you know of surviving beyond these walls. How will you protect yourself from the fair folk? How will you know where to shelter, what water sources to avoid, what plants are toxic?" Her skin pales, snow against the ebony fall of her hair, and I am glad of it. Let her understand that I have knowledge of such things. Let her feel the weight of her own ignorance. "If you were wise, you would want to travel together."

"And how does that benefit me?" she counters, eyes ablaze. "If we each want to find the sword first, who's to say you wouldn't leave me to fend for myself?"

But I would do no such thing. Because I understand what it is like to walk alone. Because I know how much darker the nights are without a fire. Because, despite my intense disdain for Harper, I cannot in good judgment abandon her to the dark. I have seen its face.

Maybe that makes me weak.

"It's your choice," I reiterate. "You are free to travel alone, if you wish." Moving to the door again, I rest my hand on the knob. "I will be in the fields tomorrow before dawn. I will wait until the sun breaches the horizon. Then I will leave, with or without you."

Harper holds herself stiffly, every harsh angle whetted by panic. Fear that I am right. Fear of what will happen if she attempts the journey alone and realizes she was wrong. "I'll be there."

"Then you'll need this." I offer her my extra dagger, which I've concealed against the small of my back. It should fit her hand well.

Her eyes widen. "What use would I have for that?"

"To protect yourself."

There was no bladesmith when I first arrived at the abbey, but in my sixteenth year, I stumbled across the old, dusty, forgotten forge. I peered through the cobwebs of abandonment at the overlooked hut, and asked Mother Mabel about its purpose.

Thornbrook's last bladesmith had passed on decades ago. Since then, no one had taken up the mantle—until me. It was Mother Mabel who suggested I wield the hammer. *Light the forge*, she'd said.

What do I remember?

The weight of that hammer, the awful ache of fatigued muscles the following morning.

What do I remember?

Smoke. How horribly I'd hacked and wheezed until I had the good sense to open the doors.

What do I remember?

The first blow against blistering metal, its singular clarity.

What do I remember?

Strength like I'd never experienced before. Strength like elation, like relief.

Lifting the dagger higher, I study it from all angles. Harper frowns, snatching for the weapon, which I pull out of reach.

"Careful," I whisper. "It's sharp."

11

ARPER AND I DEPART AT FIRST LIGHT, LADEN ONLY WITH OUR wits and whatever supplies fit into our rucksacks. We've donned our plain, everyday dresses. I've secured my hair into the tightest braid I can manage, a strip of red falling to my lower back, the heavy strands unlikely to move except in gale-force winds. Harper has arranged her own hair into an elaborate updo, something more appropriate for a ceremonial event than an extensive trek, but I hold my tongue. At least she had the foresight to wear boots.

Upon reaching the edge of the barley fields, I glance back, just once. The abbey, pale stone tucked into climbing ferns, appears in blurred pockets through the trees. I have never left Thornbrook for so long. I wonder if I will be missed.

My gaze flicks to Harper. She stares at me, blue eyes mistrustful beneath her smooth brow. We have until the eve of the tithe to return to Thornbrook. In less than two months, another seven-year cycle will reach its end. One of us will hold Meirlach in hand. And the other, unfortunately, will not.

"Do you want to leave anything behind?" I gesture to the straps cutting into her shoulders. "There's still time to lighten your load."

Harper rears back. As usual, I have affronted, insulted, offended. "If I were you," she says, dropping her voice, "I would worry about your own ability to keep up." She looks me up and down, smiles sharply, and shoves past me. "Come along, while we're still young."

Very well then.

We do not converse the entire morning. The unexpected blessing allows me space to ponder and plan. According to the map, the nymph-guarded entrance is located twelve miles south of Thornbrook. We should reach it by dusk, barring further delays.

Our route follows an abandoned foot trail through the forest, though none I have ever utilized. The air steams as the sun climbs, and the ground slopes into small hills where the trees have clambered over one another in search of sunlight. A glance over my shoulder reveals Harper struggling to navigate the numerous twisting roots.

"I warned you about the pack," I say. My back aches, but I'm used to the strain.

Harper snarls something unintelligible and fumbles to remove her canteen. Sweat slithers down her face and neck; her updo has lost its shape. Sagging against the nearest tree, she gulps the liquid eagerly.

"Slowly," I bark, hoping Harper took the necessary precautions. As long as we bless the water prior to drinking it, any taint will be cleansed, regardless of whether the fair folk poisoned the source. "We still have miles to go."

Harper tears her mouth away from the canteen, gasps out, "I liked you better when you kept your opinions to yourself," then drains the rest.

My face burns. Why do I bother offering advice when she refuses to listen? "We aren't far," I say, unfolding the map with shaking hands. At least I sound unaffected. "Only a few more miles. Do you want to break for lunch?"

"I'm not hungry." A fierce proclamation, better suited for an extensive audience. The trees are a poor substitute.

I do not believe her, but I'm certainly not going to argue. "Fine." I fold the map back into its square.

The motion draws her eye. "You say we have miles to go, but I question how much quicker we would reach our destination if someone more capable was in charge." Thus she straightens, chin lifted, a rim of gold etching her slim frame. "I'll take over from here."

When the day is done, the world dark, my journal open on my lap, these are the moments I will remember: how my heart races at her barbed words; the feeling of falling from a great height despite the firm ground beneath my soles. But mostly, I will remember this: the whisper of parchment against my fingertips as it passes from my hand to hers. The conflict I wish to avoid. The words I did not say.

Harper smiles as I relinquish the map, tucking it into her pocket. "Much appreciated."

By the time we reach the entrance to Under, the heat is well and truly boiling. Ferns carpet the bent path, each long, crenated tongue licking at our ankles. Harper pants heavily as she trudges through the green thicket. If she regrets taking on the effort of leading, she is too proud to admit it.

A few paces ahead, mushrooms encircle a massive boulder, which stands atop a grassy knoll. According to the map, this entrance will lead us to Under.

"We're here?" Harper asks. Dirt coats the hem of her dress, and mine.

"Yes." Upon further inspection, I spot a small, circular cutout in the rock. A door? Striding forward, I knock.

"Do you have an appointment?" An airy voice floats from somewhere behind the boulder. No, not behind. *Within.*

Harper and I exchange a look. She waves her hand as if to say, *Do something.* "Um . . . yes?"

"Name, please."

"Brielle of Thornbrook."

There is a pause. I bite my lip, worrying its flesh between my teeth. "I do not see your name on the list," the voice states.

Harper shoots me a mutinous glare, because of course it's *my* fault my name isn't on the list. Mother Mabel gave me no additional instructions aside from informing me to knock and offer a loaf of bread to whoever answered the door.

"Are you sure?" My question teeters on shaky legs. When did the lies become default? "It should be there."

The round cutout cracks open and pushes outward like a door. I squint into the opening, then stumble back as a creature emerges on four spindly legs, scuttling forward like a spider. Harper yelps and dashes into the safety of the ferns.

The nymph rises to stand on its hind legs, back bent. I believe the creature is male, for he appears akin to a little old man. His bald, rounded skull possesses three measly hairs, which sprout from furrowed gray skin. A white shift falls to his knees.

The nymph's bulging eyes thin. "You do not have an appointment."

"No," I admit, "but we were informed you would accept an offering to enter Under?" I present him my most sincere smile.

He blinks slowly. Sleepy, or suspicious? "We?"

Scanning the forest at my back, I spot Harper peeking out from behind a tree. I wave her closer. She hesitates, but soon picks her way over to the ring of mushrooms, upper lip twitching at the nymph's shriveled appearance, the shift's gossamer fabric shivering in strips around his bowed legs.

"We are novitiates from Thornbrook," I explain to the creature, trying my best to articulate confidently. "We seek entrance into Under, if you please."

"You and everyone else," he mutters. "So what'll it be? What is your offering?" He looks to Harper, coarse brows low, mouth mulish.

"Bread," I say.

"What flavor?"

"Rye."

He huffs and crosses his arms. "Very well."

Harper slips her hand into her pack, where the bread awaits. "But we only have one extra loaf."

"We still have fruit and cheese," I point out.

"And how long will that last us?"

We've a week's worth of food. Though we must conserve it, eventually we'll need to forage for more. Once we reach Under, we cannot consume any food or drink but our own.

"It's the only way," I whisper.

She bares her teeth. "Spoken like Mother Mabel's blind follower." Turning sharply on her heel, she regards the gnarled creature. "Will you take another offering instead?"

That stony gaze rakes Harper, then me, before settling on the dagger hanging at my waist. "What about the blade?"

"Done," announces Harper.

"Not done!" I snap.

She scoffs. "I'm to give up my meal just so you can keep your stupid knife? I don't think so. Why can't you give something up?"

The nymph glances between us. I bite the inside of my cheek until it bleeds.

"Because—" I suck in a shaky breath, praying for patience. "We need weapons. We need protection."

"Then what about those special salves you're hoarding? Don't deny it. I've seen them."

As if I would give up my mother's poultices. She never taught me how to make them, despite touting the honor of Veraness' head apothecary. By the time I was old enough to work in the shop, her days were often marked by apathy or impetuosity or both, her emotions too volatile, the clarity necessitated to run a business far beyond her grasp. Once these poultices are gone, they cannot be replenished. "You agreed to this," I say. "Give him the bread."

"Why does it need a loaf of bread? The thing looks seconds away from keeling over." She flips her long hair over her shoulder, daring the nymph to argue. He stares at her with distaste.

"Angry mortal woman," he croons, "I do not appreciate your insults. Whatever it is you seek, you will not find it here." The small round door slams shut, dust and pebbles rattling loose in the aftershock.

Harper's gaze swings to mine, dark with reproach. "Well that was a waste of time." She pats her hair into place.

The smallest, hardest lump of coal sears my chest where my heart should be. This mission is impossible enough without another obstacle tossed into our path. "If you had offered your bread to the nymph, we would have passed through. Now we'll have to find another way in."

"Why am *I* to blame? You had the opportunity to give up your salves." Hands planted on her hips, she lashes back, "You are equally at fault."

Is she truly comparing risen flour to my prized possessions? "Those salves were my mother's," I retort. "I would never give them up."

"And yet she didn't extend the same courtesy to you."

I can feel the shape of my face as it collapses, dropping into my stomach, then lower, splattering at my feet. My deepest wound, torn open afresh.

Tears slip down my cheeks, hot against my cool skin. Harper turns away, oddly quiet.

I've wondered whether my peers knew of the circumstances surrounding my arrival at the abbey. Mother Mabel would never betray my privacy. Harper must have heard it from someone who spotted me on that storm-drenched night.

"We should get moving," I mumble. Somehow, we will have to find another way in to Under.

Many hours later, we stop to make camp. Harper drops her rucksack and sinks onto a stump, drenched in sweat. Two strips of dampened fabric mark where the straps have cut into her shoulders. What is she carrying in there? The pack is nearly twice her size.

Tucking my supplies between the tree roots, I pull my canteen free and take a deep swallow. Harper drained hers hours ago, and we haven't passed a stream since. The ruby sheen of her skin snags my eye. Her lips, too, are heavily cracked.

Biting the inside of my cheek, I glance upward, seeking the spread of violet overhead, a band of cooling calm. This same sky reaches down to Thornbrook's fertile earth. Why, then, does it appear so different?

"Here." Crouching down so I'm eye level with Harper, I hold out my canteen.

She is watchful as her attention lands on the container, a bur unwittingly hooked in a stocking. "I'm fine."

"You're near collapse. Take the water." The last thing I need is an unconscious traveling companion.

"I told you I don't need it."

"You do," I reply with forced calm.

She peels away the hair plastered to her neck. It is a subtle thing, that quavering hand. "Why are you being kind to me?" A low, waspish tone whetted by fatigue. It takes everything in my power not to chuck the canteen at her head. It would certainly make a satisfying thump.

"You ask a question I do not have an answer to," I respond, equally prickly. I'm reminded of every vile word, every scornful laugh, every hurled insult I've ever endured. Ten years' worth of malice. "Is it my assistance you snub, or help in general?" Our gazes clash and hold. "Do you want the water or not?"

Harper recoils as though I have demanded she amputate a limb, so alive is her fury. But she accepts, downing every drop until it's gone.

"I'm going to search for water," I say, taking the canteen when Harper hands it back to me. "We should build a shelter once I return." Night will fall in less than an hour, and the cold will sweep in, harsh from the mountain peak. Unfortunately, fire is out of the question. It attracts the fair folk.

Newly revived by the water, Harper straightens on her perch. "I do not believe I agreed to building a shelter. Or have I suffered loss of memory in the last hour?"

Patience, Brielle. But oh, this woman surely tests it. "Unless you want to spend the night shivering, we need to build a shelter. A lean-to is simple enough to construct." If we work together, it shouldn't take longer than a few hours.

"If you want to build a lean-to," she responds, "I won't stop you. But do not think traveling together means working together. You focus on your needs, and I'll focus on mine. Deal?"

There is so much I might say were I not so cowardly.

We need to take protective measures, I might state. Or perhaps, *I will not carry you through this journey*. Or even, *You need to pull your own weight*. Yet I say nothing.

I stride off, denying Harper the pleasure of witnessing my flaming face. A scream hammers blows upon my ribs, but I refuse to let it escape. Harper's presence won't stop me from acquiring Meirlach. This I must remember.

After blessing a nearby stream, I refill my canteen and begin gathering larger branches for the roof and walls of the shelter. Dark descends with startling speed. At one point, I'm certain I spot something moving in the brush, but when I peer closer, I find the area empty, nothing to disturb the undergrowth. The buzzing beneath my skin intensifies. I regret leaving my lamp back at Thornbrook, having wanted to avoid carrying its extra weight. A light would be a blessing. They are unfamiliar, these trees. They do not reach. They loom.

It's likely nothing. Fear of the unknown etches shadows where they do not exist, yet the wind carries a scent, and I know in my bones I am not imagining it.

"Will you continue to lurk out of sight like a coward," I call, "or will you step into the light, stranger?"

An errant gust lifts the hem of my skirt. I slap it into place, surveying the darkened area with straining ears, heightened senses. The sky, too, is masked.

I drop the branches and draw my dagger. A twig snaps, sharp like a fracturing bone.

"A woman wandering alone after dark? Foolish of you."

He materializes before me, shaded by the encroaching night. The West Wind.

Flanked by two rotting trees, he strides forth with unfettered confidence, an arrogant waltz. Darkness mutes the emerald tunic to an ash gray. It is strange, but I swear something appears different about his unsightly face. I cannot put my finger on it.

"It's a long way for *you* to wander," I state with a calm I do not feel. "Won't the Orchid King come looking for you?" The West Wind has been following me. For how long? I must not shrink as a mouse would in the presence of a hawk.

"I'm curious by nature, as you know. And no, Pierus will not seek me out. Not yet, anyway." He saunters forward. "Where do you travel?"

I retreat a few paces. "My business is my own," I say, and leave it at that.

Beneath the bow of his mouth lies a duplicitous cunning. "You run from me, Brielle, yet is there not a debt I owe you?"

My grip on the dagger loosens in surprise. "There is no debt."

"Isn't there?"

"The salve you provided me was repayment enough."

"Ah, but I speak of the first debt, not the second. I gave you the opportunity to seek answers to questions in your life. A chance to change your future. But, if I am correct, you did not like the answer you received, which means my debt to you saving my life remains unfulfilled. I insist you allow me to do you one last favor."

What is he talking about? "I never asked for favors. You took me to Willow. *You*. So *you* could repay the debt you owed me after I saved your life!" His miserable, frustrating life.

Again, he steps forward, and the green of his eyes blackens in this lightless place. "Ah, but you agreed to the bargain. And to a god, one's word is binding."

How fearless might I be if I were a man caught unaware in this situation rather than a woman? I tighten my grip around the dagger with renewed vigor. "And if I refuse repayment of this supposed debt?" What will Zephyrus do, steal me away into Under? I will cut off his hand before he can touch me.

He angles his head. "Do not fret, my darling novitiate. Just allow me to fulfill my obligation to you. It is in your best interest to agree. I will not take no for an answer."

I choke on a surge of fear. "You—" The word dissolves to dust in my mouth. Why is he so adamant about repaying this debt? Why can't he accept that my aid was given without any expectation of recompense?

I shake my head, growing tired of his veiled threats. "No. This is ridiculous." My hand cuts the air. "Do not engage with me again."

"Then you accept the consequences."

It is no bluff. The words carry no carefully crafted loopholes to snag the unsuspecting, no hidden nooks. But I know this: I regret saving him that night.

The Orchid King was right. I cannot trust Zephyrus.

"We are done," I whisper, turning from the clearing.

"Brielle—"

The weight of his hand on my arm zings through me. I spin, dagger unsheathed, the blade slicing in a practiced arc toward his face. Zephyrus recoils, a hand flying to his cheek. Blood seeps between his fingers as he stares at me incredulously.

I have marked a line of blood on the West Wind's cheek, yet I feel no shame for it.

"I have told you," I growl, my voice a wisp of cold. "I have told you again and again not to touch me. This is your final warning. Next time, I will carve a line into your heart."

Zephyrus blinks, slow with shock, as my heart hurls itself against my sternum. I do not have to be kind. Not to someone who has shown so little consideration toward me.

"Perhaps, had you seen me as a person and not a tool," I say, "you would have recognized my boundaries sooner." Without a backward glance, I stride off, the branches forgotten.

Running into Zephyrus only serves to remind me how alone I am. The West Wind is no ally, and Harper is no friend. I have carried my weight, and hers, this entire day. So it is no surprise that I find Harper asleep back at camp, limbs sprawled, lines of exhaustion engraved in her face.

There is no dinner. There is no shelter. And I am too tired to care.

After unpacking my bedroll in the chilly, rot-damp night, I settle in, pulling my blanket around my body. An owl coos as I rest my head in the crook of my arm and close my eyes.

But I do not sleep.

12

GRAY SKIES, GRAY REALM. HUNCHED BENEATH THE HAPHAZARD lean-to I share with Harper, I draw my wet blanket around my shoulders, though there's no warmth to be had. It has rained for the past three days in an unceasing torrent. A cold drizzle pelts like small, stinging pebbles against my face.

The river has swelled beyond its banks—too dangerous to cross. We must wait until the rising water recedes. Until then, we're stuck. Wasted days, but then again, Harper and I haven't figured out a way forward.

I sigh and push to my feet. Everything I own is drenched. My sopping dress smothers my skin. My pack, too, is soaked: clothes, food, journal. "I'm going to see if there's another way around the river," I tell Harper.

She mumbles something unintelligible through chattering teeth, face tucked into her knees, arms wrapped around her shins.

My blanket falls to the ground with a wet slap. Mud squelches beneath my waterlogged boots as I trudge toward the River Twee, following its rapids northwest for a time. There is no way across. If the rain doesn't abate by tomorrow, I'm going to suggest Harper and I return to the nymph-guarded entrance to Under. The creature might accept another offering if we are properly remorseful. As it stands, it's our only option if we are to return to Thornbrook on time.

As I return to camp, the rain begins to taper off—a small miracle. When I reach the lean-to, however, I find my bedroll gone, my blanket along with it. Harper has snatched both and piled them atop her own bedroll as additional protection from the sodden earth, leaving me to sleep in the mud.

I stare at Harper. She stares back. One eyebrow lifts as though to say, *What are you going to do about it?* Then she rolls over, presenting me her back.

A hot shimmer infuses my skin. The heat swells: pressure in my throat, a sting across my cheeks. How dare she steal what's mine.

A hole lies within my chest, and within that hole dwells a beast. It must be soothed at all hours of the day, always denied sustenance, otherwise it would grow beyond the confines of its hovel, beyond myself. I would no longer control it. The beast would control me.

The beast is restless though, weary with irritation. Three days I have spent in Harper's company. Standing in the downpour, I consider returning to Thornbrook. I will run as fast as my legs can carry me, abandoning my companion to the wilds of Carterhaugh. Maybe something horrible will befall her. With no one to challenge me, I will become the next acolyte by default, Meirlach or not.

"I'm cold," Harper whines.

"Mother Mabel said no fire in the evenings," I gripe. It's doubtful we could produce a spark in this wet environment anyway.

She peeks over the blanket with deep satisfaction. *My* blanket. "You're shivering," she notes.

Droplets wend down my face as I duck into the lean-to and fold myself into a corner. I have every intention of yanking my blanket off her, but I don't. No fire. No blanket. No bedroll. It will be a miserable night indeed.

Abruptly, Harper pushes to her feet and tromps behind our shelter. After a while, I catch the scent of smoke.

I'm up, striding toward the bent, wizened tree shielding Harper from the downpour. Crouched beneath its branches, she nurses a small, damp fire to life.

"What are you doing?" I lunge toward the flames, intending to stamp them out, but she slams into me, knocking me off-balance. A root catches my heel, and I go down, sinking into squelching mud.

Harper stands over me, having planted herself in front of the flames. "Touch the fire, and I'll rip you to shreds."

I'm too dumbfounded to respond. Slowly, I climb to my feet, gazing at the flare of spitting flames, the enlarged pool of illumination. "The fair folk are attracted to light in darkness. You know this."

"That is no concern of mine."

"Well, it should be!" Again, I edge forward, but Harper shoves me back.

"I can't sleep without it," she snarls.

"And I can't sleep with it." My shoulder rams hers, and she shrieks, tumbling head over feet in an impressive display of athletics.

A low whine slithers through the gaps between the branches above, an eerie sound that pricks at my awareness, a gust reeking of rot.

Harper does not notice the change. A smack of fabric, and she's on her feet. Her ranting climbs in volume, arms swinging and pretty features pinched in a fit of unchecked rage. I grip her arm, hoping to calm her. She screams and flies at me. The harder I resist, the more viciously she fights, thrashing about like a fish on a line. If I'm not careful, she'll bloody my nose purely by accident.

Securing Harper's arms in both of my hands, I force her still. "Hush," I plead, breathless with dread. "Listen."

A rattling moan skates over the ferns. The leaves shiver in response.

Harper stiffens. "What was that?"

I kick dirt over the fire. Its flames sputter, smoke spewing from the ashes.

The extinguished light casts a heavy pall over the area. The trees resemble streaks of soot against the darkest sky. There is no brightness, no moon.

I straighten warily. My fingers creak as they curl around my dagger and pull it free of its sheath. I scan the dim. Two women, alone in the dark. What infests these woods? What have we called closer with our fire and light?

"What do we do?" Harper whispers.

I whip up a hand, demanding silence.

The vibrations arrive in beats of four. A momentary pause before they resume, shuddering up my legs and stirring the fabric of my skirt. Somewhere in the distance, a tree shatters, and Harper recoils, whimpering. The four-legged gait picks up speed. Whatever the manner of beast, it is massive.

"We run." It's our only option.

Harper backs away, eyes flitting from pocket to darkened hollow, searching the darkness oozing across the forest floor. A hair-raising howl crests and dies.

"We'll go north," I murmur, rushing to gather our supplies. I toss Harper her rucksack and slide mine onto my shoulders. "Do you remember the fork in the trail we took earlier? Go left. We can hide in the caves."

A bellow sends Harper fleeing into the woods. I'm right on her heels, plunging through the enclosing murk where the brush snags our ankles and calves. We veer around a tree and converge a few steps ahead. Beyond lies the divide.

"Left!" I bark, cutting down the path. But when I glance over my shoulder, Harper is gone.

13

Branches crack like bones and vines snake across the mossy floor. Springing over a collapsed tree, I veer into Carterhaugh's black depths, thorns clawing at my dress. My mind is twelve steps ahead, grasping at directions, possible options, as I crash blindly through the brush. The beast gives chase.

South, toward Harper? Or north, into the highlands? Westward, the canyon expands in folds of baked red clay with few places to hide. That leaves the Gray, sitting across the strait to the east.

I push onward. My pack slams into my lower back. My legs ache as the terrain fractures into small eruptions of stone. I clamber over another fallen tree, and the earth buckles as a wave of shattering noise crashes at my back. If I can hide until the creature passes, I can backtrack to the fork and find Harper. A high place. A low place. Any will do.

A creek runs a line of silver through the darkness ahead. The icy water burns, but I follow the current half a mile downstream before leaping onto dry land and circling back. I lose track of how many times I do this, threads crisscrossing in the dark. Panting, soaked in sweat, I sag against a tree when an ear-shattering scream rends the night.

Harper.

My wet boots slip and slide through muck as I race south, the air heavy with damp. Alabaster light leaks through the dense canopy, spotting the mossy ground.

Eventually, the terrain shallows out, and I push my exhausted body to its brink, sprinting flat-out toward a copse of trees in the distance. Meanwhile, Harper's screams reach me with decreasing frequency. I fear what that might mean.

The reek hits me first: rotting flesh overlaying thick, choking smoke. I'm leaping over fallen trunks and weaving through collapsed branches when I spot her, white skin luminous in the night.

She crouches between the roots of a vast, ancient oak, trying to make herself as small as possible among the crowded ferns. The beast has cornered her. An elongated spine forms ridges along its back, a gross protrusion that matches the bulging cage of its ribs, all clothed in heavy, streaming shadows. It hails from Under. It hails from the deep.

A second set of pitted eyes suddenly appears beyond the collapsed trees surrounding Harper. She does not notice. She is frozen, terror having bled her features of color. And I am nothing but a body in motion, flinging myself into its path.

My appearance draws the beasts' attention, and one of them snarls. I angle my hips to keep the second creature in sight, fingers tightening around my dagger—one blade, two foes.

"Your dagger," I hiss. "Give me your dagger!"

"I don't have it!" Her voice cracks. She is a whimpering dog, flinching from the hand it has bitten. "My bag—" She gestures to the lumpy sack lying between the legs of the advancing beast.

The creature eases forward. Its glistening lips peel back, saliva dripping from a collection of serrated teeth.

My world has narrowed. There is no rock, no vegetation, no earth. I am a woman standing still.

"Listen to me," I mutter, focusing on the beast before us, its smaller shadow padding closer from behind. "I'm not doing this for you. I'm doing this for me." Slowly, I lower my bag to the ground.

"I don't care who you're doing it for!" The whites of her eyes flash. "Just kill the damn beasts."

"I want my bedroll back."

"What?"

A fat, glistening tongue drags across the larger beast's upper canines. Branches snap as its companion shoves forward.

"I want my bedroll back," I state. "Agree to return it, and I will handle the beasts."

"You can keep your bedroll, keep *my* bedroll, keep it all. I don't care. Just kill the things. *Please.*"

That's as good of an apology as I will ever receive from her. "Stay low and quiet."

Harper swallows, then nods.

The larger creature faces me head-on. Its smaller companion paces to its left, more shadow than tangible shape. *Heavenly Father, give me strength.* I bolt for Harper's bag.

The larger creature lunges, those tearing fangs passing near my arm as I duck beneath its stomach and weave through its legs, putting my training with Mother Mabel into practice. It pivots, snaps at my chest. I stab my dagger toward its neck. The creature recoils with a snarl. I spring, closing the distance, and catch the bag with my fingertips as the second beast barrels toward me.

I fling myself out of range, dropping the bag in the process. Its contents scatter, including Harper's dagger. The larger beast bashes the smaller in the ribs, and it careens into a nearby tree with a thunderous crack, the force tearing its roots from the soil.

I dive into the trees, drawing the monstrosities away from Harper. One beast flanks my left, the other my right. Ahead, a gnarled old tree drips shadow. As I reach the trunk, I kick off and land facing the opposite direction, sprinting back toward Harper as the creatures overshoot my location. My chest sears with each heaving gasp. Nearly there. The second dagger lies a few paces away.

"Behind!" Harper cries.

An ear-shattering shriek erupts at my back, and I dive for the weapon. As soon as the dagger hits my palm, I whirl, a blade in each hand, one arm lashing out in a wild arc. The iron sizzles as it melts the flesh of the creature's shoulder. The beast rears back, howling, allowing me access to its hind legs. Two cuts sever the tendons there.

The creature drops. Its end is my blade, and that blade thrusts downward, plunging into the base of its skull. Black fluid oozes onto filth-caked fur. The first howling creature dies with its last exhalation incomplete. The second crashes through the brush, barreling toward me in feral-eyed rage. I twist as its jaws snap toward me, my dagger punching out to meet it.

Skin, cartilage, bone—the iron blade parts flesh, sinking through the top of the ridged snout with a hiss of smoke. The beast screams and recoils, but my hand clamps the hilt, keeping it steady despite the sting across my chest where the creature's teeth have sliced me. I shove the blade upward, into the front of its skull, between the eyes. Their polished blackness dulls, and I leap backward as the beast crumples into a motionless heap.

Nothing stirs in the close-knit air. Carterhaugh, at last, is still.

My heartbeat cannot catch its rhythm. It skips every few breaths until I begin to feel lightheaded. I brace my hands on my knees, puffing hard, curls hanging loose around my face. The beasts' carcasses bleed out, two piles of steaming, rancid meat.

I feel moments from collapse, but I fear what other creatures the disturbance might attract. We'll need to move, and quickly.

After collecting and cleaning my blades, I return to Harper. She cowers in a ball where I left her, arms clamped over her head, face tucked into her chest.

"Harper." The moment I grip her shoulder she jerks away with a scream, scratching at me with her eyes closed.

"It's me!" A hard shake clears her addled mind. "They're dead."

Her skin is pallid, sickly white. Her eyes have momentarily lost focus, bright blue rings constricting narrow black pupils. "How?"

Adrenaline has likely muddled my good sense, but I remove my cloak from my rucksack and lay it across her back and shoulders. She huddles beneath its warmth without complaint. "Dumb luck," I say. Anything could have altered the outcome.

Harper is too quiet. Shock has begun to set in.

Crouching down, I wrap the cloak tighter around her small frame. "Look at me." I cup her face in my hands. "You're alive. You're safe. We both are."

"I don't want to do this," she whispers. "I want to go home."

We can't go home. We've already lost precious time. But as we move forward, what will the cost be?

"Why would Mother Mabel send us on this mission? It's a fool's errand." The hard click of her chattering teeth sets me on edge. "Have you thought of how easy the other women's tasks were compared to ours?"

I have. I'm still not sure how I feel about it. Previous tasks included working the local soup kitchen, overhauling the abbey library's organizational system, or apprenticing with the physician to extend our healing services. None of the other novitiates were required to brave Under.

"We've come this far," I say. "Do you really want to give up so soon?"

Clarity enters her narrowed eyes. "I'm not giving up. I'm being realistic. Is an appointment worth the risk of our lives?" Another shudder grips Harper's body. "I don't think it is."

She has a point. We could have been killed. And yet—

"I will make sure you return to Thornbrook safely," I say. "We can leave at first light."

"You're not coming with me?"

I shake my head. "I'm going to find Meirlach." No matter the obstacle, I will end this mission gripping the hilt of that fabled sword.

Harper studies me, suddenly unsure. If I'm not mistaken, respect lightens her gaze.

I'm probably mistaken.

Movement on the far side of the clearing catches my attention. I shift in front of Harper, dagger out. Zephyrus ambles from the bushes with his hands raised, applauding slowly and intentionally, each clap punctuated by a brief silence.

I stare. His appearance is more rumpled than I have ever seen it. His curls sit in piles of corkscrews, a few leaves scattered throughout. Dirt deadens the green threads of his tunic, the slim, nondescript trousers.

"A mortal woman, ending those beasts with nothing but a knife?" he says. "I am duly impressed."

Realization wars with the dull horror of the implication. "You were watching the whole time?" My question wobbles. Rage? Disbelief? Perhaps both.

The West Wind shrugs, mouth pursed. "Long enough to see that you had everything under control." He glances at the fallen beasts, curious. "Your dagger," he says. "By chance is there salt on your blade?"

The change in topic momentarily confounds me. "I add salt to the water when quenching the blades."

"Ah." A vague nod. "That would explain how you were able to bring down the beasts." At my puzzlement, he elaborates, "Salt greatly weakens them. Luckily, you were quick on your feet and displayed admirable swordsmanship. Whoever your teacher was, he taught you well."

She taught me well.

My mouth hangs open for a moment before snapping shut. I understand this feeling: skin too tight, body restless. My legs seek movement. Not to walk, but to run, to extend across vast distances, and carry me away from here. "Why didn't you help us? We could have died!"

"You questioned whether you were capable of completing this journey." He surveys me as though trying to determine whether something has changed since our last meeting. "Now you know."

I am staring at a far-off wave. Nearer it comes, its sapphire back arching into a ruffled pearl collar. When the wave hits, it rips the ground from under my feet, and I tumble, caught in the churn of salt and sand.

That is how I feel, pummeled by those words. *Now you know.*

"You're an ass!" I spit at Zephyrus.

The West Wind slides his hands into his pockets. "Do you deny that it was necessary?"

"What was necessary," I growl, striding forward, "was your help. Instead, you watched like a coward in the shadows."

Lack of light imparts a leanness to his features, an effervescent quality to his skin. He appears more godlike than I have ever seen him, power suffusing his voice, brightening his emerald eyes as he says, "If I believed you were unfit to bring down the beasts, I would have intervened. You have depended on the abbey for protection your entire life. It is time you recognize you can weather what the world throws at you."

Stepping around me, he bows to my companion, his mouth the shape of laughter before it forms. "I do not believe we've had the pleasure of acquaintance," he says. "I am Zephyrus, the West Wind, Bringer of Spring."

"I know who you are." Harper climbs to her feet, hands on hips. "There are tales written about you." One dark eyebrow twitches upward. The cool, unimpressed motion gives no indication of her hysterics moments ago. "Is he the man from your room?" she asks me. I stare. "Oh, don't give me that look. You're a terrible liar."

What I wish to say is that the world would be much improved if she shut her mouth and never opened it again. Yet Harper looks at me, and she sees, and she knows.

Zephyrus drifts a few steps away before turning to face off with Harper. He stands a handspan taller, though she does not appear cowed in the slightest. "And if I *was* in Brielle's room? What are you going to do, novitiate?"

My stomach bottoms out, a sudden free falling without end.

Her grin stretches so wide I'm surprised cracks do not split her cheeks. "So you admit you two are *involved*?"

"No!" I cry, stumbling forward. "You are misreading the situation. We are definitely *not* involved. I hardly know him."

That harsh smile chisels deeper into her features, a hunger sharpening the elegant bones of her face.

"I discovered Zephyrus injured in the forest," I stammer, "and I took him back to the abbey for healing. He's a man, I know, but I couldn't leave him to die. He used my room for rest. That's all. Once he recovered, he left."

"You're forgetting the most important part of the story," the West Wind drawls, peering at me through lowered lashes. "Don't be shy. Tell your friend how we crossed into Under together."

Harper gasps, a hand flying to her mouth.

I whirl on Zephyrus. "Say nothing more."

"You went to Under with *him*?" And then she halts, realization darkening her eyes. "That's where you disappeared to last month. You know who this is, right?"

"He is the West Wind," I state.

"And I imagine the title means nothing to you. Are you aware of his reputation?"

I'm unable to shield my confusion. Reputation?

Harper laughs. "Oh, this is wonderful, absolutely wonderful. It proves everything I have ever thought about you, Brielle. What a fool you are. What a stupid fool."

My teeth grind together as hot, familiar shame washes through me. Perhaps she is right. I trust too blindly. But why and how would she know him if she has never met him before? I'm obviously missing something.

Harper tsks. "Imagine what Mother Mabel will say when she learns how you have erred."

Imagine what she will do.

Mother Mabel could send me from Thornbrook. This I know. Venturing into Under is one thing, but bringing a man into the Father's sanctuary would be seen as an act of disloyalty to Him and to my faith.

"Are you going to tell her?" My throat strains.

Harper picks at her nails. "I haven't decided. I suppose it doesn't matter if you get the sword before me. Once Mother Mabel learns of your deception, you will never be allowed the honor of ascension anyway."

That is true, which is why I must find the mythical sword first. If I can bring it to Mother Mabel, might she extend to me mercy for having momentarily strayed?

"Are you looking for Meirlach?" Zephyrus asks curiously.

"We are." Harper considers him with a sidelong glance. "What of it?"

His mouth curves. It is too sly, as is everything else about him. "I am acquainted with the Stallion and his Grotto." He slowly peruses her body, boots to waist to scowling features. When their eyes meet, Harper quirks a brow. "I can take you there," he says.

The queasy drop in my stomach sends me forward a step. "We don't need your help. We know where we're going."

"Do you?" He turns from Harper. "Let me guess. You've been using a map of some sort, only it has failed to lead you belowground."

Harper's cold glare cuts to me, as though *I* am to blame. "We have," she says to Zephyrus. "It didn't work."

He chortles as if to say, *Of course not*, and winks at Harper. It doesn't escape my notice. "We can use one of the Wells to enter."

She stares at him. "Wells?"

Now I'm certain Harper has not read a page of the Text in her life. "The Wells of Past, Present, and Future," I tell her. "They are mentioned in the Book of Origin, when the Father sought healing from their purifying waters."

The West Wind dips his chin. "Indeed. According to the fair folk, their ancestors built those wells with their own hands."

I cross my arms, then drop them. There is no mention of the fair folk in the Book of Origin. It likely isn't true. Regardless, we don't need his help. I tell him as much.

He shrugs. "It would be a shame for you to travel all that way, only to be barred from Under. You of all people know the danger in venturing below without a guide. Step off the grassy path, and who knows what dangers await."

Harper's frosty gaze swings to mine. "Is this true?" Her voice cracks out so forcefully I flinch.

"Yes," I say, "but we can't trust him."

At this, the West Wind's smile deepens. Pleased by my distress? The man is too twisted a creature. "Do you not think that the presence of a man would help you on your travels? The fair folk do love their maidens, after all."

Harper blanches. "He travels with us."

"You know nothing about him," I hiss.

"I know more than you do. You know nothing, period." She flounces nearer to the West Wind. "I'd rather take my chances with him than with those"—she waves a hand toward the carcasses—"creatures."

Grudgingly, I agree. But Zephyrus is a man whose danger lies in what he conceals, not what is evident. Harper does not know what lurks beneath his polished veneer. His company will lead to little good.

"I would be an excellent asset," he states, striding a few paces away to lean against a tree, one ankle tossed over the other. "Do you know how to reach the Grotto?"

Mother Mabel gave me directions from the nymph-guarded entrance. Unfortunately, those instructions have been rendered useless.

At my fuming silence, his mouth stretches a touch wider. "I am familiar with the unsavory areas of Under. I have connections, debts to be called in that would get us out of a bind quickly. You would not be without protection."

"What can you offer us? Pretty words?" Disdain drips readily from my tongue. "I am unimpressed."

"I assure you, my talents extend beyond what I can do with my mouth." His eyes darken, and my heart leaps for reasons unknown.

Lifting one hand, he flicks his fingers a few times, sending currents of air to stir our dresses, the fine strands of our hair. I watch a tendril of wind pluck a leaf from the highest branch of an oak tree, then tuck it behind my ear.

Satisfied, Zephyrus drops his arm. "They do not call me the West Wind for nothing."

Harper stares in open-mouthed wonder. I touch the leaf with a quavering hand, questioning all that came before this moment. Zephyrus never gave any indication of harboring any great power, aside from the ability to irk me to no end. I feel foolish for having failed to figure it out sooner. Such power would be useful on our journey. An extra set of eyes couldn't hurt either.

"What do you want in exchange for helping us?" I say, because Zephyrus' help will not come free.

He appears to ponder the question, though based on how readily he answers, he likely already had a response prepared. "Consider this my debt repaid to you, Brielle. However, if it's not too much to ask, when we reach the Grotto, I would like to go in with you."

That ridiculous debt. But . . . fine. "Why can't you enter yourself?" If he already knows its location, why go with *us* into the Grotto?

"The Grotto is protected by the Stallion, and he only welcomes mortal women into his place of rest."

"But you're not a mortal woman," Harper points out.

His mouth quirks. "No, my dear. I am not. The Stallion is blind. I can manipulate the air so your scent would mask my presence."

Harper and I exchange a look. The quickest way to Under is through Zephyrus, but I don't trust his motives. What, exactly, does he seek?

"What are you looking for? And be specific."

He stares at me for a time. "A prize that would change my life. Surely you cannot blame a man for helping himself?"

"That depends. What is the prize?" Is it dangerous? Detrimental to our health?

"I'm afraid I cannot divulge that information."

I consider him, the bright eyes and unsightly features. How convenient that he is unable to reveal his motive. But I will not knock on a door that refuses to open. I have learned that lesson too many times. There was no better teacher than my mother, who would not change no matter how many times I begged.

It is then I realize I have been staring too long at his mouth, for the West Wind's attention kindles with sudden intrigue. I quickly look elsewhere. "How long will this take?" I demand. In Under, time stretches and bends, and I fear we will spend months underground without realizing it. "We must return to Thornbrook before the tithe."

"I cannot guarantee a timeline, as you know. The more willingly you follow, however, the less time we waste."

He offers little reassurance, and yet, what choice do we have?

I look to Harper, who observes the West Wind with thinly veiled hunger, as though he is something to covet. My stomach twists with an emotion I do not recognize. She would follow this immortal, deaf and blind, into danger, yet she does not even thank me for saving her life?

"Harper," I say, trying to reclaim her attention. Though her mouth pinches in distaste, she turns to me. "I really think we should reconsider."

"The decision has been made, Brielle. If you want to stay behind, that's your choice."

"Perhaps," Zephyrus counters with a raised brow at my traveling companion, "but I do want to take Brielle's opinion into consideration."

Harper shoots me a murderous glare. If I oppose, she will likely claw my eyes from my face. I know we need Zephyrus' help. I just don't want to accept it.

"Let him do what he wants," I snap, hitching my pack onto my shoulders and striding past them. "I care not."

14

THE SHINING BLADE PARTS THE MIST ROLLING ACROSS THE DENSE wood. I whirl, arm extended, imagining the dagger carving flesh—hip, gut, chest. My weight carries me through the arcing strike.

I am a blade.

If I were tougher in nature, I would not bend, and I would not break. I'd sting and sever, slice and wound. All who met the tip of my blade would weep blood.

As I move through the moonlit glen, striking and dodging an invisible opponent, I settle into the strength of my body, the power in my large, muscled arms. Duck, twist, deflect. I grip the leather-wrapped hilt with surety. The lightweight dagger appears weak, easily overlooked. Maybe that is why I love it so.

Sweat slithers down my cheeks and neck, but the mist kisses my heated skin, the cool air disturbed with each swinging arc. And if I imagine my target as Zephyrus' head? No one but me is privy to that information.

The West Wind travels with us now. He is our keeper, our guide. I question my good sense in having agreed to his company.

To my surprise, Harper has been amenable to this arrangement, proceeding to spend the days chatting his ear off. Most of the stories are lies. No, she did not invent the spinning wheel. Neither does she know how to speak four languages. But I've held my tongue.

A flying leap around a tree, and my dagger thwacks into the solid trunk. I yank the weapon free, panting heavily, and repeat the exercise despite my wobbly thighs, the cramp searing white-hot up my back.

Why should I care about their burgeoning friendship? Zephyrus is free to converse with anyone he likes. If he chooses to speak with Harper, it is no concern of mine. Nor are his lingering glances at her; I should expect such behavior from someone whose depth goes no further than the skin.

No, my concern is Meirlach. At our current pace, we should arrive at Under in one day's time. From there, it is another four days to the Grotto—or so Zephyrus claims. Who can say for certain how many days or weeks will have passed aboveground by the time we reach our destination.

Out of curiosity, I've been thumbing through the Text for additional information about the Stallion. The Book of Power contains tales of strange creatures underground, in the blackest depths where evil lurks. Apparently, the Stallion guards a massive hoard of valuables: jewels and weapons, silks and armor and rare poisons.

I have not forgotten my mission. I must kill the beast to obtain the fabled blade. When I ponder what awaits me, I'm almost inclined to return to Thornbrook empty-handed. The true danger of this quest, I believe, has yet to present itself. And as I complete the final exercise, I end with my arm extended, the dagger's iron point catching the throat of an imaginary foe.

Drenched in sweat and thoroughly fatigued, I return to camp.

Harper and Zephyrus sit beneath the lean-to, shoulders brushing as though they have had years to grow comfortable in each other's presence instead of days. I've warned her not to trust him. Unsurprisingly, she has ignored my advice.

I pay them no mind as I search my pack. The fire snaps merrily in broad daylight, though the smell of cooked meat makes my stomach turn. We live a vegetarian lifestyle at Thornbrook. Meat belongs to the old, the infirm. I should eat the hare Zephyrus has trapped and skinned, considering our dwindling food supply, but I've little appetite today.

Harper murmurs something inaudible to her newfound friend, who releases a warm chuckle reminiscent of summer. At some point, she must have removed her cincture, for I spot the white cord dangling from a branch, holding her pack off the damp earth. I bite the inside of my cheek at the sight. She might as well spit on the church altar.

Pulling my last clean dress free, I stand and clear my throat. "I'm—"

"Tell me more about your brother, Eurus," Harper cuts in. She angles her body toward Zephyrus, who uses his cloak as a makeshift blanket, the laces at his collar loose, fabric gaping at his throat.

I swipe the dampness from my face in frustration. Harper has hoarded Zephyrus' attention for days. I can barely get a word in.

"What were you going to say, Brielle?" The overcast haze has muddied the jewels of his eyes, though they appear no less direct. I swallow, and his gaze dips, tracking the motion.

"It's obvious she doesn't remember," Harper snipes, tugging his hand toward her leg. The motion ensnares me. There are his fingers, in dangerous proximity to Harper's thigh. She voluntarily touches a man, yet condemned his presence in my room?

"Calm, Harper." He tugs free of her grip. "I was talking to Brielle."

Her teeth snap shut with an audible click.

"I'm going to bathe," I announce, my clean, dry garments gathered in hand. "I won't be long."

Harper watches me beneath lowered lashes, spite razing her features. My heart skips at the sight, but I'm likely imagining it, anticipating the lash before it falls. As I turn to leave, however, Harper's voice cuts across the clearing, her words horribly familiar.

"*Sometimes, I question my worth as a novitiate,*" she reads, with blatant mockery. "*I question whether I am needed here, whether I will ever make a difference, or if I am only taking up space.*"

My own words slap against my back. Heat flees and cold proliferates, scouring my insides, closing my throat.

Paper rustles before Harper continues, "*Today, I experienced a terrible panic.*"

I can't move. I can only receive the blows as they fall.

"*I was busy harvesting cabbage in the garden when I caught Isobel's voice in the distance. She wasn't alone. She never is. There's always someone lending strength to her voice. This time, it was Harper.*" She pauses for effect, and I whirl, catching sight of my journal in Harper's hand, her toothy grin as she relishes my mounting distress.

"*I tried focusing on my work,*" she continues, "*but it was impossible. She called my name, and I remembered all the times I'd been humiliated, an object of others' laughter and scorn. Idiot. Pig. Pathetic. My breath shortened, and the world grew dark.*"

I sense the change to my skin, how I long to retreat inward, into the very marrow of my bones. Zephyrus glances between us. Did he see her stealing the journal from my pack? Perhaps he turned a blind eye to the transgression.

"Give it back." The whisper emerges limp and threadbare.

Harper merely returns to reading. "*Now here I am,*" she whispers, still smirking. "*Chest tight. Sheltering in bed. Door locked for the first and only time since I arrived at the abbey.*"

I remember that day. I remember feeling so overwhelmed I thought I might vomit. The darkness, Isobel's callous laughter as she cornered me. I could not bear it, and fled to the dormitory.

I wish I'd done things differently. I wish I'd stood up to Isobel. I wish I'd drawn an uncrossable line. But I'd yielded to the weakness in me.

"That's enough," I croak. "Give me my journal." I stride forward haltingly, hand outstretched.

"If you want it," she says, "you'll have to take it from me."

Reaching over, Zephyrus presses a hand across the pages, temporarily shielding the cramped, scrawling ink. "Return what is not yours." Though he speaks to my companion, his gaze rests on me.

Her nostrils flare. "If she didn't want me reading it, she shouldn't have left it lying around."

"It was in my bag," I snap. "You went through my things."

Zephyrus flips the cover shut, for which I'm grateful. Snatching it from Harper's possession, I shelter it against my chest. How much more did she read? Is this her first offense, or has she rifled through my belongings before, while I've been sleeping? My chest pinches fiercely, and I can't breathe, I can't *breathe*.

As if sensing my affliction, Zephyrus begins to push to his feet. "Brielle—"

I run.

The River Twee glimmers in pockets between the trees, a bright line drenched in the afternoon sun. Its eastern branch widens, transitioning into multiple tranquil pools lined with smooth rocks. Brush and boulders fringe the largest basin.

Placing my belongings between two rocks, I peel away my clothes, the chemise momentarily sticking to my chest. I bite back a hiss as the skin tugs painfully.

The water's reflection reveals my pale, round face and freckled skin. Above my breastband, a thin scratch where the beast's claws caught me draws my attention. Two days ago, it was pink. Now yellow-green ooze seeps from the puckered scab. Gently, I press the pads of my fingers around the area. Its slight heat melts into a burn that carves deep.

My hand drops away. I'm panting, seized by that vicious pain, or is it the shame of having been stripped bare by Harper's cruel game?

After tossing aside my soiled garments, I lower myself into the cool water with a groan. It's shallow enough to stand, my toes gripping the slippery, pebbled bottom. I sink lower until the water encloses my skull. Let these thoughts empty out: Zephyrus, Harper, this unsettling awareness of their togetherness, the memory of his hand on her leg.

Forgive me, Father.

The night Zephyrus slipped into my room, I'd unbuttoned my gown and exposed my naked back to his hands. In that moment, the thought of a man's touch did not disgust me.

My head breaks the surface of the water, and I wipe my face, slick back my heavy russet hair.

The West Wind stands at the pool's edge.

I scream, recoiling against the far side of the basin, my face redder than an overripe tomato. "I'm bathing!" I send a splash toward him for good measure.

Grinning, he crouches on the balls of his feet. The water shimmers with dew-drop clarity, and I worry that the paleness of my skin against the dark rock will draw attention to my shape, the curves of my breasts, stomach, and thighs.

I tighten my arms over my chest. How much of my body has he seen?

"You forgot your soap." He holds up the bar of tallow soap.

"You can place it on the ledge there," I state, sinking lower so the water laps at my chin. "Thank you."

There's a distinct tightening in my lower stomach as he continues to peruse me.

"You can leave," I clarify, leaving no room for him to misinterpret my dismissal.

The West Wind twirls the soap lazily. His long, naked fingers possess remarkable dexterity for someone who I've never seen handle a weapon.

"Zephyrus—"

"What were you doing under the water?"

An unwelcome tingle rolls across my skin. "Praying." Of a sort.

His impolite snort puts my back up.

"Do you have an issue with that?" I snap.

"Your friend has humiliated you by reading your journal and you choose to *pray*? Seems rather avoidant."

How little he knows of me, my situation, and my world. "Harper and I are not friends."

"You give her too much power," he says.

He dares speak of power when he is the one pulling strings? "I give her nothing."

"Then what was that story about Harper and Isobel?"

I do not have to answer him. I do not have to even acknowledge his question, not for something as private as the heart. "I'm not discussing this with you." My legs cross in an attempt to conceal the secret place where they meet. If I had more courage, I'd wipe that smirk off his face with the palm of my hand. Traversing the pool, however, is not an option.

He shrugs. "She will only use your jealousy against you."

My mouth parts in astonishment. "Jealousy?" The word breaks, too loud, too revealing. "*Jealousy?*" Surely this is a joke.

The Bringer of Spring, however, does not laugh. He awaits my reply at his leisure.

"Why should I wish for anything Harper has?" I demand.

"You do not like the attention I give her. I have seen it in your eyes."

"You are delusional." A voice of cold I do not recognize flows unhindered across my tongue. "What I feel is certainly not jealousy."

"Then what is it you feel for me?"

Why does this sound like another question entirely?

"You exasperate me to no end."

"I do." His eyes sparkle, and I'm momentarily stunned into forgetfulness as he eases forward, a trouser-clad knee digging into the soil. "Tell me more."

"You infuriate me. You refuse to think of anyone's well-being but your own. Your voice is your favorite sound in the world. You—"

He sidles nearer to the water, then stops. "I what?"

The dappled glow upon his face reveals both light and darkness. It is fitting. No matter how homely I find him, I'm unable to look away.

"Nothing." I shake my head. Water sloshes into my mouth.

"Come now, Brielle. We're friends, aren't we?" The lovely melody of his voice seems to rein in the encroaching shadows.

"No."

"I gave you my special salve," he points out. "That was a friendly thing to do."

"Yes." He could have let me suffer. "Though you were the cause of my punishment in the first place." Let's not forget that particular detail.

The curve of his mouth loses shape. After a moment, he nods. "I was, and for that, I'm sorry."

How little his sincerity moves me. "Please leave. I'm sure Harper is eagerly awaiting your return." A shiver puckers my skin beneath the water.

Still holding the soap, he begins to round the pool toward me, his boots soundless on the damp stones.

"What are you doing?" When he does not slow, I move toward the center of the pool to avoid being cornered, my entire body submerged save my head and neck. The water ripples with my movements, but it cannot hide my shape, the curves I display for no one but myself. "Stay away."

"Regardless of what you believe you feel toward me," he goes on, completely disregarding my stuttering command, "I am certain that the attention I pay to Harper irks you." His golden curls catch the light, and for a moment, I swear his face changes shape. "But why would you care, I wonder?"

"I don't." Zephyrus is free to flirt with whomever he wants. I hold no claim to his affection.

With every purposeful stride, he nears. My throat tightens. He will see. It is forbidden, but he will see.

"Why?" I whisper. "Why do you torment me so?"

After removing his boots, Zephyrus lowers himself onto the ledge, hangs his legs into the water. "Because you intrigue me," he says, "and I want to know why."

He slides fully clothed into the pool.

My back hits the rocks. Indecision winds through me and tightens to the point of pain. "You would touch a woman against her will?"

The West Wind's eyes darken. "Never against her will. Never without her permission." He says, "Tell me to go, and I will."

"I've already told you," I grind out.

"I'll need you to repeat it, I think. My memory isn't the best." He tosses me an impish grin.

I stare into the water. "If you please—"

"Look at me."

I'm helpless to do otherwise. What power is this, that I cannot even control my own mind? "You can't be here," I whisper. If Harper were to see . . .

"Can't I? Let your mind open. Let it experience the vast range of possibilities." Pushing off the wall, he glides through the water. Another step closer brings him within arm's reach. The water warms between us, as though he carries sunlight in his grasp. His soaked tunic clings to his contoured chest, the lean strength of his arms.

"Your gaze is bold today."

My face heats. I glance away, but only for an instant. "I apologize," I stammer, "for staring. I did not realize . . ."

His lips curve. They are like soft pink petals, concealing those pretty white teeth.

"Do not apologize for what you desire, Brielle."

Look at him. His muscular neck; the wet, curling tips of his hair; the hint of stubble along his jaw; the lovely dusk of his skin.

"If I might offer a suggestion?" He all but purrs.

"Is the suggestion," I whisper, tongue darting out to lick the water from my lips, "that you will leave me to bathe in peace?"

He tracks my tongue with his gaze. "Quite the opposite, actually."

That stare unnerves me. It takes every effort not to break it. "Well?"

"A kiss."

I rear back, forgetting about the sharpened stone behind me. A collection of points digs into my spine, and I wince. "No man may touch a Daughter of Thornbrook."

"But you're a novitiate," he says, sliding closer. "You have not taken your final vows. Don't you want to be selfish, Brielle, just once? Don't you want to claim something for yourself?"

My arms tighten around my front even as my breasts begin to grow sensitized. Zephyrus and I are of a similar height, but in this moment, I feel small. It's so rare a feeling I'm momentarily taken aback.

Admittedly, I think of these things. The life of a novitiate isn't easy. We are given the basics to survive, but nothing more. I remember a time before the abbey. My mother and I, curled in bed, her delicate fingers stroking my tangled hair. Sometimes I ache for that memory so much I cannot breathe.

But then I think of what followed. How her hands would tighten, dragging at my scalp. The shrill quality of her voice when her grasp on reality warped. Her giddy highs preceding the inevitable crashes, days lying in bed. A young daughter forced to care for her mentally unstable mother.

Another shift brings his mouth closer to mine. His trousers brush my thighs underwater, and the coarse texture sends a dart of heat through my core.

"You don't actually want to kiss me," I whisper. His smell, like rain on baked earth, lifts to cloud my senses.

"Is that so?" Curled lashes dip over his eyes, shielding them from view. "I have thought of your mouth since our last parting. I have thought of it too often."

"You lie." My voice wavers.

"I do not."

Suddenly, he is that much closer. He exhales in one long stream, his breath slipping into my open mouth.

"Why?" I hate the insecurity a single word can hold. I should not care. I have Thornbrook. I have the Father, and my smithing, and the Text. It has always been enough.

"Because you are an enigma," he says, eyes gentle. "Because you are most generous. Because you are discovering what lies beyond your abbey walls, and I find myself drawn to your bravery."

"I'm not brave," I stammer, searching his gaze for deception. I find none.

"Aren't you?"

If I were braver, I would turn my back on people leading me down unfulfilling roads. I would have fought for myself years ago. Being swept up in the whims of others? That is not bravery. That is complacency.

Zephyrus hesitates, then says, "I am old, Brielle. Very old. The world does not hold the same allure for someone who does not age."

Pulling away, he lifts himself from the pool, water dripping from his clothes to splatter onto the rocks. "I have enjoyed watching you experience life," he says, features shadowed by unexpected grief. "Do not take it for granted, because soon enough, it will end."

15

I EAT LITTLE OF THE DINNER ZEPHYRUS PROVIDES BEFORE ROLLING into bed, dragged into unconsciousness before my head hits the ground. My dreams grow talons. Sweat oozes from my pores, and a dull ache throbs alongside my bones. Then: dawn.

I pull myself upright, shivering as I store my belongings and shoulder my pack. Even in these early hours, the light glares potently, my eyes cracked to the barest sliver against it.

Cheese and apples comprise breakfast, but I do not partake, considering the awful metallic taste in my mouth. Zephyrus and Harper stride ahead, chatting merrily, unaware that each of my steps falls slower than the last.

Noon arrives and departs with equal lethargy.

As the afternoon wanes, the earth, springy and wet, begins to stink of rot. I find myself reaching for low-hanging branches, the treacherous ground pocked with holes. Blackness streaks my vision. I stop, swaying dizzily in place.

"I need a moment."

Despite the softness of my voice, Zephyrus hears me. I would recognize that long-legged stride among the marching gait of a hundred men as he doubles back to help lower me onto a stump, worry creasing his face. "You're pale."

My mouth is so dry I fail to swallow. "I'm always pale."

"Wan, I should say." He shifts nearer. "When did you last eat?"

Yesterday returns in flashes of color, sound, and light. "Last night. Dinner."

"Oh? You mean the single bite you took before falling asleep?"

I frown at him. "Yes." I was not aware he had been paying attention to my eating habits.

Harper retraces her steps through the brush, glowering at me from a patch of sunlight. Zephyrus catches my chin. He stares into my eyes, but I struggle to focus, so I look at his nose. That impossibly crooked nose, a blight on his features. Strangely, it comforts me.

"You have lost your appetite," he says.

What does that have to do with anything? "We've been hiking all day. I just need to rest for a bit."

Prowling over, Harper circles me, black hair freshly combed despite the long, sweltering hours trapped in Carterhaugh's humidity. "I said if you fell behind, I would not wait for you."

"It's probably a cold," I say, slumping forward to rub at my pounding head. "It will pass."

The West Wind continues to study me. He does not seem to notice Harper's proximity, much to her frustration. "Are you injured?"

As usual, he thinks he knows things. "All my limbs are in working order."

"You're certain you weren't hurt during the chase the other day?"

"Are you suggesting I don't know my own body?" I'm too fatigued to put any heat behind it, though it irks me all the same.

"No." He exudes a calm that is quite unlike him. "But it was dark. Our eyes miss things. And yours are very mortal."

An oversight. No fatal wounds or severed appendages, but a scratch. A hairline cut parting the cotton of my dress.

Fumbling with the button at my collar, I slide it from the eye loop while the forest respires in great warm heaves around us. Harper leans closer despite feigning disinterest.

We've traveled so quickly, and I've been so weary, that I haven't paid much attention to the ache at my sternum. My arm twinges as I awkwardly tug the sleeve over my shoulder, the skin across my chest tearing painfully. When I reveal the slice above my breastband, Zephyrus pinches his mouth closed.

Yesterday, the scab had been intact, stretched by the yellowing pus gathering beneath. It has since burst, widening to an open wound stuffed with graying flesh. A subtly sweet reek lifts from the sore. Harper gags.

My fingers quaver as I trace the sooty black veins branching from the glistening wound. The salve I slathered on it has cracked, leaving behind a white residue.

"It looks infected," Harper states.

"It's not infected," Zephyrus says. "The creatures you fought are called darkwalkers. Brielle has been envenomated."

This news ... it sounds serious, and yet I feel nothing. I've been sucked dry of emotion. Not even Harper's sharp gasp can rouse me.

"That explains why the salve didn't work," I murmur, carefully buttoning up my dress. I'd rather not look at the gruesome display. "How do we treat the wound?"

A restlessness stirs the air despite Zephyrus' lack of movement. "There is no cure, Brielle." A woeful tone. Harper's gaze cuts to me, but I can't look at her. I'm afraid of what I'll see. Satisfaction. Pleasure, even, at my misfortune.

"How long?" I whisper.

He rubs at his jaw. "It takes around five days for the venom to work its way through the system."

We have been traveling together for four.

Sadness passes as a cloud over my heart, for I am helpless to turn back time. It is done. Soon, I will be, too.

"These darkwalkers. What are they?" Not that it matters. With my fate carved in stone, knowledge for the sake of knowledge will make no difference. But it comforts me, knowing the what and how and when.

"They hail from the Deadlands—my eldest brother's realm. In simplest terms, they are the corrupted souls of the dead." He toes the ground with his boot. I'm watching his face, witnessing pain he seeks to keep hidden. What tortures him? "Last I heard, the darkwalkers had been cleansed from Boreas' territory. It seems some managed to cross into Carterhaugh."

Deadlands. Darkwalkers. I've never heard of this place, these creatures. "The Deadlands? They don't come from Under?"

"They do not. The Deadlands is where those who have passed on await Judgment. There, they find their final resting place."

What absurdity. Everyone knows the dead ascend to the Eternal Lands—those who are worthy, at least.

"What will happen to me, as the venom spreads?" What a question to ask, and so matter-of-factly. But I'd prefer to shed the veil of this unknown.

Zephyrus squeezes the bridge of his nose. "It will not be pretty." His response is subdued, tight with reluctance. "Your fever will continue to climb. You will crave water no matter how much you drink. Your flesh will blacken with decay."

Harper stumbles backward in horror. "By the Father." She retreats among the ferns, arms wrapped around her torso.

My attention returns to Zephyrus. "Go on."

"Brielle—"

"Do not spare me, Bringer of Spring." My eyes sting, but I refuse to let the tears fall.

The Text teaches us not to fear death, yet I am afraid of departing this good earth having failed the task I've been given. I'm too young, too untried. I question what lies beyond this day, not in fear, but in tentative curiosity, even wonder. My hands shake as I straighten. No. I will not shrink in light of this reality. I will face this upright as I should have faced all my trials, days, weeks, months ago.

Zephyrus hangs his head. His hands spear through those honey-brown curls. "The venom will reach your organs last. It will be . . . very painful. They say a quick death is preferred." He swallows, lifts his eyes. "Do you taste metal at all?"

I nod.

"Then the final stages have already begun to take effect."

Is this where I will die? In the depths of Carterhaugh, a place crawling with unspeakable horrors, not even a candle to bring me comfort?

"I wish you would have said something," murmurs the West Wind with far more compassion than expected. "This could have been prevented, had your wound been treated within the first forty-eight hours."

How was I to know? It makes me twice the fool, I suppose.

"You're sure there's nothing we can do?" I hate how my voice shakes. "No cure? Nothing at all?"

His expression tightens in what I believe to be conflict, or pain. Perhaps my imminent demise upsets him. I did not think Zephyrus cared for me. Indeed, I believed he cared for no one. "I wish there was something I could do for you. Because the darkwalkers hail from another realm, the fair folk lack the proper ingredients required to nullify the beasts' venom. You ask whether there is a cure. Unfortunately," Zephyrus says, "there is not."

Hearing it aloud, without ploy or trickery, guts me. I swipe at my eyes, yet one tear manages to escape, sliding down my feverish cheek. Zephyrus frowns. He leans forward, reaching toward my face. The pad of his thumb brushes my cheek, catching the droplet. I meet his gaze. Together, in this moment, we are still.

Eventually, he leans back, though the frown remains. "Is there someone you'd like me to inform afterward?" he wonders. "Family?"

"No." I stare at the ground. "I'm an only child. I never met my father. As for my mother . . ." I've little to say about my mother. Dead or alive, I know not.

I shake my head. "There is no one. The abbess has acted as my mentor for the last decade. She will want to know of my passing." I look to Harper. Once I'm gone, she can claim Meirlach for herself.

Zephyrus follows my gaze, then nods. "I will make sure your abbess learns of this. You have my word."

It is the smallest reassurance. "Thank you." I lick my painfully dry lips, the cracks stinging where the skin has peeled free. "Will you continue onward without me?"

He lowers himself onto the ground beside me, one leg extended outward, the other pulled to his chest, an arm wrapped around his shin. "I will not leave you."

Relief courses through me, though I try to hide it. That he has considered my comfort is more than I expected from him.

"Plus, I'm terrified of being alone in Harper's presence," he tacks on.

Against all odds, my mouth curves, and I snort. Harper, a vague shape in the fringe of my vision, walks away, head bent while Zephyrus' chuckle softens into a smile.

"Her presence does not appear to have bothered you until now," I point out, more harshly than I intend.

He shrugs. "Any conversation is better than no conversation."

His tone gives me pause. "What are you implying?"

"If you chose to speak with me, maybe I wouldn't feel the need to talk to Harper."

I stare at the West Wind with dawning realization. Perhaps he enjoyed our discussions as much as I did. "I didn't know," I say. Disappointment hits, unwelcome and uncomfortable.

"You didn't know?" A small, rather sad smile flits across his mouth, then is gone. "And here I thought I was being obvious in my affection."

My throat tightens with an odd, bereft sensation. Though I do not think Zephyrus lies, I cannot be sure. We must have a different interpretation of the word *affection*.

He scans my face. "Is there anything I can do to make your time left more comfortable? Anything you need?"

I bite my lower lip. *Rest.* Blessed slumber croons in my ear, but if I am to die, it seems pointless to rest, knowing the hole into which I will fall contains no bottom. "Could you just stay? And talk?" A blush scours my face. "I don't have many friends to converse with." I consider leaving the thought unfinished. "Actually, I have no friends," I admit. Not one.

"No friends?" He frowns. "I find that hard to believe."

"Making friends doesn't come easily to me." I never know the right thing to say, how best to connect with my peers. Many of the older acolytes don't even know my name. "But you—" The West Wind can draw people in, make them stay. Make them *want* to stay. "It is easy for you. The way you interact with others . . . I can't do what you do."

"Easy?" A bark of startled laughter claps the air. "My darling novitiate, nothing comes easy to me. It never has. I'm just adept at appearances."

To my eternal frustration, another tear slides down my face. Baring my soul was never the plan, yet my defenses have caved, my exhaustion is too great. So be it. Let Zephyrus see. I no longer care enough to pretend otherwise.

"Do you have regrets?" I ask.

A weary sigh escapes him. He appears bent in this moment, as though a great burden rests upon his back. "The better question, I think, is what do I not regret." When his eyes catch mine, I forget to breathe for a moment. "What are your regrets, Brielle?"

I shouldn't say. Even the thought is too wicked to conceive. My mouth, however, has other ideas, and promptly runs away from me.

"I'm thinking of that couple we stumbled across during our visit to Willow." Their twined limbs and insatiable hunger for each other.

Zephyrus emits a low rumble in his chest. It is less of a sound and more of a sensation. It sweeps low through my stomach, and despite lying on solid ground, I experience a feeling of falling, however brief.

"You regret not partaking in sexual acts?"

"No!" By the Father, I should not be having this conversation. "But the kissing . . ." My mouth is so dry it is difficult to swallow. "I suppose a part of me wonders what it would be like." I feel my ears burn.

"Is that what you want?" he asks, gaze unreadable. "A kiss?"

If I do not acknowledge it, perhaps the desire will leave me. But no. I want this. Of that, I am certain. "If I am going to die, what does it matter if my vows are broken?" Though that is not entirely true. Perhaps this is the selfishness in me. "I would like to experience it, I think. Just once."

I have not yet seen this sadness in him. Indeed, I could not have believed Zephyrus could feel with such depths of sorrow toward my plight, but I cannot recognize the emotion that shifts his features as anything else. He nods, and leans forward. "Then I would be honored to bestow this gift upon you." He lifts his hands and, deliberately, rests them on either side of my head, effectively caging me in.

A small sound squeezes past my tightening throat. Fear? Despair? Humiliation? My teeth chatter as a rising cold licks through my chest. *Deliver us from temptation.* With this touch, I will never know peace.

Slowly, he lowers his face to mine. As always, he smells of sun-warmed grass. I will miss his scent when I am gone.

"Brielle," croons the West Wind. "Let yourself unwind."

I'm too spineless to keep my eyes open. Lack of sight heightens the forest sounds: the rough, coursing river; leaves rustling fragile as moth wings; and the wind, sightless and scentless, winding knots through my hair.

Something brushes my mouth. I pinch it shut on reflex.

Obedience, purity, devotion. Here, on the eve of my demise, my vows will shatter into a thousand unknowns. I feel sick with shame, but I want to live, fully, with whatever time remains.

"Trust," he whispers against my mouth. "Let your heart guide you."

My lips part of their own volition, and I inhale. Lemon and herbs. My pulse gallops wildly, a slow flush suffusing my overheated skin. His tongue slides against mine, fleeting, before he pulls away.

My skin tingles with the aftershock of his touch. All the world is darkness until I open my eyes to find the West Wind staring down at me.

"I see it in your eyes," he whispers.

All thoughts have fled. I am a woman made vacant. "See what?"

Leaning forward, he touches his mouth to my ear. "The hunger."

16

"IT'S A SHAME YOU'RE GOING TO DIE."

Harper perches on a large, smooth stone near the fire, gazing at me with her enormous, all-seeing eyes. They shimmer like orbs of pristine lake water in her small face.

I lie in my sweat-soaked bedroll, shivering, every warm breeze scouring me like the iciest wind. Initially, I fail to process her words. Zephyrus departed hours ago, seeking a herb to help dull the pain as the venom works its way through my system. Last night, my health began its sharp decline. I scribbled in my journal for a time, noting my final thoughts as my fever intensified, my lips cracked and bleeding. Despite my fatigue, I pushed on. Only in pouring my heart into my journal do I feel secure, loved. It is a compulsion that cannot be stopped.

Here at the end of my days, the fight has all but gone out of me.

"For once in your life," I rasp out, "can you show a little compassion?" Allowing space for compassion should never be a burden.

"You know people don't buy your little act, right? Perfect Brielle, who can do no wrong. What a joke."

An edged pain jabs beneath my sternum. "I wasn't aware it was an act," I grit, trembling from the spasm. "Why should I not treat others as I wish to be treated? They are our brothers, our mothers, our sisters, our children. That is what the Text teaches us."

Harper scoffs, which only agitates my irritation to further heights.

"Have you even thought about what becoming an acolyte means?" I ask her. "Have you considered how you'll use your mantle for the betterment of Thornbrook, and the world?"

If Thornbrook is a pillar of faith and goodwill, then novitiates are its bedrock. We are responsible for the day-to-day tasks required of keeping the abbey doors open. Acolytes, however, actively shape the surrounding community. They travel to Kilkare, to Aranglen, to the smallest towns on Carterhaugh's border, spreading the Father's word. *Come*, they urge. *This is the way.*

"And I'm to believe you have?" she snaps. "I was not aware there was any space in your head for such thoughts, considering your nose is stuck in the Text every spare moment."

Again, this disdain for my continued studies. I do not understand it. Abbey and community—stronger together, weaker apart. But Harper, a woman who sees nothing but her own reflection? She covets the prestige gained in wearing the red stole and nothing beyond it.

"Not every acolyte is required to break their backs seeking lasting change," she says, leaning forward on her perch.

"You do not think He expects your best effort?"

"Just because I haven't thought of some grand plan doesn't mean I will do any less good." She crosses her arms. At least she's returned to wearing her cincture properly, the white cord knotted at the front of her wrinkled cotton dress.

I cough into my hands. "Spoken like someone who has given little thought to the responsibility."

I'm surprised steam doesn't billow from Harper's nostrils. She drags her pack closer and begins yanking out her filthy clothes, folding and unfolding them, as if busying her hands to stop herself from walloping me in the face.

"What are your ideas," she snips, "if you think they're so much better?"

I flip onto my side to ease the pain radiating through my bones. The summer's warmth presses heavy hands against me. It is so oppressive I struggle to retain clarity of mind. I fumble for the buttons on my dress, manage to wrench the sleeves down, then my chemise, exposing my sweat-drenched upper back to the air.

When I look toward Harper, I find her face oddly pale, mouth slack. That's when I remember Mother Mabel's lash, the marks spoiling my shoulder blades, the length of my spine.

Teeth gritted, I slowly rebutton my dress. How could I have forgotten my penance? Then again, what does it matter? In a few hours, Carterhaugh will begin to bruise with approaching twilight. I wonder if I will even see the morrow.

"I never said my ideas are better than yours," I state. "For that to be true, you'd have to have your own ideas to begin with."

Tension grips the lines of her body, and I do not imagine the heat rolling in waves off her skin. "Well," she murmurs, eyes reduced to haughty blue slits, "you are certainly opinionated today."

At this point, I've nothing to lose. "Do you want to hear my ideas or not?"

She flaps a hand. It's the only consent I can hope to receive.

"I was thinking along the lines of an apprenticeship," I say.

"Elaborate."

"Thornbrook has an excellent relationship with Kilkare," I say, too weak to do anything but lie in stillness, "but what of the smaller towns to the north and east?" I think of Veraness, its scattered remains. "Many of the children in those parts go hungry, having received no proper schooling. We could teach them how to harvest grain, how to read and write and complete simple mathematics, how to mend clothes, forge weapons. In return for work, they would receive food, shelter, and the means to provide a better life for themselves and their families."

In my younger years, I visited Kilkare every few weeks to apprentice with their local bladesmith. Three years later, I graduated with an arsenal of skills, the means to create any manner of blade. Providing children with the same opportunity could greatly benefit the community as a whole.

Harper appears contemplative. Perhaps I've given her something to ponder. And yet, I'm imagining what will occur once my heart ceases to beat. Harper, sauntering into Thornbrook, Meirlach hanging from her waist. Mother Mabel's grief at my passing overshadowed by the acquisition of that remarkable sword. Another red stole bestowed upon someone less deserving than I.

I think, *I am going to die.* Why fight when the Eternal Lands await? But in my life, there are still so many things left undone.

"You claim Mother Mabel favors me," I whisper hoarsely. "What do you think she will do when you return to the abbey with the news of my death, sword or not?"

Harper crams the clothes into her pack. Then she sits, glaring at me. She understands my logic, and she hates it. Alas, that is nothing new.

"I hate to be the bearer of bad news," she says, though her tone suggests otherwise, "but novitiates are a drop in the bucket to Mother Mabel. Dozens pass through Thornbrook every year. Do not think you are irreplaceable."

Harper is wrong. I am a valued member of the abbey. Only I can shape the blades that protect us from the fair folk. "Even if you become the next acolyte," I counter, "your mantle will be forever tainted by my death."

She scoffs. "You volunteered to take this journey. You knew the risks. Mother Mabel wouldn't fault me for your demise."

"Wouldn't she?" I feed her dubiety, crumb by crumb. "I imagine there would always be certain reservations."

She brushes dirt from the front of her dress. "You think too highly of yourself. You are nothing more than a pair of hands, like everyone else."

It takes mettle to hold the gaze of my tormentor, but I force myself to do it. At this point, I'm out of options. "I think," I say slowly, "you underestimate Mother Mabel's affection toward me."

"I'm confident I do not. If the abbess truly favored you, why pass you over for others less diligent? She only gave you the opportunity to try for the position because she pities you."

Harper knows exactly what buttons to push. Still, I refuse to cave. "Maybe you're right. Maybe I am just another *pair of hands*, as you put it. But if I am not?"

"You are." Trembling.

I shrug.

Lurching to her feet, Harper stumbles toward the nearest tree. She braces a hand there, back bowed with the force of her breaths. Only the seed requires planting. She can see it all unravel, this dream of hers, before it has even occurred.

"What do I have to do?" she whispers. "I've worked too hard to botch this opportunity."

"You save me," I tell her. "Otherwise, you'll be left with nothing." And that, I've realized, is something Harper cannot bear.

A fraught silence sinks into place, then all at once, she deflates. "But Zephyrus said there's no cure."

I give her my blandest stare. "And you believe him?"

Frowning, she searches my gaze, and in this moment, she appears as deeply uncertain as I do, caught unaware by the support I've given. She considers this, then strides over to Zephyrus' bedroll.

"What are you doing?"

Harper loosens the tie on his satchel and begins to rummage through his possessions. "Searching for leverage," she states, as though it were obvious. She pulls out a small book, frowns, and shoves it back inside.

The only thing Harper loves more than proving a point is . . . well, nothing. At least she finally agrees with me. The West Wind is too cunning, too keen.

"And here I thought I was doing a good deed," drawls the West Wind.

He emerges from the thicket in shades of gray. Crossing into a patch of sunlight brings color to his green cloak, the simple brown trousers. He moves so swiftly he is gone when I next blink.

Dropping the pack, Harper whirls on him, blade out. She is the most bull-headed woman I've ever met. Why else would she pull a blade on the West Wind?

He halts a hair's breadth from her outstretched hand, not alarmed in the slightest. She may as well hold a feather to his throat. "Do you even know how to use that thing?" he asks.

Harper's low, throaty laughter washes out in a cascade of sound. "I stick the pointed side into your flesh. What more is there to know?"

His mouth smiles. His eyes do not. "Did you find what you were looking for?"

"And if I did?"

Zephyrus examines Harper as I have done many times before, with the understanding that the one you address hides many untruths, and you must search in every crack and crevice, down to what lies beneath.

"Let me speak plainly," Harper says. "We need Brielle for this mission. If she dies, so does the opportunity to acquire Meirlach. She will ensure our time is not wasted."

I stare at my surly traveling companion in astonishment. Never has a word of praise flowed so naturally from her mouth, and certainly not about me. As always, she speaks with conviction. Even I believe her.

She tosses the dagger toward her pack, as if having decided it's not worth the trouble. I wince as it hits the dirt. The blade will need to be cleaned. "Our only option is to save her life."

The West Wind's attention shifts to where I lie prone. Another shiver rattles my insides, and he frowns at the sight. "As it turns out, I agree."

"Oh." Harper blinks, then straightens. "Very well."

"Someone owed me a debt," he says, "and that debt has been repaid. This"—he lifts a vial of pale liquid—"is the answer to your prayers. I know a hedge witch in Carterhaugh. A master healer. This is one of her more potent remedies. Although, it required a trade: a few drops of your blood." He lifts my hand, and I notice a small bandage wrapped around my thumb. "Hopefully you don't mind."

"That will cure me?" I croak.

"It will."

Harper speaks from behind. "If you knew this was an option, why didn't you visit the hedge witch sooner?"

She has a point.

"I wasn't certain that I could obtain the remedy," Zephyrus says. "The hedge witch travels great distances to procure ingredients and cannot easily be reached."

I want to believe him. Harper, too, appears suspicious as she shifts into my line of vision. Then again, she believes nothing. "How convenient that you managed to acquire it at the eleventh hour."

"Yes," he replies with a bite. "It is."

Every feature of my tentative ally pinches in wariness. "Very well." She waves a hand. "Heal Brielle and be done with it."

Zephyrus approaches my side, the vial squeezed in his fist. He kneels. Sunlight halos his springing curls. A warm breeze stirs the branched canopy overhead.

"Open your mouth," he says.

With his attention focused wholly on me, I struggle to form words. It is his voice, his scent, the heat of his leg through his trousers. Too easily, he overwhelms, even more so in my weakened state. "I can dispense the cure myself," I say, holding out a hand for the vial.

A pout softens his lips. "You would deny me the honor of healing you? Or is it my touch you shy away from?" He traces the line of my sleeve, drags his finger upward toward my collarbone. "But why? After all, we have already shared a kiss."

The air falls like a dead weight against my skin. I can neither move nor think. I do not want to look at Harper. I must look at Harper.

She stands stiffly, with a stillness that reminds me of a large predator. The gleam of her eyes twists my gut into knots. She is ravenous, too eager.

Oddly calm, Harper says, "A kiss?"

"I can explain."

She offers me a sugary smile. "I'm sure you can."

Plucking the vial from Zephyrus' grip, I uncork it and dump the contents into my mouth.

The result is instantaneous—relief in the purest form. The weight on my chest lifts. My lungs open, my breath flows free.

"I thought I was going to die," I tell her. "He didn't touch me but for the kiss."

"Did you ask him for the kiss?" Arms folded across her chest, she regards me unblinkingly.

"Harper—"

"Did you, or did you not, ask for the kiss?"

The West Wind's eyes rest on my face. My heart quakes in light of this truth. "I did," I whisper hoarsely.

Spinning on her heel, she plunges through the ferns, and I do not have the voice in me to call her back.

17

THE FOLLOWING MORNING, I'M SURPRISED BY THE LACK OF INSULTS from Harper.

She will not look at me. Neither will she speak to me. But her eyes, those lake water pools—I cannot shake them free. She knows. And I know. The kiss was a mistake.

But that is not the truth, is it? The truth is this: I wanted it. Deep down, in an old, abandoned corner of my heart, I wanted to know what it felt like, just once, to be desired.

Midway through the afternoon, we stop for a break. It could not have come at a better time. Carterhaugh is particularly dense, holding close to the warm, stagnant air, its walls of greenery shuttering any distant sound. Zephyrus strides off to relieve himself, leaving Harper and I alone.

She sags against a fallen tree, clothing bagging around her slim frame. Once again, Harper has run out of water. Since we cannot afford the delay of a potential collapse, I set aside my irritation and approach her, canteen in hand. "Here."

To my surprise, she accepts it without argument, draining half the container in one swallow.

"Slowly," I snap.

A gasp rings out as she rips her mouth free. "Don't think this will stop me from informing Mother Mabel about that kiss when we return to Thornbrook." She takes another greedy pull.

For a heartbeat, I'm caught in a free fall. There is the excuse, there is the lie, and there is the truth. "I can explain."

A hair-raising cackle scatters the birds roosting in the trees. They soar off with raucous caws of distress. "By all means, go ahead. Explain how you were lured into a sexual act with a man. I'm sure the abbess will understand."

I have always found Harper disagreeable, but here, now, I realize how horrible she truly is. She is bitter enough to drag me down into the blackest waters and let me drown. And I will, if I do not start fighting for myself.

"I thought I was going to die," I say lowly. "It was harmless."

"You think Mother Mabel cares about that?" Her mouth pinches. "You are sullied, and I will ensure she knows of it."

Helplessly, my eyes begin to sting. What is worse, the venom she spews, or my belief in it?

Do I regret kissing Zephyrus? That, I cannot answer. For from his mouth, I received life.

"Go ahead and tell Mother Mabel," I choke. "The only reason you're doing this is because you can't stand the idea that Zephyrus might find me desirable." My fury crystallizes, a sharp, burning core alive inside me.

"He does not desire you," she hisses. "Is that what you think? You are so simple, Brielle. I feel sorry for you. Honestly, I do. Zephyrus is playing you, don't you see?"

Tossing the canteen at my feet, she hauls her rucksack across her back and dives into the brush.

My hands shake as I gather my belongings. To choose desire is to choose oneself, and to choose oneself is to walk a path separate from the Father. Zephyrus did not put his hands on me, but why should that matter? He kissed me. I wanted it. That is something I am unable to reverse.

By midafternoon, the sun screams with heat, and not even the shade can curb its oppressive weight. The canopy reveals pockets of white and blue. A rush of cooling air sweeps in, relief against my red, patchy skin, and I glance up in time to see Zephyrus drop his hand, fingers colored silver from the breeze he has conjured.

I offer him a grateful smile. "How much longer?"

Something softens his expression, if I'm not mistaken. "See for yourself."

As we push through a break in the trees, my footsteps falter. A squall hits us from the east, and I gasp. Blue sky above, and beneath, rock of deepest red.

It is an ocean of emptiness. A gulf that continuously unfolds so its vastness seems to expand in countless directions. Sunlight hammers the striated rock, squeezing out veins of quartz and gold, stone splitting beneath the pressure of a thousand years. A layer of sizzling air skates over the landscape.

I have heard of the world's endless stretch, but I never imagined *this*: the widest, deepest canyon, with plunging valleys and curved, mammoth walls. Look at how it bursts its seams.

Harper tromps up to my side, surveying the vista. Then she turns away, utterly unimpressed. Kneeling on the ground, she removes the map from her rucksack and opens the oiled parchment. "I don't see a way to cross."

"There is," I murmur reluctantly, though it's not inked on the chart.

She lifts her head to look where I point. A narrow rope bridge stretches across the ravine, creaking in the humid breeze.

Harper pushes to her feet, folds the map, and studies the hanging bridge. She appears neither frightened nor concerned. "This is the only way to cross?"

Zephyrus speaks from behind. "It is."

This cannot be our only option. I study the canyon, every wide, meandering curve. A shaded copse shimmers on the opposite side of the gulf, a dark green border where the sweltering red rock ends.

Harper passes me the map. "Might as well get it over with."

I tuck the parchment into my pocket. "You're not afraid it will snap?"

She lifts those lovely, curved eyebrows in challenge. Even trekking through Carterhaugh, they are never less than expertly groomed. "Are you?"

Yes, because the bridge looks as if it hasn't been repaired since its construction, however many centuries ago that was.

My palms begin to sweat beneath my gloves. "If we go the long way around—"

"We don't have time. We've only until the tithe to return. We're already behind."

"Maybe we wouldn't be," I point out, "if you had bothered to help set up and break down camp the last three nights." I gathered firewood, erected our shelter, cooked dinner, dug the latrine, despite my slow recuperation from my near-death experience.

Harper hefts her pack higher onto her back. "Spare me your righteousness, Brielle. I've done my fair share on this journey. You're not the only one capable of contributing."

I don't bother mentioning that without my aid, she likely would have collapsed after the first few miles.

"Ladies." Zephyrus steps between us. "Can we save the sparring until we reach the other side?"

Harper pays him no mind. She says to me, "If you're too afraid to cross, you'll have to go back alone. I'm going ahead with or without you."

She's right. If I cannot cross the bridge, this entire journey will have been for naught. And that is not an option.

As she brushes past me, I catch her sleeve. "Can't you reconsider?"

She sighs. "Oh, Brielle. When will you learn? People act out of their own selfish needs, and I am no exception. Neither are you." A hard yank rips her arm from my grasp. "I'll be sure to put in a good word to Mother Mabel for you—or not."

With a cruel smirk, Harper plants one foot onto the nearest plank. The bridge sags beneath her weight, creaking like an old door in the wind. I watch it all without taking a breath.

Plank by plank, she shuffles forward. Her hands clamp the rope railings strung waist-high across the gulf. The bridge holds, but Harper is half my body weight. The lines would surely snap if I attempted to cross.

I can't do it. I can't put my trust in this shoddy contraption, one sneeze away from collapse. Helplessness—a feeling I know well.

"Close your eyes." The command flutters near my ear, brimming with unseen power.

I cannot. A few planks of wood bound together with fraying rope is all that would separate me from the drop, those vicious rocks jutting from the bottom of the ravine. A screaming gust wrenches through the canyon.

"Brielle." Warmth at my back, followed by the wind's cool caress. "Let me guide you."

"I'm not crossing the bridge."

"You are going to cross the bridge," Zephyrus says. "And I am going to help you."

"I just said—"

"Then why are you here?"

That stops me. Why *am* I here? I thought I knew. But that was *before*. Before the darkwalkers, my illness, each excruciating second spent in Harper's presence, our unnecessary battle of wills.

"I shouldn't have left Thornbrook," I murmur. "I should have stayed where it was safe."

"That sounds dreadfully boring." Then he sighs. "What is it you want, Brielle?"

I release a shaky breath. Harper has nearly reached the other side. "To obtain Meirlach. To prove my worth to Mother Mabel. To give my life to the Father."

"Then you will cross the bridge. If you cannot confront this fear, you will continue to feel small. Is that what you want?"

What can the West Wind know of fear? He is a god, immortal, prevailing. He could shape the world in his image if he chose.

"Close your eyes," he repeats.

It is easier to speak truthfully when I am blind to other things, and yet—"I can't."

"Why not?"

The answer is an old wound, and I fear it has not healed as well as I had hoped.

"The dark," I whisper. "I fear the dark."

He falls quiet, yet the wind unleashes itself, a great, howling, emotive creature. I do not realize I'm leaning into Zephyrus until his breath stirs the fine hairs on my nape, and I lurch forward to put distance between us.

"Steady," he murmurs, placing a hand on my hip. "The dark is not inherently dangerous on its own."

I lick my lips, forcing out, "I'm aware." By the Father, this will not be easy. "What do you fear?"

He makes a sound in his throat as the wind bleeds into a low hum. "I fear the fall."

The hand on my hip remains, his touch muted by the fabric of my dress. It feels strange to lean on him. To lean on anyone, really.

"I believe fear lies in all of us," he continues. "We ask ourselves if it will hurt. We wonder if we could have done something differently."

What does he refer to? Here, now, me, this bridge, something else, something more? I do not believe he speaks of falling in the physical sense. More of a fall from grace. That is a fear I know well. "What part of falling do you fear?"

"What comes after."

"And what comes after?"

His hand tightens on my hip. "The understanding that what has been broken can never be repaired."

My surroundings fade, and I feel only a man's body against mine as my eyelids flutter shut. "You know this from experience?"

The fingers on my hip squeeze slightly. I'm startled by the tingle of heat in my belly. "Where are all these questions coming from?" He presses against my back.

I shuffle forward, peeling away from his slender strength. "You redirect."

A soft, wry laugh. "I underestimated you, I think."

"You think me meek."

"I did. But I'm learning."

Rocks scatter beneath the toes of my boots. I do not understand how he can smile and laugh so freely, while beneath resides a darkness I cannot see, only sense in waves of sadness, frustration, guilt. Against all odds, it is those lightless places I'm drawn to.

He pushes me forward another step, and the plank beneath me shudders. Somehow, we've made it onto the bridge.

I stiffen, but the hand at my hip directs me ahead, always ahead, the West Wind's body acting as a barrier against my retreat. The contraption sways wildly. My legs quiver, on the threshold of collapse.

"Take me back," I croak.

"We can't turn back." He continues to nudge me along. My heart hammers so ferociously its pulse hums against my sweat-coated skin.

"We can. We absolutely can." My voice ratchets to a shrill pitch. "Zephyrus!"

"Quiet your mind, Brielle." A subdued incantation, meant to soothe. "It will all be over soon."

I grab hold of that promise and cling to it for dear life. The quiet place nestled in my heart brims with overflowing roses in a tranquil garden, a sweet perfume, a swing upon which I sit, swaying beneath the shade of a massive tree. When the world is obdurate and cold, I return here, to an evergreen spring.

"You asked me of my experience." Zephyrus draws me in step by step, shepherding me across the vast canyon. "There's not much to say, for it was long ago. I was an insecure, selfish fool, and someone paid a terrible price."

What terrible price does he speak of? Death? Injury? Loss? This person he mentioned sounds important to him.

"How much farther?" My right hand slides along the rope as the bowed planks wobble beneath me. I can't think. My mind spins.

"Don't worry about the distance. Think only of the next step."

"You are the least helpful man I have ever met."

He crows a laugh. "From you, I think that might be a compliment."

The bridge falls quiet as my feet pass onto solid ground.

"Well done," Zephyrus says, and releases me.

My eyes open. Harper leans against a collection of boulders, arms crossed, nonplussed at our arrival. In the distance, trees erupt to brush the sky. She glances between us, yet says nothing.

Zephyrus skirts the rise of massive stone, gesturing for us to follow. Those long, limber strides flow without interruption to a patch of grass shaped in a perfect circle. A stone well squats in its center. Surrounding the grass: baked red rock, the wavering air of a place where little flourishes.

"This," Zephyrus says, resting a hand on the structure's rough edge, "is the Well of Past. Each of the Wells requires an offering to the Gods of Old in exchange for entry."

"You mean the Father," I clarify.

"No," he replies. "I mean the deities the fair folk have worshipped for centuries."

I bite my cheek in an attempt to hold my tongue. "There is no mention of this in the Text."

Harper emits a low sound of derision. I ignore her, maintaining focus on the West Wind, who studies me with frustration.

"Who the fair folk worship has nothing to do with your liturgy. They may not be your gods," he says, and his gaze is old in this moment, and sad, "but they are someone's gods. The fair folk have their beliefs, too."

It's not intended as an insult, but it feels like one nonetheless. "How can the fair folk possibly have something as advanced as organized religion?" I argue. "They're vile, wretched—"

"Different?" Zephyrus counters.

I fall silent. The thought of offering anything to a god other than the Father sits like an abrasion upon my skin.

Harper brushes me aside. "We do what we must. Either accept it, or don't." She turns to Zephyrus, fingers curled around the straps digging into her shoulders. "After the offering, what then?"

In answer, he draws up the wooden bucket from inside the well, the metal pulley creaking with each rotation. "You will need to be lowered down."

The West Wind is fond of jests, but I do not think this is one of them.

"The rope was recently replaced." He flicks the braided twine. "Within the last hundred years, at least."

Harper blanches. A cold sweat slides down the groove between my breasts.

"The longer we stand here, the more time we waste." He claps his hands encouragingly. "Let us begin. We must all make an offering—something we have kept close to our skin."

It means nothing. The offering is but an object. It holds no importance, no symbolism. I must remember that.

Following Zephyrus' lead, we circle the well, then each toss in an object. I pull a button off my dress. Harper gifts a coin. Zephyrus tears a strip from his cloak hem, the dark green fabric fluttering as it drifts into the cavity.

The ground shudders in response, then stills.

"Lastly, since this is the Well of Past, you must offer it a story from your life." Zephyrus tosses my companion a warm smile. "Harper?"

"Brielle will go first," she states, chin angled my way.

I'm too overcome with nerves over the upcoming descent to argue. "When I was seven years old, I accompanied my mother to the market one morning. We lived in a small town, and figs were only in season for a few weeks during autumn."

This memory, I remember, does not end favorably. It ends in tears, the hoarse screams of the conflicted. And now I question why I chose to speak of it. How long will it take Harper to weaponize this story against me?

"Later that night," I continue, "my mother accused me of eating the figs she bought, having forgotten she had traded them for a block of soap. When I tried to explain, she grew angry." My hand lifts to my right cheek.

The West Wind's pupils narrow to pricks of shade. "Did she hit you?"

Never before had my mother laid a hand on me. Looking back, I think I knew something wasn't right. The rage. The rapid, often incoherent speech. The exhaustion and mental fog. Business had grown slow in recent years, yet I do not believe that to be the underpinning of her change in behavior. The source of her sickness seemed to originate from within, the slow deterioration of her own mind.

"She apologized a few days later," I mumble.

A gust of hot air slithers mournfully through the canyon at our backs. Zephyrus' focus is so acute I turn away. I'd believed that I had buried that memory ages ago, but it remains. I wish I had asked my mother why. *I am your daughter*, I would have said. It is too late now.

"Harper—your turn." Zephyrus' quiet command.

She sucks in a breath through her nose, then peers into the well. "There's not much to say. I grew up in a household where I wanted for nothing. My father was a silk merchant, my mother a florist. My sisters and I attended the most prestigious academy for women's education. They sought to become great seamstresses. I was on track to become a healer."

I frown at this new information. Why did Harper dedicate her life to the faith? Generally, a woman seeks the church during times of hardship. Harper's childhood sounds positively idyllic.

"As a girl, I had always wanted a dog, though my parents would never allow it. I found one abandoned in the old mill the summer I turned twenty. I named her Lily, because of her white coloring." She folds her hands at her front, voice subdued. "I loved that dog and spent many months secretly nursing her back to health. But there came a day when I found the mill door open, and Lily gone."

Harper drops her eyes. To my surprise, tears cling to her eyelashes.

"For days I searched, but I could not find her. One morning, however, as I passed by the church, one of the acolytes offered to help me search for her. We combed the woods left and right, and eventually found Lily, caught in a bear trap."

I gasp, the cincture squeezed tight in my grip. Harper glances at me before continuing. "She was near death. Nothing could be done. But the acolyte was kind to me. She gave Lily a draught to ease her passing. Never had I witnessed such compassion toward a stranger. I believed it was a sign to give my life to the Father. The following month, I joined Thornbrook as a novitiate and haven't looked back since."

She sniffs, brushes her hands across her front. Whatever sadness she expressed moments ago has dried up along with her tears. I turn toward Zephyrus expectantly.

He lifts a sly brow. "Yes?"

"You claimed the Well of Past requires a story—from each of us." When he does not volunteer his thoughts, I wave a hand. "Doesn't that apply to you as well?"

Another broiling gust screams over the scorched red rock. I am ashamed to discover my attention slipping toward Zephyrus' mouth, its slight upward curve. As though noticing my ogling, his smile deepens, a flash of white, even teeth.

"My story is one of brotherhood, I suppose." Zephyrus shifts his weight, as though uncomfortable being the center of attention. "It was on the eve of a great battle, the coup that would bring change to my homeland. I remember standing with my brothers beneath the starry sky. Boreas, our leader. Notus, quiet and withdrawn. Lastly Eurus, who craved blood. We gazed at one another and promised to always stand as one." There is a pause. "It was the last time my brothers and I were together as a family."

"How long ago was that?" I ask. Though I do not have siblings, I recognize the longing marking his expression.

He says, in a melancholy tone, "Many centuries ago."

A beat of silence passes before I hear it—a low drone from the well's center.

Zephyrus nods. "We're in. I'll go first. Brielle will follow. Harper, you bring up the rear."

"I'm not going last." She steps forward, regards him with a sultry expression. He meets it openly. "I'll be in the middle."

I bite back a retort. Is my sanity worth the argument? Probably not. What do I care if they ogle each other? I don't.

Zephyrus manages to fit into the bucket with ease, crouching on the balls of his feet as he takes the rope and lowers himself down, curling hair vanishing from sight. A few minutes pass before the empty bucket reappears.

As Harper grips the rope, I reach out, snagging her arm. "Wait."

I'm fully anticipating a counterattack, but here, a rare glimpse of weariness, a momentary doubt, each stamped onto my companion's pointed face. "What?"

"There are things you must know before passing into Under."

She shrugs off my hand, yet gives me her undivided attention—an unprecedented occurrence.

"Firstly and most importantly"—I lower my voice so it doesn't carry—"you cannot speak your name, or my name, aloud. If any of the fair folk overhear it, they will forever have power over you, and me. Understand?"

"If this is so important," she snaps back, "why didn't Zephyrus mention it before?"

That is a valid question. Do I dare take it as a sign that the Bringer of Spring cares more for my safety than Harper's? "Your guess is as good as mine."

"Very well. Is that all?"

"Secondly, you must not eat or drink anything offered to you."

"Fine." Her eyes narrow at the delay. "Anything else?"

"You cannot trust Zephyrus."

Harper inclines her chin, fingers clamping the rope, but I do not miss the way her gaze darts to the well's opening. "You've already said this."

"There are things he wants," I say. "Things he has not made known. He is tied to Under, and he wants out."

"Why should I care about that?" Harper asks.

And she calls *me* the naive one. "You are a tool to him. We both are. At some point, he will manipulate the situation to his advantage."

She rolls her eyes. "If you had bothered to read anything other than the Text, you would already know of his reputation, the stories of all the women he's lured into Under. His depraved behavior does not surprise me."

I'm still reeling when Harper climbs into the well without comment and lowers herself down. Again with Zephyrus' reputation. I do not want to believe he's lured women into Under, but I have lived the experience.

The empty bucket returns to the top. I wait a moment longer, but eventually, I, too, climb inside. My thighs are too large to fit, so I perch on the lip, my boots resting in the bottom of the container. It lurches with a squeak, then begins to descend.

The light above shutters. *Breathe.* In through the nose, out through the mouth. I hang suspended in eternity, my hands cramping from how tightly I cling to the rope, the chill of the underground radiating through my clothes. When the bucket hits the ground, I exhale and climb out on wobbly legs, my boots settling onto the springy soil of the grassy path.

It is dark like a mouth, dark like the world before the Father. Shades of coal smudge the stone chamber—walls, ceiling, floor. A darker strip, shimmering slightly, can only be the underground river, which the grassy path leads to. Water laps against the cave walls, womb-like.

Zephyrus stands at the bank, nudging an arrow-shaped boat with his boot. "We will reach the Grotto via the River Mur." He lifts the long, slender pole resting atop the vessel's bench seat. "Sit toward the back, near the stern."

"The River Mur is located many miles east of here," I point out, failing to smooth the tremors in my voice. "Surely you are mistaken."

"Am I?" He sweeps a hand out in front of him. "This, too, is the River Mur. It flows in the opposite direction of the one aboveground, but its waters are the same."

And that, I decide, is officially too confusing for words.

Harper and I scramble into the vessel. It is cramped, forcing us into close proximity, but for the time being, I accept the solidity of her back against mine, her warmth an odd, if undesired, comfort as we push off into the swallowing dark.

18

A SET OF SPIKED WINGS PROTRUDES FROM THE BLACKNESS AHEAD. Initially, the beast's features lack distinction. The closer we drift in the low-ceilinged tunnel, however, the larger it appears, perched on the heavy iron gate that lies before us. Sharp, puncturing tips jut upward from bent bones, and tapered coal feathers fall in a cascade of lustrous black edged in violet. Never have I seen a creature with so vast a wingspan. They are like dark mountains, these wings, peaked atop the heavy gate below.

Red light bleeds upon the black bars ahead. The water pools like oil before us. A gleaming silver lock bars our passage.

Angling the pole near the stern, Zephyrus drags the end through the mucky riverbed to cut our speed. Harper and I remain quiet, pressed thigh to thigh, shivering in the clammy air pushing through the long tunnel.

I've lost track of the hours beneath the earth. Twice I have slept, shallowly and fitfully. Zephyrus assures we have been traveling for three days, but it feels longer, the hours frayed to threads, and my nerves along with them. Soon, we will reach a place of openness, light. I have to believe it.

Eventually, we drift to a complete stop. Harper shifts beside me, her breathing erratic.

"Hello, Bringer of Spring."

A voice slithers from the shroud of encompassing darkness. It is ancient: the oldest seas, the cleaving earth, a time predating the Text, when all the world was a void. It sounds like an end. To what, I cannot say, but an end nonetheless.

Zephyrus inclines his head. "My will is yours."

A pulse in the gloom skates across my skin. "So you remember." The voice softens. "It has been some time."

"A god never forgets."

The air whispers as though the dim has become tangible. "Gods? No. But those who worship us? The world shines brightest for mortals. Every day brings something new. Forgetting is to be expected. But what brings the Messenger so far from his master?"

Even at a distance, I sense Zephyrus' rising tension. "We request safe passage."

"I assumed as much. Brave of you." Something faint clicks against the rock. "And terribly foolish."

I struggle to control my breathing, but I fear the creature hears my increasingly fitful gasps. This cannot be the Stallion, can it?

"The tithe nears, Bringer of Spring. Whatever it is you're planning, I urge you to reconsider." The clicking unfolds with rapid punctuations. It reminds me of a thousand insectile legs scuttling over rock. "Do not underestimate Pierus' wrath."

"Let me concern myself with that," Zephyrus snaps.

Something splashes in the distance. "Very well." I hear the smile in its voice. "You are aware, then, of the payment."

A dagger appears in Zephyrus' hand that I'm certain wasn't present a moment ago. He digs the tip into his palm, twisting. Blood wells black within the hollow. Tilting his hand, he allows three droplets to fall into the water.

The ruby shine streaking the walls softens to a rich pink. A sigh of relief fills the cave, and a moment later, the gates groan open.

Zephyrus directs us through with stone-faced resolution. We are nearly through the opening when something twitches above. I tilt back my head, scanning the top of the tunnel. A wing curls inward, limp feathers rustling. Whatever creature those wings belong to is not quite dead.

My head snaps forward. Harper hasn't noticed the movement, her gaze downcast. I remember my first visit into Under, the ways its perverse nature had pried open my mind. Willow. The two fair folk coupling beneath the tree. Zephyrus' voice commands my thoughts more often than not these days. *Closing your eyes will make no difference. You have already seen.*

A frigid breeze wafts through the space. I rub my arms in an attempt to regain warmth, but to no avail. The sweet reek of rotting plants billows from the cavern ahead.

"I thought you said only mortal women could enter the Grotto," I whisper to Zephyrus.

He pushes the pole through the current, angling it so we drift into a turn. "This is not the Grotto," he replies. "We are entering the wilds of Under, where Pierus' influence has failed to reach. Those who live in these parts are mostly water-dwelling creatures. They live by their own rules."

"And the Orchid King has no issue with this?" For a man bloated on power, I would assume no corner would be left unmarked by his hand. Once more, I question the why and how of Zephyrus' relationship with him, the events leading to the Bringer of Spring's unwilling participation in that gruesome ritual I witnessed.

"Sometimes, the best manner of control is to let people think they are free."

"I see." My attention drifts to the River Mur, black on black, bend upon endless bend.

"Don't touch," he murmurs. "It will likely be the last thing you ever do."

Taking a deep breath, I settle in for the remainder of the journey. The darkness has thickened since we passed through the gates. It is like none that I have experienced. We could be traveling in any direction. The river could suddenly drop off and I would not know until the fall.

"Why do you fear the dark?"

Zephyrus' voice, coaxed from the shadows.

I stare down at my gloved hands. It's so opaque I cannot make out their shapes. "I never used to." In truth, I loved nothing more than to wander the forest on the threshold of eve. "But that was before the storm." Before a lot of things, really.

"Storm?"

I shy from his gaze. "It's the reason I lost my mother. The spring of my eleventh year, the weather was particularly harsh. Sometimes it hailed. There were long spells of drought, which killed the crops."

My eyes close as those weary, hard-edged memories wrench free.

"The storm was sudden. Clear skies, then the strongest winds you could imagine. It splintered trees, turned entire structures to rubble. Our home was destroyed. My mother and I fled deeper into Carter-haugh." A few heartbeats pass before I'm able to continue. "She took me to the mountain's base. An old tree had rotted through, and she told me to hide inside its trunk, told me I would be safe there while she searched for help."

We drift, passing quietly through eternity. I pretend I am elsewhere: a bright, open field, free of the earth's crushing weight. "For three days, I awaited my mother's return. It was dark. Raining. I heard the abbey bells marking the hour. On the evening of the third day, she returned, but I did not know that things had changed." Or that it was the last time I would ever see her.

Zephyrus has stopped propelling the boat. By the Father, I swore I would never return down this road. My mother's behavior had deteriorated, lapsing into the erratic, the far-fetched, the reckless, all motivation rooted in paranoia. She could not yank me out of that tree fast enough, hauling me toward the pealing bells in the distance, Thornbrook's white spires.

"I do not fear the dark because there is no light," I tell Zephyrus. "I fear the dark because of what it means to me: solitude."

And that is the most I have ever spoken of this weakness—to anyone.

The tips of his fingers brush the top of my forearm. "Give me your hand."

Once I loosen my grip, he places something in my palm. Round, light, delicate as a flower petal. I squeeze it in curiosity. It has no give. "What is this?"

"Tap the side."

A faint ring echoes, and I blink against a sudden rosy light. "Oh." How lovely. And familiar. I'm positive he showed me this object prior to entering the Orchid King's lair.

"It's called a roselight." His face, caught within the disk of illumination, softens. I frown, peering closer at him. For a moment, I could have sworn his features had altered. "Once Under's roses reach maturity, their petals are harvested into a substance of eternal light."

"It's beautiful." I lift the object higher, let the brightness devour the gray as the walls open up and the River Mur empties into a vast underground lake. Holding its heartbeat in my hand, the darkness recedes, and I calm. This roselight, yet another unsolved mystery surrounding our immortal guide. There is much I do not know about the West Wind.

"You mentioned before you favor the bow," I say. "But I have never seen you carry one."

"Ah." Lowering the pole across the length of the boat, he crouches next to me, Harper at his back. "My bow is long gone, unfortunately. I gifted it to my elder brother's wife."

This statement is made of pieces, and I mentally examine each one. If he believes people are inherently selfish and goodwill is naught but smoke, what was his motive? There, I think, is a story yet to be told.

"Wren is a gifted archer," he continues. "I know she will care for the weapon. But I regret the manner in which I gifted it to her. As such, I am barred from Boreas' realm forevermore."

"Why?"

Zephyrus taps a finger against his leg. Tension climbs, cresting to cloud his eyes with what I believe is regret or grief, perhaps both.

"Because I made poor choices. Because I was selfish. Because I did not learn."

It tells me nothing. I want to know. I *must* know. Again, I demand, "Why?"

"Let me ask you something. Do you ever wonder why some people have all the luck?"

"All the time," I reply truthfully.

"Doesn't matter what they do. The world unfolds before them, shaping itself into the most pristine path. Others may try to do what is right, but their attempts are twisted, impure. Any progress is countered by another obstacle." There is a pause. "My brother is a good man. He's made mistakes, but haven't we all?" His throat bobs, and he runs a hand along his jaw, the hiss of skin on stubble loud in the dark. "He's moved forward and built a beautiful life for himself. He deserves it. Me? I question whether anyone could love someone with a past like mine. Someone like me."

It is perhaps the saddest thing I've ever heard, and yet I understand to a frightening degree what Zephyrus feels—the inadequacy.

"Cold?" he murmurs.

Despite his smaller stature, his hands swamp mine. They sit like wheaten gold against my slim brown gloves, flushed pink by the rose-light.

Though I have not answered his question, he lifts my hands to his mouth to blow on my fingers. Even through the leather, his hot breath engulfs my icy skin.

Our eyes lock across the shroud inundating the underground lake. There is a thickness to the air that wasn't present a moment ago. Another exhalation streams across my palms, and the sting begins to thaw into a pleasant tingle.

Zephyrus lowers my hands. "Better?"

My voice has fled. I can only nod. And I have officially been staring for too long.

Shifting out of reach, I turn toward Harper to see how she is faring. The boat, however, is empty.

I whirl around. "Harp—"

Zephyrus catches my shoulder in warning. "Take care with your friend's name."

"Where did she go?"

A beat of silence passes. "She cannot be reached."

"What?"

Grave is his expression, entrenched in the weight of mortality. But it is not his own mortality he fears. For Zephyrus, Bringer of Spring, cannot die. "They have taken her."

"Who has taken her?" My eyes strain as I scan the open water. What manner of creature dwells beneath the surface? "How?" We would have witnessed her abduction, right?

"The naiads," he whispers. "Nymphs who dwell in fresh water. They are shrewd creatures, able to manipulate the air and water to mask sight and sound."

Something has frozen inside me: my heart, or my stomach, or my lungs. The air *had* changed. I did not imagine it. I see nothing. I heard nothing, not even a splash. She could be just below the surface. I lean over the side of the vessel, searching—

A firm yank drags me backward, and I land hard on my rear, rocking the boat. The roselight hits the bottom of the hull with a crack and rolls beneath the bench. "Naiads paralyze their victims upon contact. A numbing kiss, they call it. She will drown once the paralysis wears off."

"Paralysis?" Was my distraction the reason she was taken unaware? If I had been more attentive, if I had resisted Zephyrus' allure . . . "How long does the paralysis last?"

With a kindness I have not often encountered, the West Wind says, "It is not a painful death. She will have no awareness of what is happening."

I may dislike Harper, but to perish in water, away from life-giving sunlight, her soul will be forever barred from the Eternal Lands. I wish that fate upon no one.

Slowly, I push to my knees, adjusting the skirt around my legs. I then reach for the roselight, grasp its sleek, cold shape. What do I need? Time, and it is already gone.

"Look at me." Zephyrus grabs my arm, but I shake him free. "It's too late for her."

"It's never too late," I say, and dive into the oily black lake.

19

Down and down I sink. The embracing cold shortens my breath and cripples my lungs, my hair slithering through the gloom like strands of fiery grass. Squeezed in my icy palm, the roselight dissolves the dim into fragments. Strange, ethereal creatures slink along the silty bottom. They possess unmistakable female anatomy, dips and swells beneath shreds of wet cloth, limbs shaped into fins. The naiads peer at me with enormous milky eyes.

Harper drifts at the bottom of the lakebed.

Her hair, as thin and insubstantial as mist, hangs like a shifting veil around her face. Two naiads guide her in this listless state, bubbles trailing from her slackened mouth and boots dragging through the silt.

I kick upward, head breaking the surface of the lake. Zephyrus screams at me from the boat, but I'm already diving, propelling myself forward with sturdy kicks. The deeper I swim, the greater the water's crushing weight. Another hard kick closes the distance.

As my fingertips brush her shoulder, cold slime wraps around my ankle. I glance down. One of the creatures grips my leg with webbed appendages. Bubbles burst from my mouth in a scream, and I kick once, twice, until the naiad releases me. Once free, I catch Harper's waist. Her weight sags against me. We begin to sink.

My ears pop painfully, and pressure thrusts at my eye sockets. We hit the sludge-filled lakebed. I push off hard, Harper in tow, and swim with all my strength. The hazy surface seems an impossible distance. My head feels like it will split open, but we are nearly there. I can almost taste the air on my tongue.

Long, brittle fingers snag my hair, and something rushes past at the edge of my vision. I twist to meet my newest foe as the grip on my skull tightens, my hair drawn up by the roots. Snatching the dagger from my waist, I lash out, striking one of the creatures in the shoulder. The blade plunges into soft, rubbery flesh, and the naiad recoils with a low wail, a stream of smoky liquid clouding the water.

A second creature crowds my back. I spin, cutting low to give myself distance as Harper slips from my grasp. I feel my lungs begin to wither, pain coiling into a white-hot star.

Kicking away from the advancing mob, I regroup. My head pounds with unrelenting agony as the naiads writhe, dragging up silt, fogging the water. One strikes out with curled nails. Pain erupts across my shoulder, and I swing the dagger in a wild arc. The creature rears back, the seam of its lips wrenching open to reveal triangular teeth ringed in rotting gums.

Another lunge with the blade, and the creatures scatter. I dive, grabbing the back of Harper's dress with one hand, and begin hauling her toward the distant light. In the corner of my eye, I spot Zephyrus gripping Harper's other arm, lending strength to the task. Amidst the turmoil, I did not notice him dive into the lake.

My head breaks the surface in a spray of droplets. I gasp, sucking in a mouthful of frosty air. The boat has drifted farther downstream, knocking against the far wall.

"Bring her to shore," he manages.

Together, we drag Harper's limp body onto the sloped, rocky bank. I'm already kneeling at her side, knees digging into sharp rocks, hands clutching her pale, waxy face. I give her a rough shake. No response. I slap her once, twice. Nothing.

"There's no point."

"Hush." Her sternum, the plate of hard bone, bows beneath my weight. I once watched the physician revive a man by pressing on his chest. I give two hearty pumps, and her head flops with the motion. She appears shrunken beneath her dress, the white, knotted cord squeezing her waist into nothing.

Zephyrus' soaked boots enter my periphery. "She was under for too long."

Harper will live, if only so that I can hold this over her head for the rest of her life. I switch to hammering blows against her back. It might dislodge the water in her lungs.

"It won't work. The paralysis—"

"Let me tell you what I promised this woman on the first day we met." I do not stop the rhythm. "I was alone, terrified, grieving. She saw my loneliness and took advantage. Tripped me in the middle of the refectory, causing food to splatter the front of my dress. I told her I would never forget her cruelty. And I would never let *her* forget it either." She cannot die. It is too sweet a temptation to see her live, and witness her failure when I eventually gain Meirlach for myself. Whether or not Mother Mabel learns of my broken vows, I will have my triumph.

A scream breaks free of my chest. "Breathe—you—wretched—cow!" I slam a fist against her heart.

Harper's eyes snap open. She stiffens, her head wrenching sideways, water gushing from her mouth. Her fingers scrabble at the rocky shore.

I sit back on my heels, weary to the bone with trembling. When her lungs have emptied, Harper slumps to the ground, hair tangled in her own sick. She squints at me, features twisted with conflicting emotions, as though she understands how near to death she was and yet cannot comprehend the sight of her savior: dripping water, clothes plastered to my skin, color riding high on my face. But—she is alive. It is enough.

"We need to build a fire," I say, lifting my eyes to Zephyrus. He studies me, dumbfounded. "Is there something we can use for fuel?" When he does not immediately respond, I snap, "Zephyrus."

His mouth twists, and the motion pulls at the discoloration patching his skin. For whatever reason, it appears to have evened out somewhat. "There is a sea-nymph village," he concedes. "It's not far. But don't expect a warm welcome."

"I thought those creatures in the lake were sea-nymphs."

"Those were naiads—freshwater nymphs. The sea-nymphs are their distant cousins."

I struggle to keep track of the sheer variety of creatures. Sprites, naiads, dryads, sea-nymphs. What else? "Will we be safe there?" I can no longer feel my fingers or toes. "We need to get warm."

Harper's limbs twitch erratically. Grasping her face, I survey her features. Bloodless skin and blue-tinged lips. She stares right through me, the color of her eyes dulled.

And then I realize something else. The grassy path has disappeared.

"The trail." I look to Zephyrus. "What happened to it?"

His gaze drops to the ground. "Under likely anticipated our arrival a few miles downstream. It did not expect you to jump into the lake." He quirks an eyebrow at my alarmed expression. "Don't worry. As long as you two stay close, nothing terrible will befall you."

"And the village? Is it safe?"

The West Wind's hesitation concerns me, for he has always acted with unflappable conviction. "That is open to interpretation. Keep your guard up. If something were to happen to me, you would have to find another way out."

Trusted guides are difficult to come by, but I would not consider Zephyrus one anyway. "We don't have a choice, unfortunately." After wringing out my dress, I stand. "Take us to the village."

Huddled beneath my cloak, I struggle to muffle my heavy breathing as Zephyrus propels us down the River Mur. The dim remains unchanged, altering neither in color nor form. Cupped between my palms, the roselight offers little reprieve from the darkness and even less warmth.

"How is she?" Zephyrus asks quietly.

Curled in the bottom of the boat, Harper lies with eerie stillness, muscles twitching every so often in an attempt to warm her sodden limbs. She is present in body, but not in mind. The unfocused, small-pupiled eyes betray her mental retreat. "No recent changes."

I wait in anticipatory silence, but Zephyrus adds nothing more. He has not asked after my well-being. I try not to let his lack of concern bother me, though the sinking sensation in my gut is a most unwelcome visitor.

"Will she recover?" I haven't inquired until now, fearful of his answer.

Water splashes as the West Wind lifts the pole, allowing the current to drag us around a hairpin corner. "That depends on how the sea-nymphs react to our arrival. Their clan has the means to revive her, but the matriarch has the final say."

"You don't think the matriarch will help us?"

"She might help you, in exchange for something of value. But me?" A coarse, raw noise. Laughter, I realize. "Probably not."

I turn to glare at him. "What did you do?"

He meets my gaze without flinching, almost as if he expected this question. "I have done a great deal." His mouth crimps beneath that large, crooked nose. "I, too, have regrets."

I grow weary of his evasiveness. While others plant their feet, Zephyrus flits from hill to knoll, each landing brief.

Facing forward, I demand, "What will happen if Harper is beyond help?"

"She will not die, but who is to say she will not be changed in irreversible ways? No one can know what the long-lasting effects will be."

Irreversible change? I sincerely hope she will recover. I can't return to Thornbrook with a senseless companion, but I can't return without her either. The decision to enter Under was shared, yet I can't help but feel responsible for Harper's misfortune. My involvement with Zephyrus led us here. Then again, we would not have been able to enter Under without his help.

Something squeals in the distance, cutting through the silence of the cave. I clench the roselight tighter, watch the pink light seep through the spaces between my fingers.

"We're close," Zephyrus murmurs.

I pray there is a fire, or at least an extra set of warm clothes.

"Do the fair folk who live in the wilds participate in the tithe?" I wonder.

Zephyrus slows our passage through the water. When I sense his gaze on my back, I shift on the bench to face him. "Have you ever attended the tithe?" he asks curiously. But there is something else in his voice, too. Shame?

"No. I was ill the last occurrence."

I'd hoped Mother Mabel would select me as one of the twenty-one participants, but I'd barely had the strength to walk, much less make the journey belowground. Fourteen years old, and already my dreams had been dashed.

He appears relieved by this. "Those in the wilds typically do not participate. They do not agree with the Orchid King's rule in these parts. You can understand why their presence would irritate Pierus."

"He cannot govern those whom he cannot control."

"Exactly."

I think of what Zephyrus said, and then I think of what he has not said. "What would you change, if you were in the Orchid King's position?"

Hushed is the underground, the long, coiling gullet through which the channel courses. Zephyrus' silence says much, and yet—

"Everything," he says. "I would change everything."

As the conversation tapers off, we ease around a bend, and the tunnel widens, the River Mur stretching outward. A rocky shelf juts out over the river, a village perched on top of it.

I study the fair folk from the safety of the boat as we drift nearer to shore. These creatures are lean, but wide in the belly. They dwell in squat grass huts whose roofs rise to blunt points. The men wear trousers shorn at the ankle, their torsos bare. Fish-pale skin and milky eyes give them the appearance of long-limbed salamanders.

"What's wrong with their eyes?"

"The sea-nymphs are among the most ancient of the fair folk and have dwelt in Under's deepest grottos for centuries, seldom exposed to sunlight. They have adapted over time to make do without their eyesight, sheltering in caves and deep water when traveling toward the sea. Though I should warn you," he murmurs, "their sense of smell is keen as a bloodhound's."

A group of sea-nymphs busy their hands winding twine into fishing nets. One angles its head toward the river, its wide, slitted nostrils flaring with each inhalation. The group follows suit, abandoning the nets at our approach, straightening their long, reedy bodies. Zephyrus calmly docks and gestures for me to remain seated.

He disembarks, his movements so smooth the vessel does not rock from his departure. Harper stirs, her gaze flicking from creature to creature. Though my hand drifts to the dagger at my waist, I do not draw the blade.

A woman—or at least I believe it is a woman, judging by her garb— steps forward. "Bringer of Spring. It has been some time." Her voice emerges reed thin, the words choked as if by fluid in the lungs. A blue tinge coats her rheumy eyes, which shift without sight.

Zephyrus eases along the outcropping, though I sense his desire to put space between himself and those congregating. "Annag."

The woman I assume is this clan's matriarch holds out a waiting hand, palm up. A long, grimy dress hangs in strips around her shins, clinging to a body more skeletal than not. From her shoulders sprout small protrusions akin to broken coral.

Zephyrus sighs and draws his dagger. A prick at his fingertip produces a drop of blood, which he lets fall into her outstretched palm.

The sea-nymph brings it to her nose with a deep inhalation. "Such strength," she whispers, before lapping her skin clean. "How have you fared since our last encounter?"

"Well enough." After wiping the blade on his trousers, he returns the dagger, freshly cleaned, to its sheath. Those gathered monitor his movement, their small, pointed ears twitching as the metal slides into its case. "I hear we share an acquaintance."

"The sailor." She nods. "Ten years in Troy. Ten years at sea. The man was stronger than we first assumed, and clever. What was his name?"

"Odysseus."

"Odysseus, yes." A slow cant of her head. "That witch, Circe, warned him of our presence. She ordered his sailors to stuff their ears with beeswax. They tied Odysseus to the mast of the ship." A few of the female sea-nymphs chuckle in response.

Annag smiles. Her teeth remind me of fragmented shells. "Oh, how he begged. We sang to him the loveliest ballad. A feast for us, it would have been. But alas, things do not always go as planned. They refused to be swayed."

"I heard." Zephyrus scans the crowd before retreating to the edge of the overhang. Harper and I continue to observe from the boat.

"I admit, I was surprised to learn you'd helped Odysseus." She picks at something caught between her teeth. "Unless I am mistaken?"

"I did my best to steer Odysseus back to Ithica, but men are fools, as you know. His sailors released the bag of winds gifted to them, which sent them hundreds of miles back out to sea. They alone are responsible for their misfortune."

"A pity." The sea-nymph's eyes track slightly to the left, unable to pin his exact location. "But let us discuss the present. You have brought company. It is not every day we encounter mortal women."

Zephyrus angles toward us. Dark are his features, shrouded in secrecy. "One of the women is in need of a healer. Both require warm clothing."

"And you expect my clan to provide this for you?" A smile sweetens her voice despite the lack of curve to her mouth. "You expect a lot, Bringer of Spring."

"I understand this will not come free."

"Indeed." A long, insectile tongue pushes between her lips, fluttering with gentle undulations against the air. "One of the women tastes of fire. The other, salt."

"We encountered the naiads a while back," he explains.

"If it is a trade you seek, I would rather trade with the woman who tastes of fire."

"No." I've never heard a command so sharp from such a honeyed tongue. "Your business is with me."

A small, serene smile graces the sea-nymph's mouth. He's revealed too much, I fear. "Very well," she says as the crowd at her back spits out a guttural language I cannot understand. "Let us discuss."

"And my companions?"

"I will allow them to take refuge in our guesthouse until an agreement has come to pass. They will be kept warm."

Zephyrus catches my eye, and I give him a nod. "Thank you, Annag. I appreciate that."

"I'm sure you do," she says quietly.

As the matriarch draws him into one of the huts, two female sea-nymphs approach the boat, skinny arms laden with baskets of cloth. Their large, round, white eyes stare straight through us.

"We smell your filth, human women." They speak simultaneously. "Come. We will show you to the baths."

I disembark, thankful for the solid ground beneath my feet. Harper, however, hasn't moved. I shake the boat to get her attention. "Come on."

Her expression blurs into an unfocused vagueness. "I won't," Harper mumbles through chattering teeth. "Have you seen those things? They're hideous. How do you know they won't drag us off to some distant corner and strip the flesh from our bones?"

"I don't." The farther we stray in this dark realm, the less I know and the less I am certain of. "But you need to get well. They can help us."

"You trust Zephyrus' word?"

He has gone great lengths to ensure our safety. Maybe I misjudged him.

She scratches at the wood, then stops, her breathing shallow. "I feel the water on my skin. The voice in my ear . . . I do not think it is the Father's."

I lay my hand against the hunch of her upper back. "You hear a voice?"

She lifts her face. A sheen films the whites of her eyes. "You don't?"

"Harper," I whisper, making sure her name will not carry. "I'm here." She clutches my hand with iron strength. She will not let go.

A wave of concern moves through me with startling intensity. A weakened Harper, an uncertain Harper, a frightened Harper. None sit well with me. "Come." I coax her from the boat onto the rocky shelf.

The two sea-nymphs lead Harper and I to separate huts. Clay walls, fired red by the single candle sputtering in the room's center, enclose the circular interior. A tub full of steaming water awaits, and a change of clothes rests on a sturdy wooden chair. Once I remove my boots, the sea-nymph departs to give me privacy.

My knees creak as I hobble toward the tub, but I'm unable to unbutton my dress, so stiff and icy are my fingers. Blast this fabric. I step into the tub fully clothed, sinking into the scalding water with a helpless whimper. Once I regain use of my limbs, I'm able to slide off my gloves, unbutton my dress, and peel it from my soiled skin. They have provided soap, which I use to scrub away all remnants of that nightmarish lake. I briefly remove my undergarments and wash those, too.

Skin pink with irritation, I climb from the tub and don the long linen dress provided, my cincture and gloves, and a burgundy cloak. Then I go in search of Harper.

She huddles near one of the cooking fires, hair wet from her bath. Instead of wearing the clean clothes provided, she has changed back into her filthy, sodden dress. She shivers, blue eyes locked on the dancing flames, and she does not appear so certain of herself in this moment, her spine curved and wariness abloom in those dark pupils. Well, good. That makes two of us.

With a sigh, I remove the cloak from my shoulders and drop it onto Harper's lap. She stares at it before handing it back.

"Take it," I snap. "Otherwise you'll freeze to death after I've gone to such lengths to save you."

Her fingers tighten around the fabric. After a moment, however, she tugs it around her body.

Sinking onto a nearby log, I join her in studying the lash of red-orange flames. The air reeks—fish and char. "Did you let them heal you?"

"They gave me a tonic." The words are mumbled. "The voice stopped. I should recover without any adverse effects."

I'm relieved. I hate that I am relieved.

Our packs sit at Harper's feet. Someone must have brought them from the boat. Tugging mine closer, I pull out a few strips of dried hare. When I offer some to Harper, she shakes her head.

"Why did you save me?" she whispers.

I stow the food in my pack, taking the opportunity to think of an appropriate response. "How do you know it wasn't Zephyrus?"

Harper snorts, hunching lower, and stares at the ground. "Why should the West Wind care for me? All I do is irritate him."

I'm not going to argue with that.

Along the shore, a trio of sea-nymphs drags a net from the water. It bulges with writhing, eel-like fish. The clan eats what the River Mur provides them.

"To be perfectly honest, I don't know why I saved you. If you ask me, it was a senseless decision to save a woman who has spent the last decade doing everything in her power to make my life miserable."

Harper frowns, hands clenched in her lap. "That's not—"

"Don't say it's not true," I growl. "Don't you dare say it."

She falls quiet.

What, exactly, compelled me to desert the safety of the boat and dive into those dark unknowns? We believe water acts as the entrance to Hell and eternal woe. Those who drown may never know peace. Yet I leaped without regret.

A stone rises to block my airway, warping the emerging sound. "Maybe I should have let you drown. The Father knows you deserve it. But I suppose I can't stand to see someone die, however cruel that person is."

Harper will not look at me. Neither will she speak. She is not heartless. I have witnessed her kindness, however twisted, however rare. Maybe she's just heartless to me.

"Nothing to say? Not even a *thank you* for saving your life?"

"I'm sorry," Harper whispers.

Clumps of fabric wad between my clammy hands. "I've spent the last ten years waiting for those words." One glimpse of remorse, genuine regret at her actions. It's all I've ever wanted. "But it's not enough."

Her head snaps up. In the shifting light, a distinct sunken quality distorts her cheeks.

"You're apologizing to appease whatever guilt you feel," I say. "But you don't mean it. You don't care. You've never cared."

Maybe that was my downfall. I, Brielle of Thornbrook, have always cared, and because I care, I place others before myself. I become timid. I am reduced to the inked markings in my journal. I forget the parts of myself I actually like. I forget my dedication. I forget my skill with a hammer and blade. I forget my kindness. And I have failed myself, not once, but again and again in lacking the conviction to assert my boundaries, having believed I didn't deserve that grace. How sad I feel for that girl now.

"Why me? Why was *I* the target of your vitriol? Was it because you felt threatened by me? Because Mother Mabel favored me over you?"

With each word spoken, a weight lifts from my chest. How long have I carried it? Years. But today, now, I cast it far and wide.

"Or maybe it was insecurity. Deep down, you don't actually have what it takes to become an acolyte. You don't study. You shirk your duties. You treat the other novitiates like dirt. You barely respect the current acolytes." My voice—my entire body—shakes at Harper's muteness.

"And do you want to know something truly sickening? For so long, I wanted to be your friend. I wanted to be accepted into your circle." It seems silly, yearning for something that would never come to pass. "But I've felt like a stranger at Thornbrook for a decade, and that is your doing."

Harper's mouth quivers, then flattens to a line. Still, she says nothing.

"The thing is," I whisper, "I look at what you've become and I feel sorry for you. You may acquire Meirlach first. You may even become the next acolyte. But I will fall asleep at night knowing I did right, even when I didn't have to."

Pushing to my feet, I stride off, abandoning Harper to her own wretched company. I cannot continue on this path. I cannot bare my stomach for someone else's blade. That life was mine, but no longer.

Not anymore.

20

GUESTS ARRIVE BY THE HUNDREDS. DRYADS AND SPRITES AND every manner of creature drift toward the sea-nymph village on their narrow vessels, propelled forward by long, slender poles. Men with feathered wings. Women with hooves and small, curved horns. Children with their eyes plucked out and their skin stitched over, and elderly fair folk so shriveled they appear to have baked in the sun for a century.

From the bench where I sit writing in my journal, I notice a man with snowy skin marked by black stripes flitting among the clustered arrivals, brandishing a long coat that clinks as he walks. He accepts coin for payment in exchange for what appear to be empty glass bottles. Only after he meanders off do I realize the man was likely trading in stolen mortal names.

A trio of women surrounds a flat stone upon which three goblets rest. Two of the women, with their flaxen hair, are undoubtedly fair folk. The first wears a stuffed vulture atop her head. The second possesses short antlers. The third, however, appears quite normal. Mortal, even. Tucked between the two bright-haired creatures, she sits demurely, a long, black braid snaking over one shoulder, hands folded in her lap.

I haven't seen Zephyrus in hours. As the night progresses, the celebration devolves into absolute frenzy, and I am not even sure of its purpose other than merrymaking, which the fair folk seem exuberantly fond of.

We shouldn't linger. After all, Meirlach awaits, and who can say how many days will have passed when Harper and I return to Thornbrook?

Against my better judgment, my attention returns to the woman with the ebony braid. She sips from the goblet offered by the lady with antlers, who wipes her mouth with a square of cloth as though she were a child.

"Do you desire a mistress, or master?"

My head snaps sideways, and I flinch from the massive shape looming over me. It is both a man and a bear. Small, curved ears poke through the dense fur atop his blocky skull. He wears a pair of loose trousers. His bare chest is wider than two men standing abreast.

When I fail to answer, he leans closer. "Well?"

If I were to retreat any farther, I'm afraid I'd fall off my seat. "I don't understand."

"That mortal woman you're staring at? She's a pet. Those two banshees are her mistresses."

Slowly, I shift my gaze back to the trio. I am familiar with banshees. Their lamenting wail supposedly foretells the deaths of those who hear it. And the third woman? Mortal. How is that possible? And what does the creature mean by *pet*?

When the hulking creature settles beside me, I slip my journal into my pack. My hand then drifts to my iron blade, and I swallow to draw moisture to my mouth. "Are there many pets in Under?"

"Oh, yes. It's more common than you might think."

I cough into my hand. The beast's breath reeks of decaying flesh. "So, the fair folk take advantage of these humans?"

"You misunderstand. That woman *voluntarily* entered Under. She sought out a new opportunity, a different life." I stare at him blankly. "You mortals are always running from something. Down here, it is easy. You gift your name to another, and all your troubles and worries disappear."

For the first time in weeks, I wish Zephyrus were around. He knows how to navigate sensitive topics of conversation. "But that woman has no control over her life anymore."

"It is the sacrifice one makes." He looks me over. "Pets are well cared for. They are akin to your small, triangular-eared gods."

It takes a moment before the inference sinks in. "You mean cats?"

"Cats, yes." He beams. "Haughty things, aren't they? *So* self-absorbed."

Indeed, they are, even the nastiest barn cats.

"If you seek a master," the beast goes on, "I can be of service. You would be cared for in all ways." His great bear paw settles atop my thigh.

My gut churns in warning, and I clamp my dagger with a trembling hand. I don't want to use it. I don't want to draw attention. If I scream, who will come to my aid? I doubt anyone would care.

But the creature removes his hand and says, "Here." He offers a glass chalice full of clear liquid. "You look thirsty." He points to a vat simmering over a fire. "We collect water from the river. Once boiled, it is potable."

Zephyrus mentioned not to drink anything, but surely water is an exception. This is the River Mur, the same river that flows aboveground. If I bless the water prior to drinking, I should be safe, and I *am* parched. With a forced smile, I accept the goblet.

"Stop!"

Someone slaps the glass from my hand. It shatters on the rock, and the scent of cherries hits, momentarily veiling the cloying odor of rotting plants. When I glance at the spilled drink, I notice the liquid is now red, not clear as it had been.

"Get out of here." A tiny creature shoves the much larger beast from its seat. "Go!" The bear-like brute trundles off in obvious disappointment.

My savior turns.

I blink, stare into a pair of smooth, ebony eyes, in contrast to the snowy hair and skin. "I remember you," I whisper as the sprite's name comes to mind. "Lissi."

Those slime-coated gums flash. Small, cracked teeth protrude from their moist pulp. "And you are Zephyrus' companion," she replies, cupping my rounded cheek. "I did not think I'd see you in Under so soon before the tithe. Do you seek a violent end?"

Lissi plops onto the rock beside me. Her long white dress pokes beneath her battered overcoat. "Do not fret, sweet. You will not remember the tithe once you return to your own realm. What occurs in Under, stays in Under. But do tell me, are you participating? Miles Cross is not far from here."

"I don't know." Mother Mabel has yet to select the twenty-one women for the ceremony. Or at least, she hadn't when Harper and I left Thornbrook. "It hasn't been decided."

"Do let me know if you'll be in attendance. Perhaps we might sit together." She sidles closer, linking her skinny arm through mine, and props her head on my shoulder. "How are you enjoying my village?"

"Oh." I was not aware Lissi lived here. "It's . . . quaint."

She beams at me. "See my home over there? It's small compared to your larger mortal dwellings, but I don't need much, just enough space to sleep and store my poultices. The matriarch is fond of my tinctures. She offered me housing in exchange for my healing services. But tell me. Has Zephyrus been a decent guide?"

"For the most part, yes." When he is honest. When he does not act in his own self-interest.

"And your mortal companion? She has been sitting alone the entire evening." Lissi pairs that with a salacious smile. "It is rare we encounter a face so lovely belowground."

With her pale skin, black hair, and azure eyes, Harper is indeed comely. Unfortunately, that means enduring the fair folk's attention. A pair of horned, bare-chested men currently circle her fire.

"Do not be fooled by her beauty," I inform Lissi, voice darkening. "Her heart is rotten to the core."

She laughs. "Even better. I imagine she would taste delicious."

"My companion is not for eating, I'm sorry to say."

"Well, poo." The sprite swings her legs back and forth. "I admit I am curious. Why return? It seems like an unnecessary risk."

Information has always been the fair folk's preferred currency. But she will receive no payment from me.

"My business is my own," I say, and leave it at that.

Lissi appears thoroughly pleased by my avoidance. "You are learning. But I must warn you," she says, an edge to her voice. "If word gets back to the Orchid King of your presence, he might get involved, and that is the last thing you want. The agreement between Under and Thornbrook is quite clear. Mortals are only allowed to enter on the eve of the tithe."

"I was granted permission by my abbess. Surely that is an exception?" I struggle to maintain slow, steady breaths.

"Historically, the Orchid King and your abbess have not had the most affable relationship. But if you claim she granted you permission, well, then the Orchid King is likely already aware."

And if he is not? Nothing is certain. That frightens me. "Will you keep our presence here to yourself?"

Lissi tugs on one of my curls, watching it spring back when she releases it. "That is quite the favor." A small, secret smile plays across her mouth. "You are too pure for this world, and I would not see the Orchid King crush a flower in winter. Yes, I will keep it to myself, but for my own safety, this must be the last time I speak with you. I do not want to be punished."

Zephyrus' initial warning resurfaces: trust no one. The fair folk, however, cannot tell a lie. Thus, Lissi speaks the truth.

"I understand," I say, and push to my feet. Someplace quiet, I think, will do. "Best to you, Lissi."

Her stony eyes take me in. "And to you, my sweet."

Skirting the edge of the village, I retreat deeper into the cavern, relieved when the rock softens to grass, which eventually empties into a glen sheltered by towering oaks, brightened by the yellowing enchantment of the moon. With a sigh, I unlace my boots and tug them free. The cool air feels wonderful against my sweating feet.

"I see you and your prickly companion came to a head earlier. A bit harsh to speak to a friend that way, wouldn't you agree?"

Zephyrus slides into my line of vision, clothes rumpled, hair unkempt. Moonlight paints his skin a lovely, sun-kissed gold, cheeks infused by a rosy flush. Angling toward him, I notice that the irregularity of his skin has smoothed, as though it has healed itself. My eyes dip lower: the trailing laces of his tunic, its collar open at the throat. Chest hair, slightly darker than the curls on his head, sprinkles the toned pectorals.

"Harper and I are many things," I snap, hating the burn beneath my fire-hot skin, "but we are not friends." With stiff movements, I sit, adjusting the skirt around my legs.

"Careful," he murmurs.

My stomach twists. Right. In my frustration, I'd forgotten to keep Harper's name to myself. "Maybe she deserves to have her name stolen," I mutter.

"She is your only ally belowground. I would not be so quick to toss her aside." Drink in hand, he saunters closer, the hem of his emerald green cloak swaying around his legs. "Might I suggest attempting to bridge that gap?"

"Why? So she can craft more insults?" He does not understand. If I were to write out every horrible offense Harper has hurled my way, there would not be enough time in the day to list them all.

The West Wind considers me before settling at my side. "Why do you think she has targeted you?"

"I don't know!" A low hiss of frustration flames across my tongue. "If I knew, do you think I would be in this predicament?"

"You have never asked?"

As if I would bare my neck to Harper's blade.

"You know nothing about me or my situation. You know only the surface and haven't bothered to look any deeper than that." My eyes narrow, daring him to argue. "I don't have to explain myself to you."

Placing the glass near his feet, Zephyrus draws his knees to his chest, slings an arm around the front of his shins. "She continues to beat you down, yet until today, you've refused to do the same to her. Why?"

I shrug. It is true what they say. Misery loves company. "It's not in my nature to be cruel." My mother taught me to place loyalty and kindness before anything else, but what did she know? Her last words to me: *Be good, Brielle.*

"Maybe I'm just weak," I mutter.

"Soft does not mean weak," he responds, with a sadness that does not suit his smiling mouth, "but does your faith teach you to be kind, even at the detriment of your own self-worth?"

"We are Daughters of Thornbrook," I explain. "Our mission is not to build ourselves up. Our mission is to serve the Father, no matter the cost."

"The cost being your own individuality."

He has no idea what he's talking about. "No one is more accepting of individuality than the Father. There is nothing I want for myself that He can't provide." In my darkest years, He stood by me. He did not abandon me when the world grew dim, the ground unstable, my childhood turned to dust.

Zephyrus studies me beneath lowered lashes, that penetrative gaze roaming over my legs, mapping out each curve, before coming to rest on my pinkened face. "Not even that kiss we shared?" His voice deepens, running hot fingers across my skin.

I swallow, glance around. We alone occupy the glen. "The kiss was a mistake."

"Because you enjoyed it so thoroughly?"

"You misunderstand," I stammer.

The brightness of his teeth provides temporary relief from the darkness, and a breeze teases the curls of my hair. "Do I?"

"I thought I was going to die. I would not have agreed to it otherwise."

"If only I believed you."

I straighten, fully prepared to defend myself, when I notice the drink he holds, the subtle sway of his body against the overgrown grass, the glaze of his green eyes.

My mouth flattens in distaste. "You're drunk."

"Enchanted," he corrects, lifting a finger. "I am *enchanted*."

"I thought you said the wine doesn't affect you."

"It doesn't. Well, not in the way it affects you."

"Then why drink it?"

"This isn't wine." Raising the glass, he swirls the gold liquid around, lifts it to his mouth. "What you see here is a taste from my homeland. This, as it turns out, is the last of it."

His words alone do not give me pause. Rather, the longing behind them. "Is it a liquor?"

Tilting back his head, Zephyrus stares up at the strange, oily sky, beyond which lies the earth, grass, Carterhaugh, all veiled behind a blackness without end. "It is not, though it does alter one's state of mind." He leans back, supporting himself with one hand, and considers me. "But we both know you would never broaden your horizons in such a manner." With a satisfied smirk, he downs another swallow.

Oh, he dearly loves to push my buttons. Who defines my character? I do. No one else.

As he takes another mouthful, I swipe the glass from his grip.

Zephyrus lurches forward, blinking a few times. When he spots the drink in my hand, his eyes glimmer, as though delighted to have been proven wrong. "I have spoken too soon," he murmurs.

"What would happen if I were to try the drink?"

His eyebrows climb toward his hairline. "Perhaps you should see for yourself," he hedges.

"Perhaps I will."

"Then by all means." Zephyrus gestures for me to proceed.

I take a small—very small—sip, and frown. "It tastes like . . ."

"Beets," he says.

It tastes nothing like beets. "It tastes like freshly baked bread," I correct him.

"To you, yes. But to me, it tastes like beets." At my look of confusion, he elaborates, "Where I come from, we call it nectar. It tastes like one's favorite food. Thus, the taste differs depending on who consumes it."

I see.

"Your favorite food is *beets*?"

Zephyrus looks affronted. "Do you have something against them?"

"They taste like dirt."

Slowly, he crosses one ankle over the other. Ponderous. The effect suits him. "I agree. I wonder what that says about my tastes?"

"That they are poor."

Zephyrus smiles, as do I—the first we have shared.

"I wouldn't say poor, exactly." His grin widens. It eases the awkward planes of his face and allows them to slip into something more harmonious. Pleasing, even. "After all, I kissed you, and I thoroughly enjoyed that."

Despite my burning face, I force myself to maintain eye contact. His dancing gaze meets mine, and slowly warms as silence ensues. At some point, I have managed to relax in the West Wind's presence.

Lowering the glass into my lap, I examine the gold substance, if only to avoid some undesired realization coming into sharper focus. "This is the last of the nectar?"

"In my possession, yes."

It seems a shame to waste the drink on someone who will not savor it. "Here." I offer it back to him.

He straightens from his languishing, abruptly suspicious. "You do not want it?"

"No." Not after learning that it cannot be replenished, this reminder of his home.

The West Wind moves as though afraid he will frighten a rabbit back into its burrow. He reaches toward me. Warm, clever fingers curl around mine. However briefly, we cradle the curved crystal in togetherness.

An enthusiastic screech from the distant festivities shatters my paralysis, and I relinquish my hold on the drink, watching his throat work as he swallows the last dregs.

Zephyrus sets aside the glass with unusual care. Gone is his previous amusement. "To answer your earlier question, I drink because the nectar helps dull the pain."

I am drawn to this version of him, this grave immortal who has seen the world. My attention is his to manipulate, his to bend. "What pain?"

"The pain of life. What else?"

There is a certain ambiguity to the response, which tempts me into questioning him further. Zephyrus has never given me so much in so few words. "Life isn't just pain," I tell him quietly, although much of my life has been marked by it.

"How young you are. How little you know." Before I can defend myself, he says, "Imagine this: A god, beloved and adored by all. A hero, in some regard. Yet one mistake was enough to tear down the legacy he'd built, leaving his name forever tainted. Coward, they called him. Murderer."

My eyes widen. *Murderer?*

"That is my pain," he murmurs. "I am the West Wind no longer. Now I am simply Zephyrus: outcast, prisoner." His head hangs. "You deny the pain of life? That is very naive of you."

"You aren't listening," I snap. "Of course we experience pain in our lives. That is the nature of our world. But if you find your life to be *only* pain, *only* suffering, then I question the manner in which you live." I point to his hand. "You continue to gift your blood to this place. Why? Why must you harm yourself for the Orchid King? Will you spend an eternity suffering for his benefit?"

"You must understand. It is the price I must pay."

"For *what*?" That is the question that remains unanswered, that plagues me during my sleeping and waking hours, that I have brought forth into the light for careful study, yet still I lack an explanation. "Why are you bound to the Orchid King?"

Murderer.

"It occurred long ago. I've accepted my situation will not change." When his eyes lift to mine, they shine with clarity. All traces of the nectar's enchantment have vanished. "I am not like you. My beliefs are full of holes. The water pours through."

It hurts me to see those with little faith—in anything, really.

"But you do believe in something," I press. "Right?"

One of his hands slides on top of mine, pressing it into the grass. I stare at the place where we touch, and my toes curl inside my boots. Despite my gloves acting as a barrier, his wide palm imprints heat into my skin.

"You ask what I believe?" His lashes dip, gold fringed in the dying light. "I believe there is more to you than I first assumed. I believe you have many shades, not just one."

"That's not—" I falter, unsure of how I feel about his admission. It warms me even as it frightens me. "That's not what I meant. Belief in a higher power. Faith in the good forces of the world."

"Why can't I believe in things that move me? Are you not a good force in this world? Do you not spread kindness and compassion wherever you go?"

I'm helpless to stop the blush reddening my skin. I didn't realize Zephyrus viewed me in such a favorable light.

"You," he says, "are a bright, willful woman who understands the sacrifice true dedication requires. It takes strength of character to extend compassion to so many, even those who don't deserve it."

Bright. A word gifted to things touched by illumination: knowledge, a star. I had not believed Zephyrus capable of seeing deeper than one's skin, of hearing anything aside from his own laughing voice.

"We are all deserving of compassion," I say.

"Are we?" And then the despair manifests, fully formed to dull his eyes. "I have questioned myself more in your company than I have in the last thousand years."

"Is that so bad a thing?"

He frowns, takes a breath. "I believe there are few good things in this world," he says, "but the kindness of your heart might be the best thing I have ever experienced, in any lifetime."

My throat tightens. I am not sure whether to weep or fling myself into his embrace. Never have I received so thoughtful a compliment, and so generously gifted, without the expectation of reciprocation.

"Thank you," I whisper hoarsely.

His gaze drops to the grass with a rare shyness. "You are an incredibly special person. I just want you to know that."

I understand, as I had not previously, what it means to desire. How the wanting is a flood. It does not seem so terrible a thing in this moment.

"My darling novitiate," Zephyrus murmurs. "I would very much like to kiss you."

A puff of warmth washes across my mouth, and the sweetness of his breath lures me nearer. Mossy rings encircle the welling blacks of his eyes.

"You've already kissed me," I say.

"That was not a kiss." He slides one hand forward, loops it around my wrist, where glove and sleeve meet. "I would kiss you the way a man kisses a woman he hungers for."

I am not thinking of my vows. I am not thinking of my faith and what a betrayal it would be to accept the West Wind's mouth. I am thinking of all the truths I have never before considered, including this: his kiss is an offering I cannot refuse.

Because I have been a good servant this last decade, haven't I? I have never, not once, strayed. It is true that no man may touch a Daughter of Thornbrook, but what of a man who views me as a woman first, a novitiate second? What of a man who encourages me to consider my own needs, those separate from the Father's?

Lowly, I whisper, "What of Harper?"

"We are traveling companions, nothing more."

My lips purse. Light and laughter from the festivities trickles through the shifting meadow grasses. "You picked a funny way of showing it."

"What can I say? I enjoy getting under your skin." His eyes flash, full of impish cunning. Again, the sense that his features have softened, become something else. "It's the most fun I've had in ages."

At my droll look, he laughs, drawing my hand up so it rests on his thigh. My skin leaps at the heat there, the hardened muscle beneath, as I say, "Tell me the truth. When I was bathing in the river, did you truly want to kiss me, or were you just toying with me?" As he does with everything else.

For a time, he considers me. Then: "Let me ask you this. Would you deny a parched man water from the cool mountain stream?"

The gall of this immortal. I should challenge his claim, yet I'm ashamed to admit that I had wanted his mouth, sought to relish his taste, however brief.

"No," I confess. "I would not."

The green of his eyes deepens, as though a shadow has fallen across the moon. Framing my face, he tugs me forward, nose to nose and breath to breath. "All right?" he murmurs.

This is not the first time Zephyrus has touched my bare skin. Am I to burn in the blackest depths of Hell? "Y-yes?"

"Is that a question or an answer?"

"Um." I bite my lip. Each of his fingertips are a brand upon my face. How can something that feels so right be a sin? "Answer."

Leaning closer, Zephyrus bypasses my mouth, skimming the tip of his nose along my cheek, across my jaw. The fragile, butterfly-wing whisper spreads warmth down my neck. I hold still, trembling, awaiting his touch. And when his mouth brushes mine, I catch fire.

A wash of heat explodes across my tongue, pulls down my throat, fists in my lower belly. The drag of flushed lips. The scrape of stubble across my skin. I try to follow Zephyrus' lead, but I have no idea what I'm doing. My fingertips dig into the soil—an anchor. Then I'm swept far and wide, sucked beneath waves I cannot climb, arches of white foam collapsing over me in dizzying sensations: sight and sound and taste and, by the Father, his *smell*. My mind, my entire being, spins out of control.

I break away, shaking from head to toe. My body has seized, the energy coiling so tightly inside me it ruptures, shockwaves extending down my limbs.

"Sorry," I whisper through chattering teeth. "I'm no good at this."

"Do you see me complaining?" he asks with a raised eyebrow.

"No." But the insecurity creeps through me regardless.

Zephyrus rubs my upper arms in soothing strokes. I'm likely twice his weight, yet in this moment, I feel small. "We can take it slow. There's no rush."

I cannot see where this door will lead. But I understand that passing beyond its threshold means leaving the vows I swore to uphold behind. To become intimate with a man, *this* man ... I choose this for myself. "I've never done this before."

His eyes soften. "It's an incredibly frightening thing, letting someone in. We move forward if and when you choose to."

His patience helps soothe my frazzled nerves. The West Wind can be incredibly accommodating when he wants to be. "Is there a better way to ... you know."

"Better way to ... ?" Zephyrus regards me expectantly.

He will make me say it, the fiend. "Kiss you."

A bit of playfulness lightens his expression. "Do whatever feels good."

"That's not helpful!"

"How will you know unless you try it?" It emerges as a throaty purr. "Do you dare test your boundaries?" At the next breath, he catches my mouth with his own. And when my lips part, peeled open by his eager tongue, I whimper.

He makes a sound in turn, his taste so much more potent now. The slow, indulgent kiss is worshipful, absorbing all my concentration in a way I have only experienced in deep prayer.

Tilting his head, Zephyrus begins to find a rhythm. I'm shocked by how good it feels, this need to press forward, rub catlike against him so the heat sparks fire. My mouth throbs, raw and abused, as the kiss deepens.

"Give me your tongue," he murmurs.

"H-how? I don't know how." I squirm in place, trying to ease the tightness coiling between my legs.

The West Wind presses a brief, chaste kiss against my chin. "Relax." One of his hands envelops the front of my throat like a warm collar. "Part your lips ... Yes, like that. Ease your tongue past your teeth. Good girl."

Everything we have done thus far, each deliberate unfolding, piles into rich extravagance. Together we climb and together we fall. For the second time, I break away, swaying.

"You're lovely," Zephyrus says. "So perfectly pristine." The hand at my throat tightens slightly. When I swallow, my muscles strain against his grip. "And yet, I find myself wanting to do filthy, depraved things to you."

My heart knocks against my ribs so forcefully I'm certain his immortal ears catch its harrowing rhythm. "Like what?"

The banked heat in his eyes reveals the impious corners of his mind, the fiercest cravings. "I will show you," he murmurs, nipping at my jaw, "in time. For now, let us indulge."

The West Wind coaxes my mouth open too easily. The slide and curl of his tongue. The hard plundering that follows, which drags all those rough, embarrassing sounds from my throat. My breasts brush his chest, and I whimper.

"*Brielle.*"

I'm spiraling, too far gone to care that he has spoken my name aloud in a place that would surely snatch it. Zephyrus claims he is faithless, but my name rings like the holiest of prayers.

"Tell me how it feels," he murmurs, lips tickling the shell of my ear. "Tell me I am your undoing."

His hand skims up my shoulder, down my arm, across my stomach. His fingers skirt my chest, return to my heaving back, where his palm sinks between the shoulder blades. I cannot deny him, for it is true—his touch is my undoing.

My body bows toward Zephyrus as he shifts his attention to the curve of my neck, a press of damp heat above my collar, mouth always in motion. *Yes. More.* As soon as the thought forms, it evaporates. My thighs clamp tighter around the budding throb that lies between.

As Zephyrus grips my hips, the timbre of his voice drops. "Sit on my lap." He squeezes my waist—the area I've always been most insecure about. It freezes me in place.

"I'm too heavy," I tell him.

"Says who?"

"Everyone."

He is too quiet.

The inward retreat has already begun. My weight has never mattered to me. It has only ever been a topic of contention for others.

"Your body," Zephyrus murmurs, eyes intent, "is beautiful. I have always admired it."

"You don't care that I'm larger than you? That I could carry you without breaking a sweat?"

"Absolutely not." He drags his hands down to my wrists, fingers encircling them like bracelets. "I love your shape. I love your curves and the muscle in your arms. I love how physically strong you are. The differences in our bodies? That is the headiest allure."

I lick my lips nervously, and my stomach clenches as Zephyrus' eyes lock on to the motion.

"Sit on my lap," he says again.

I do not fight the temptation. I'm too far gone. Straddling his waist, I ease my weight against him.

He sinks his fingers into my hips, the fabric of my dress so thin it may as well not exist. "Do you trust me?"

Over the course of this journey, I have come to better understand him. I may not trust the West Wind with my heart, but there is trust enough for this: allowing him to bring my desire to life. "What will you do?"

"I will show you that exploring one's body is not selfish. I will show you that indulging is no sin."

As if reading the uncertainty in my expression, he rains soft kisses down to my jaw. The sensation suffuses my skin with an unbearable heat. I hold still, poised on a knife's edge, a trembling deep in my belly.

When his mouth slants over mine, I am prepared. Eagerly, I feed the kiss, edged in these feelings I dare not name. My head tips back, and Zephyrus drinks deeply of everything I offer. He then shifts me to the side, one of his legs slotting between mine, and he holds me there, rocking his thigh against my core until the sensation takes root and I begin to move.

Oh. My eyes roll into the back of my head, and all at once, my body loosens, contouring around his hard, flexing muscle. Then, a brightness, something igniting in my core. I falter.

"Let it unfold," Zephyrus whispers.

Whatever *this* is, I can't control it. I shift my hips harder against him, his hands securing me in place. The pleasure sharpens as it nears its peak, and though my body seeks to chase it, I am desperately afraid of what awaits me at its end. Abruptly, I go cold.

"That's enough," I gasp.

Immediately, Zephyrus stops.

My thighs continue to tremble, muscles locked tight. He studies me—this panting, red-faced, wide-eyed woman. "Did I hurt you?"

"No." I shake my head. "I just . . . need space."

Expression grave, he nods and loosens his hands from around my waist.

I slip off his lap. The ground is cold beneath me. For whatever reason, I want to cry. How can I miss his touch when I'm the one who demanded distance?

"Sorry." I've never offered a more pitiful apology.

Zephyrus catches my hand, gives it a reassuring squeeze. "Don't apologize. You did nothing wrong."

Then why do I feel so inadequate?

"I thought—" A helpless sound escapes. "I thought I wanted to do . . . *that*. But—"

Despite the abrupt shift in mood, his eyes soften. "You don't have to explain anything to me." Reaching out, he cradles my cheek, brushes his thumb across its curve. "Rest," he says. "I'll watch over you."

Curling into the grass, I lay my head on Zephyrus' thigh. He weaves his fingers through my hair, pushing the curls away from my face. The meadow, the stars, and the West Wind—infuriating, too clever by half, yet at times unexpectedly sweet.

When my eyes close, I dream of spring.

21

MY EYES OPEN TO A DARK SKY. THE STARS HAVE WANED, AND LOW, sinuous clouds drag their bellies across the forested canopy.

"Zephyrus?"

Pushing upright, I peer around the glen. An imprint in the grass beside me suggests someone has lain there. The West Wind, however, is nowhere in sight.

A chill courses through me, though the air itself is pleasantly warm. In the distance, the fires have died. Night sounds, hushed and drowsy, blanket the village. As suddenly as it manifested, the gathering has reached an end.

My attention shifts to where the shadows are thickest. Nothing stirs. The air holds itself in suspension. I am alone. And yet, I am certain someone or something watches me.

Climbing to my feet, I brush off my grass-stained dress, limbs loose and mouth bruised. My glove-clad fingertips press softly into my lower lip, tender to the touch. I remember the drag of the West Wind's tongue, the abrasiveness of his unshaven cheeks. His taste lingers, a honeysuckle sweetness.

I touched a man. Kissed him. Ran my fingers across his muscled torso. It was a reckless act, driven by emotion rather than logic, too rash for the life of a novitiate. And if it ever comes to light, I will lose—everything.

Brielle.

I whirl around. No sign of whoever called my name. "Hello?"

Where are you, Brielle?

The call seethes through the forest undergrowth, rough with pain. My stomach takes a sharp dive. It sounds like Zephyrus, though he knows better than to speak my name aloud.

Grabbing the hem of my skirt, I race across the clearing, plunging into the wood, the trees closing at my back.

A few paces ahead, the grassy path appears, brown with age. By the time I reach the trail's end, my breath draws short and I stand before the entrance to a cave. My name drifts from its cold, black depths.

Nervous energy jitters beneath my skin. It tells me *no*. It reminds me of all I have to lose. But if Zephyrus is in need, who will help him, if not me?

I duck into the low-ceilinged tunnel. Keeping my hand to the cool, damp stone, I follow the warren as it descends beneath the earth. Thankfully, Zephyrus' roselight keeps the gloom at bay.

When the tunnel empties into a large, moonlit chamber, my footsteps falter. I have been here before. A field of pink flowers embraced by silver-painted walls.

I quickly scan the vacant chamber. "Zephyrus?"

"He is not here, young novitiate."

My attention snaps upward, and I lurch back with a frightened cry.

The Orchid King clings to the ceiling with his grub-like roots, those horrible, open-mouthed buds oozing a clear liquid. He hangs suspended in the vines, the gleaming white skin of his upper torso rippling with strength as he twists around, evaluating me as though I am a particularly compelling enigma. A messy silver braid snakes over the curve of one muscled shoulder.

"Do not be frightened," he soothes. "You are safe here."

"You will not punish me?" One of the carnivorous blossoms erupting from his shoulder snaps its mouth shut. "I'm forbidden to enter Under except on the tithe."

The Orchid King finds amusement in my concern. His eyes cut like shards of ice. "I do not care to punish you, my dear. My relationship with Mother Mabel takes precedent. I do not wish to taint it by penalizing one of her charges."

I do not trust his word, though his reasoning makes sense. "Where is Zephyrus," I say once my pulse slows, "and why was I called here?"

The Orchid King cants his head in puzzlement. "You tell me. You arrived—uninvited—into my home. There must be a reason for it."

"A voice called my name," I say with far more calmness than I feel. "I followed it."

"Whose voice?"

"Zephyrus'."

A vine drops to the ground with a slap, followed by a second, third, and fourth. Grunting, the Orchid King lowers himself from the ceiling, the span of his roots extending from wall to wall. I shuffle backward to put distance between us.

"How curious," Pierus replies, and the tip of a curved, blackened nail dimples his chin. "Have you considered whether the voice was your inner self nudging you in this direction?"

"Why would my mind lead me here?" I swore after witnessing Zephyrus' torturous ritual never to return, but the entrance I came through held no familiarity. This time, there was no waterfall to pass behind.

The Orchid King shifts his bulk through the field of flowering grass, then clambers atop the mound of dirt heaped against the back wall. "Who is to know? The world is full of mysteries."

He settles in, white roots diving into the soil like hungry worms. Blue eyes placid, he sinks down with a sigh.

"If Zephyrus is not here," I say, "then where is he?"

"I cannot answer that question, my dear. Has he finally abandoned you?"

A long moment passes before I'm able to speak.

"Zephyrus gave his word to help me find Meirlach. He would not break that promise."

"Meirlach." He drags a claw idly down one cheek, expression ponderous. "This is why you have returned to Under?"

At once, I realize my error.

The Orchid King sits as an asp in its nest, flush from its recent meal. "You do not seek this weapon for yourself. Who sent you? Mother Mabel?"

I am remembering Pierus' visit to Thornbrook, how my peers flinched in the presence of this peculiar creature, neither plant nor man, something caught between two worlds. But mostly, I am remembering the clench of Mother Mabel's hands at her front, her obvious disdain for him.

"Do not fret, my dear. You do not have to answer. I understand your need to protect those you love. But I'm concerned for your safety. You see, I do not think the Stallion will welcome you, not after its last visitor. Oh, it was long ago, but a kelpie's memory is longer still."

Does he imply I will be unable to enter the Grotto? If this is an attempt to throw me off-balance, I daresay it is working.

"But," he tacks on, "perhaps this time will be different. You are, after all, a novitiate. A servant, lowly in the church. Perhaps the Stallion will spare your life, if you ask nicely."

"I am not in the habit of asking nicely for that which is rightfully mine," I say with impressive finality. "I know only that the Stallion guards Meirlach, and I am to obtain the blade."

The Orchid King sighs, the bridge of his nose pinched between two fingers. "I would not expect Zephyrus to divulge such an important detail. After all, he wants to ensure you reach the Grotto. Without you, he's completely out of luck."

It makes no sense. If visiting the Stallion puts my life in danger, wouldn't Zephyrus be in danger, too? Although, Mother Mabel's order to kill the beast makes a lot more sense now. Better it dead than me.

I voice these thoughts to Pierus.

"He is a god, my dear. Immortal. He cannot die."

"Even so, that doesn't explain why he wouldn't warn me of the steps I'd need to take to reach the Grotto safely. Withholding information puts me, and his own opportunity, at risk. I'm going to find Meirlach. He knows this."

"And how do you expect to acquire Meirlach?" He searches my gaze. When I do not immediately respond, he nods, as if my lack of comprehension was to be expected. "I imagine the Stallion would allow you to take something if you provided a decent replacement, though I doubt you will view it as a fair trade." He peers at me with those piercing blue eyes. "But Meirlach? A sword forged by the gods, for the gods? It will not part with a treasure so rare. You are wasting your time."

"Enough," I growl, stepping forward. "You're trying to confuse me. It won't work."

Tilting back his head, Pierus briefly studies the ceiling, the distinctly human gesture of a man seeking patience. "I understand we have not known each other for very long. I'm aware you do not trust me, and believe that I lead you astray. But have you weighed the risks in allowing Zephyrus to accompany you on this journey?"

"I am aware of the risks." Deep in my core, the trembling manifests, first as hairline cracks, then greater waves. "He has his reasons for traveling with us."

"And those are?"

"He didn't say. Just that he seeks something that will change his life."

At this, Pierus smiles. "Have you considered that Zephyrus wishes to claim the sword for himself?"

The idea forces itself inside my mind, past my defenses, and slots into place, a suspicion I'd previously denied. Why would Zephyrus wish to claim Meirlach? I've asked myself this question before.

A cant of Pierus' head as he takes me in: curling red hair, my borrowed, ill-fitting dress. "Tell me what you know about the sword's properties."

I cross the room, needing space from the Orchid King. The small, gnashing teeth of those opening buds escalate my disquiet. "It is said to pierce any armor. It can cut through walls, shields. It claims mastery over the winds." Since Zephyrus already has power, it seems pointless he'd want to acquire more of it. "It also demands the truth when held to the throat of another."

As I speak, I pace. I cannot run, not when there remain questions unanswered. No, I must see this through to the end.

"You know nothing else?" Pierus inquires. I shake my head. "Then let me inform you that should Zephyrus claim Meirlach, he will be able to sever our contract by killing me. Only a weapon forged by the gods can kill a god."

"I see."

"Do you? My dear, let me explain. As soon as Zephyrus gets his hands on Meirlach, he will no longer have any use for you."

A chill creeps along my skin. "He wouldn't betray me. We had an agreement."

The Orchid King shakes his head in mild sympathy. "You do not know the West Wind as I do. For a chance to free himself from his captivity, he would stop at nothing."

Zephyrus knows how much becoming the next acolyte means to me. Whatever my reservations, I've moved past them. I have given him pieces of myself. Was that a mistake?

"I told him he could accompany us to the Grotto, but I could leave him behind, right? He wouldn't be able to follow us." Since he is neither mortal nor a woman, he would be barred from entering the Stallion's lair. I could ensure Harper and I reach Meirlach first.

"That depends. Does he have access to your blood? Entering the Grotto requires an offering of mortal blood to the River Mur."

"Of course not."

Pierus inclines his chin, as if he anticipated the pushback. "Are you certain?"

My pacing slows. Something nags at me, sliding deeper, so deep I am forced to peer inward, down and down and down. My sickness. Zephyrus mentioned requiring my blood to barter for the remedy needed to heal me after I was attacked by the darkwalkers. I thought nothing of it.

"I don't understand. Why blood?"

The tips of his talons connect, forming a bridge in front of his mouth. "The blood of a mortal," he says, "contains powerful properties. You humans and your beliefs. They are strong enough to take a life. Strong enough to save one, too. If the Stallion is feeling generous, your blood would appease him, for however short a time."

I brace a hand against the wall. I feel old in this moment, the years of a bygone era pressed upon my shoulders. I'm not sure whether to cry or scream, deny or repent. How could I have known this was Zephyrus' plan? If I cannot trust the Orchid King, if I cannot trust Zephyrus, or Harper, then who can I trust?

Pierus must know how I've grown to rely on Zephyrus. He has his reasons for planting this uncertainty. What does he seek? Control. He will do whatever is necessary to keep those spidery fingers wrapped around the West Wind's neck.

"No." I push away from the wall. "You're trying to manipulate me." Raised chin and crossed arms. Why, I can almost imagine myself as Harper in this moment.

The Orchid King wrenches his roots free of the soil and slithers forward, pushing upward to give himself additional height. "I am not trying to deceive you, young novitiate. Zephyrus is a god, and gods do not change."

Quiet: a place where doubt takes root.

More frightening than standing here alone with Pierus is the knowledge that the West Wind, the person I have come to know these past weeks, has revealed only a shade of his true self. What has been true? What falsities have erected the image of Zephyrus in my head? With no evidence to hold its shape, my image of him begins to crumble.

The Orchid King crawls toward a shelf carved out of the damp, glistening rock. He removes a small book, saying, "From what I understand, you suffered a great loss as a girl. It is a terrible thing, wandering the earth motherless."

I did not think it possible to shrink further. "How do you know that?"

"I have known Mother Mabel for years. At times, she has confided in me. She has told me of her loyal, red-headed bladesmith, and speaks of you fondly. Your abbess is concerned for your well-being."

I'm not sure how I feel about Mother Mabel informing the Orchid King of my painful past. He offers me the book, which appears to be a diary. "I've marked the page. Read it. Let history guide your decision."

Curling my fingers around the soft leather, I slip it into my dress pocket.

"There is good in Zephyrus," I say, more to myself than Pierus. "I have seen it." With that, I take my leave, striding toward the exit.

"You have seen what he wants you to see," the Orchid King calls to my retreating back. "You and I both know your trust in the Bringer of Spring is tenuous at best. What has he given you except his lies?"

Something splinters in my chest, a great fissure within me. The world is vast, and there is much I do not know. The tithe nears. Harper and I must return to Thornbrook, Meirlach in hand. I cannot presume Zephyrus has been telling the truth. If I am wrong, everything I've fought for will be lost.

I turn to face Pierus, his long, angular face awash in wan moonlight. "What is the quickest way to the Grotto?"

He seems pleased by my question. Those scarlet blossoms gush from his alabaster skin like fresh wounds. "You will need to take a boat upstream. When the River Mur diverges, go right. Eventually, you'll pass through a gate and reach an island of sand, where you must disembark. It marks the boundary to the Grotto." He takes me in a moment longer. "Another word of advice? Offer the river your blood. The Stallion will at least hear you out before deciding to kill you."

22

I RUN STRAIGHT FROM THE CAVE TO THE BOAT MOORED AT THE village's edge without stopping. The rope thumps against the bottom of the hull, and I'm off, using the pole to direct the vessel across the water, pushing as quickly as I dare. When Harper wakes, she will notice my absence, but I intend to return. I will not abandon her to the fair folk. As for Zephyrus, he will know I have gone, perhaps sooner than I would like.

When the River Mur branches off, I steer the boat into the dark tunnel. Then I settle onto the bench, roselight squeezed tightly in hand, and pull the book from my pocket, letting the current carry me toward the Grotto.

A small piece of cloth has been tucked between the pages. I flip to the bookmark, squinting down at the markings. Inked words bleed beneath the roselight's faint pink glow.

Day eleven, second month of spring.

I was right. It *is* a diary. And if I'm not mistaken, this is Mother Mabel's elegant script. So how did it fall into the Orchid King's possession?

Hunching nearer to the page, I begin to read.

Tragedy has struck Carterhaugh.

A message arrived from Veraness. Seemingly overnight, the entire popu-
lation was wiped out, having succumbed to a storm the likes of which I've

never seen. Days ago, I watched the tempest approach Thornbrook. Low, roiling clouds swelled with thunder and the bright clap of lightning.

My charges were frightened. I told them to pray, that the Father would take care of the rest. But sometimes, His kindness comes at a price. For though we were spared, the people of Veraness were not.

My eyes snag on a single word: Veraness. The town that had once been my home.

Once the storm cleared, I took my charges to Veraness, or what was left of it. We searched for survivors. There were few. I sent a message to Pierus, asking if he knew the storm's cause. Supposedly, the West Wind had attempted to sever his bond. As one of the Four Winds, his power was unsurpassed. Although he was unsuccessful, the damage Carterhaugh sustained was immense.

A sense of foreboding slinks through me. The Four Winds. I wondered why the name sounded familiar when Lissi first mentioned it. I have read of this event not in the Text, but in the history books held in the abbey library.

My hand shakes as I flip to the previous page and note the date inscribed on the top right corner—three days prior to my mother's disappearance. According to Mother Mabel's personal account of these events, Zephyrus is responsible for my home's destruction, the event that triggered what followed: a harrowing journey through a storm-drenched night, waiting in the hollow of an old tree, my abandonment on the abbey steps.

I shove the diary into my pocket, my breathing choked. Curse Zephyrus. Curse the Orchid King. Curse this vile place, its rotten core. And curse my own frustrating naivete. Is that what Zephyrus saw upon our first meeting? Was it then that he decided to exploit my goodwill?

"Eternal Father." The strained plea comes unbidden. "Lead me to your quiet waters."

Pushing to my feet, I reclaim the pole and steer around a corner where the current drags. The tunnel curves ahead, cast in the glow of the flickering roselights. My vessel drifts past the open gate the Orchid King mentioned. The air smells of old growth and decay.

"Grant me protection, and in your protection, strength."

As I round the bend, the current slows, and a shallow strip of beach comes into view. Once the boat bumps against the sandy shore, I scramble onto dry land.

The rush and retreat of the river has dissolved the tunnel's limestone walls into vast pockets and warped pillars, the ceiling scooped hollow. Ahead, the Grotto lies partially submerged in the black water of high tide. It boasts an impressive archway inlaid with rubies, their color darkened to rust in the frail light. I cannot see what lies within. It begins and ends in obscurity.

"May your light be my guide," I whisper. "May you walk with me through darkness. In your name I pray. Amen."

The tips of my boots brush the water's edge. I will have to swim across. I have no choice. I've come to meet my fate, whatever form that might take.

But first, an offering.

The point of my dagger produces a spot of blood on the pad of my finger. I let the red bead drop into the water, shallow ripples disturbing its glassy stillness.

Toes, ankles, shins, thighs—the icy water drags at my dress. Beneath, sharpened pebbles line the riverbed like teeth, the smallest bones. My boots skid along the bottom. As the water hits my waist, the roselight tucked inside my pocket gutters.

I'm halfway across the channel when a long, shallow ridge of water emerges, hurtling toward me in an elongated, unbroken wave.

My heart leaps, and I scramble forward, my arms cutting through the chest-high water, which crashes against the walls of the echoing chamber.

A rounded snout breaks the surface. Two large nostrils flare, exhaling steam. I bite back a scream and plunge blindly through the churning river. My boots gain traction. I shove upward, ripping free of the water's hold. My knees fold. I collapse onto the shore, shivering, puffing hard. At my back, the River Mur settles.

A mortal woman. It has been a long time.

My skin pebbles in the stale air, for a voice blossoms inside my mind.

Pushing to my feet, I glance around the expansive cavern, its smooth floors laden with gold: mounds of sloping hillocks, towering peaks crowned with gem-studded collars and tarnished diadems. All gleam beneath the rosy glow pulsing from the roselights in the main chamber. The most lovely tapestries paint the walls, their colors undimmed. One section contains an extensive array of shelving stuffed with bound manuscripts, piles of loose parchment, scrolls secured with velvet ribbons, precarious stacks of dusty tomes. Silk garments drape a coat rack in one corner. And still, there is more. Cluttered arrangements of chalices, goblets. Gold-spun thread. The treasure of a thousand lifetimes.

Pulling my eyes away from the collection, I search for whoever spoke. The weight of my dagger reminds me I am not without defense. "Are you the one they call the Stallion?"

I am. A thread of intrigue colors the voice—male, I believe. *But I admit I do not know who you are. Why have you come, mortal woman? It is a long way from your abbey.*

A half-turn toward my right. I'm certain something moved, but upon closer inspection, nothing appears out of the ordinary. An ornate mirror leans against a heap of purest emeralds. It reveals a scene, almost as if I peer through a window: the climbing white spires of a city perched atop a mountain's crown, a shadow cloaking the base of its valley.

"How do you know I'm from the abbey?" I ask, continuing to scan the area, my every sense heightened. No sign of a sword that I can see.

The Stallion makes a light humming sound. *You smell of the incense they burn on the Holy Days.*

"We burn it," I explain, "to clear the air of impurities."

So I have heard.

His voice fades as abruptly as it manifested. Water patters from my soaked clothes, chipping away at the silence.

"Will you show yourself?" I ask. "I have traveled far to meet you."

As do many who believe they are capable of besting me. They send the strongest, the swiftest, the cleverest. None can. You seem neither strong nor quick, unfortunately.

I force myself to stand tall. "It is true I am not the swiftest, or strongest, or cleverest," I state, backing toward a wall, "but I have made it this far. Surely that is a testament to my will."

Your will means nothing to me. You, Daughter of Thornbrook, are not welcome. Pray to your god, girl, for your death will be neither quick nor painless.

So the Orchid King was right. I am not welcome here. It seems my blood didn't appease the Stallion either.

"Why do you wish to kill me?" I search the water again. I'm certain something lurks beneath the surface. "Does my faith offend you?"

It is not your faith that offends me. It is your interpretation of it. A faith that sanctions stealing from others? I will have no part of it.

"We do not steal," I snap. Formidable creature or not, I will defend the Father by any means necessary. "We spread good and kindness through His teachings."

Then why must I defend my cache against yet another Daughter of your faith?

I glance upward, peering into the chamber's farthest corners. "I do not understand."

Only once before has a mortal entered my Grotto and escaped with their life, a stolen treasure in hand.

No wonder the Stallion doesn't trust me. "I'm not here to steal from you. I'm here to bargain."

Nothing you offer interests me. You are young, girl. Untried. Too innocent for this world. I will extend to you this mercy: leave, if you cherish your life.

"I won't go." Not without Meirlach.

Then you have welcomed your own demise.

The river shatters into a thousand lapping waves. I stumble back, retreating farther into the cavern as the Stallion emerges in pieces: long snout, tapered head, water pouring from its massive hindquarters, and an impenetrable coat of glossy pitch. River grass hangs from its equally dark mane and tail.

The towering steed extends perhaps twenty-five hands, maybe more. Its rheumy eyes are filmed in white, without pupil or iris. Zephyrus was correct. It is blind.

The Stallion clops toward me. Muscle shifts beneath the coal flesh encasing its musculature. I scuttle backward, dagger in hand.

"You will not even hear what I have to offer you?" I stutter, wide eyes pinned to its sleek, oily coat. "I thought kelpies enjoyed a good bargain."

You wish to bargain? Climb onto my back, the Stallion's voice says inside my head, *and I will gift you a treasure from my cache.*

Indeed, I have heard the tales. Water-horses that prey on women. Once I mount its back, it will return to the river and drag me down.

"I wish to fight you for the opportunity to win an object from your cache," I say. "A duel. That is fair." And by the end, my blade must be buried deep into its heart. "Will you flee?"

Flee? The horse shakes its head. Water sprays, flecking my cheek. *What have I to flee from? Come, girl. Climb onto my back. Let the bargain be fulfilled.*

I retreat until my spine hits the wall. "I will not."

Water drips in the quiet pooling between us. *Very well. You request a duel? Then let us fight.*

Air ripples around the creature, and when it settles, I blink in surprise. The Stallion is neither a man nor a terrifying beast. He is a child, on the cusp of adolescence.

He wears brown trousers and a thin white tunic. He stands with a relaxed posture, hands loose at his sides. A flop of pale hair falls across his brow. He is all bones, yet staring into his white eyes, I understand that I am quite young in comparison. For those eyes are old. They have seen things.

The kelpie pads forward on bare feet. "Are you frightened?" His attention rests slightly to the side of my face.

A trickle of sweat slithers down my neck. "Yes."

The boy smiles. "Good." His teeth are small and square. "You should be."

Killing a kelpie is one thing, but a boy? I will not do it. I do not care if the Stallion merely wears a human skin. Somehow, I will have to gain Meirlach without slaying the beast.

I push off the wall to face the Stallion.

Tucking his hands at the small of his back, he begins to circle me. "Before we begin, let us discuss particulars. What treasure of mine do you seek?"

"Meirlach."

He shakes his head, continues his circling. I turn, reflecting his movements. The last thing I want is to expose my back. Despite his lack of sight, I sense the boy would strike with precision. "Meirlach is not for the taking, I'm afraid, but you are free to select something else." He flutters a small hand toward the eclectic display.

I readjust my grip on my dagger. Its leather wrapping clings to my damp glove. "I came here for Meirlach," I state. "I will not leave without it."

"Then you will not leave," the Stallion cries, expression twisted in irritation.

Calm, I think. Yet my heart thunders with the knowledge that things are not unfolding as I imagined they would. "You said I could choose any object in your collection." Round and round and round he goes.

"Any object," he counters, "but Meirlach."

"Why?"

"Because it is mine. That is reason enough."

I swallow, squinting through the half-light in an attempt to locate the shining pommel of a sword. Mounds of treasure pile against the Grotto's curved walls. A few precarious towers extend all the way to the stalactites overhead. "Do you fear I will beat you in a duel?" I dare ask.

Silence stretches and reforms around this statement, as if the Stallion considers the question from all angles. He stops, his arms crossed, mouth mulish. "It has been long since I have battled."

If the Text has taught me anything, it's that we are all born with equal potential. I am but kindling that has yet to burn.

"Don't you tire of your loneliness?" I press. "Don't you seek to connect to another, however briefly?"

The Stallion releases a crow-like laugh. "I have lived a thousand life-times, girl. What you offer is nothing I have not already experienced."

"You seem certain. But I ask you this: what do you know of me aside from my mortality and faith? I may surprise you."

There is a pause. "I cannot decide whether you are brave or merely foolish." He shakes his head. "At the very least, you are entertaining. Very well. I will give you the opportunity to win Meirlach, Daughter of Thornbrook." A sword appears in his childlike hand. The long, elegant blade pulses with an ethereal light. "Lovely, isn't it?"

It is a weapon worthy of a song. The hilt has been shaped from gold. A ruby winks from the disk capping the pommel, and the guard, a collection of spiraling strips, shapes a protective sphere around the Stallion's hand.

"If you draw first blood, the blade is yours." The Stallion gives Meirlach a twirl. "However, if I draw first blood, you will climb onto my back and dwell within my Grotto forevermore."

Never have I desired anything more than Meirlach in this moment, with the aftermath of recent betrayal roiling hot in my belly. I have the will. Of this, I am certain. But if the Stallion draws blood first, I am as good as dead.

Slowly, I raise my blade. He studies me with that adolescent face, those primordial eyes. In his mind, I am a child. Even when my body becomes dust, he will likely still be here, guarding his cache.

There is little I can do now. I'm committed. From the moment I stepped beyond Thornbrook's walls, I vowed to return with the sword or die trying. I have trained for this. Besting the Stallion is but the last obstacle on this journey.

Planting my feet, I take stock of my opponent. His sword offers greater reach. A dagger, however, is the most versatile of weapons, a many-faced foe. What I lack in speed, I make up for in strength. Let him think me untried.

I do not see him move.

A rush of air stirs to my right. I swing on a half-turn, meeting his blade. The clang peals out.

The Stallion deflects, lunging for my left flank. Our blades kiss before he spins away in a ripple of darkness. He returns, hacking at my neck with frightening calculation. A complex pattern of counter cuts keeps the Stallion at arm's length, but he is ancient, this creature. He is no mere boy. I must remember that.

His next strike whacks my blade with back-breaking force. The impact rattles my arm, the roots of my teeth. Once more, he whirls away to enfold himself in the shadows. I scan the cave, weapon raised, my heartbeat marking the passing time. He has disappeared.

A droplet of sweat rolls with aching slowness down my spine. Tumbled gemstones, gold bricks, and shimmering silver ripple in waves of color beneath the roselights.

I am a blade.

A dark shape rushes from a murky corner. I pivot around his strike, yet slip on a few scattered jewels, crashing into one of the golden mounds. Coins plink across the floor. The Stallion lunges. I spin out of reach. A glance over my shoulder reveals his sword buried in the mound up to the hilt. By the time he yanks it free, I'm already across the room.

He reconvenes, brushing a lock of hair from his sightless eyes. His other senses must be highly attuned if he's able to pinpoint my location so accurately. At the next attack, I leap sideways, stabbing toward the Stallion's thigh. He skirts free with a high, tinkling laugh.

"You'll have to do better than that if you wish to escape this place alive," he says.

Again, he disappears. My attention leaps from mound to mound, blade at the ready. By the time I sense movement, his sword hacks with brutal severity toward my unprotected neck.

A clash rings out. Shock roots my feet to the ground, for Zephyrus has inserted himself between me and the kelpie, a sword hewn from air in his hand.

As they rain blows upon each other, I look beyond them. Harper stands in the arched entryway, eyes wide, a cloak clutched around her slender frame. I turn my back on her.

Zephyrus cuts toward the boy, who swipes low, nicking his opponent's thigh.

"This fight is mine," I snarl, striding forward.

Zephyrus attempts to gain the upper hand despite his poor swordsmanship. His strategy is to continually evade, never landing a blow directly. It reeks of cowardice.

"Your fight," I call to the Stallion, "is with me!"

As Zephyrus pivots toward the archway, I ram him from behind, and he slams face-first into the wall, his sword clattering on the ground. He claps a hand over his face, blood pouring from his nose.

Positioned between two piles of gold, the Stallion advances, his nostrils flaring, taking in the coppery scent. I meet his aggression with equal fervor. The West Wind's presence changes things. My strikes land with greater weight, my parries fleeting, memories before they're made known. Blade to blade, we battle for dominance. Meirlach will be mine. It is a symbol, after all. And symbols hold power.

The Stallion ducks, and the flat of my dagger passes over the warm heat of his skin. I complete the drive upward, cutting across his face, forcing him into retreat. His back hits the wall, my dagger at his throat.

The boy pants through his teeth. Sweat sheens his skin, the color feverish in the low light, but he is not the one I wish were on the receiving end of my blade.

He must recognize this. "You will not kill me?" the boy whispers, and he does not seem so old now, with dirt streaking his ripped trousers and a slice reddening his cheek.

Wrath boils holes into my stomach, and yet, the Stallion is not my foe. Merely a scapegoat for my fury.

"A life is a life in the eyes of the Father." Stepping back, I lower my dagger. "I will not kill you."

Something like respect lines his features. "It is clear you are no helpless mortal." He hesitates a moment. Then, holding out his hand, he offers me the blade. "Meirlach is yours."

As soon as the hilt touches my skin, a warm current licks at my fingers and slithers up my arm. The sword is far lighter than it appears, its pommel a perfect counterweight to the steel blade.

My eyes lift to the Stallion as his bloodless lips curve. "Take care with that sword. Power is a dangerous temptation, after all."

I am well aware.

"Farewell, Daughter of Thornbrook." He transforms back into his equine form, eliciting a gasp from Harper. A blink of those sightless eyes and he vanishes into the river.

Footsteps, carried on a loam-soaked breeze. I turn, sword in hand, to study Zephyrus, who halts a few paces away.

"Are you all right?" There's a harried look about him, the curls of his hair clumped with sweat and blood. Fool. He's lucky he can wear his immortality like armor.

"Fine." I brush past him. Harper and I will need to return to Carterhaugh as quickly as possible. I only hope we have not lost too much time to Under—months or, dare I think, years.

"Wait," Zephyrus calls.

There was the old Brielle, the green, narrow-minded novitiate of Thornbrook. But the Brielle of today is a much wiser creature. She understands the difference between choice and obligation.

Slowly, I pivot to face the Bringer of Spring. His features have altered in such a way that they bear little resemblance to the man I rescued in Carterhaugh. The skin is smoother, the bone structure sharper, with an agreeable symmetry that wasn't previously present.

"If it is a fight you seek," I clip out, trying to mask my surprise, "you will have to look elsewhere. I earned Meirlach fairly."

"You did," he concedes. I do not fail to notice how his attention fixates on the weapon. "You fought well."

I already know this. Ten years ago, Mother Mabel put a blade in my hand. I have not wasted that time languishing. "What do you want, Zephyrus? Be honest, for once."

A muscle flutters in his jaw. Anger? Not quite. It is something decidedly more deadly. "Why did you leave for the Stallion alone?" He searches my face. "You are not usually so rash."

It seems I will have to spell it out for him. "Ask me what I learned, Zephyrus. Go on."

His pupils dilate, swimming against the mossy rings surrounding them. A hare, I think, caught in the eye of a snake. "What did you learn?"

Admittedly, I'd believed myself capable of civil conversation. In my mind, I would lay everything out, every hardened fact. Information would be picked over, torn apart, arranged in its proper location, where all made sense.

But it cannot be done. Between one heartbeat and the next, tears sting my eyes, and my breath comes short.

"The Orchid King told me of your plan. How you would lead us to the Grotto. How you would use my blood to gain Meirlach for yourself. How you would then kill Pierus, thus breaking the curse that binds you to him." *How you would betray me.*

"You sought him out?" Zephyrus seems frightened—*for me*, I think. "Pierus is dangerous."

"How dangerous can he be when he speaks the truth?" The words grow broken and coarse. "Do you deny it?"

He steps forward, palms lifted in repentance. "I can explain."

"You lied to me." The accusation spews out, thick and sour enough to choke me. "You lied, and you lied, and you lied! I trusted you."

For that is the true hurt, after all. I warned Harper of Zephyrus' motives. I reminded myself to maintain distance. Daily, I thought, *Do not trust him.* Yet I could have sworn I'd witnessed change in him. I believed, truly believed, my feelings for Zephyrus were reciprocated. If I cannot trust my own heart, what can I trust?

"All this time I thought you were here to aid us in our quest, to repay your debt, to gain your *own* prize. But you weren't, were you?" I weep openly. "You wanted Meirlach. It didn't matter that we wanted it, too. *Needed* it. Everything was for your own gain."

For the first time, I see the West Wind clearly. The promises that break, the vows that bind. "I have given you every opportunity to show your true self," I whisper. "Why—" My throat closes as I stare into his eyes. "What kind of person manipulates someone who has only ever been kind to them?"

His expression falls slack. Mourning something that will never come to pass? It matters not. Meirlach will remain in my possession until I present it to Mother Mabel. Zephyrus will have to pry it from my cold, dead fingers before I ever let him touch it.

"Nothing to say?" I demand. "I want the truth. Tell me that the only reason you agreed to help us was to acquire Meirlach for yourself."

"It's not—"

"Say it!"

He looks physically ill as he replies, "Initially, that was my intention. When I learned you sought Meirlach, I planned to go along until the opportunity presented itself. But as time went on, as I came to know you, I began to question what was right."

A likely story. "It didn't stop you, though."

"You have to understand my dilemma. I have been captive for centuries. I would have done anything to free myself."

"And whose fault is that?" I fire back. While I do not know the reason for his captivity, I am almost certain it is justified. "You have only yourself to blame."

"I know." His voice has never been smaller. "But Meirlach was my last hope. Only a god-touched weapon can fell a god."

"You're saying you have no access to any other god-touched weapon? What of your dagger?"

"It is a mortal-made weapon. I had a bow once. I told you this. But I gifted it to my brother's wife."

For a good, long while, I stare at this man. Freedom: a captive's greatest, most elusive hope.

"It didn't have to be this way," I quaver, fresh tears wetting my cheeks. "Had you simply *asked*, I might have agreed to part with the sword." For a time, at least.

He stares at me. "You wouldn't have given up Meirlach."

"You don't know that!" I cry, flinging up a hand. "You assumed things of me. You shoved me into a box and your mind did not change. Instead of being honest from the start, you deceived. You thought little of me."

But I am not through with him. On the contrary, there is so much I might say, had I the time to do so. But I strike where he is weakest. Fell him with a single blow.

"You once asked if anyone could love someone like you," I whisper. "Me—I could have, had you given me the opportunity. But you are a bird so enchanted by its own song that it remains deaf to the calls of others. That is why you are alone, why you will continue to be alone for the rest of your long, miserable existence."

Pain fractures his expression. "I'm sorry."

"Sorry you were caught," I spit. "Sorry you will return to the Orchid King empty-handed, no nearer to freedom."

"Brielle, please." He eases forward, yet I raise Meirlach, its blade luminous despite the darkness of the Grotto. He is too careless, tossing around my name. He must be truly desperate for my attention.

"One more step, and I will slit your throat, immortal or not." My voice trembles with restrained rage. "Let this be your final warning: if you ever show your face in Thornbrook again, I will kill you. I don't care what it takes or how complicated the steps. I will find a way to end your life."

His eyes widen. Zephyrus, however, says nothing more.

After today, I will return to Thornbrook and I will not think of the West Wind ever again. With Meirlach in my possession, I can move on with my life. I doubt Zephyrus will be let off his leash anytime soon, if ever. A just punishment if I have ever heard one.

His attention slides to the blade, perhaps debating the likelihood that I will carry out my promise. "You need me to guide you back to Carterhaugh. It's not safe."

"I don't need you, Zephyrus." A lesson I have learned too late and at the cost of my trust in another. "I never did."

Turning my back, I wait until his footsteps recede. And when stillness coats the Grotto's every darkened hollow, I break. My knees hit the ground. Dagger and sword slip from my grip, impacting the stone with a harsh clatter as my hands lift to cover my face, sound shattering up my throat.

Why must I suffer so? Have I not been a dutiful servant? I think of that eleven-year-old girl left on Thornbrook's doorstep. I am still that girl, even now.

Something warm and heavy settles across my back. I startle, peering up through my fingers in confusion. Harper stands above me. I did not hear her approach.

"You're shaking," she says before looking elsewhere, as though uncomfortable at the sight of my distress.

I then realize Harper wears only her gray cotton dress. The cloak she wore earlier warms my body—the same cloak I bestowed onto Harper last night near the fire.

"I'm sorry," she whispers.

Sorry. I'm growing sick of that word. "Did you know?" Tears continue to slide across my knuckles, down into the grooves between my fingers. "What he planned to do with the sword?"

"I swear to you I didn't. I honestly believed he cared for you."

I scoff. "Right. And I'm sure Zephyrus told you to say this, considering you two are such close friends now."

A prolonged pause follows. "I know I've given you no reason to trust me," she says, voice soft with what I believe to be regret, "but that is the truth of it."

Then we were both fools.

"Here, you dropped this."

I glance at the object she offers me. The roselight throbs like a pale rosette in the center of Harper's palm. It must have fallen from my pocket during the match.

Something goes cold within me. Snatching it from her hand, I heave the orb far into the darkness. It hits the stone with a chime, then bounces, rolls, before coming to a stop somewhere in the murk. I wish it had shattered.

Harper studies me in concern. "What now?"

I have traveled farther than I could have dreamed in my lifetime, but I am tired. I believe I could sleep for years if given the opportunity. "It's time to return to Thornbrook," I whisper flatly. "We have been gone long enough."

PART 2

THE
FAITHLESS

23

IT IS MORNING. GREEN, GOLDEN, WARM. AS I STEP INTO THE HOT, close air of the forge, the tightness in my chest unravels. Here lies familiarity and comfort, the quiet of solitude, every piece of this workshop touched by my hand. It is the only place in Carterhaugh where I can breathe freely.

With the tithe a mere week away, every moment counts. We understand its significance. The blood of twenty-one Daughters gifted to Under, so that Thornbrook may lease the land for another seven-year cycle. Mother Mabel has requested five additional iron daggers for the event, bringing the final count to twenty-six. *For the Orchid King*, she'd explained, *as a gesture of goodwill*.

Needless to say, I'd held my tongue.

Slipping on my apron and toolbelt, I tend the fire and shape the metal without complaint. Time spins out. My back twinges as I drive the hammer down, the impact shuddering up my arm, into my shoulder joint. The cowhide apron chafes the front of my thighs, and heat blankets me like damp cotton.

Uncomfortable thoughts begin to intrude. They appear as flashes of light and darkness: the gleam of a metal sword, the curve of straight white teeth. My heart thunders sickeningly. I swiftly block them out.

I'm beginning to shape the bevels into the blade when a shadow falls across my worktable. I startle so hard I almost drop the hammer on my boot.

Harper, her coal hair clasped in an elaborate updo, stands in the doorway backlit by the sun. A warm halo softens her shoulders in buttery light.

"I don't know how you can stand to work in these conditions," she remarks, waltzing in as though she has every right to. Her nose wrinkles. "I'm melting already."

As usual, Harper's commentary is unwanted. "Is there something I can do for you?" My attention returns to the blade's fiery tip, my tongs clamping the tang to hold it steady against the anvil.

"Am I not allowed to visit? This isn't your forge, you know. You just work here."

I scowl at her. "If you're here to start an argument, I will forcibly remove you from the area." Flipping the metal over, I finish shaping the tip. "And to be clear, this *is* my forge."

Bowing my head over the anvil, I return to hammering, effectively ending the conversation. Maybe Harper will finally leave me in peace.

Shaping a medial ridge requires an aggressive slant of the hammer, pushing the metal rather than drawing it out. This ensures the angles marking the ridge do not cross at the center, which thins the blade, thus weakening its structure.

Harper watches me work for a time, a dark shape in my periphery. "Do you mind if I look around?" she asks.

Lifting the dagger to the light, I examine the ridge. Almost perfect, but not quite. "Mother Mabel requires these blades by the end of the week. I can't afford a distraction." Back onto the anvil it goes, the hammer impacting the edges with short, punchy clinks.

"I won't distract you."

I cut her a sidelong glance, my suspicion evident.

Harper sighs. "I want to see the work you do. That's all."

And she does not view this as completely out of character?

"I wouldn't recommend it." Again, I inspect the ridge. Much better. The spine is sharply defined, and the angles do not cross. "You'll dirty your alb."

THE WEST WIND • 237

Harper smooths a palm across the pristine white fabric. She wears her red stole atop it—displayed diagonally over her chest to represent her service to the Father—and has for the past fortnight. Following initiation, acolytes are required to wear them for twenty-one days. The cincture, tied into three knots, hugs her waist.

"I'll live," she says.

Who am I to deny Harper what she wants? "Fine. But keep your distance."

With the medial ridge in place, I begin hammering in the bevels so its shape maintains uniformity. I heat the blade in sections, tip to base. At the next blow, another vision flashes: a tanned hand cradling a glass of golden liquid. My stomach turns.

"You really made all these?"

I falter, glance over my shoulder. Harper studies the line of daggers and knives hanging from the wall.

"I did." I would have thought that was obvious.

She reaches out. A touch, finger to blade, dragged down the peaked center where the bevels meet, across the swirl of silver and darker iron. Pulling her hand away, Harper pivots to face me. "I didn't realize your skills were so extensive."

"You never cared to know."

She picks her way around the various worktables. "You're right." I do not imagine the regret softening her admission.

With a heavy sigh, I set aside the partially finished dagger and shove my hammer into my toolbelt. It's impossible to concentrate with Harper present. Better to address the cause of her visit. I can work on the dagger when she leaves.

Grabbing an old rag, I wipe the sweat from my burning face, toss it into a nearby bin piled high with dirty cloth. "Why are you really here, Harper?"

She sets a small container on the table separating us. "The lunch bell rang. I didn't see you in the refectory, so I brought you something to eat."

Her unexpected benevolence takes me aback, and I lift a hand to my chest, rubbing the twinge there. Since my return to Thornbrook, I have had little appetite.

"Thank you." Of all the recent oddities, none are stranger than Harper's kindness. We are not friends, exactly. But neither are we enemies. "If that's all . . ."

"Actually, I wanted to ask your opinion on something." She moves as if to perch on one of the rickety chairs, then draws away, likely noting its dusty state.

"Very well." The sooner she asks, the sooner she can depart.

Harper again glances at the vacant seat, frowns, and sits. The sight pleases me. "I've been speaking to Mother Mabel about Thornbrook's future. I wanted to ask about changes you'd like to see implemented. We're to begin planning after the tithe."

Sinking into the opposite chair, I study the woman who was once my most abhorred rival, yet who has recently become someone I might one day respect. A leader of the faith.

She squirms beneath my gaze. Crosses and uncrosses her arms. "Well? Do I need to repeat myself?"

There is the Harper I know. "Mother Mabel requested this of you?" Once a year, the abbess meets with the acolytes to outline proposals regarding the allocation of funds, renovations, community presence, and miscellaneous projects. While novitiates do not vote on final decisions, we are often petitioned for suggestions on ways to make improvements.

"No," says Harper. "I approached her myself."

"You remembered our conversation from Under." When we spoke of duty, responsibility, neglect. It feels like a lifetime ago.

"I did." She straightens, hands arranged artfully across her lap like lovely porcelain figurines. "Is that a problem?"

"I think it's admirable you want to implement change." Unwittingly, my face softens. Faith is not stagnant. Neither is Harper, it seems. "Have you spoken to the other novitiates?"

"I have. They've given me much to consider."

Knowing Harper, she will not leave until I comply with her wishes. "I mentioned the idea of an apprenticeship program. I believe such a program would benefit not only Thornbrook, but the entire community. If you could bring that to Mother Mabel's attention, I'd appreciate it."

"Consider it done."

Since Harper's ascension, I've seen little of her. This new post requires long days on the road, traveling from town to town, spreading the Father's word. Admittedly, it was a beautiful ceremony. A hush blanketed the church as Mother Mabel drew the red stole across Harper's white alb.

I cannot deny my envy. That could have been me. It was I who obtained Meirlach. But I was not the one to gift it to Mother Mabel as proof of my worth.

"How have you been?" Harper abruptly asks.

A bead of sweat trickles down my temple, which I swipe away. "Well enough." Though I have not opened the Text since my return. It sits on my desk, gathering dust. "And you? Hopefully Isobel isn't too put out that you've moved out of your dormitory room, now that you're an acolyte." Whoever next enters Thornbrook will have the pleasure of cohabitating with Isobel.

"Actually," she says, "Isobel and I are no longer friends."

"Truly?" Now that she mentions it, I've noticed they dine separately during meals. They no longer arrive to service together either. No wonder the halls are quieter.

She shrugs. "Our values don't align as they once did."

Years Harper has spent feigning assurance. And now the walls have crumbled, vulnerability displayed without artifice ... She has transformed in ways I did not believe possible. "Do you miss her?"

"It's not Isobel I miss, exactly. It's the security of her presence."

"You're lonely."

Harper swallows, then nods. Whatever animosity I once felt toward her is gone. I feel only sympathy, the faint ache of repressed pain.

"I do not regret distancing myself from Isobel," she whispers. "Serving the Father as an acolyte has made me feel closer to Him. I feel more certain of my place."

"I am glad." A strained smile is all I can offer. "It's what you always wanted."

"But I didn't earn it." She holds my gaze until I look away.

We have had this conversation before. "You earned it," I say quietly. "We both entered Under. We both faced terrible things."

"But you bested the Stallion," she argues.

"Luck, pure and simple." It sounds like the truth. It tastes like a lie.

"It was not." She speaks gently and with newfound compassion, another positive change since her appointment. "You knew what you were doing wielding that blade, just as you knew what you were doing when you ordered me to take the sword to Mother Mabel and claim it was I who had found it."

My attention slides to the open doorway. Since my return from Under, Mother Mabel has not visited me in the forge. Neither has she approached me in the halls. She has given me space, as if suspecting I need the solitude.

"You are an acolyte." My gaze returns to Harper. "I thought this was what you wanted."

"It's also what you wanted," she points out.

Wanted—a word stuck firmly in the past.

The truth is this: I no longer know what I want or what drives me. Under broke something in me, and I fear the damage is irreparable. "It did not seem appropriate to move forward when I was questioning my place here."

Indeed, I questioned much when Harper and I emerged from Under weeks before, bruised and battered beyond belief, my heart in tatters. I had given my life to the Father. How could He lead me astray? How could He have allowed me to trust Zephyrus blindly, only to have him sink a blade into my back? Had I not been a steadfast follower? Or was I punished for involving myself with a man?

"Isn't it in times of uncertainty that we need Him the most?" Harper counters.

"You know, I think I liked you better when you were unbearable."

Harper laughs. Surprisingly, I do, too. It is not a true belly laugh, but it is something. When we grow quiet, I say, "Once the tithe is done, I will reconsider my place. Until then, I'd rather not think about the quest at all."

"About that." Her mouth flattens into a line. "There's something I think you should see." Pulling an object from her pocket, she sets it in her palm, a glass orb in a flood of morning light.

My heart knocks once against my ribs, then stills.

When I last saw the roselight, I threw it as hard as I could into the Stallion's Grotto. Miraculously, it remains whole. Not even a crack. Harper must have retrieved it prior to our flight from Under.

"You see it, don't you?" Harper murmurs.

Inside the delicate casing, the soft pink glow I've come to expect has muddied to gray murk and bloodshot scarring—a hemorrhaging.

I lean back in my chair, needing distance from the orb. The color worries me. Something is not right. "Why would you take this? It belongs to Under. Nothing good can come of it."

"Call it an impulse." Harper taps a fingernail against the glass, the chime momentarily brightening the cloud that has drifted over me. "Things ended messily between you and Zephyrus, but I suspected it would not be the last you saw of each other. You may still have need of this."

A familiar dread oozes through my gut. "That was not your decision to make."

"It's been four weeks, Brielle."

"And? Why does that matter? I'm never going back." As for the Bringer of Spring, he may rot.

Harper takes her time responding, perhaps remembering our return trip to Carterhaugh. Under's strange enchantments offered us safe passage via the grassy path. We returned to Thornbrook unscathed. She did, anyway.

"I've watched you," she says. "You're listless, unhappy, unmotivated. You sleep and work in your forge. You do nothing else."

She is wrong. I spend hours in bed, it's true, but I am wide awake, my heart galloping despite my listless state. When the sun finally breaks over Carterhaugh, I wipe the crust from my eyes and go about my day. I think only of numbers. Ten knives, twenty, forty, more. Numbers do not lie. Numbers are absolute.

"I think you need closure."

"What I need," I growl, hands clamped around the arms of my chair, "is to be left in peace."

"Is it peace you're after," she challenges, "or denial?"

I've half a mind to chuck a hammer at her head, though her skull is so hard I doubt it would leave even a dent.

With some effort, I pacify myself. I'm not angry at Harper. I'm angry because she asks all the right questions.

"So you don't want this?" she demands. "You do not wonder why the roselight has dulled?" Another tap against the glass. When I fail to respond, her face falls. "Very well." She heads for the door.

I'm halfway out of my seat before I realize I've moved. "Wait!"

Her pitying gaze weakens my knees, and I fall into my chair as Harper returns, offering me the roselight without judgment. As soon as I grasp the cool sphere, my heart begins to palpitate with increasing distress. There is a sluggish pulsing against the glass—a flagging heartbeat. "What happened to it?"

"I wish I knew," she says. "It's gotten worse since we returned."

What would cause the West Wind's roselight to change color? I recall Zephyrus' cry of pain as the Orchid King assaulted him. Pierus, whose limbs gorge on blood.

I return the roselight to Harper. My palm stings where it touched the glass. "It's no longer my concern."

"Even if this roselight signals that he's in trouble? You would turn from him in his hour of need?"

What of my needs? The West Wind didn't care for them, only his own, and shattered my trust in the process. "I would. He doesn't deserve my help, or anyone's help, for that matter. The West Wind only acts out of self-interest."

"I'm not so sure about that."

A muscle pops in my jaw as my back molars grind together. Harper has no idea what she's talking about.

"Remember when we arrived at that village after you saved me from the lake? The matriarch wanted something in exchange for aiding us."

"What of it?"

"I overheard Zephyrus speaking to the matriarch. She wanted his eyes, Brielle. His *eyes*."

Shock worms through me, though I give no outward sign of my distress. "He didn't agree, did he?"

She gives me a knowing look, which I ignore. "No, but he did agree to gift his blood once a month for the remainder of his life."

I hate the relief that stirs in me. "So he made a deal. It's what he does, Harper. He sees what he wants, and he does whatever it takes to get it."

"It wasn't just that. He could have let me die. I was disposable. Oh, don't give me that look. You know I'm right. You were the stronger candidate. You would have done whatever it took to reach Meirlach. Zephyrus knew this, yet he put his life on the line to ensure my recovery. He didn't need to do that."

The twinge in my chest returns. It feels uncomfortably like guilt. "It doesn't matter. It's done."

Harper shakes her head. "Even to yourself, you lie."

"Enough."

"I know you want nothing to do with him—"

"I said enough!"

I blink, and the world comes into focus. I'm standing, fists raised, prepared to land blows.

Harper watches me steadily. "You care for Zephyrus."

My knees wobble, and I lower myself onto the chair. It's pointless to pretend otherwise. "I wish I didn't." I drop my gaze to the floor, the scuffed wooden planks.

"But you do. So now you must decide what to do about it."

I've already made my decision. "I'm going to finish these daggers for Mother Mabel, and once the tithe is done, I will not think of Under ever again." In time, I hope to return to my old self. One day, that red stole will rest upon my shoulder, if I am fortunate.

"Even if it means denying your heart?"

The heart, I've learned, can never be trusted.

"I broke my vows, Harper."

Perfect Brielle, who can do no wrong. Those words linger like a smear on my skin.

"But they were your first vows," she says, "not your final vows."

It shouldn't make a difference. Obedience, purity, devotion. Here they rest in pieces. My only saving grace is that Harper didn't inform Mother Mabel of what transpired on our journey. Then again, she doesn't know I nearly gave my body to Zephyrus on the grasses of a moonlit glen. "Nothing is more important than our faith. Mother Mabel says so."

"What if Mother Mabel is wrong?"

My head snaps up. "You can't say things like that."

"And why not?" A haughtily arched brow, arms crossed as she surveys me.

"Because—" Oh, I haven't the slightest idea why. "Because it is written. Because it has been foretold. Because it is truth. Isn't that why you joined Thornbrook? You said so yourself you joined after one of the acolytes helped you search for your lost dog. The Father spoke to you then. There is no other explanation."

An uncomfortable emotion passes over her tightened features. "Brielle." She rubs a hand across her eyes, mouth pinched in reluctance. "I made that story up."

"What?"

"I lied. I never had a dog. But the well needed a story from my past, and I was too ashamed to tell the truth."

I'm speechless, but rather impressed the Well of Past did not sense the deceit. "Then why did you become a novitiate? Why give yourself to the Father?"

Her fingers tense atop her thighs, then relax. "My home life was awful. Yes, my sisters and I attended a prestigious academy, but I neglected to mention that they were superior to me in all ways, and I failed after the first year."

I stare at her in astonishment. I had no idea.

"My parents could not tolerate my inability to live up to their standards. They considered me a stain upon their reputation, and punished me accordingly once I returned home a failure. Some days, I was whipped so severely I fainted." Her eyes go cold.

"Harper—"

She lifts a hand. "I need to say this. Please." With a deep breath, she continues. "My home was poison. Most nights I slept little, so deeply rooted was the dread. But on the Holy Days, my family would attend church at the abbey. I witnessed the Daughters' kindness to others. I felt safe there. And I decided their life must be better than the one I was living. A few days later, I packed my bags. I told no one where I was going. That was ten years ago. My family probably thinks I'm dead."

Those who embrace the devout life all seek to gain that which they lack. I sought acceptance. Harper sought belonging. We are not so different, she and I.

"Mother Mabel is more of a mother to me than the woman who birthed me," Harper continues. "I crave her approval. I want to *matter*, do you understand?" Before I can respond, she says, "I have always felt threatened by you. No matter what I did, there was always Brielle— bright, shining Brielle—who could do no wrong. No matter my efforts, I forever stood in your shadow."

An awkward silence descends. All this time, she struggled with feeling small, just as I did. "I didn't know you felt that way," I murmur.

"I couldn't compete. You were too good, too diligent, too pure." A shake of her head.

"I did not realize it was a competition."

She lifts a hand, touches the base of her neck in what I imagine to be a gesture of self-compassion. "You're right. It shouldn't be, yet I still viewed it as such, even after you *saved* me. From the darkwalkers. From the lake. At times, from my own stupidity. I—" Her eyes flutter shut. "I never thanked you, not once during that long journey." Harper opens her blue, blue eyes. "Thank you," she says with an openness I have never before witnessed, "for saving my life."

Her sincerity washes over me, and embraces my hurt with newfound tenderness. I did not expect this, but I cannot pretend that the bruised, wounded girl I'd been hadn't hoped for Harper's acknowledgment.

"You're welcome," I say.

"You showed me there is always room for improvement. Since my appointment, I've learned that faith does not have to be rigid. It can change. It can be reinterpreted. If we do not remain the same, why should our beliefs?"

The idea doesn't sit comfortably with me. Not because I disagree, but because I have pondered exactly that.

"If you are truly a Daughter of Thornbrook," Harper says, "you will find your way back to the Father."

I have questioned many things, but never the Father. Never my god. How can the world, so vast and complex, exist without the touch of a divine hand? Thornbrook saved my life and gave me purpose when I had none. Is that not a miracle?

"I appreciate your honesty, Harper," I murmur, "but I would like to be alone." I do not know my way forward. I am frightened and unmoored. I seek only my thoughts. "I've a lot of work to do."

Harper dips her chin, visibly saddened. "All right." She pads to the doorway, but stops at the threshold to look back. "I misjudged you, and for that, I'm sorry, truly sorry, for all the pain I have caused you. There were times I treated you no better than a dog. I was shortsighted, selfish, and cruel. It shames me to know we could have been friends, had I not behaved so horribly."

The apology manages to worm its way inside my heart. I hold it there, warm and healing, as her footsteps recede into the bright morning.

24

A DAY BEFORE THE TITHE, I HAMMER THE FINAL BLOW. ITS RING shimmers with clarity inside the hot, stuffy forge, dawn creeping across the threshold in strips of dappled violet and gold.

My arm shakes as I lower the hammer onto the anvil. Seventeen hours from shapeless metal to sharpened blade and it is nearly done. Grasping the hilt, I drive the dagger into the bucket of salt water at my feet. A hiss of steam erupts where water and hot metal collide. When it clears, I hold the blade aloft, inspecting its tapering from every angle, the lovely, flattened gleam. It will do.

I hang it on the wall to cool with the others. Twenty-six daggers, all iron-forged. A six-month task, now complete.

The sun continues its climb behind the mountain as I emerge into the brightness of full day. The wind does not blow. It hasn't for many weeks now. I have wondered why, and I worry.

Upon reaching the abbess' house, I knock on the door.

"Enter."

Pushing it open, I step inside the foyer and head down the short hallway where Mother Mabel's office is located. She sits at her desk, penning a message. Beside the open window at her back, Meirlach hangs from a wall mount, a pillar of sharpened steel capped in gold.

At the interruption, she lifts her head, sets down her quill. "Brielle. What can I do for you?"

"I've finished the last of the daggers," I say, nudging the door open further. "They're ready for transport into Under."

Her smile is brief, gone within the next heartbeat, but the affection in her eyes lingers as she gestures to the vacant seat across from her desk. "That's wonderful news. All twenty-six are accounted for?"

"Yes, Mother Mabel." I perch on the edge of the chair, hands folded in my lap.

"Excellent. Your hard work has not gone unnoticed. This will benefit all of Thornbrook. Pierus will appreciate your contribution as well."

I do not care to benefit the Orchid King. I forge the daggers so we may continue to lease Thornbrook's land for another seven years. "I'm happy to serve Thornbrook in any way I can."

The skin around her eyes smooths, all fine lines pressed into dewy youth. "Indeed. What would we do without you?"

I've asked that question myself. In time, the Abbess on High would train another novitiate to replace me. Someone needs to light the forge.

I push to my feet. "If that is all."

She holds up a hand. "Forgive me, Brielle, but I have to ask. Are you all right?" Concern shadows her gaze. "You seem troubled."

My body feels heavy in uncomfortable ways. There is much to say, but I'm not sure whether I have the strength for this conversation. I feel myself spiraling, warmth in my face and sweat on my palms.

"When you returned to Thornbrook, it was clear the trials of your journey had changed you." Though not the gentlest woman, Mother Mabel speaks kindly, perhaps sensing my distress. "You stood taller. You walked with surety. You did not cower in the face of adversity. But there has been a deadness to your gaze that concerns me."

A deadness. That sounds about right.

She shifts the quill and parchment to the corner of her desk, making room for her hands. The long, belled sleeves of her alb hiss as they pass over the naked wood. "Do you know why a novitiate must complete a task prior to taking their final vows?"

"To prove their worth?"

"To an extent." Fingers interlaced, she leans forward, commanding my attention with little effort. "Because many women join Thornbrook at such a young age, it is unfair to assume they seek the same life once they become adults. The task is a catalyst. It helps a novitiate determine what future they seek. A life in service to the Father? A life beyond that?"

The mission *did* test me. It snapped me into pieces and forced me to question if they fit together as seamlessly as they had a year before. Mother Mable cannot know the agony of the experience. How out of place I feel. How confused.

"I gave you space," she continues, "because it was clear you needed to process what had occurred. However, there has been little change since you returned." Set beneath pale eyebrows, her black eyes lock on to mine, apprehension swimming in their depths. "Will you tell me what plagues you?"

Facing Mother Mabel is never easy. In the morning bright, it seems impossible. She has given me council in my darkest hours. She made room for me at Thornbrook despite my questionable upbringing. I feel that I've failed her. "I've been struggling, Mother Mabel. It's true."

A brief nod. "There's no shame in it. Have you spoken to the Father about this?"

"I have not." My guilt is too great.

"Remember that the Father loves you. We only need to ask for His forgiveness."

"What if—" Shame hurtles up my airway and sticks at the back of my tongue. How could she possibly have known of my needs? Even I did not know. "What if I do not deserve it?"

At once, she rises, skirting the desk in a cloud of sweet incense, hands gentle on my shoulders. "Brielle."

My heart thunders from the abbess' intense scrutiny.

"Have you broken your vows? You have not given your body to another, have you?"

I cannot bear the disappointment, nor the accusatory tone. She knows. I have never been able to hide what I feel.

"Are you still pure?"

I hesitate. Technically, I am still a virgin, so I nod. "I am."

The deepest, most soulful sigh leaves the abbess. Surprisingly, she is smiling. "Please do not despair if you made a mistake. We all do. That you still wish to be a shepherd of the Father proves your loyalty despite your trials." She strokes my cheek. The display of affection is more than I could have hoped for.

"Thank you," I whisper.

"You have a good heart, Brielle. I hate to see you suffering." She frowns, drops her hand. "Promise me you will speak to the Father tonight."

"I will."

Satisfied, Mother Mabel returns to her desk. "Speaking of the quest." *Tap, tap, tap* goes her fingertip atop the desk. "Can I ask what happened in the Grotto? I admit I was certain you would obtain Meirlach first."

Revealing these underlying truths—that I do not believe I deserve the station, that I fear my altering mind—puts my past, present, and future into question. I must gift Mother Mabel the truth, but just enough to avoid further inquiry. "Harper entered the Grotto, as did I. She is equally worthy of the spot."

"She slayed the Stallion?"

"The Stallion is not dead."

Her eyebrows climb high onto her forehead in permanent fixation. "You're telling me you and Harper managed to escape the Grotto without taking the Stallion's life?" Before I can respond, she shakes her head, mouth slanting into her cheek with wry amusement. "You were undoubtedly lucky. Kelpies are a conniving lot, and the flesh of a virgin is an undeniable temptation."

Was it luck? I bested him fairly, blade to blade. He questioned my will, and I proved mine would not bend. Something nags at me though. "May I ask, Mother Mabel, how you know so much about the Stallion?"

"You are not the only one to have entered his Grotto and survived."

I am frozen in sudden memory. What was it the Stallion had said? *Only once before has a mortal entered my lair and escaped with their life.*

How did Mother Mabel acquire the necessary information to best the Stallion? I would expect the fair folk to know such details, not a woman from Carterhaugh. Then again, she was held captive in Under, long ago. Was her visit to the Stallion connected with her escape?

"But," the abbess continues, unaware of my mental backflips, "the question remains of how Harper claimed Meirlach first. You and I both know she hasn't the means to defeat a creature as shrewd as the Stallion. She barely knows the difference between a knife and a fork."

Mother Mabel's opinion of Harper doesn't sit well with me. It borders on disrespectful. "Harper may have her faults, but she has her strengths, too." Despite her complaints, she faced Under tenaciously, plowing forward with fierce resolve. It's hard not to respect someone who defies the rules so easily.

"I had complete faith that you would return to Thornbrook victorious," Mother Mabel says. "The position was always supposed to be yours."

Does she sense my dishonesty? Yes, I won Meirlach, but when the time arrived, I insisted Harper take ownership of the sword instead. Anyway, if the position was supposed to be mine, why pit me against someone else?

"Well." She sighs and folds her hands atop her desk. "There is always next year."

Next year. It rings hollowly. Will I have to complete another soul-destroying quest to prove my worth? The thought tires me.

My attention shifts to Meirlach. The ruby-inlaid pommel winks like a fiery eye.

Mother Mabel notices the direction of my gaze and smiles. She appears more relaxed in the weapon's presence. Reassured, even. "Beautiful, isn't it?"

"It is." A true work of artistry. The fuller is the straightest I have seen, the rounded groove extending the length of the blade.

"Meirlach has been in the Stallion's possession for a long time. So long, in fact, that its existence passed into myth." Opening a drawer in her desk, she pulls out the Text. "Admittedly, I was not aware of its existence until my captivity. An unfortunate, if fortuitous, turn of events."

My skin prickles in sudden awareness. Rarely does Mother Mabel speak of that time. In all my years as a novitiate, I have only heard her mention it once.

"Seven years," she whispers, "and all I had was the Text. The Book of Change was my salvation. It told me of Meirlach. It reminded me all was not lost. Days after I learned of its existence, I met another prisoner, a mortal man who was an adept swordsman. He taught me how to wield a blade. He reminded me I was strong. I vowed to continue my training once I returned aboveground, and I have."

I'm arranging pieces of information into a natural flow. Seven years may have passed in Carterhaugh, but how many lifetimes did Mother Mabel experience in Under, trapped in the strange enchantment of the realm? At some point, Mother Mabel visited the Grotto. She also escaped with her life. Whatever she stole from the Stallion, it wasn't Meirlach. Perhaps she was unable to outwit it. I communicate these thoughts to the abbess.

"Brielle." The sound is caught firmly between fondness and exasperation. "Are you suggesting I lacked the cunning needed to steal Meirlach? If so, I don't appreciate having my shortcomings pointed out. You should know better."

I am twenty-one years of age, yet in this moment, I feel like a child. *Know better.* I have weathered this chiding before. "I apologize, Mother Mabel."

She sighs. "No, you're right. I was unable to take Meirlach from the Stallion. That is why the acquisition is so vital. With this blade"—she sweeps an arm toward the weapon—"we can guarantee our protection."

Something she did not have when the Orchid King stole away those three novitiates decades ago. We, as women, must go to greater lengths to protect ourselves. To work twice as hard as any man but reap only half the rewards.

"Is that why you sought the Father?" I ask. "For protection?"

Silence.

Tucked into my lap, my hands bunch, sweaty skin growing warmer with every heartbeat. I've overstepped. Mother Mabel's bristling gaze is evidence enough. "I apologize—"

"To an extent," she clips out. "I grew up poor, Brielle. Very poor. We lived in a one-room hut on the outskirts of Aranglen. I never knew my father, not really. He left my mother days following my brother's birth.

"It was a difficult life, as you can imagine. When I was a girl of fourteen, my brother took ill following an unusual cold snap, then my mother." Though her face tightens, she maintains composure. "They were dead within the month, and I was orphaned, with no prospects for work."

I had no idea. "I'm so sorry."

Her nostrils flare, and she holds up a hand. "Do not pity me. We all face trials in life. Those just happened to be mine."

I stare at the abbess, a mortal woman who has not aged since her escape from Under decades ago. Whatever words of comfort I might offer, she does not want them.

"Luckily," she goes on, "a woman noticed me wandering the market one evening and brought me to Clovenshire—Aranglen's abbey. I began as a novitiate. Two years later, I took my final vows. I stayed as an acolyte for another decade, deepening my relationship with the Father. Following my thirteenth year at the abbey, I was elected Abbess of Thornbrook. I've been here ever since."

It makes perfect sense that Mother Mabel would climb the ranks. Those of us abandoned by the world must work hard to put down roots. "Do you ever consider returning to your old life?"

"By the Father, no. Who would I turn to? Where would I call home? Those who do not have His will in their lives . . . I pity them." The tips of her fingers skim the Text's leather cover with reverence. "They are lost, as I was, as you were."

I'm not so sure. Kilkare's residents do not seem lost. They are mothers and painters and carpenters and bakers and merchants and

254 • ALEXANDRIA WARWICK

brothers and believers. Most welcome the Father in their lives, though not to the same extent as the Daughters of Thornbrook. It is enough for them.

Mother Mabel leans back in her chair, studying me. "Is that what you want, Brielle? To go out into the world and leave us?"

"N-no," I breathe, horrified by the thought. "Of course not." My heart thuds, but I'm uncertain where the fear stems from. "It was a curiosity, nothing more."

She nods, appeased. "Thornbrook is your place. It will always be your place."

My place, but not my home. I do not miss the distinction.

For I am a bladesmith, but I did not place a hammer in my hand. Mother Mabel did. I did not choose to come to Thornbrook. My mother abandoned me. The Text tells me how to interpret the world, what is acceptable and what is not, what morals shape a woman or a man.

I love the Father, but can I not love Him without the title of novitiate? I'm not rushing to leave. I don't *want* to leave. But I wonder what else awaits me out there, what shape my life would take if I chose differently.

"Have you given thought to my proposal?"

I refocus on Mother Mabel. Last week, she asked if I was interested in participating in the tithe tomorrow evening. It would give me an excuse to return to Under and search for Zephyrus. Alternatively, I could abandon the West Wind as he abandoned me. I could stay here, in Carterhaugh. I could forget.

"If I could offer you some advice?" It is kindly, her tone. For whatever reason, my throat tightens with impending tears. "Go to the church tonight. Speak to the Father. Maybe He can help guide your path."

I gaze out the window. A blue sky speckled with wistful clouds, the perfect day for a morning stroll. How quickly my mind returns to a green-eyed god.

"It is your choice, in the end," Mother Mabel says. "Should you choose to participate, we will gather in the quadrangle tomorrow at dusk. Take the day to think about it."

Bowing my head, I reply, "I will."

Pushing to my feet, I make my way to the door. Before I depart, however, I've one more question that needs answering. "Why did the fair folk let you live?"

Mother Mabel stares at me coldly. "They did not *let* me live. Seven years I was trapped in Under, enduring countless horrors, without hope of ever escaping. I did what I had to do to return to Carterhaugh, and I don't regret it." A thin, dark smile crawls across her mouth. "It turns out, there are some things not even Under can break."

25

Later that evening, I light my lamp. The wick catches, a star sheltered within the thin, curved glass, etching fine shadows across the contents of my bedroom. My heart beats rabbit-quick, yet my hands are steady as I push open the shutters to hang the lamp in my window, as I had once done months before.

The bell tolls, marking the eighth hour. Beyond the window, the air hangs static and warm from recent rain. I'm not so naive as to believe Zephyrus will see the lamp. After all, I have not sensed his presence in weeks. But if not him, then perhaps someone across the strait who seeks a light in the darkness, as I do.

After gathering clean clothes, I hasten for the bathhouse, soap and washcloth in hand. Though curfew isn't yet in effect, my peers have begun their evening prayers in the privacy of their dormitories. As for me, I've shut my emotions in rooms with locked doors, but tonight, I am ready to face them.

Upon reaching the bathhouse, I step into the tiled entryway. Empty, as suspected. A large, sunken tub claims the floor, three curved steps descending into the still pool.

My dress and undergarments fall away. I submerge myself in the chilly bathwater. Remnants from recent washings swirl in greasy clouds. Shivering, I force my head beneath the surface.

Obedience.

The water holds peace. Cold and muted it may be, but it casts no judgment. When my lungs pinch, I surge upward, head breaking the surface. I drag my soapy washcloth across my skin, prying every speck of dirt free until I am pink, flushed as a newborn.

Purity.

Dressed in a clean, dry alb, I head for the church. Its massive doors lie open, the nave's expansive belly resting in shadow broken by wells of light—the altar candles, which burn eternal.

Devotion.

Pews, arranged in tidy rows, await the warm bodies of tomorrow's Mass. The windows of brightly colored glass have extinguished. A rug unfurls, fern-like, down the center of the space before pooling at the altar's base: white marble draped in crimson cloth.

I rinse my hands in the lavabo. Once purified, I stride toward the low railing separating the presbytery from the sanctuary. There, I kneel upon the long, embroidered cushion, heart thundering. The roselight pulses weakly in my pocket.

Bowing my head, I rest my interlaced fingers on the wooden railing where we take Communion. I have found myself in these walls not once, but again and again. I seek the church because I am adrift and hope to find a bit of rock to cling to for a while.

"Hello, Father," I murmur. "It has been four weeks since my last visit." And I have borne that weight each passing day.

"First, I must say it was not my intention to ignore you, but much has happened since then." My voice, stricken with shame, hoarsens. "I have made questionable decisions. I brought a man into the abbey, but I confess that is the least of my transgressions."

The altar candles flare despite the lack of breeze. I tighten my sweaty fists until the shaking subsides. It must be said. I will shed all that I have carried, this fear of a slow altering within me. I will squeeze the confession from my tightening throat, every last drop wrung free.

"I had sexual relations with this man, Father." It sounds appalling when spoken aloud. "His name is Zephyrus. He kissed me, touched me, and I confess that I wanted it. It's wrong, I *know* it's wrong. A Daughter of Thornbrook must never yearn for man's flesh. But I hungered for him."

I shrink in place, tensing as a cold wind cuts across the crown of my skull, stirring the damp red curls. The Father is not pleased. That is to be expected.

"I know I shouldn't have trusted him. I told myself to keep my distance. And yet, I felt my will weakening in his presence. He is not like you, Father. He is selfish and self-serving, manipulative and careless." And sad, and desperate, and perhaps unwhole. "I confess that I care for him, despite his betrayal."

The shards inside my chest grind painfully. I gave all of myself only to learn I knew nothing of him, this Bringer of Spring.

"I came to you, Father, because I fear something terrible has befallen Zephyrus." As my throat cinches, my voice pitches high, ridding itself of the confession. "He is a man grown, far older and more experienced than I, but something bids me to go to him. I don't know what to do," I whisper, hunching farther over the railing, nearer to the altar and its trio of candles. "Tell me what to do, *please.*"

I am not certain. I am not strong. I am neither obedient, nor pure, nor devoted. There was a time when I was committed to those morals. They were, in all ways, my anchor.

Obedience: to abide by my duties as a novitiate.

Purity: the simplest vow, yet quickest to deteriorate.

Lastly, devotion. I'd planted this seed most readily. A devout life gave me purpose. It masked my loneliness—for a time.

It was never my intention to break my vows. I had truly believed I would live out my life on these grounds, my days spent on my knees before the church altar, my purpose one of singular importance. But I have exhumed new facets of the world, and I wonder: is Thornbrook still right for me?

"If my duty is to spread goodwill, then I ask you, Father, how I can turn away from someone in need, even if that person has betrayed me? Even if he is a man? A god?" It would be reckless to return to Under, and I'd risk more than my life. But I must know. I must understand *why*. "Will you not guide me through?"

The church seems to hollow out. My ears ring from the change in pressure. I receive no answer, no reassurance, no forgiveness. I came here for clarity, but I only feel more confused, a woman kneeling in an empty room, all the world's warmth deserted.

It is the greatest effort to stand. A greater one still to look upon the altar and understand what the silence means. I have erred. Regardless of my repentance, I made a choice, and the Father made His. There is no response as I depart the church, the altar candles swallowed by darkness. I fear there never will be again.

I do not return to my room. My feet carry me through the cloister, downhill toward the overgrown outer wall, the forge tucked at its base. Cooling air blankets the deep greenery, but it lasts only as far as the forge's threshold.

There the daggers hang, twenty-six blades, rows upon rows of glinting black teeth. I gather them woodenly, deposit them into the cart sitting outside the doorway. The clatter of metal splinters the still eve.

Tomorrow, I'll distribute the weapons at dusk. Once the Daughters of Thornbrook gather, Mother Mabel will look to me with a question: stay or go? I am still uncertain, and I begin tidying the space to keep busy when a shard of metal catches my attention in the back corner.

I kick aside a pile of old, rotten beams and lift what is most definitely a broken sword. Another segment peeks from underneath a pallet of wood. I drag it out, lift the pieces so they fit together.

I remember this blade. At the time, it had been my most ambitious work, but I'd hammered the metal too thinly. I still recall the sound of its fracturing, clean and sudden and cold.

My chest twinges at the memory. There had been tears, a furious sweep of them, as I'd knelt at my cot that evening for prayer. I'd wanted to be great. *Known*. For three years I'd apprenticed, toiling in that sweltering forge until my blisters burst and calluses collected in layers of toughened skin. I was a bladesmith, but I wasn't good enough. Not then. Not yet.

For whatever reason, I hadn't tossed the sword. I'd discarded it in a corner, and over the years, tools and material had piled atop it, burying the evidence of my failure.

Moving toward a worktable, I lay out the two segments. The blade's profile is quite good. My error occurred in the distal taper, or the reduction of the blade's thickness from hilt to tip. Ideally, one desires a gradual thinning of the steel. I'd hammered it with too much enthusiasm.

My hand tightens around the unfinished tang. I didn't stamp this blade with my touchmark. I was too young then, not yet a master. Now? I see the faults clearly. I understand the steps needed to repair this break. The sword lies in pieces, but if they fit together once, can they not do so again?

I get to work.

Gone is my exhaustion, the weight dragging at my bones. I begin by piling slow-burning kindling into the forge's stony mouth. Thick white smoke drifts through the cracks. Once the kindling catches, I layer it with additional coal, smothering the flame.

Tonight, I am awake. *Hungry.* How could I have forgotten? The charged air changes shape around me. My muscles lengthen and contract in a rhythm that is both grief and exaltation.

The heat climbs as I work the bellows, putting all my strength behind the motion. The fire speaks. It demands more, though sometimes less. When it cries *enough*, I know to step away, let it settle, before building it higher and brighter than before. For the blade to become whole again, everything must be melted and reshaped.

It takes the night. I heat the metal to a burning orange. I hammer it out before allowing it to cool, the metal strengthening. Again and again, I follow this process as the fire grows, exhaling mouthfuls of blistering heat.

I shape the point, then the blade's profile. The distal taper, then the bevels. I drive the blade into the fire, heat soaking into the searing metal, before setting it atop my anvil. The steel cools, white to orange to deep umber. Lifting the hammer above my head, I drive it down, the impact tossing sparks into the dark, to forge what was once broken into something whole and new.

26

Twenty-one Daughters of Thornbrook gather as the sky blackens and the evening bell tolls its final lament. Cloaked, hooded, devout, each carries an iron blade. They are my peers, but tonight, as I instruct each woman how to grasp the hilt, how to draw it safely from its sheath, they are my pupils. Their eyes exist as slots of darkness, watchful beneath their hoods.

Carterhaugh rattles and seethes beyond the outer wall. I can sense it—the hunger. The tithe calls for blood, and tonight, the price will be paid.

At the corner of the grassy quadrangle, Mother Mabel ties a scabbard at her waist. Hours earlier, I'd watched her sharpen Meirlach from my bedroom window, a high whine cutting the atmosphere as she dragged the whetting stone down the blade's edge.

"You skipped me."

Turning, I take in Harper, that haughtily lifted chin. Her long ebony braid snakes free of her raised hood.

When I do not immediately respond, she takes it upon herself to point out my misstep. "You showed every person how to draw their dagger but me. Why is that?"

I lift an eyebrow. "I thought you already knew what to do." At her blank expression, I elaborate, "You stick the pointed side into flesh?"

Harper blinks in surprise, then snorts. "Not my brightest moment, admittedly."

Indeed. It's comical that she once thought to best a god with nothing but a paltry blade. "Give me your hand."

As I did with the others, I lead her step-by-step through the motions of drawing the dagger from its sheath. In the background, the women stir nervously, a few choosing to walk the cloister while we wait.

"If you need to draw it," I say, angling closer so my voice doesn't carry, "hold the dagger like this." I rearrange her fingers so they curl around the hilt, her thumb brushing the top of her index finger. Harper's eyes meet mine, wide with uncertainty. "Just in case."

"Brielle." Mother Mabel glides toward me, hands linked at her front. Meirlach's ruby pommel emanates a pristine scarlet hue. "I take it you spoke with the Father?"

Harper retreats to give us privacy, and I force myself to meet the abbess' depthless gaze. "He helped set me on the right path." With some effort, the tension eases from my face. My mouth curves slightly. "My place is here."

She smiles in return. In all my years, I've never seen one reach her eyes. Tonight is no different. "As it should be."

Moving off, Mother Mabel directs everyone into position. We stand in two columns, our white albs peeking beneath the hems of our heavy wool cloaks, my pack sitting discreetly against my lower back. The novitiates wear white, the acolytes, red. We wear our trinity necklaces, our gloves. Harper and I stand shoulder to shoulder near the back.

A cold wind drags across the spiked blades of grass, and the mountain's chill settles. I've done all I could to protect what's mine. I placed milk and barley on my windowsill, at the threshold of my bedroom door. I've armored myself in iron.

"You all know why you're here." Mother Mabel lifts a hand to address the group. Not even the bone-white pallor of her skin penetrates the deep cowl of her hood.

"Tonight, the barrier between realms is at its thinnest, and another seven-year cycle draws to a close. Our journey will take us to Miles Cross.

Please understand the importance of your commitment. Participation in the tithe will allow us to retain ownership of Thornbrook and its surrounding lands for another seven years. The price is blood.

"For those of you who have never participated, please listen carefully. Do not speak. Touch nothing but your daggers. If someone offers you food or drink, you decline." Down the line she goes, looking each woman in the eye. "Do not step off the grassy path. When the time comes, you offer one drop of blood, nothing more." At the back of the line, she stops, voice ringing against the old stone pillars. "Lastly, do not take off your necklaces. Keep them safe."

Mother Mabel then strides back to the head of the columns. "Remember. Although we have protections in place, we venture into unfamiliar territory. The rules of Under are not ours to control." She scans the group. "Any questions?"

Our names, I think. Why would she not mention our names?

"I already warned the others about speaking their names aloud," Harper murmurs with a sidelong glance in my direction, though she, too, appears confused by Mother Mabel's oversight.

I'm so surprised by Harper's consideration I can only nod mutely.

With a wave of her hand, we fall into step behind the Abbess on High and depart Thornbrook beneath the gatehouse archway, its black points cutting as cleanly as knives through the dark.

As we make our way toward the entrance, Under thrums beneath our boots, hungry for mortal flesh. A dull roar announces the River Twee. Clumped together on the sloping bank, we stare at the lashing current galloping downstream. Harper leans into my side, shaking. I'm not certain she's aware of it.

"Deep breath," I whisper.

She snaps her head toward me, pupils blown. "Are you afraid?"

"Yes," I whisper, but not for the reason she thinks. The West Wind draws me to this realm's edge. I must know of his welfare. I must accept that I have changed. "It will be all right," I tell Harper.

Not far from where we congregate, the water splits. Floating a foot above the rapids, slender wisps of water spiral upward, merging into the pinnacle of an ornate archway, beneath which rests a set of translucent doors fashioned from sheets of falling water. Like panes of wavering glass, they cast reflections in the low light.

Those nearest to the river clump even tighter together. "By the Father," someone whispers. None of us have ever witnessed an enchantment such as this.

Two gilded handles materialize, and my heart begins to pound with increasing urgency. As the rushing current tapers off, the river recedes to reveal a handful of flat stones leading to the strange doorway.

"We will enter in pairs," Mother Mabel informs us.

Something brushes my hand. I glance down to see Harper's gloved fingers twined lightly around mine.

Lifting my head, I meet her wide-eyed gaze. As the doors crack open, the sweet reek of decay rolls forth. How could I have forgotten this scent? Growing things trapped beneath the earth.

Harper's pale, sweaty face flashes beneath her cowl. She remembers what it feels like inside the beast's belly. She remembers, as I do, the hair-trigger awareness of having become prey.

My fingers tighten around hers. We may not have entered Under as a team months ago, but even the prickliest rose still blooms. Tonight, we stand together.

Mother Mabel enters first with one of the acolytes, their forms swallowed by the sheets fluttering beneath the archway. In their absence, the women stir uncomfortably, reluctant to brave the enchantment.

"You're next." Isobel shoves a pair forward. They stumble, recoiling from the strange, ethereal phenomenon of water falling without a source.

The older woman reaches outward, and her hand passes through without the slightest splash. "It's dry!"

The two loiter with indecision, then forge ahead. Pair by pair, the Daughters of Thornbrook enter Under. Then, it is our turn.

I am a blade.

Harper and I pass beneath the archway, entering a lush grove carpeted in ferns, their crenated edges just shy of being fully opened. The grassy path curves right, a paler stripe through the rich forest undergrowth. Mother Mabel counts heads and, once satisfied we are all accounted for, gestures for us to follow, her cloak sweeping across the dense understory.

The sky marks a trail of twinkling light as we navigate glens and the widest, deepest rivers. Every so often, something scuttles through the underbrush, tearing screams from the women, who whip their knives free with a complete lack of finesse.

"Stupid fools." Harper slaps the wrist of a younger girl. "Put that away," she snarls, and the novitiate is so terrified she returns the dagger to its sheath without question.

"Can't believe I'm back in this wretched place," Harper mutters.

I push aside a low-hanging bough, waiting until she passes by before asking, "Then why did you volunteer?"

"I wasn't going to." She sniffs, brushes specks of pollen from her scarlet cloak. "But Mother Mabel said you might participate, and I thought it important for me to be here, too."

Unbelievably, it sounds like an admission. "Are you saying you're here for moral support?"

"So what if I am?" Arms crossed, she forges down the path, jostling the younger novitiates with far more aggression than is necessary. "Someone has to watch over you."

I bite the inside of my cheek, though the smile tries its hardest to break free. "Are you forgetting who defeated those darkwalkers?"

"Are you forgetting who convinced Zephyrus to save your life after you were envenomated?"

Fresh nerves stir in my chest at the mention of his name. Harper notices my plummeting mood and sobers. "I'm sorry. I know returning isn't easy for you."

There must be something wrong with me, to feel this softness in my heart for the prickliest woman I know. "It will be over soon," I say. I *hope*.

By the time we reach a broad plain, muck coats my boots and the hem of my cloak. In the distance, a bridge arches over a wide, glassy waterway. The River Mur, I assume.

"Nearly there," Mother Mabel calls over her shoulder. We hurry in single file, crossing the bridge and delving into a vast network of underground tunnels, the walls stained in dim scarlet light. The deeper we journey into the warren, the slower we shuffle, the women dragging their feet as the odor of rot and decay intensifies. Someone gags, and gooseflesh pimples my arms.

Then—light. The tightness in my chest loosens as we enter a soaring stone chamber, its heart claimed by a pond nestled in wild-flower-studded grass. Lily pads float upon the crystal pool, and turtles gather on the banks where moonlight pours through the opening above.

Miles Cross.

It's beautiful. A picturesque painting edged in the softest pastels. And yet, all light must end. Beyond the circle of illumination, the fair folk lie in wait, cloaked in shadow. I glimpse a long-fingered hand, the curve of a ram's horn. A peal of laughter erupts beyond sight, and the group shudders.

Mother Mabel grips Meirlach's hilt and scans the area, catching sight of something lurking in the gloom.

A long, milky root slithers from its depths.

My fellow peers shrink as the Orchid King drags his bulk forward. Sweat gleams on his pale torso, every muscle chiseled to perfection. We remember his visit to Thornbrook. We have not forgotten.

"Mother Mabel." Pierus spreads his arms, flashing a set of straight white teeth. "Welcome."

The gloom retreats momentarily, revealing a great, three-tiered amphitheater surrounding the field. It appears as though the entirety of Under is present in the audience, every manner of creature and beast.

"Pierus." Our abbess glides forward with regal authority, her hood pushed back to uncover the pale strands of her hair. Mother Mabel and the Orchid King speak in low tones for a time, and I glance over my shoulder to the tunnel we emerged from. Once the tithe begins, I will be unable to leave. It must be now.

Ensnared by the vicious beauty of Miles Cross, my peers barely stir as I shuffle toward the back of the group. From there, it's a stone's throw to the tunnel, the darkness cloaking me from sight.

I walk with haste. I do not run, for the sound will draw attention. Back straight, chin high. I'm nearly to the end.

"Brielle."

My hand spasms around my dagger. The mental image of what awaits me beyond the cave slams shut as I gird my stomach for a difficult conversation. Tucked inside my pocket, the roselight pulses erratically.

Reluctantly, I turn. Harper steps forward, hood pushed back, bright blue gaze searching mine. "What did I tell you about speaking names aloud?" I whisper.

She stops, clearly taken aback by my admonishment. Then her eyes thin. She peers left, right, ahead, behind. Slowly, so as to make a point. The tunnel is deserted. We are alone.

"No one is around to hear us," she states.

"That we can *see*."

Harper's attention shifts to my blade. "What are you doing?"

She knows. And I know. There is little point in voicing it aloud.

"There's not much time," I murmur. "As it is, I'm afraid I'm already too late."

"You're going to find Zephyrus."

I swallow, fighting the urge to deflect, and nod. I'm not sure how long I'll be gone. Once I leave the safety of Miles Cross, I forfeit Mother Mabel's protection.

All I know is this: I cannot go on living a lie. Ten years I have dedicated my life to Thornbrook, but lately, my heart has yearned for something more. I have grown to care for a man. He lied and he deceived and he betrayed, yet something compels me to find him.

Harper glances over her shoulder before striding closer. "I understand you want to help him, but if you leave, we won't have enough women to complete the tithe. You would leave us vulnerable?"

I bristle at the implication, yet hold my tongue. If our positions were switched, I would demand the same. "The Orchid King said twenty-one

Daughters of Thornbrook, right?" She nods. Harper is correct: without my presence, the total number of volunteers to gift their blood would fall to twenty. However—"Mother Mabel is a Daughter, too." Granted, she has achieved the highest station one can attain, but she is still a Daughter nonetheless.

Harper considers this detail with pursed lips, then rubs her forehead hard enough to leave a mark. "She will notice you have gone. She's too observant."

"Not right away." The abbess has Pierus to contend with, and I'm certain she will track his every motion with her hawk-like gaze. As for my disappearance, she will not notice it because she will not expect it.

"What about the grassy path?" Harper gestures to the ground—bare, shadowed rock. "How will you get back? How will you know where to go?"

"I don't know." Hoarse laughter punches out of me. It's not funny. It's the farthest thing from funny. "You were right. Is that what you want to hear? Zephyrus is a wretched, manipulative ass. He cannot be trusted."

"But you care for him. Maybe even more than care for him."

I will not consider the depth of my feelings. I've already questioned too much. "I know it's wrong," I whisper, "but something about him calls to me." It's time I accepted that. "I'm tired of fighting its pull."

At once, her expression softens. How young she looks in this moment, and how comfortable in her own skin. "What do any of us want in life? Love, security, acceptance. There is no shame in desiring such things."

Except Zephyrus does not offer me these things. He offers me only the promise of the unexpected and brokenhearted. I must be absolutely out of my mind to help him.

Harper crosses her arms, looks me up and down. "Give me your cloak."

Following her instruction, I pass her the white fabric. She passes me the red. The cloak, warm from Harper's body, settles across my shoulders. I draw up the hood, and she does the same. Harper is much smaller than I am, but Mother Mabel is so preoccupied with the tithe I doubt she'll notice a difference. "Thank you," I say.

"I should have done this a long time ago." She fiddles with the trio of knots at her waist. "Been your friend, I mean."

We are human, and as such, we make mistakes. I've seen a change in Harper, and I know it to be true. I'm ready to let go. I'm ready to heal this wound.

"I forgive you," I tell her. "For all the hurt you have caused me, I forgive you."

The loveliest sheen coats her eyes. "Will you return?"

I bite my lip to stop its trembling. Leaving the comfort of all you know is no easy task. "I don't know." I have every intention of returning, but who can say what trials Under will present? "Only time will tell."

"Then I wish you luck," Harper murmurs. "Say hello to Zephyrus for me."

27

BLACK SKY, BLACKER WOODS. THE DEEPEST, LIGHTLESS POCKETS OF the forest quiver ominously as I race along the twisting path, following the river beyond the bridge. Clamped in my hand, the roselight pulses weakly. Feeble, to be certain, but bright enough to avoid tripping over any lurking creatures. Depending on which direction I hold it, the light either flares or dims. If the roselight is connected to Zephyrus, surely it will help guide me to his location?

Eventually, a cave comes into view. My legs twinge with fatigue, yet I increase my pace, diving into the cave's dark mouth blindly. With the Orchid King preoccupied at Miles Cross, I've time yet.

The tunnel opens into a moonlit cavern—Pierus' lair. The mound of soil where he normally holds council is vacant. For whatever reason, the field of pink flowers appears wilted and gray, as though it sags beneath a coating of ash.

Across the way, a motionless lump draws my attention to the floor.

Zephyrus? My mouth shapes his name, but no sound emerges. The sight before me has killed it, wholly and completely.

He is pale. So, so pale, that resplendent, sun-kissed skin having bled of color. Limp lashes droop against wan cheekbones, curls of hair plastered to his clammy skull. A short beard darkens his jaw. He is naked as the day he was born.

I stumble forward, dazed. Carnivorous blossoms have fastened their small, searching mouths to his body: arms, stomach, even the insides of his muscled thighs. They drink in prolonged swallows, the attached vines undulating with each mouthful. The skin where the tiny spines have taken root bulges, sore-like with irritation. It's subtle, but his chest stirs. Breath in his lungs? I'll take it.

My hands hover near his body, but I don't dare touch him. If I listen closely, I can hear the sound of draining fluid. A ring of white cakes his mouth from how tightly his lips press together, and I watch, repulsed, as a collection of rust-colored petals wrenches free from his ribs with a wet gurgle, revealing the small tattoo I'd spotted months ago—a trio of hyacinth blossoms.

My concern surrounding the vines deepens. I wonder, yet again, why Zephyrus is subject to this horrid anguish. I fear he has been here all this time, hours, days, weeks. I'll need to safely remove the parasitic flora. Then distance. Shelter. A place to rest until I can figure out the next steps.

The flowers, however, are deeply imbedded. When I attempt to pry one of the buds free, the needles slide deeper into flesh, sucking eagerly. Black veins distend his parchment-pale skin.

The scuff of what might be a shoe echoes through the tunnel—someone approaches.

I spring toward a niche in the far wall as a tall, willowy woman glides into the moonlit chamber. She wears a flowing white dress and carries a pack across one shoulder. Mortal, she is not. A luminescent glow brightens her deep brown skin.

Five cloaked creatures trail the woman. Their raised hoods shimmer like the purest jewels—ruby and citrine, emerald and sapphire and amethyst. Flat, stony eyes sit within heavy folds of copper skin, and large, ornamental rings hang from their noses. Their faces bear eerie resemblance to goats.

The dark-skinned woman crouches at Zephyrus' side before retrieving something from her leather satchel. With her back to me, I cannot see what object she removes. The cloaked individuals observe her from afar.

I've half a mind to fling my blade into the woman's spine, but she departs the cavern as quickly as she arrived, along with her colorful companions. When her footsteps fade, I return to Zephyrus. Nothing appears to have changed.

Gently, I tug on the vine attached to his right shoulder. The West Wind twitches and falls still.

This plant is a living organism. Even if I were to sever the vines, the mouths would likely remain fixed to his body. If I disentangle Zephyrus, will Pierus sense it? He is connected to this horrible plant, after all. But I suppose it matters not.

Sliding the pack from my shoulder, I rummage through my supplies, pushing aside my journal and cache of food until I find the flint and steel, a piece of cloth, and a small vial of oil. All combine to create a torch in miniature, which I set ablaze.

Orange light fills the space as I hold the torch beneath one of the vines. Flames lick hungrily, the waxy skin beginning to char.

A scream shatters through the cave. Its blood-curdling pitch sends me to my feet, the nightshade roots lashing toward me.

I sidestep, driving my dagger in a vicious downward swipe. Sharpened iron peels through the vine's flesh. Blood—Zephyrus' blood—spews from the incision. The root recoils with a desperate shriek.

Screams compound as the blaze leaps from vine to vine. Smoke, dense and roiling, stings my throat. Within a few moments, the nightshade plant disintegrates. What remains? Red-bitten skin and a half-dead god.

I shrug off my cloak and maneuver Zephyrus' arms through the sleeves so the garment conceals his nakedness. Then I crouch low and heave the West Wind's body over one shoulder. Bladesmithing has its benefits. Tonight, I'm able to carry both our weights.

We reach the mouth of the cave without incident. Village lights shiver in the distance, but I continue onward, plunging through the impermeable forest with blind fear. There is no grassy path to guide me safely. Eventually, the soil fissures and the trees transition to the exposed clay deposits of an eroded cliffside. By the time I stumble upon adequate shelter, my back aches fiercely and sweat soaks my underarms.

Carefully, I set Zephyrus beneath an overhang. He should be safe until I return. After one last look at his face, I race back the way I came, my sights set on the distant village.

A rapid *rat-a-tat-tat* against the door, knuckles on wood. Three heartbeats later, the door eases open. A round, black eye peers through the crack.

Lissi's pale skin drains to a bloodless hue. "What are you doing here?"

"I need your help."

"No." The word spikes with fear. "You must leave." The door snicks shut.

"Please." I lay my gloved palm against the wood, its rough grooves catching the leather. My heart limps from the long, arduous run. Lissi is my last hope.

"The tithe has begun." The door muffles her voice, though not its bite. "The rules are plain. We cannot interfere."

"I would not come to you unless I had need."

"You are mortal, sweet. I will not stretch out my neck for you."

A cool wind stirs at my back, coaxing me to turn. The village is steeped in a fog of desertion, windows shuttered, the river an oily pool in the distance.

"I know I'm endangering you by returning," I say lowly, tightening my hand around the knob, "but I swear, this is the only time I will ask for your help." She cannot know what it means that I am here at all, placing my trust in the fair folk.

"Unfortunately, the answer is no."

The hollow moan of a woodwind instrument carries from a great distance, and a wave of cold sweeps through me, pebbling my skin. It sounds like a dirge.

My voice croaks out. "What if I were to offer you a trade?"

Silence hangs between us. "A trade?" Lissi's girlish voice brightens with excitement.

I slide open my pack, pull out the old, worn pages of the Text. "My most prized possession," I say. "It's yours if you help me."

The door swings open. Lissi's eyes dart over my shoulder, side to side. She has exchanged her usual waistcoat for a cherry scarf and lumpy wool hat. "Come inside." Grasping the front of my alb, she hauls me over the threshold.

A hiss of pain escapes me as my head knocks the top of the ceiling of the single-roomed structure. A pile of blankets identifies Lissi's sleeping area. It smells of herbs, a bright, clean scent.

Lissi tugs my arm impatiently. "Show me."

As I hand over the Text, I understand this is the last I will ever see of it. I've no room in my heart to grieve. The decision has been made. A steadfast comfort, now passed on to another.

Lissi stares at the heavily bound manuscript, unimpressed. "Your prized possession is a book?"

I try not to take offense. "Don't you like to read?"

"Read?" She giggles. "How boring. I prefer the more salacious activities, if you know what I mean." Lissi offers an impish wink, and I can't help but smile in response.

"I suppose it's not that salacious," I admit, although the Book of Night contains a few hair-raising tales.

"What about that?" She points to my chest.

My necklace? I catch the pendant between two fingers, the pad of my thumb pressed into the trinity knot. Mother Mabel said to never take it off. "It's not for trade, I'm afraid."

She pouts, yet glances between the necklace and the Text. "I do not care for a book, sweet. Keep it." She returns the Text, much to my surprise. "Now, what need do you have of me?"

I sag beneath the most profound relief. "Zephyrus is injured," I say, shoving the tome back into my rucksack. "Will you tend to him? You mentioned you were knowledgeable in the healing arts."

Her mouth curls, stretching around those dull, slime-coated gums. "You are a good girl, sweet. Why risk your life for the West Wind? I've warned you he cannot be trusted."

"I'm not here to have my decisions questioned," I state flatly. "Will you help me or not?"

Lissi considers me beneath lowered eyelids. The sprite is tiny, but no pushover, if the fire in her gaze is any indication. "Very well. Let me grab my supplies." She brushes off her hands, selects a nondescript bag by the door. Pulling back the heavy drapery, she peeks through the window. "How far away is he?"

"A few miles."

"Then we will move quickly."

Lissi wastes no time herding me back through the forest. I lead her to the overhang, beneath which lies an unconscious West Wind. She halts, a childlike hand covering her mouth. "Oh, dear."

The red cloak gapes at his chest, revealing livid teeth marks where the flowers had been attached. Filth clumps his head of curls. He has not moved since I left.

The sprite kneels next to Zephyrus while I hover in the background. She passes a hand over one of the wounds, traces a black vein running up his inner forearm. "These are from the nightshade plant." She lifts her gaze to mine, wary, questioning.

I hesitate, unsure of what information to divulge. I do not wish to endanger Zephyrus further, or Lissi, but I fear the consequences of withholding vital information, so I nod. "I took him from the Orchid King's lair."

She exhales sharply and removes her hand from Zephyrus' body. "Foolish of you, but there's nothing we can do about it now. Do you know how long the flowers were attached?"

Though the guilt ebbs, inevitably, it returns. If I had known of his torment sooner, would I have come? "I fear it has been many weeks."

I explain the roselight's change in color, why I believe that it signals Zephyrus' declining health. Lissi takes the glass orb in hand, her expression grave. "That is a perceptive observation, sweet. You may be correct."

"He cannot die, can he? He is immortal."

After returning the roselight to me, Lissi begins unpacking her supplies. "You forget Zephyrus is not from this realm. His body reacts differently to Under's influences. He will not die, but he can be harmed, and scarred." A variety of tools, jars, and bandages stuff the many leather pockets of her bag. She selects a small flask, pulls away the stopper. A viscous substance clings to the container. "How were the flowers detached from Zephyrus? Was the ritual complete?"

Ritual? A frisson of nerves wends itself through the confusion. "I'm not sure what you mean."

Lissi frowns, mouth pinched beneath the overwhelming vastness of her great stony eyes. "You are not aware of Zephyrus' circumstances? Why the tithe is necessary for Under?"

I shake my head. Our participation is required to ensure the continued lease of Thornbrook's grounds, but I've been told nothing beyond that.

"In order for Under to thrive," the sprite explains, "a pool of energy must feed the realm. Long before the fair folk were driven below-ground, the land produced its own energy from which we drew. It powered Under's enchantments, its weather patterns, the cycle of its sun and moon. But since the Orchid King's arrival, Under's power has weakened. He has absorbed that power into himself, leaving little for the realm. Thus, we require a donor."

As her gaze catches mine, a sense of foreboding trickles through me. "Zephyrus," I whisper.

"Yes. His blood provides the power necessary for the realm's existence. But mortal blood is powerful, too, in its own way, especially those of the faith. Only the blood of the truly devoted is able to draw forth the power of a god, especially one who has fallen so far from grace. After all, what are gods without disciples? This is why the Orchid King has manipulated the abbess into contributing to the tithe."

She knows of Zephyrus' suffering. They all know, all choose to shy from it, and reap the rewards at the cost of another.

"And you do nothing to stop this?" I grind out, unable to hide my disgust.

She shrugs her thin shoulders and says, "What can we do? The Orchid King is formidable. No one would dare challenge him. As for our more immediate concerns, the West Wind's declining health likely explains the diminished roselight. The Orchid King is voracious. He knows the tithe will deplete Zephyrus of his power for the foreseeable future, so he drains as much as he can for himself in the days leading up to the ceremony."

So Zephyrus is essentially a sacrifice. This must be how he pays the debt owed to the Orchid King—his power used to perpetuate the realm. Centuries of enslavement, no better than worm fodder.

I had no idea. None.

"What happens during the tithe if he's too weak to give his power? How does that work?"

"I don't know," Lissi says. After soaking the cloth in salve, she begins to dab at his wounds. "Based on these markings"—she gestures to the thin, sickle-shaped discolorations on his neck and chest—"it appears the ritual finished prematurely." Her eyes shift to mine with disconcerting gravity. This I know: whatever I have done, I will likely live to regret it.

"What is it?" I whisper. "Tell me. I can handle it."

"I am not certain of that, sweet."

She removes a second bottle from her supplies. "During the cleansing ritual, a small dose of venom is injected from the flowers' spines into the host. This ensures he or she remains unconscious, thus mitigating any pain. However, if the flowers are removed prior to the ritual's completion, the nightshade plant injects a high dose of venom into the bloodstream—enough to kill."

"I thought you said he couldn't die!"

"He will not die," she repeats, "but for some, death is a welcome relief. Once the venom reaches his heart, it will paralyze him indefinitely."

This cannot be. How was I to know the consequences of my actions? I could not let the West Wind weather that gruesome state a moment longer. "How long until the paralysis is total?"

Lissi untwists the cap from the second bottle before setting it aside. "Difficult to say. I have a tincture that will bring him to a conscious state, but eventually, he will succumb to the venom." She places a third bottle full of green liquid on the ground, a clink of glass on stone. "I estimate we have a handful of days, at best."

What, exactly, defines a handful? Three days? Four? Do we measure the time aboveground, or below? All is obscured, and I cannot bear it. "There's nothing you can do?" I urge. "No cure?"

"None that I'm aware of. The venom can only be flushed from his system if Zephyrus returns to the Orchid King. Only nightshade can reverse the effects."

"He can't go back." That is not a life. That is not even existence.

Lissi peers at me as though I am a particularly petulant child. "You would risk your life, your livelihood, for a disgraced god?" When I fail to respond, she continues, "Once the Orchid King realizes Zephyrus is gone, he will do everything in his power to find him. The tithe remains incomplete without the West Wind."

A difficult decision? Not particularly. A foolish one? Absolutely. My mind, however, will not change.

Reclaiming the second bottle, Lissi pours what appears to be ointment onto his wounds, and there are many. The inflamed skin begins to scab with hardened blood. Afterward, the sprite tips the green liquid down his throat, clamping his jaw shut so he's forced to swallow.

"He should wake within a few hours," she assures, returning the empty bottles to her satchel. "I cannot stay."

As I expected. Nevertheless, I am sad to see Lissi go. "Thank you," I say. "You have done more than I have a right to ask for. I will not forget it." As she pushes to her feet, I catch her hand, waiting until her eyes meet mine, curious, amused. "If ever there's a need, you will always have a friend in me."

A smile ghosts across her wide, lipless mouth. "A mortal and a sprite, friends?" The chime of her laughter shivers through me as she takes her leave. "These are strange times indeed."

28

I'M BUSY TENDING THE FIRE WHEN ZEPHYRUS WAKES.

A lick of warm air stirs against my back. My heart quickens, lifting free of its prior weight. *Breathe, Brielle.* My hand tightens imperceptibly around the stick I've been using to stoke the fire. A dagger is preferable.

Turning, I find his eyes resting on me. The slash of his eyebrows forms a bridge above his nose, which I swear appears smaller, less crooked, though the wavering light may be to blame.

I'm not ready. That is immediately apparent. I assumed I'd have more time to decide what, exactly, I would say to Zephyrus when he regained consciousness. I'd gathered my thoughts, penned them onto the pages of my journal, harvesting them one by one: thorny anger, the bruised trappings of hurt, heartache's shredded tatters. I would lay out every fault, every wrongdoing, before prying him apart. The West Wind would learn the game had changed. I, Brielle of Thornbrook, was a lamb no longer.

Fury sears my throat with violent velocity. *Now,* I think. Now is the time to strike—when the man is down. It would be nothing less than Zephyrus deserves.

But looking into his face, I see the weariness of a man who has built cities, only to watch them crumble.

The fire in my heart banks to a simmer. He and I are alone in Under, without friends or allies. We have only each other in this wretched place.

Unfortunately, navigating its underbelly will require trust in the West Wind—and in myself.

"How are you feeling?" I ask quietly.

Zephyrus pushes upward with a wince and rests his back against the overhang. Harper's cloak gapes at his chest, revealing the many puncture wounds, livid against his paler skin. "Tired."

What does it mean that I have missed his voice?

He peers beyond the fire, scanning the shadowed hillside at my back, the dark of isolation. His fingers shape into a fist, and the air pops in my ears.

"I've created a sound barrier around the camp," he explains, appearing even more fatigued following that display of power. "We may talk freely." His gaze pins mine. "What happened?"

He can probably guess, given his lack of clothes, but I fill in the larger holes.

Eventually, those bright green eyes return to mine. "What of Pierus?" he asks.

I poke the fire to keep my hands occupied. "He was already at Miles Cross. When I found you in his cavern, there was a woman in a white dress. Dark hair, dark skin. She was accompanied by five individuals wearing jewel-toned cloaks."

The corners of his mouth droop in unhappiness. "Her name is Oly. She assists Pierus when he is elsewhere. The others you saw are akin to Pierus' council, though they're more like lackeys than anything else."

"What did she do to you?" I ask.

"What do you mean?"

"I think she dispensed something into your mouth, but I didn't see what it was. A tincture, maybe."

"Ah." He nods in understanding. "Usually, I'm given something to numb the pain. Well, most of it, anyway." The cloak hem disappears inside his fist. He holds it there, like an anchor. "I would not have wished you to see me this way."

He thinks me prudish. "I have seen nakedness before." Granted, only the other Daughters in the bathhouse, never a man, though he doesn't need to know that.

"I meant the wounds." He pokes the underside of one wrist. A clear substance oozes from the opening. "I don't understand how I'm awake. I should be unconscious."

"You know this from experience?"

The West Wind peers into the fire, tugging on his beard in a preoccupied manner. It has clearly been weeks since he shaved. "Twice before," he says, "I attempted to escape the cleansing ritual prior to its completion. I did not get far before I blacked out." He frowns and turns to me. "There remains the question of how I'm here, conscious, and—if I'm not mistaken—quite far from Pierus' lair."

"I had help from a friend." Better to keep Lissi's identity a secret. The less Zephyrus knows, the less Pierus can use against me. And I owe Lissi a great debt. She even surprised me a few hours ago by dropping off clean clothes for my charge, in addition to a pair of boots in his size. Then she'd left. *For good this time*, the sprite had said.

His hand twitches atop his thigh. I recognize the motion for what it is: the desire to grasp a weapon. "I thought better of you, Brielle."

"Excuse me?"

A low growl of frustration darkens his response. "You have everything you could ever want. A home. A purpose and a place. You obtained Meirlach," he says. "You're an acolyte."

"I'm not an acolyte," I mumble.

He stares, green eyes blank beneath his mess of curls. "Yes, you are." He gestures to the scarlet cloak concealing his nakedness.

"It's not mine." My voice softens further. "It's Harper's."

Slowly, Zephyrus shakes his head. "I'm not following. You bested the Stallion. You acquired Meirlach. The title was yours to claim."

"Harper delivered Meirlach to Mother Mabel, not I."

There are words, and then there are the spaces between words— that which has not been said. The only way Harper could have delivered Meirlach to the abbess was if I gave up the sword. Zephyrus knows this. "Why?"

"I have my reasons." I jab the stick into the logs. The tip catches, and I shove it into the ground, cool, moist clay extinguishing the flame in a curl of smoke.

"You've worked toward the position for ten years, yet when the time came to claim it, you gave the opportunity to someone else. Tell me why."

Leather creaks as my gloved fingers curl inward. Rancorous, spiteful, cold-blooded, my ire possesses many faces, not just one. "I did what I thought was right at the time. I would have rather given the position to Harper, who held no uncertainty about claiming it, rather than take it for myself when I had begun to question my faith." Even though it broke me to do so.

A muscle pulses in his jaw, its slow tic mirroring my agitated heartbeat. "You were free, Brielle. *Free*. Yet you returned to Under, placing yourself in unnecessary danger, and for what? To save the skin of a disgraced god?" The words prod, a knife to the spine. "It was foolish."

"Saving your life was foolish?" Of all the boneheaded things to say. "A *thank-you* would be more appreciative."

His expression shutters, closed and cold. "You are wasting your time."

"You're an ass." I chuck the stick into the fire, and sparks flare like dying stars against the overhang. "Do you know what I went through to get here tonight? The emotional turmoil I've experienced?" If he did not look so pathetic lying there, I daresay I would leap over the fire and bash his head into the rock. "But maybe you're right and this has been a complete waste of time. Should I have left you to Pierus' cruel ministrations? Perhaps you wouldn't be in this situation had you not deceived me. I—" My throat closes. "I thought you cared for me," I whisper. Strong in conviction I have been, but not strong enough.

"Brielle." He lets out a long, weary breath. "I do care. I promise you, I do."

"Not enough to put someone else's needs before your own."

He clenches his jaw, fights to neutralize his features. "All right," he says. "Maybe I deserved that."

"That is the least of what you deserve." My voice roughens with rising emotion, the desire, like a frenzy, to tip back my head and howl, sound shattering up my throat. "You—" I must say it. "You are the cause of my misfortune."

His hand drops. "*I'm* the cause of your misfortune?"

"Spring, ten years earlier. You do not remember?" How easily my fingers curl, driving deep into the flesh of my thighs. "Think back, Zephyrus. Remember the story I told you. Remember the storm that destroyed Veraness, my home. Remember that my mother will never return."

Fire—chaos and light—is all that separates us. "Veraness." He frowns at the hands clenched in his lap. "I have not heard that name in a long time." Then he looks up. "Veraness was your home?"

I'm shaking. Had the Orchid King not gifted me Mother Mabel's journal, I would never have known the part Zephyrus played in my abandonment. And yet, I am here. I've sacrificed much to save him. I fear my own motivations despite the hurt harbored in my heart. "Do you deny responsibility of its demise?"

He appears dazed. "I tried to sever the bond that day." His recollection rolls forth with slow contemplation. "I used all my strength. There was . . . much destruction."

His attempt at escape left thousands dead, my home unsalvageable. Three days later, my mother was gone. It was then that I learned love was temporary.

"Your mother died?" he whispers, searching my gaze.

I look away, let the void overhead soak my vision black. "She isn't dead," I mutter, "or she wasn't. I don't know where she is now."

"I'm sorry."

"You have no idea what it means to be sorry. To you, *sorry* is a scapegoat, a means to avoid accountability for your actions. It's no wonder you are alone."

His shoulders roll inward, and I vow not to display a shred of pity for him. He may be a beaten dog on this night, but weeks before, he held the leash.

The fault is yours, I nearly cry. It will be the club I wield, brought down with shattering force.

But that is simply not true.

I try to swallow, yet despair lodges in my throat, a snarled old knot. The West Wind was the perfect scapegoat. If he is responsible for my sad tale, then I do not have to accept what I have feared all along: I was not an important enough reason for my mother to stay.

"My mother had been ill for a long time," I begin. "Her mind lacked the clarity necessary to make sound decisions." And when Veraness had been ripped from beneath our feet, who can say how severely it damaged her fragile mind?

Zephyrus drags a thumb along his lower lip, studying me as he did on our very first meeting, when he had yet to decide who I was, who I might become. "The story you told at the Well of Past. Was she of stable mind then?"

"Mentally, I think she was beginning to degrade, but I did not know it at the time." I was only a child, without the answers to life's problems. Back then, she did not mumble nonsense about the end of the world. Neither did she hoard tinctures, convinced of her premature death.

"She hit you."

"She did." I do not excuse my mother's behavior, but she was troubled. If she could not help herself, I could not help her either.

"She abandoned you." As he searches my gaze, I witness in him another realization, like a candle taking flame. "That's why you've been at Thornbrook for so long."

I bite the inside of my cheek. A trembling manifests in my core, rippling outward, and tears well before I'm aware of them, salted tracks sliding down my face.

"My mother was sick," I choke. "She was sick for a long time, and I could not help her, could only watch as she deteriorated, and changed."

"Brielle." The West Wind's tone gentles. "You were a child. It was not your responsibility to care for your mother."

The dam has broken. The flood will not cease. "She wouldn't seek help. I tried. Every day, I tried. But over the years, it grew worse. She claimed she never had a daughter. Said I was a liar, that I was only pretending to love her to steal her money, though we had none to spare. Business slowly declined, and eventually, she was forced to shut down the shop." No employment, no means to support a family. And when the storm hit, no home. My mother could not differentiate between reality and illusion. Her mind was too far gone.

My chest caves, and my head drops into my palms. I remember the gates, their glinting iron points, Thornbrook's massive front doors, the church bell ringing so sweetly. Finally, my mother's retreating back as I stood upon the rain-slickened stoop, a child of eleven.

"I try not to think about that day," I sob into my hands, "but how can a mother treat her daughter so cruelly? How could she leave me?"

I was defective. I wasn't enough. Not for my own mother to choose love over fear. I am, a decade later, still mourning.

Rising to his feet, Zephyrus circles the fire to crouch at my side, placing a hand upon my back. The gesture wrenches open the wound, my heart in pieces.

"I loved her. And yet, some days I loathe her. I *hate* her." Spite licks at my skin, seeking an outlet, even as my shoulders curl forward, attempting to repress that foul emotion. "But as much as I loved her, she didn't love me."

"I do not believe that."

He is wrong, I know it in my soul, yet I can't help but ask, "How can you know?"

"Because—" He catches my chin, draws it upward so I'm forced to look into his eyes. "If anyone is deserving of love, Brielle, it's you."

Deserving of love. What does that even mean?

"How can I feel this way about the woman who birthed me?" My chest heaves. "She gave me life. Is that not the greatest gift?"

Zephyrus takes my hand in his. Our fingers lock, an effortless slide. "We do not have the privilege of choosing our parents, unfortunately. Not everyone is adept at the job. As such, we must sometimes carry this pain throughout our lives."

His face loses focus behind my swimming vision. At times, the West Wind is unbearable. Now he is knowing, sage.

"I understand why you hold to faith so tightly," he says. "In your darkest hours, your god did not abandon you. He offered you light when you had none."

Yes. It is exactly how he describes. It is everything.

"I also understand why my actions hurt you. How poorly I treated you. Why your trust in me was broken."

My throat squeezes, and I choke out, "I did trust you. I didn't want to, but I did."

"I know," he whispers. "I'm sorry." He releases a slow exhalation. "Selfishness is a flaw in me, one I have long recognized. It is difficult for me to nurture honest relationships."

Difficult, or impossible? "Why are you bound to the Orchid King? And I would like the truth." If ever there was a time to be honest, let it be now.

Zephyrus holds my stare. I'm satisfied when he shies away first. "The truth has never come easily to me."

"Sounds like a coward's life."

He snorts, yet the sound holds no humor. "I suppose you're right."

Pulling away, he returns to the opposite side of the fire, settling the cloak around him. The flames have burned low, and I appreciate the whole of his face, every ridge and curved bone, the angles more harmonious than I have seen previously.

"Will you tell me why you run?" I ask the West Wind.

Emotion tautens his features. I recognize it instantly. Am painfully familiar with the reluctance of having to claw away something rooted deep. "All right, then. I will start from the beginning."

Easing back against the stone, Zephyrus stares into the fire and begins.

"I was born in a realm far from here called the City of Gods. My brothers and I mastered the changing seasons. Boreas, the eldest, is the North Wind, and controls the north's brute chill. Notus, the

South Wind, reigns over the hot summer winds. Lastly, there is Eurus, the East Wind. The storms do love him."

Boreas, Zephyrus, Notus, Eurus. The Anemoi.

"There's not much I can complain about in those early years. Wine flowed and our great city blossomed. I was, above all else, beloved." His entire demeanor softens, and for a moment I can imagine the man he used to be, prior to his banishment. "And then I met Hyacinth."

I'm appalled by the spike of jealousy that shoots through me. In all the time I've spent in Zephyrus' company, I've never heard this quality to his voice, as if he speaks of something so precious it must be cherished, shielded from the world's harsh winds.

"He was a prince from a neighboring realm, visiting our city to bargain with the Council of Gods. Those first few months, we spent every possible second in each other's company. The smell of his skin, the sound of his laughter. It was overwhelming."

My stomach twists uncomfortably, for the yearning in his gaze is plain. Yearning for someone else.

"I loved him," Zephyrus says. "But unfortunately, I was not the only one entranced by the youth." Strain folds the corners of his eyes, that capricious mouth. "His name is Apollo. God of music, truth, and light. One afternoon, I discovered Hyacinth and Apollo tossing a discus in the park." He drops his gaze, takes a long breath, dredging up strength for the tale's end. "Watching them interact, I questioned everything. The way Hyacinth looked at him . . . It hurt," he says, "to think that what we had was something he could find so easily with another. It pained me to realize he would leave me for Apollo—bright, shining Apollo—and that, ultimately, I was not enough."

I feel the sadness in him, which in turn draws me in, petals unfurling, naked heart exposed. If ever there was a time when I felt connected to Zephyrus, it is now, all walls tumbling down.

"It was my gravest mistake," he murmurs. "The moment in time I wish I could reverse, but not even gods are all-powerful." A beat of silence passes, and I wait.

"As Apollo released the discus, I sent a strong wind through the park. I was aiming for Apollo. But when the wind caught the discus, I lost control. It slammed into Hyacinth's skull instead."

Wet and torn, the breath catches in his chest. I don't move. I can't.

"Hyacinth fell," Zephyrus whispers, "and did not rise."

"You killed him."

Zephyrus swallows, and his eyes swim with tears. "It was not my intention."

"Then what was your intention? You claim you loved this man, yet putting someone in harm's way is not love. To give up everything you are, to choose another's life over your own? *That* is love."

"You are correct," he says dully. Shadows slither nearer to our depleting circle of light, but I've run out of fuel to feed the flames. "It was not love. It was possession."

Against my better judgment, the indignation softens in me. No use beating a man already down. At least he's aware of his wrongdoing. "There was nothing to be done? Even in the City of Gods?"

"No. His death arrived far quicker than I anticipated. Anyone who might have been able to reverse what had occurred did not wish to help me." Parting the top of the cloak, he points to the marking near his ribs. "When Hyacinth's blood fell to the earth, flowers bloomed in its wake. This tattoo is in memory of him."

I stare at the tattoo, its trio of flowers. Beneath lies his skin, dusted gold, and flexing muscle. I drag my focus away, though it takes effort. "And Apollo?"

"Apollo was inconsolable. I had not considered how deeply his feelings for Hyacinth ran."

As I shift these details into their proper places, the image grows clearer. What was it Pierus once said? *It will never be enough. I had hoped you would realize that by now.* "Does Pierus have any relation to Hyacinth?"

He sends a gentle stream from his fingertips to wake the dying fire. It flares, painfully bright, then gutters. Nothing remains to catch and burn. "Hyacinth was Pierus' son."

At last, I see the whole of this tangled web. The reason for Zephyrus' enslavement. A father's vengeance stretched eternal.

"What happened afterward?" For I sense that we have not reached the end of this tragic tale. Hyacinth's death is the dawn, but the day is long.

Zephyrus studies the glowing coals. "At first, nothing. I expected Pierus to demand a trial, but months passed, and the Council of Gods did not send for me. Over time, Hyacinth's death weakened my resolve. I lost sleep. I was not eating properly. The grief was too fresh."

He drags at his lower lip in thought, then says, "To keep my mind occupied, I joined Boreas' efforts in organizing a coup with my brothers. We attempted to overthrow our parents, who reigned over our great city, but we failed. Once the dust settled, we were banished from our realm, cast off to the four corners of this new world, never to return to our shining home."

"And how long ago was that?"

He shrugs. "Centuries? Millennia? Time passes strangely in Under, as you know."

It is another moment before he goes on.

"Although I was exiled to Carterhaugh, Pierus did not believe my punishment was just. After appealing to the Council of Gods, he was granted permission to cross over and oversee my sentence. They gifted him my name, the power to control me. He essentially stole Under from the fair folk and proclaimed himself its king."

There is so much information here my mind struggles to process it all. Does Mother Mabel know of this? And did the tithe exist prior to Pierus' arrival, or did he implement that on his own?

"For killing his son," Zephyrus croaks, "I am forever in Pierus' debt. The power in my blood feeds Under so the realm may continue to exist, and at the close of every seventh year, I am sacrificed. I do not die, not in the sense that mortals do, but I am emptied. I become a shell, a god made vacant of power, until the dawn of a new cycle, when I am revived."

"There's nothing you can do? No way to sever the ties binding you?"

Leaning forward, Zephyrus drags the pile of clothes Lissi provided onto his lap. "No methods worth pursuing. Once the tithe is complete, I will be bound for another seven years."

I can't accept that. If he's bound, why in seven-year cycles? What else must I know to get to the bottom of this mess? Fumbling in my pocket for the roselight, I pull it free. "Look." Its feeble glow is but a ghost of color on glass. "Do you see what Pierus is doing to you? What this horrible ritual perpetuates? There has to be another way."

Yet the West Wind stares at the roselight as though it is the sun rising after the longest, darkest night. "You threw it away," he says quietly. "Weeks ago."

I've carried the roselight since Harper's visit to the forge, though I've considered flinging it down a well. Twice, I nearly did. My fingers refused to let go. "Harper retrieved it," I say, and leave it at that.

Still he watches me, expression guarded. "Why did you come for me?"

There is no singular answer. Because of the way he is in this moment, all defenses brought low. Because he is more than his faults. Because beneath that shining immortal skin, Zephyrus is just a man. Despite all that he's done, I believe, as the Father believes, that people can change. They can begin again.

"Everyone leaves me," he murmurs, "but you . . ."

My heart squeezes in response. "I came back."

His throat dips, and I watch the tension ease, and settle into a deeply profound peace. "You came back."

29

"TELL ME EVERYTHING YOU KNOW," I SAY, STIRRING THE FIRE TO life. "Leave nothing out."

The West Wind, dressed in clean, dry clothes, watches the flames gorge on the dry wood. While he rested, I had gone to collect firewood and scout the area. I'd observed no signs of intrusion, but I didn't linger, returning to our shelter in fear of something catching my scent. A block of cheese from my bag settled my gnawing stomach.

Tossing a branch onto the fire, he says, "Without my blood, the tithe will remain incomplete. I'm sure Pierus has already learned that I'm gone, and why, though he will stall for as long as he can. He hates to appear foolish."

It's been hours already. Mother Mabel must know something is amiss.

"Wouldn't he call for you?" As far as I know, Zephyrus cannot deny the compulsion, not for long.

"He would, but he hasn't. My return is not enough. He would want to punish those responsible for helping me escape the cleansing ritual as well." Crossing his arms over his chest, he slumps lower against the outcropping. "That can only mean he's sent for the hounds."

"The hounds?"

"Unfortunately, you are now marked by the Orchid King."

A chill licks at my flesh beneath the heavy wool of Harper's cloak, which Zephyrus has returned to me. "What does that mean?"

He pinches the bridge of his nose in a rare sign of distress. "Pierus will do everything in his power to hunt you. Your only chance at survival is to leave Under and never return."

"I'm not leaving without you."

"You're not listening. You cannot outrun the hounds. No one can. They are bred for one thing only: to catch their prey. The tallest peaks, the widest rivers, the deepest chasms. No matter where you run, they will find you." His hands fist, long fingers enclosed within the strong, callused palms. "I would not see you torn apart by darkness."

It begins subtly: a prickle in my throat, dampness beneath my arms. Nerves fray, and I struggle to catch my breath. "They wouldn't kill me. Mother Mabel would never allow it . . ."

"Brielle."

My name drifts like a fog, and the fire spins into threads of color and light, the ground sliding out from beneath me.

"Look at me."

I turn, and there is the West Wind, the heat of his breath thawing the chill tightening my cheeks. Grasping my braid in one hand, he pulls the tresses free, allowing his fingers to slide through, cupping the back of my skull.

My chest sears with sharpening pain. "My heart—"

"Is beating steadily," he says, pressing his palm to the rise of my breast. "You are safe."

Knotting my fingers with his, I crush his hand harder against my sternum, as if it might punch through skin and bone, take the place of this failing organ. Beneath his gaze, my pulse slows, descending from its treacherous high. Then the blackness retreats, giving way to fire and light.

Watchful and troubled, he tucks a russet curl behind my ear. "My darling novitiate, will you sit with me?"

The endearment stirs a flutter behind my ribs. "I'm already sitting with you."

"I'm afraid I must disagree," he says, that old charisma returning. "You sit next to me, but I wish you to sit *with* me."

Now I understand. The difference lies in the choice.

I nod, and he tucks me against his side. Quietly, he asks, "Do you want to talk about it?"

I am no stranger to my body's reactions, however ill-informed they are. Do I want to talk about it? Not especially.

"I can't remember a time when I did not feel overwhelmed." I rub the back of my hand across my eyes. Unsurprisingly, it comes away wet. "It's hard to describe."

"You write a lot in your journal." A pointed gaze, nonjudgmental, merely curious—the simple desire to know.

"Yes." I remember the humiliation of Harper reading my private musings. Likely Zephyrus does, too. "Putting my thoughts to paper helps when I feel myself spiraling."

"Does this happen a lot?"

How often is a lot? Weekly? If so, then yes, but I am used to it. At this point in my life, it is woven into the fabric of myself. I am not Brielle of Thornbrook without it. "I started experiencing these episodes when my mother's mental health began to degrade. Gradually, it bled into other parts of my life." Confrontations, looming decisions, things vast and complex and beyond my grasp.

His expression turns inward for a time. "That makes a lot of sense. I struggle with a lack of control in my life as well."

This isn't about me. I will survive, as I have always done. If the Orchid King has sent his hounds, I will face them. But I worry for those I love.

"What about Mother Mabel, the Daughters of Thornbrook? Are they in danger?"

"I doubt it. Pierus wouldn't risk tainting his relationship with your abbess. The power in my blood is paramount to Under's survival, but the blood of virgin mortals is equally necessary. Your faith strengthens this realm. It is something the fair folk lack."

The reassurance settles me. Their safety means more to me than my own. "Then we have the advantage. We have time to plan our escape."

I expect enthusiastic agreement. In the end, I receive lukewarm resolve. "Maybe we should reconsider."

"What?" By the Father, he's serious. "Why would you say that?" And after everything?

He gazes out longingly, trees blanketing the ground from sight. "Although your friends will be safe in Mother Mabel's company, I cannot say the same for you. Pierus could kill you and blame it on an unfortunate accident. I would not put it past him. If we return to Miles Cross, he will probably let you go, provided that you leave in the abbess' company."

"What about you?"

"Unlike you, I cannot walk free so easily." It is grim, his smile. "I will face the consequences of my actions."

"You would still be bound to Pierus," I argue. "That is no life."

"I am aware of what awaits me." The words seethe, too cold for comfort, and I stiffen against him. "If I do not return and complete the ritual, I will waste away to nothing. What is a mind without a body to do its bidding? I would rather not subject myself to that torment."

"You are a *god*," I state. "Are you telling me there's not a single person who could help you cure the paralysis?"

Zephyrus lifts a hand. Together, we watch short bursts of air weave around his fingertips, silver thread in the darkness. "Two people come to mind, but I have seen neither in centuries."

Two prospects. It's a start. "How are we to find them?"

With a sigh, he drops his hand. "The first is my brother Notus. Unfortunately, I'll likely succumb to the venom before we reach his realm."

A handful of days if we are lucky. And we've already wasted the night. "How far is it?"

"Difficult to say. We would need to venture beneath one of the mountains to the south. One of the four original entrances into Under lies there. It will lead us to Notus."

"These entrances. Does each lead to one of your brothers' realms?"

"They once did, yes. But as far as I know, my brothers remain unaware of their existence."

I nod in understanding. "What of the second contact?"

"His name is Yakim. He's a poison dealer in the wilds of Under. It's possible he'll have an antidote, something that could slow the venom until we reached my brother's realm."

The tips of his fingers drift up my side, a slow, indulgent touch that draws warmth to my cheeks. "How do we find him?" I ask, a bit breathlessly.

"Oh, I know where to find him. The problem is whether he would agree to meet with me."

I wait until Zephyrus' gaze returns to mine. His attention is heady in a way I've never experienced before. I don't shy from it. I welcome its touch. "Let me guess," I say, with a sigh of exasperation. "You wronged this person in some way."

"He and I had a falling out long ago. I'm not sure if he would remember." Then he tilts his head, considering his words. "Actually, there's a good chance he will."

I will not question the why and how. Obstacles have never stopped the West Wind before. If nothing else, I have confidence in his ability to manipulate a situation, place his pawns where they are most beneficial.

"If Yakim is our only means of reaching your brother's realm in time," I say, "I think we should find him. What have we got to lose?"

"For you? Everything."

And here marks the struggle, the desire to remain tight-lipped, invulnerable, and the compulsion to bare all. "Zephyrus," I say, with all the compassion I possess. "I have lost more in my life than I care to admit. I will not lose you, too."

He turns to me then, sweeping his palm over my cheek. He does not speak, but what need have I for words when all is clear in his eyes? It means something that I care for him. It means more than he lets on, I believe. Whether or not Zephyrus reveals what lies in his heart, I know this to be true: I am seen in all ways, and perhaps, if I dare to consider it, loved.

Catching his hand in mine, I lower it onto my lap. "Where can we find Yakim?"

He hesitates. "It's not safe, Brielle, not for a mortal. It's best if I go alone."

The moment I reforged that broken sword, I made my decision. "I'm going with you," I say. "And whatever awaits, we'll face it together." Just as the Father shadows me in life, so too will I walk this path with the West Wind.

The dilapidated two-story house squats over a massive spreading bog, its foundation submerged in murky water. A wide wraparound porch skirts the front of the structure. The front door hangs off its hinges like a broken limb.

"Yakim lives here?" My voice emerges in a half-gasp, for the reek of this place forces me to breathe through my mouth.

Standing beside me on the drooping boardwalk, which connects the house to a handful of muddy islands, Zephyrus responds, "The Estate acts as a crossroads. For some, it is a gambling den. For others, it is a tavern, a place to order a hot meal and unwind. For the select few, there are lodgings within that cater to only the most exclusive circles. Yakim is one of their preeminent clients."

It had taken half the night to reach the bog, endless miles crossing difficult terrain, the trees clumped like shadowed specters, hunched with age and rot. Zephyrus sent a message to Notus via a stream of air—apparently an effective method of communication between the Anemoi. Despite all odds, we've made it, sunrise still hours away.

Someone pushes aside a curtain from one of the second-story windows, revealing the silhouetted curves of a woman's body.

"Right on time," Zephyrus murmurs.

"Who is that?" I ask, more suspiciously than I intend to.

He lifts a hand in acknowledgment, smiling as the woman pushes open the window and calls out, "You were never fond of knocking, old friend!"

"How did you know it was me?" he hollers back.

"Roses. Nothing smells that good around here."

He laughs.

I wrap my arms across my stomach, glaring at Zephyrus from the corner of my eye as my mood darkens. Who is this woman, that she is able to pull a shred of unspoiled joy from the West Wind?

"I hope my arrival isn't an inconvenience," he says.

The woman grins, a white crescent against her shadowed face. "None at all. Come on up. And bring your friend." The window slams shut.

Zephyrus is still chuckling when I demand, "Are you going to answer?" After saving his skin, the least he could do is acknowledge me.

His eyebrows wing upward in surprise at my waspish tone. "You have to ask a question in order to receive an answer."

It's not intended as a blow, but I endure it as such. "I did," I choke out, "or were you sleeping when I said, *Who is that?*"

His eyes clear. For a time, he regards me. "You're jealous."

"I am not."

"You are." He sidles closer, eyes dancing.

I hold my ground. "If you want to stare at a naked woman, that is your prerogative, but after the trouble I went through tonight, I would have expected you to be more concerned with your deteriorating health." I've risked everything to be here. I'd hoped he'd realized that.

Pushing past him, I tromp down the boardwalk, avoiding the sagging planks. Zephyrus captures my hand, tugging me around to face him.

He draws me close, pressing my palm flat over his heart. It taps an eager pace. "I *am* concerned," he says lowly. The pad of his thumb brushes the back of my hand in soothing strokes. "Her name is Ailith. You will have to trust me when I say there has only ever been friendship between us. Anyway, her wife would castrate me if I ever behaved inappropriately."

My face burns brightest red. "I assumed you two . . ."

"Never. She loves women. Always has. Can't really blame her, can you?" He winks, and against my better judgment, I'm charmed. "To be honest, I'm partial to redheads."

"Stop." My voice drops, and I lick my lips. "You're trying to distract me."

His thumb slides beneath my palm, pressing into the callused flesh inside my glove. "Is it working?"

"No."

He grins. "Liar."

The lies surface more readily, it is true. I'm not sure how I feel about it.

"Shall we?" The West Wind offers me his arm, which I accept, allowing him to steer me along the boardwalk.

The woman, Ailith, awaits us on the front porch. She isn't naked as I first presumed, but she might as well be, with her dewy olive skin exposed but for scraps of sapphire cloth covering her chest and backside. The curve of her stomach reveals a brutal scar. Small white horns protrude from the top of her skull, cutting through her inky tresses.

She frowns as we climb the steps onto the porch. "That's certainly your unruly hair and flouncing gait," she says, examining Zephyrus in confusion, "but what happened to your face?"

"It's not permanent." He rubs the tip of his crooked nose with a grimace. "At least, I hope not."

"I see." Her frown deepens. "Shouldn't you be at the tithe?"

He smiles. I'm impressed by his ease. "Nothing to worry about, my dear."

"I will have to take your word for it." Though she addresses the West Wind, her dark, uptilted eyes rest on me. I'm so fixated on her presence I don't think too deeply on the exchange she and Zephyrus shared. "You've brought company," she mentions. "A mortal woman? This pleases me."

"Calm yourself, Ailith." The words thrum with suppressed amusement, yet warning, too. "We're not here for your services."

"You bring your pet to my place of business, dangle her before me like ripened fruit, and claim no interest in my services?" Her gaze slinks eagerly over my ample chest. "What a waste of beauty."

"She is no pet." His kindness has frozen into a far more dangerous expression.

Low conversation drifts through the open door. Someone pulls aside the curtain, peeks through the wide bay window, then vanishes.

"I see." Ailith retreats a step with a muffled clack. "If she is not your pet, then what is she?" Two of her fingers skim up my arm, across my shoulder, where they alight like small birds. "Because as far as I'm concerned, she is too good for the likes of you."

"You would not be wrong. She is a Daughter of Thornbrook," he responds, and the woman's smile reveals a pronounced gap between her two front teeth.

"One of the faith? Even better."

Zephyrus snorts, though remains close to me, a hand on my lower back. "Do you have a minute for a pair of weary travelers?"

Ailith winks. "For you, my dear? I will give you seven."

The front porch, cobbled together from buckling boards, creaks as we cross the threshold, the yellowing door stripped of paint. A bell chimes upon our entrance.

Despite the neglected facade, the Estate's interior is well-maintained and tastefully decorated, with white satin curtains draping the tall windows, the space cloaked in the haze of candlelight. A lemony fragrance offers relief from the putrid reek outside. Unlike the front porch, the wooden floor gleams with fresh polish beneath the rugs, and the bar tucked against the far wall shines impressively.

The fair folk gather around low tables, busy smoking, gambling, drinking, and conversing. A blaze blackens the central fireplace, having attracted a group of sprites relaxing in upholstered armchairs, passing cards from hand to hand.

"Back in a moment," Ailith says. "Make yourselves at home. Drinks on me at the bar, if you wish."

As I press nearer to Zephyrus, the hand on my back slips lower, grazing the curve of my backside, and I momentarily cease to breathe. "Has Pierus called for you yet?" I murmur.

"No." He scans the area, taking in the patrons observing us with open curiosity. They see the West Wind, and something changes in them. Their spines straighten. Their meals go cold. "And I think I know why."

He crosses the room, and I follow, my attention drawn to the charcoal sketch he rips from the wall, a portrait which bears a startling likeness to his face.

A bounty for the West Wind.

What was it Zephyrus said about this place? *It's not safe.* "Should we leave?"

"No." A few patrons return to their gambling. "It is merely a scare tactic. The hounds are my greater concern."

"How long before they reach us?"

"Hours." He does not sound particularly enthused. "The quicker we meet with Yakim, the quicker we can leave." Turning, he meets the eyes of those still staring, smiles charmingly, and saunters toward the hallway Ailith disappeared down.

I stick close to his heels. "I thought Ailith said to wait here." We climb a set of curved stairs overlooking the great room, the air warming the higher we go.

"Ailith says a lot of things."

Once we reach the second level, we turn right down a hallway plastered in yellow silk paper. "Did you spot Yakim?"

"Not yet." Nudging my lower back, Zephyrus directs me to a door with a brass knocker. "He's been coming to Ailith's for the last four hundred years. I would be disappointed if he had changed his habits." Lifting his hand, he knocks.

The door swings wide, and Ailith stands on the other side, hands on hips, the curve of her leg peeking through a slit in the tiny skirt covering her ample backside. I blink in shock. The woman's slender ankles end in hooves.

"Why do you always fail to follow instructions?" Her smile hardens. "That was a rhetorical question, by the way." Nonetheless, she waves us inside with a murmured, "The Blue Room."

The space is aptly named. Silken sapphire walls. A floor patched with rugs in various shades of blue. A large window overlooks the smoking marsh, and a collection of turquoise armchairs shapes a half-moon around the fireplace.

"Please," Ailith says, shutting the door behind us. "Take a seat."

Zephyrus and I select two neighboring armchairs. After clearing away what appear to be financial documents spread across a low table, Ailith pours herself into the sofa across from us, her soft thighs filling the space like water in a glass. She stares at us until I begin to feel sweat prickle my hairline. In the wilds of Under, I am mortal, and I am weak.

"What can I do for you, Zephyrus?" the buxom woman purrs.

He leans back, swings an ankle up to rest on his thigh. "Does Yakim still conduct business here?"

"He does." The click of her long, curved nail against the wooden sofa back prevents the silence from ever truly settling. "I thought you parted ways long ago." Her gaze flicks to me, then back to Zephyrus.

"We did, but I have need of his services again."

"Why?" The tapping pauses.

Zephyrus offers his most inviting smile. "Ailith. You know the importance of confidentiality."

"You two did not part on good terms. Who is to say he will not seek vengeance in some way?"

"Two centuries is a long time to hold a grudge." He shrugs. "I'm sure it will be fine."

"Zephyrus." Her small, pitying sound rushes forth. "The fair folk never forget."

I shift uncomfortably in my seat. Ailith crosses her legs, and my attention snags on her hooves.

"I'm a faun, dear." She winks at me. "No need to fret."

I glance away sheepishly before my gaze finds Zephyrus. "So, what *did* you do to Yakim?" I ask him.

My question draws Ailith's and Zephyrus' attention. There was a time when the West Wind would evade the subject, refusing to step fully into the light, but I'd like to think we have become better versions of ourselves since then.

"I may have"—he lifts a hand, lips pursed with casual disregard—"swindled him out of money once or twice."

Ailith and I share a look of wordless exasperation.

Errant conversation drifts from the level below, slipping like steam through the cracks between the floorboards. Every so often, clinking glass breaks the monotony of the muddled hum. "You ask for my cooperation," Ailith says, "but offer me no information. How am I to know what danger you invite into my home? People depend on me for protection."

"You have my word," Zephyrus promises with rare solemnity. "Whatever it might be worth. I will not bring danger to those you shelter. I simply seek a meeting with Yakim, and a safe place to do so."

"Safe? My dear, you are a fugitive." A cool voice floats from the open doorway, and I catch sight of an equally stunning buxom woman dressed in flowing white trousers and a frilly pink blouse. Red bumps distort the complexion of her heart-shaped face.

Zephyrus nods to the newcomer stiffly. "Soria."

Padding to the back of the sofa, the woman wraps her long arms around Ailith's neck, propping her chin atop the faun's head. Ailith's wife, I presume. "All of Under is aware of your escape from the Orchid King," Soria says. "Pierus has already placed a bounty upon your head, and there are many who wouldn't think twice about turning you in. Wherever you go, danger will follow."

"Be that as it may," Zephyrus counters, "Yakim would be foolish to attempt to capture me here. Anyone would." Reclining into the plush blue cushions, he grins lazily, no better than a cat in the sun. "A lifelong ban from the Estate is a steep price to pay. Everyone knows your drinks are the best in Under."

Ailith preens at the compliment. Her wife, on the other hand, remains unimpressed.

"You always do this," Soria snaps. "You waltz in here acting like the sun shines from your ass, toss out a request, and expect our cooperation."

Her voice drops to a roughened pitch. "Let me remind you, Bringer of Spring, that this is Under. Your divine privilege extends no farther than your fingernails."

Eyes narrowed, Zephyrus studies Soria, then Ailith. When he finds no support, he turns to me. I gaze at him calmly. "She's not wrong," I murmur. The West Wind possesses an unfailing streak of self-importance.

"Let's try something different." Soria paces toward the window and returns. "Why don't you ask for our help as your friends, instead of using us as a means to an end. A difficult concept for you, I know. But the fact is, your options are few. Why mistreat those who can help you?"

Pride gleams in Ailith's eyes as she takes in her wife. Zephyrus, however, bows his head.

"You're right. I think of you both as my friends, and I should have treated you as such. For that, I apologize." A wayward curl falls into his eyes; he brushes it away with a shaking hand. "Please, if you can help me, I would be grateful. If not, I will leave you in peace."

Once more, Ailith taps her nails on the sofa back as she considers him. "I'll make an exception, just this once. But if anyone comes to harm under my roof, you will suffer the consequences. I like you, Zephyrus, and I would hate to lose a friend, but those are my conditions."

His eyes close in apparent relief. "Thank you both. I won't forget this."

"A likely story," Soria mutters.

Ailith lays a hand on her wife's arm. "As luck would have it, we are expecting Yakim shortly. Normally, we place him in the Red Room, but we will inform him it requires cleaning. He will wait in the great room until it is done. That should give you the opportunity to approach him."

"Excellent."

"And what of your companion?" Soria questions.

Ailith's whetted gaze takes me in. Indeed, she did not overlook my presence. Merely tucked me aside until needed. "It is true he cannot resist mortal flesh. If you're willing to take the risk, the payoff could be to your benefit. But your pet will need to participate."

The West Wind's eyes darken as he turns to the faun. "I already stated that she is no pet," he warns.

Ailith shoots him a conspiratorial grin. "Why does Yakim need to know that?"

30

"A RE YOU CERTAIN THIS IS NECESSARY?" I WHISPER.
Ailith meets my gaze in the mirror, her hands filled with my springing curls, a few already pinned in place against my scalp. Maneuvering my hair into sections, she piles the red tresses so they frame my face. "Quite certain. When I'm through with you, Yakim will look nowhere else."

I blanch as she feathers the ends of my curls with a comb. Do I regret agreeing to this outlandish scheme? Maybe a little. I've tossed myself into the sea without first checking its depth.

Tonight, I am to play the part of Zephyrus' pet.

Once my hair is properly styled, Ailith bustles to a small table littered with cosmetics. The vanity mirror is so large I'm granted an unencumbered view of Ailith and Soria's bedroom. Pale pink silk plasters the walls. Aside from the enormous four-poster bed, there is a small sitting area to my right backed by a tall bookshelf.

I've no personal touches at Thornbrook. I never wanted them. This bedroom, however, reflects the couple's nature. It must be nice, I think, to make a space your own.

"You are quiet," Ailith states, plucking a shade of lip cream from the pile, holding it up for scrutiny, and discarding it amongst the impressive collection with a shake of her head. "Do you not want the West Wind's attention?"

"His attention?" They are sharp, these words. It is too late to temper them. "Why would I want that?"

Her gaze angles toward my left hand, which claws the arm of my chair. I loosen my grip, sink back into the cushions with a soundless exhalation.

"Why indeed?" she drawls.

I neither want nor need Zephyrus' attention, or any man's attention, for that matter. Zephyrus is a distraction. Always has been. If he happens to stir certain yearnings in me, well, I can worry about those later.

I say, "Why did you ask Zephyrus if something had happened to his face?"

Cosmetics in hand, Ailith crosses the room with a sway of her generous hips. Tubes, pots, brushes—all clatter onto the table.

"He did not always appear so unsightly," she replies, opening a tube and smoothing a pale cream over my cheeks. "I'm not sure what trouble he got himself into. Knowing him, he probably deserved it."

"What did he used to look like?" Truthfully, I find Zephyrus handsome, despite his awkward features, though I am convinced his nose is straighter than it was when we first met, his skin more luminous.

She spends an absurd amount of time lengthening my eyelashes. Only when they are curled to her satisfaction does she reply, "Too pretty to be real."

I gaze into the mirror. Dark brown eyes hazed in kohl regard me calmly. This woman appears arrogantly unaffected. Hair teased, freckled skin spritzed with perfume, small pearls shining at her ears. An emerald gown, cut scandalously low, accentuates the length of her neck, softens the shape of her strong shoulders and upper arms.

Her name is Brielle.

"You don't think this is a little much?" I hedge to Ailith, who applies a gold-tinted cosmetic to the outer corners of my eyes.

"My dear," she says through her laughter, "I could do so much more. With your hair, your skin, your curves . . ." She trails off, mouth quirked. "Your gloves, however, clash with the outfit."

I clench my hands in my lap. The brown leather does not particularly match the green, it is true. "I must keep them on. My faith requires that I do."

I'm greeted by a look of pure skepticism. Ailith is not the first to respond in such a manner, nor will she be the last. I do not expect others to understand, and I made peace with it long ago.

"Well," she goes on, substituting one powder for another, "as long as it makes you happy."

It does make me happy, or it did, rather.

"So, there's really nothing between you and Zephyrus?" the faun presses.

My eyes cut to hers. Pink colors my neck and climbs into my face.

"He's a friend," I croak.

"A friend. How quaint." She's smiling as she rubs rouge onto my lips. "The way Zephyrus looks at you, I'm not so sure your relationship is as chaste as you think."

I vow not to question her further, but it has been a long, arduous road. Today, I am weak. "How does he look at me?"

Wiping an errant smudge from the corner of my mouth, she leans back to study her handiwork, darkly amused. "You'll find out soon enough."

From the top of the stairs, the great room spreads below in shades of gray pocked by small islands of candlelight. Countless patrons have since arrived in the time Ailith spent *embellishing* me. Her words, not mine. The guests crowd around the tables, slurping stew or sipping wine from finger-smudged glassware as the front door opens and closes with increasing frequency.

I am a blade.

I do not see Zephyrus. He left me in Ailith's capable hands, claiming he would nurse a drink in the meantime. I force myself down the stairs, one hand fused to the railing, the other lifting the heavy skirt of my gown. The stairs creak with my descent. My attention flits from darkened corner to shaded nook, drapes partitioning off smaller sections in the larger space. I smell him—nectar and sunlight. The perfume of his skin.

Down and down and down I go, nearer to this evening's purpose. There on the bottom step, my world goes still.

Across the room, the West Wind lounges in an armchair near the fireplace, body arranged in artful repose. Lifting a tumbler of amber liquid to his mouth, he watches me lazily over the rim. In the time we were apart, he has clearly shaved, the scruffy beard now gone. His green-eyed gaze holds candlelight, and darkens subtly in the passing moments.

Zephyrus' mouth shapes a faint upward curve. The arrogance in that smile stirs things in me despite my attempts to defend myself against it. The West Wind: devious, clever, undying. A god.

Tipping back his head, he drains his drink to the dregs. A rush of heat tightens my skin as he unfurls from his sprawl with grace. He circles the tables, slipping through space with complete mastery, no evidence of the numbness likely eating at his legs. Then again, I am not the only one playing a part tonight.

A bead of sweat slithers down my spine as Zephyrus halts at the bottom stair, drinking me in. "You," he murmurs, "are a wonder."

"It was Ailith," I stutter. "She did all the work."

The West Wind leans forward, and I suddenly forget to breathe. "Darling," he murmurs into my ear, "I have always thought you beautiful. I did not think that was a secret."

My nipples pebble beneath my corset, pained and chafing, and I quickly cross my arms to conceal the evidence. "You never mentioned it," I manage with breathless nerves. "You never once made it known."

"Didn't I?" His eyebrows hike upward, and the mossy rings encircling his pupils sparkle. "Think carefully. What is it you remember?"

He is too close, but I do not demand space, even when his sigh brushes my mouth. "You teased me," I murmur. "You toyed with my emotions, always seeking a laugh, with me at the center of it all."

Head canted, his attention slides across my waist, up to my chest, where it lingers, before returning to my face a heartbeat later. "I spoke truth in those times. You decided my words were false, having thought yourself unworthy of a man's attention."

"How could I believe you," I quaver, "when every other word from your mouth was made in jest?"

He falls into contemplative disquiet. Beyond his shoulder, one of the patrons, an old, bent crone, returns to the bar with an empty glass.

Zephyrus steps closer then, his sternum pressing into my upper arm. "I apologize if I made you feel unwanted or undesired. That could not be further from the truth."

I swallow so hard I'm certain he hears my throat click. I'm absolutely going to Hell for this, but I must know. "Then what is the truth?"

His eyes shine like fresh lacquer. If I were not staring so intently at his face, I would have missed the flare of heat there. "Do you remember your first visit to Under?" With hypnotic sensation, the tips of his fingers skim the flowing silk of my skirt. "The couple beneath the willow tree?"

Naked limbs and sweat-slickened skin. The forked end of a man's tongue. My insides curl from the recollection, and I bite the flesh of my cheek, give a fitful nod.

"Do you remember what I said?"

"You told me closing my eyes would make no difference," I whisper as his fingers sink deeper into the folds of fabric. "That I have already seen."

"Indeed. And once I tell you, the truth will be known. Are you sure you want that?"

I used to regard truth as a burden. I chose blindness. I accepted what I had always been told, what I had read, what I had heard.

We are attracted to things that lie outside of our lived experience. We crave something deeper.

"Tell me," I demand.

I startle as his fingertips alight on my outer thigh and begin to trace tentative circles there. "Shall I inform you of the nights when camp was quiet," he says, voice resonating like the lowest church bells, "and I watched you, asleep in your bedroll?" The touch skims upward, across my hip bone, where it rests, a scalding permanence.

My hands tremble. I clamp them together at my front. His allure unfolds with dizzying calculation. Bringer of Spring.

"Hours I spent in your company each day, watching the sway of your body as we hiked." His lips brush the side of my neck. "What a temptation you were."

Heat feeds into my bloodstream. I fight for air, or sanity, or both. I am Brielle. I have not forgotten. What manner of enchantment has taken hold?

"It was the most delicious torture," he goes on, grasping my thigh with a firm hand. "In the evenings, I retreated to a quiet place to attend to my needs. I worked myself over slowly, wishing it was your hand around my cock."

My stomach plunges straight through the floor.

Zephyrus turns his head, and his breath coasts across my naked collarbone, bare skin prickling in the wash of heat. "It was your face in my mind's eye."

"You—" My voice cracks. All that I might say turns to dust.

Up his hand drifts, across my abdomen, skirting the soft swell of my chest. For a moment, I'm overcome by the urge to angle my breast into his open palm. I question what he might do next. Squeeze the nipple, perhaps, or circle the nub until it aches.

"Someone will see you," I whisper.

"No one is paying any attention to us."

My cheeks burn, but I peek beneath my eyelashes, searching the room. He's right. Everyone is too focused on gambling and drinking to notice.

"Shall I go on?" Zephyrus asks, a knowing gleam in his eye.

He must sense my yearning. He must smell it on my skin, taste it on my breath, feel the shuddering waves of longing running through me, down to the pit of my stomach, the soles of my feet.

"Shall I describe to you what it felt like," he goes on, "imagining the expression on your face, the sounds you'd make, how sweet your touch would be—"

I slap a hand over his mouth, breathing hard. Our eyes lock and hold: green to brown, god to mortal, captive to the free.

I don't know what to say. How does one properly respond to indecency of the mind? I'm afraid to admit to my cravings, to learn of those things, too.

Slowly, he lifts a hand, curls his fingers around my wrist, and pulls my palm away from his mouth. "You asked me why I run," he says, "but perhaps the better question, darling, is why you run from something that cannot be denied? Do you not feel this?" He presses his hand against my thundering heart. "Do you not wish to see where it might lead?"

My mouth open, then clamps shut. I do, and I don't. How to explain these complicated emotions?

Suddenly, his eyes widen, and I move before I'm aware of it, catching him around the waist as his knees buckle. My legs engage as the full weight of his body sinks against mine.

Panting, he stares at the threadbare rug, shock having frozen his features.

"The venom?" I ask.

He nods, just once, and gasps out, "Help me to a chair."

With his arm tossed over my shoulder, we shuffle toward the armchair he vacated earlier. The fireplace roars behind the metal grate.

I deposit him onto the cushions, and he emits a low oath as he runs his hands up and down his legs, massaging the stiff muscles. Perching on an adjacent chair, I consider how best to manage the kink in our plan. "How bad is it?"

"It's already passing." He lifts his head, manages a small smile. A worthy attempt, to be certain, but bleakness stamps shadows over his expression.

It was the same during our trek to the Estate. Every few hours, numbness claimed his legs, dragging him to the earth. He told me the waves would hit with increasing frequency over time. Eventually, the numbness would remain, a paralysis of unfeeling permanence.

"Let us not think of this," he says. "Yakim should be arriving any moment. Until then, let us enjoy ourselves."

Nodding in agreement, I settle back, fully assuming Zephyrus will do the same. Instead, he perches on the arm of *my* chair, body angled toward me.

"Don't you want your own chair?" I suggest with a strained smile. "It would probably be more comfortable."

His mouth curves fiendishly. "Am I making you nervous?" The shadows from a moment ago have vanished, as though he has beaten them into submission.

I will not give him the satisfaction of affirmation. "Isn't this inappropriate?"

"To you, maybe. To the fair folk, this is positively chaste." His hand slips beneath my hair to curl around my nape. The touch is a shock. "Imagine we are meeting for the first time."

His knee bumps my outer thigh, and I startle, clambering for my bearings. *Imagine.* What a treacherous word. He asks me to experience, for however long, a life that is not mine, but that perhaps I yearn for in some darkened corner of my heart.

"I arrive here on business and spot a woman I've never seen before." Against my nape, his thumb skims upward, tracing the sensitive tendon. "I wonder who she is and where she comes from. I ask myself why she is here."

He pauses deliberately, allowing me space to respond.

"I am here to visit my sister," I say quietly, though I have no siblings.

He nods in encouragement. "Go on."

I swallow with difficulty. Thornbrook is all I know, all I've ever wanted to know, but the West Wind is a force, and helplessly, I'm swept downstream.

"While I wait, I decide to eat dinner. During my meal, I notice a man staring at me from across the room. Our eyes meet, and I feel . . ."

What I'd feel then is what I feel now. Namely this: overcome.

"Tell me," he coaxes in a tone I know well. It is deep-rooted, old. It demands I listen.

"Seen," I relent. "I feel seen."

Catching my chin, he angles my head so I'm forced to meet his eyes. They brighten the gloom with emerald warmth. Though it is a story, it's too similar to reality for me to pretend otherwise.

"You are," he whispers. "Seen."

My tongue slips out to wet my lips, and Zephyrus eases forward a fraction.

A bell chimes, and he drops his hand, turning toward the front door. "Right on time."

I follow his gaze to a tall, lanky man wearing a maroon vest tucked into the waistband of his trousers. In one hand, he carries a leather briefcase. In the other, a scarf, despite the balmy temperature.

"Don't let his manicured appearance fool you," Zephyrus whispers. "Yakim is ruthless. Remember that."

Admittedly, I was expecting someone a bit more bloodthirsty. He possesses a full head of long, sable hair tied in a low tail, only a few shades darker than his stippled skin. Yakim could be forty or seventy. It is difficult to say.

As he crosses the room, my attention falls to the long, thin tail trailing his heels. Once Yakim reaches the bar, he folds himself onto one of the three vacant stools.

"Yakim is a demon," Zephyrus murmurs into my ear. "Blood is necessary for his survival." He watches the newest arrival carefully, as does every other patron in the room. "Normally, he would acquire blood through a pet, but when he is unable to procure one, he must purchase it."

Yakim does not ask for a drink. One simply appears. Wrapping his fingers around the glass, he lifts it to his mouth as Zephyrus says, "He must drink every four hours to keep the madness at bay."

The tumbler hits the countertop with a dull *thunk*. Eventually, patrons return to their conversations, their dinner, their gambling, though the tension in the room lingers. "What do you mean *madness*?"

As Yakim's gaze passes over Zephyrus, he does a double-take, frowning.

"Switch places with me," whispers the West Wind.

"What?"

He's already drawing me upright. "Here. Sit on my lap."

I'm standing without knowing how it happened. He tugs me onto his lap, and my legs sprawl across his thighs, the emerald fabric tumbling like falling water, his face unnervingly close. I shove against his chest to put space between us when Yakim rises from the bar, eyes locked on the West Wind.

"He's coming over," I hiss.

"Calm, darling." He squeezes my hip to comfort me, though he continues to survey the approaching demon. "Keep your eyes on me."

I try, I really do, but my apprehension morphs into an ugly, deep-seeded fear. Why did I agree to this? Why did I leave Miles Cross, abandon my peers, sacrifice the certain for the uncertain?

As I shift into a more comfortable position, Zephyrus lets out a strained moan. Firm thighs, the cradle of a man's hips, a solid chest at my back, and this: a long, hard ridge pressing into my backside.

My muscles lock. I may be a virgin, but I know what happens when a woman lies with a man.

"Give me a moment," he says.

"Sh-should I move?"

"No." His hand spasms around my hip. "That will only exacerbate the issue."

"Right." The word squeaks out.

He blows out a breath, then laughs, his forehead resting between my shoulder blades. "This is not going to plan."

We had a plan? I'm wound too tightly to remember. "I don't know if I can do this," I whisper. Those loitering in the demon's path scuttle out of range. "What if I say the wrong thing? What if he kills you?"

Hooking his thumb at the edge of my jaw, Zephyrus turns my head to face him.

My breath catches. Our surroundings fade, and I imagine fabric enveloping our private corner, muting sight and sound but for the West Wind, a vision of bright clarity. The bones of his face appear more defined, whetted by shadow and light.

"Whatever happens, remember this: it is not real. Understand?" The pads of his fingers slip beneath the neckline of my dress with frightening ease. "These are the parts we must play until the deal is done."

We discussed this, Zephyrus, Ailith, and I. The West Wind is my master, and I am his pet.

He studies me a moment longer. "Try to stay in character. If you feel yourself becoming overwhelmed, settle back and I'll take over. All right?" He tucks a lock of hair behind my ear.

A wave of longing sweeps through me so fiercely I do not even consider how many times he's touched me without barriers in the last hour. Sitting sideways on his lap, I watch the demon close the remaining distance, the curled end of his tail wrapped around his left leg. Zephyrus' hand slides to my thigh and settles there. My mouth goes dry.

Yakim halts a few paces away, peering down his nose at the West Wind. Flecks of silver glitter within his black eyes. "Zephyrus." The coarseness of his voice reminds me of crushed rock.

Zephyrus inclines his head in response. "Yakim." The demon's gaze skips to me and draws a leisurely path from my bared ankles to my chest.

A pet signals status, Ailith had told me. *It is an object representing ownership and power. A pet,* she added, eyes alight, *is the ultimate form of possession.*

When Yakim's gaze lifts to my face, a small, sated smile curls his mouth. "Is this your pet? She is lovely."

"She is." Tightening his hand around my thigh, Zephyrus drags it higher so his fingers catch the fabric, displaying his most recent acquisition. "Poor thing was being traumatized by a horde of nymphs before I found her. Not sure how she got here." He grins, his teeth growing points before my eyes. "Lucky me."

"Indeed." Yakim settles into a vacant armchair and places his briefcase at his feet. "Have you claimed her?"

"I have." If I'm not mistaken, his canines elongate further. "It was almost too easy."

"You always did love a pretty face." He runs his skeletal fingers over the polished surface of the side table. "It has been some time. I almost didn't recognize you across the room. The look suits you." He gestures to Zephyrus' nose, though it is smaller than it was weeks ago. "A better reflection of your personality, to be certain."

Zephyrus inclines his head. "I appreciate that." He flags the bartender, who delivers him a glass of wine, as well as a glass of blood for Yakim. The demon smacks his lips heartily and sets the drink on the table.

With my hands folded over my lap, I do my best to remain unobtrusive, but every so often I lift my hand to the West Wind's chest, presenting the image of one enamored by her captor. His arousal still pokes at my rear. My mind never strays from it for long.

Swirling the wine, Zephyrus takes a swallow, then deposits his glass on the table. "Thank you for not killing me at the first opportunity."

"Well." The demon smiles briefly, and to my surprise, his teeth are white, like small, dazzling pearls tucked among pink gums. "I'd like to believe I've mellowed over the last century or so. What's done is done. After all," he adds, a bit of malice hardening his tone, "it's just business, right?"

Slowly, Zephyrus tugs me nearer, his chest warming my spine, almost like a shield against the obvious threat Yakim poses. "No hard feelings I hope," he purrs. "You of all people understand the stakes of a gamble."

"It was no gamble," Yakim snarls, blood outlining his shining white teeth. "You double-crossed me."

"And you're saying you weren't planning on doing the same?" He snorts. "Face it. You're just angry I fooled you first."

Before Yakim can respond, the West Wind plants both hands on my legs and pulls, spreading them wide. My instinct is to stiffen, wrench myself free, but beneath his touch, I soften, my head falling back against his shoulder. Yakim's attention drops to where the fabric hangs between my thighs.

"As much as I appreciate tedious small talk," the demon drawls, eventually shifting his attention to Zephyrus, "it is no coincidence you're here. Let's not pretend this meeting wasn't premeditated."

"Now that you mention it," Zephyrus says, "I am here to make a deal." Gently, he nudges my legs closed. The pose apparently served its purpose.

The demon laughs, and the conversation at the adjacent table cuts out, for it is a chilling sound, thin and cruel. "How utterly unsurprising you are." He steeples his fingers together, peering over the point. "Very well. Seeing as you went to all this trouble, I will hear your case."

"I'm in the market for a powerful antidote, something able to reverse the effects of nightshade." Yakim's dark eyebrows quirk. "Do you have something in your collection?"

"An antidote for nightshade." He speaks deliberately, a jagged fingernail scraping the arm of his chair. "Interesting."

"Yes, yes, it's all quite interesting." Zephyrus waves a hand. "What is the cost of the antidote? Assuming you have one at your disposal."

"To start, twenty thousand gold coins. Ten thousand for the antidote itself, ten thousand for the trouble of an unscheduled meeting."

My heart begins to thunder, because I have never seen a single coin on Zephyrus' person. Debts and unfulfilled promises are the West Wind's currency of choice.

"Twenty thousand seems a steep price to pay."

"The antidote contains the grounds of a bezoar stone from a goat born in the seventh hour on the seventh day of the seventh month," Yakim says. "You will find nothing more potent, no other guarantee to stop the venom. Granted, it can only be taken at sunrise."

My attention snaps to the window as the fingers at my hip flex. It's still dark. But we don't have long before Under's enchanted sun rises, if it decides to rise at all.

"I see," Zephyrus mutters.

A cold smile blooms, lips thinning beneath Yakim's sharp nose. "If you do not have the payment, well, that *is* a shame."

The demon cannot know how near to paralysis Zephyrus is. Even now, another wave of numbness recedes beneath his skin, a faint trembling the only indication.

"I only have twelve thousand at the moment," he says to Yakim. "Will you accept a trade instead?"

Yakim leans back in his armchair, viciously pleased. "Throw in your pet, and you've got a deal."

That slaps me awake. "Excuse me?"

Pets can be bought, Ailith told me. *They can be sold. They can be traded and set free. Only one's master has the power to decide.*

Yakim considers me. "So, you do have a voice. I must say it is as lovely as the rest of you."

It takes two attempts before I'm able to speak without retching. "Zephyrus will pay you whatever amount for the antidote, but I am not part of the deal."

"You are, my dear." How calmly Yakim responds. "I determined it."

It is then I realize Zephyrus no longer touches me in reassurance. "There must be another way."

"While I appreciate a woman who speaks her mind"—the demon's low, silken cadence makes my stomach turn with dread—"the decision is not yours to make." There is a pause. "We will have to break you of that habit."

Panic swells beyond my control. It bears a mouth ringed by jagged teeth.

"How desperate are you for this antidote," Yakim murmurs, "old friend?"

Zephyrus wouldn't turn me over. He would not handle my life so carelessly.

"That is your price?" Zephyrus demands. When I reach for his hand, he nudges me away.

"It is." The demon glances between us. "The only question is whether you are willing to pay it."

Was this the plan all along? Use me, trade me, dispose of me when

I no longer served his purpose? To think I've abandoned my peers back in Miles Cross for him—and now this.

"And if I am?" Zephyrus holds the demon's gaze.

Picking up his briefcase, Yakim props it on his lap, opening it toward himself so we are unable to view the contents. He selects a vial with a cork stopper, holding it out. Small particles rest at the bottom of the glass.

I dig my fingernails into Zephyrus' arm. "Not this," I whisper.

He won't meet my eye. "It's the only way."

"It's *not*." There must be another solution we have yet to think of.

Yakim offers the vial between his long fingers. "It can be yours," he murmurs. "All I need is your pet's name."

"Give me the antidote, and you will have it."

The vial disappears into the demon's grip. "You are the last person I would ever trust. Who's to say you will not flee once the antidote is in your possession?" He clucks his tongue in disappointment. "We do the exchange my way, or not at all."

"My way," Zephyrus counters, "or you can forget about my pet."

Yakim laughs his cold, brittle caw. "I have no great need for a human companion. Yours is lovely, but there are others I can obtain by easier means."

He wouldn't. He can't. But I have forgotten who Zephyrus is: a once-beloved god. He is used to catching others under his thumb, going to whatever lengths is necessary to obtain what he desires most.

Nudging me into a standing position, he directs me toward the demon. Panic spikes again as he removes his hand from my back. The trap, I finally understand, was never for Yakim. It was for me.

"Brielle," the West Wind states. "Her name is Brielle."

31

"BRIELLE," THE DEMON CROONS, FLASHING THOSE BONE-WHITE teeth. "How it rolls off the tongue."

I am still, caught within a perpetual echo. *Brielle.* The most carefully safe-guarded secret, bargained away, no more significant than a bit of dented coin.

The trade is made, the antidote passed into the West Wind's possession, and twelve thousand coin given to Yakim, plucked from the air itself. Zephyrus also tugs a glass bottle from his pocket, similar to the ones I witnessed being sold at the sea-nymphs' celebration, and hands it to the demon. With dread, I realize what it must contain: my name. But how? Has he had it all this time? I am not familiar enough with the process to understand. The great room drifts out of focus, a melancholy blur tinged with sweet-smelling smoke.

Yakim collects his briefcase, downs the remainder of his drink, and turns to me.

"I can understand why Zephyrus wanted you for himself." He peers down the blade of his nose, a spot of blood crusted at the corner of his mouth. "Your old master did not recognize what a treasure you are, but what can you expect from an arrogant, self-serving god?" That sharp smile makes a reappearance. "His loss."

Tears sting my eyes. Fear has dogged my heels for the last ten years, but I have learned to live with it. I *will* get through this. Once Mother Mabel learns I'm missing, she will come for me.

"Don't be frightened, my dear." The demon's gaze, bright with greed, cuts to Zephyrus. "I care for what's mine." He trails one thin, elongated hand down my bare arm.

Over his shoulder, Ailith has emerged from a nearby hallway. She waves him over. "Yakim. A word, please."

His expression tightens with obvious irritation, yet he turns and smiles prettily at the faun. "I'm a bit preoccupied at the moment."

She cocks her hip. "I'm happy to discuss your financials in front of my patrons, if that is what you wish."

Yakim snarls.

Ailith's smile spreads with slow satisfaction. "Meet me in the Red Room," she states, and flounces down the hall.

Yakim steps away, briefcase in hand. "A moment, Brielle. You are not to leave without my permission. Not that you would get far. You are bound to me now." He dodges a nearby table and vanishes down the corridor. A few patrons observe his departure, and only when he's out of sight do they visibly relax.

"Brielle." The West Wind catches my hand. "Look at me."

I lurch from his hold, collapsing into the opposite chair. The silk skirt billows in green clouds before sagging around my trembling legs. "How could you?" My gut churns with the horror of what he's done to me. I should have known better. Why do I not learn?

"I need you to look at me—"

His voice bleeds into the hum of background noise: clinking dishware, thudding boots, the roar of the fireplace. At this point, I'm uncertain of my way forward. How is Mother Mabel to know where to find me? Would she risk her life, the lives of my peers, to bring me back to Thornbrook safely?

Slowly, I lift my head. "Why?" I thought I'd seen a change in Zephyrus. How deep does my naivete truly run?

"Come." He glances over his shoulder. "We don't have much time."

"Did you not hear what he said?" I spit. "I can't leave. You gave my name away!"

You must never speak your name aloud, Brielle. Ever. Should any of the fair folk hear your name, they will have power over you. More power than you can ever imagine. Keep it safe.

My fingers curl into the arms of the chair. If I could exchange nails for claws, I'd gouge out those green eyes without a second thought. "I trusted you."

The West Wind studies me, completely unaffected by my hurt. "Can you move your limbs?"

"What does that have to do with anything?"

Deeper and deeper I spiral, down into a lightless pit. Where will the demon take me? What will he make me do now that he has control over me? I am afraid. But more so, I am sick with rage.

Spearing his fingers through his curls, Zephyrus glances down the hall where Yakim disappeared. "Will you just try? Please?" A few patrons look on. I've not forgotten the bounty on Zephyrus' head. Neither have they.

"What are you not telling me?" I demand.

"Walk to the door."

"But—"

"*Please.*" Another furtive peek toward the hallway.

I stay put. "Tell me why." I'm tired of his secrets.

Zephyrus pivots, gaze stony, and strides to my chair. He leans over me and slips a finger beneath my neckline, pulling the trinity knot pendant free. "The Father shields you."

The gold piece shines against his tanned hand. Lifting my eyes, I peer into the West Wind's gold-flecked gaze.

It's not real.

"Was I ever in any danger?" I whisper.

"Had you lost your necklace, or had someone snatched it, you would have been vulnerable. But I may speak your name freely when you wear it. I did not tell you because it was better to proceed with caution, and I feared the ruse would be too transparent if you knew. Yakim is not easily fooled."

I suppose it makes sense. The fair folk, while not able to speak untruths, are able to sense them in others, though I do not agree with Zephyrus' method of trickery. "What about the glass bottle you gave him? What was inside?"

"I'd like to think my powers are strong enough to create a bit of shimmering air."

"Oh." Quiet, uncertain.

He is somber as he says, "I would not betray you, not again." He stares at me a moment longer before pushing away. "We must go. Hold this for me. Keep it safe."

He passes the antidote into my hands. I slide it into my pocket, yet hesitate, fingers curled in my heavy gown. "I can't run in this."

He yanks me from the chair and slings my pack onto his shoulder, having stowed it near the fireplace. "You don't have a choice."

We run—across the great room, out the door, down the stairs, navigating the wet, buckling boardwalk spanning the steaming bog. We leap onto a strip of high ground, which leads to a dirt lane cutting through the marshland.

We're halfway down the road when a shriek of rage erupts at our backs.

Zephyrus jerks me along, our escape aided by the weak propulsion of air he buffets at our heels. I try to keep pace, but his long legs propel him faster, farther. A few steps later, the wind fails, and he begins to pant, sweat sliding down his face.

He cuts right, plunging off the road into the swamp. We sink knee-deep into the putrid water. Slime sucks at my boots as I trudge forward, the drag of my dress catching on whatever lurks in this dead, water-logged place. The sky lies vague and shadowed above.

A crash behind us draws Zephyrus' attention. "Grab hold," he pants.

As soon as I grab his hand, a robust wind stirs around us, and we are flying through the air, up into the sweeping boughs of a nearby tree. There, we settle down to wait.

A beast thrice the size of a horse enters the clearing. Four limbs, a dripping maw, its spine pushed so severely against its thin skin I swear I see bone.

"Is that Yakim?" I whisper.

Zephyrus nods, a finger pressed to his lips. *Watch,* he mouths.

The demon lurches below, winding through trees, scenting out our trail. The fog overlaying the swamp must help mask our scents, because after a time, it moves off.

"What now?" I ask.

"The way I see it, we have one option." Crouched amongst the branches, Zephyrus rubs his palms against his trousers, his cheeks pale despite the hard run. "We'll have to kill Yakim."

I hesitate, a bit uncomfortable with the implication, but if Yakim's death makes room for Zephyrus' life, surely the Father would make an exception.

I pull my dagger from the small of my back. "Tell me how."

"No." The word thrums with authority as Zephyrus catches my wrist, forcing me to lower the weapon against the folds of green fabric veiling the branch I sit on. "I'll go alone. It's safer that way."

"What about the venom? The numbness?" I see it in his eyes, the apprehension of another wave hitting him while he's vulnerable. Until the sun appears, Zephyrus can't risk taking the antidote. "We should stick together."

He falls quiet then, eyes downcast.

"What is it?" I shift closer, grabbing onto a higher branch for balance.

"You thought I had given you to Yakim. You thought I'd broken your trust." Beneath the sopping tunic, his chest heaves erratically, each breath tripping into the next. "I have given you every reason to doubt my word, yet here you are. Maybe that's why I fear placing the burden of my life onto you. I do not want to believe you might care for me out of fear that you do not."

"Zephyrus." I take his hand in mine. "Of course I care. Why do you think I'm here?"

"Who is to say you will not abandon me?"

How wrong he is. How like a child in this moment. "Look at me." Reluctantly, he lifts his eyes, and my heart aches for the man he'd once been, the man he still carries with him despite the passing centuries. "If you think I would abandon you to a demon," I murmur, "then you don't know me at all."

He slumps against the trunk, clothes mud-spattered, in complete disarray. "It would be nothing less than I deserve." After removing my pack from his shoulders, he tucks it between the branches and drops neatly into the water. "I'll be back."

As I watch him go, I understand that life is a collection of choices, and here is one more I must make. Enveloped in these branches, I am safe. And yet, Zephyrus lacks a weapon. His power flags. My iron blade might be all that can defeat this demon.

Only I can decide what path my life will take, I realize. I hold the power. I have always held the power.

After tying back my hair, I grab my rucksack and climb down the tree, following the direction Zephyrus went, the path littered with broken branches and massive, clawed footprints. I push forward, but the dress is so heavy, the corset so tight, that it's impossible to catch my breath.

Ahead, something large and menacing shifts between the trees. The beast slinks toward Zephyrus, ears flattened against its skull. Crouched at the edge of the clearing, I palm my dagger, thumb pressed against the frayed leather wrapping. Zephyrus stands alone, unarmed.

The demon hurtles forward with a roar, and I am running, dagger in hand, toward the West Wind's back. I am not afraid. The Father guides me over pressed grass, drowned muck. Knocking Zephyrus aside, I leap forward and bury the dagger into the beast's chest.

It recoils, falling back with an ear-shattering shriek. The motion wrenches me forward, my blade firmly imbedded. A short twist of my arm frees the weapon. I stumble back as the demon lurches upright. Its skin sizzles, melting from the touch of lethal iron.

"Brielle!"

That sharp-toothed maw drives toward me. It rams into a solid barrier, as though Zephyrus has fashioned a wall of air to separate us. At the next lunge, it crashes through the partition. I dodge, fighting the drag of my soaked dress, and slash the dagger toward its throat. It rears back, colliding with an ancient cypress. Then it's up, charging, steam curling from its slitted nostrils. A slither of air coils around a hind leg and binds tight. The demon strains against it in a fit of gnashing teeth.

Darting around Zephyrus, I plunge the dagger into its torso a second time, then slash the blade across its throat. Blood pours forth, and the bog shudders as the demon collapses.

My chest heaves, my hand shakes, but I refuse to turn my eye from the beast. It might not be dead. It could rise again.

"Brielle."

"What if it heals itself?" I demand. "We can't take any chances."

"Yakim is dead."

I whirl, and there Zephyrus stands, a single scratch marring the otherwise smooth skin of his cheek. He is handsome. Beautiful, even. What manner of sorcery is this?

"Your face." I'm still staring. It hovers on the threshold of perfection, indescribable splendor, sharp enough to cut. "How?"

He collapses with a cry.

As his head vanishes beneath the surface of the bog, I lunge, catching him around the collar and hauling him upright. He sags into me, dragged down by his weakened legs. By the Father, I wish the sun would reveal itself.

"The tree," he grinds out. "Bring me to that tree."

I drag him to the tract of dirt, where an old cypress oversees the sprawling wetland. He grabs a low branch, glaring at me like an irate kitten. "That was the stupidest thing you've ever done," he growls.

"It was going to kill you. You just stood there—"

"I was going to end it with my power," he retorts. "It had to be at the last possible second. A single strike to the heart."

"How was I supposed to know?"

"I told you not to interfere."

My blood hums dangerously, and my fingers twitch around the dagger, drawing his eye. We have been here before. I'm beginning to wonder if he prefers death. "I saved your life," I hiss. "A simple thank-you would suffice."

"Thank you?" He laughs, yet the sound fractures, becomes something else as his face crumples. A tear slides down one cheek, shocking me to the core.

I step forward, suddenly uncertain of my place.

"I can't watch someone I care for die again," he says hoarsely. Silver streaks his green gaze. "I don't think I could bear it."

His admission softens me and saddens me. He has experienced much strife in his immortal life, but haven't we all? The difference is, I've had support—Thornbrook, my peers, Mother Mabel. Zephyrus is alone.

Lifting my hand to his face, I say, "We will get through this. I have faith." My thumb catches a tear where it trembles, dewdrop clear, against his cheek.

"I lost faith long ago," he says.

"That's all right. I have enough faith for us both."

Zephyrus abruptly releases the branch, his nostrils flaring. The numbness must have passed, for he's able to stand without aid as a mournful cry, low and eerie, winds through the moss-draped trees.

"The hounds," he murmurs.

A chill overtakes me—body, mind, heart.

Snagging my wrist, the West Wind yanks me deeper into the marshland at a run. A tree blinks into existence an arm's length away. I lurch sideways, veering around its gnarled trunk as Zephyrus leaps with my arm in tow. My shoulder joint wrenches, then sears, forcing my back to curve to alleviate the pain. "Zephyrus!"

"Run, Brielle, unless you want to die."

I'm tossed forward, the wind momentarily bearing my weight. My feet hit the squelching mud, and I stumble, my boots catching in one of the twisting roots.

"Faster," he pants.

My pack slams my lower back. My calves cramp from strain, and my sopping clothes drag me toward the mucky earth. A massive crack echoes through the bog.

My foot slips. Down I go, crashing through the water. I'm dizzy, weakening, but then I'm up, I'm limping along for seven, eight, ten steps. The weight of my body, however, is too much.

"Zephyrus." My knees fold, and I drop into the mud, fighting tears. "I can't go on." The hounds yelp with heightening frenzy, likely sensing their flagging prey.

Bounding over, he grips my arm, panting, "You can't give up. The bog will end. It's only a bit farther." He tries to haul me onto my feet, but my legs refuse to cooperate.

"You're not listening to me." My voice climbs, and cracks from compounding exhaustion. "It's not that I won't go on. I *can't*. I am physically incapable of outrunning those hounds." Tears cut hot pathways through the cooling mud on my face.

With staunch calm, he kneels beside me. In this moment, his eyes are old. They have seen things I likely never will: life and death and the heartbreaking reality of a world that changes while he alone stands still. "I don't want you to die in this place," he says, bringing his hands to my shoulders.

"I don't want that either." I swipe the dampness from my cheeks, only to smear more filth across my freckled skin.

Zephyrus takes in our surroundings. A few muddy islands interrupt the span of gray water. The scent of rot drifts steadily nearer, and a dog bellows nearby, though I can't pinpoint its direction.

I follow Zephyrus' eyes as he regards one of the islands. "That could work. There's a burrow over there, see it? We'll hide until the hounds pass."

Who is to say we will not be rabbits flushed into a trap? "You've forgotten their sense of smell."

He tosses me a wry smile. "I assure you, I have not."

He's gathering up mud in handfuls, he's smearing it across his face, he's slopping it over his thighs and dragging the mess beneath his tunic to coat his skin.

His gaze meets mine. "Now you."

I'm too drained to lift my arms. Neck, breasts, then thighs, Zephyrus smears the sludge over every curve and into every crevice until I'm covered from head to toe. The chilled grit encases me in its foul reek.

Using Zephyrus' hand as a guide, I manage to squeeze into the hollow, losing sight of the bog in the process. The tunnel leads to a slightly larger chamber, half submerged under several inches of water, where the West Wind crouches. Roots dangle from the ceiling, eerily similar to strands of hair.

"All right?" He watches me in concern.

"Yes." Leaning against the soggy walls, I collapse into a breathless heap, arms and legs askew, supplies crushed beneath my body, skin shivering from the fear firing my blood. As my vision adjusts to the burrow's darkness, Zephyrus settles beside me, his shoulder brushing mine.

Huddled together, we wait. Small vibrations in the ground announce the hounds' arrival.

They sniff and snort and growl above, water splashing as their limbs disturb the stagnant pool. I squeeze my eyes shut, retreating to the placid green garden tucked inside my heart. *Please, Father. Help us.* If we are caught here, my soul will never know peace.

After a time, the hounds move off, yipping and howling their frustration. When the sound dies, I release a fraught breath. "Now what?"

"If they don't return within the next ten minutes, it's probably safe for us to continue. We're near the edge of the bog. I can smell greenery in the distance."

My head jerks awkwardly, not quite a nod. It is both relief and sustained agony. Under offers no guarantees. We might never reach the end of the wetland.

"I want to thank you, Brielle." Zephyrus draws his knees to his chest as a child in need of comfort might. "If not for you, I would have had to face yet another tithe alone."

I've never heard words so bitter. "After what happened with Hyacinth, you never loved another?"

He turns his head. In this position, our noses align, mouths separated by a small span of dusk-colored air. "I have been alone for a long time. It is safer for me, for everyone."

"You don't desire companionship?"

"The problem with living forever," he responds quietly, "is that the people you grow to care for will eventually leave you. A mortal body ages. Bones fall brittle and organs fail. Do I desire companionship?" A forced smile takes shape upon his mouth. "Yes. But I am well aware of its costs."

I had not considered companionship from the perspective of one who lives forever. What a sad thing to experience. "I'm sorry."

"Do not pity me. I accepted my fate long ago." His attention returns to mine. "Is that what you want? To walk through life with another?"

It's silly to even consider the possibility. I am a Daughter of Thornbrook. Once I take my final vows, there can be no man in my life save the Father.

But I have thought of it, briefly. A passing notion that will never come true.

"I do wish that," I admit, "sometimes."

His chest deflates with a slow expulsion of air, which smells of the earth. His eyes are very dark. They remind me that these woods are not safe.

"Have you thought of the qualities this companion would possess?" he asks, a shadow of his old playful self.

I'm ashamed to imagine the possibility at all, but cowering in this burrow, far from civilization . . . no one from Thornbrook ever has to know.

"This man would be kind," I murmur, because what is love without kindness? "He would act selflessly. He would treat those around him with compassion and respect. He would always seek to better himself and would give his life to the Father. He would face conflict readily and speak honestly. His intentions would be nothing less than pure."

This man is ideal. Unfortunately, he does not exist. When I think of the person whose presence makes my heart skip, I see only a pair of vivid green eyes.

Zephyrus appears saddened by what I have said. "And you would deserve nothing less."

I bite my lip shyly. It means more than I can say, his words. "What about you?"

"I'm a simple man, Brielle. All I want is for someone to know my heart is theirs. That is all."

I'm still considering this when he draws away. "It's time," he says.

I force myself to nod. Ready or not, we must act.

"We'll split up, and I'll draw them off. The hounds never miss a scent twice." He slides out into the open, then sticks his arm back into the burrow. A wave of nausea rolls through me, but I grasp his hand, allowing him to pull me from our shelter. I'm remembering what it feels like to become prey.

"I'll draw them north," Zephyrus says. "Go south. Once the bog ends, find whatever shelter you can. I'll return for you."

The moment he pulls away, the air sweeps in with a disconcerting chill. His gaze catches mine, and holds.

"Stay safe," I whisper.

His attention drops to my mouth, where it lingers. "And you, Brielle of Thornbrook." Then the West Wind vanishes through the low-hanging fog.

It feels as though the wind nudges me onward with increasing urgency as I splash through the marsh, clouds of insects descending, then scattering at my arrival. The baying of the hounds snaps at my heels, yet my legs leap forward with seamless togetherness. I move like the Bringer of Spring, a god whose motions aid the wind.

A break in the trees ahead reveals a well-trodden forest path. I follow its trampled curve as the terrain ascends, until I realize how close the yelps truly are, growing louder by the minute.

It is not Zephyrus' scent the hounds have caught.

It is mine.

32

I N THE LIGHTLESS WOMB OF THE BOG, I RUN.

Leaping over collapsed vegetation, I plow through the murk, doing my best to avoid the deepest waters, the areas of marshland devoid of risen earth. My stomach cramps, snarling into a knot beneath my right hip bone. It is beyond pain, beyond the most excruciating agony. *Rest,* my body demands. I cannot.

I've pushed myself to the very edge of what I can sustain, yet my weighted legs continue to move. I crash through stagnant pools and rotten debris, my dress in tatters. The air lies dead against my skin.

Ahead—a break in the trees. Light punctures through every gap and hollow, sweeping wide across a long plain of short yellow grass elevated above the waterlogged grave of the swamp. As the baying reaches new heights, I glance over my shoulder. Shapes crowd the undergrowth, too many to count.

I careen forward with a choked sob. Death awaits. I'm not ready. I cannot die here, so far from the sun.

Halfway across the clearing, my boot catches on a depression in the soil. I hit the ground hard, rolling twice before slamming onto my back.

My dagger appears between one breath and the next. Pushing to my feet, I face the pack, iron blade steady despite my heaving lungs. The hilt bites into my palm, and the pain grounds me. I am not dead. Not yet, anyway.

The hounds close in, beasts wrought by the realm's insidious darkness. Nothing remains of their snouts except small cavities. Their rib bones gleam white, bare of muscle or skin, revealing the scooped-out hollows of their stomachs. I glance between them in rising panic, for the circle closes at my back, cutting off my escape.

The first hound lunges with a snarl. I pivot, slashing across its eyes. It yelps and falls back, riling the pack into a great howling mass that snaps at my legs.

I kick out, catching one in the snout, then punch my blade through another's back. There must be thirty surrounding me in total. They take turns nipping and retreating, stirring me into blackened terror, where there is neither thought nor clarity, where the blade is all that matters.

Another hound strikes my leg. I spin away from its attack and kick out. As my foot connects with the ribcage, its teeth sink into my thigh and I scream, driving the blade into the back of its skull. The creature drops, twitching.

I whirl to catch another hound mid-leap. It slams into my chest, and I go sprawling, the dagger knocked from my grasp.

A spiraling squall whips through the clearing, and the pack scatters.

Something slides beneath my arms. "It's me," Zephyrus whispers. "Hold on."

Up we go, the wind dragging us into the trees. I'm too exhausted to protest, allowing Zephyrus to maneuver my feet upon a high branch, my back to the wide, sturdy trunk. He's a mess. Mud still cakes his ripped trousers, and his tunic hangs limp and dingy around his frame. A cut on his chin, newly opened, weeps blood.

"Thank you," I whisper. At the base of the tree, the hounds plant their paws onto the trunk, yelping their protest.

Crouching at my side, the West Wind relieves me of my rucksack, setting it aside. He then adjusts the fabric of my dress so it covers my bare legs. "It seems I'm not the only one who is lured by your scent," he whispers.

"I'm tired, Zephyrus." My voice strains. I could sleep for a thousand years if given the opportunity.

"I know." He tucks a damp red curl behind my ear, the tips of his fingers brushing the heated skin there. "I'll take care of it."

I catch his hand in mine. "There are too many." Wan is his face, and drawn. Hour by hour, the West Wind fades.

"You worry too much, darling." He offers me a smile, however forced. "Am I not the West Wind? Do I not call forth spring in all forms?" Yet those mossy eyes have dulled.

Quietly and with feeling, I whisper, "I don't want you to die."

"Brielle." Equally quiet and aggrieved. "At this point, I would welcome death."

He is gone within the next heartbeat, dropping onto the grass below. Out punches four spheres of air in rapid succession. Three hit their marks. The fourth veers wide as Zephyrus sidesteps, evading a rogue beast.

I've never seen anything like it. He is music in tangible form. The wind is his to forge, and he hammers it effortlessly, noosing another two beasts, decapitating a third with a sword hewn from the air itself. But immortal or not, the West Wind is unwell. I cannot allow him to face this alone.

As I drop into the meadow, the air—fashioned into two massive, circular blades—careens forward, slicing the grass to bits. Blood sprays as the dogs scatter. When the aftermath settles, four are dead, sliced to ribbons. Their white bones dissolve into dust.

The baying spikes with newfound hunger. As the drove regroups, Zephyrus retreats until his back hits a tree, legs sinking into a half-crouch, hands raised. Air erupts, then dies to a mere breeze that goes no farther than his reach. His eyes widen as the hounds surge toward him and he disappears from view.

Terror like I've never known surges through me. "Zephyrus!" Snatching my dagger from the ground, I race toward him.

Under shudders in warning. I manage two more steps before my ears pop, and out sweeps a roar that buckles my knees. There is a scream.

Gale-force winds pound upon me. I lift my head, pushing against the force as entire trees are uprooted, tossed far and wide. Through my slitted vision, I watch the West Wind unfurl. Flowers blossom at his feet, a blooming field infusing color throughout the land.

He hums an eerie tune set in a darkly minor key, the wind tearing at his hair, snaking around his arms in protective bands. The air alters scent: sweetest honey and warmest sunlight. His eyes, no longer green, glow liquid silver. He is something I cannot comprehend.

Zephyrus flings out his arms, tossing the hounds skyward. Then he brings his hands together with a world-shattering crack.

A massive stem erupts from the clearing's center. I stumble back, losing my balance as another tremor rocks the ground. Long, vicious thorns rupture through the stalk to pierce the hounds on their descent.

The melody eases into a collection of haunted chords, the gentle rise and fall of modulation. As it changes key, new shoots penetrate the beasts' shadowy skin, gouging into flesh as worms carve through earth. With another crack, what remains of the hounds dissipates.

"Zephyrus!" I do not recognize my voice, its shrill cry. I hurry toward him. Blood stains his clothes black.

He stumbles, face taut with pain, and stares at me with those odd, silver eyes. He is strange and he is a stranger.

"It's me," I whisper. "Brielle."

Silver dims, giving way to sweeping green. "Brielle." He scans my body, the lines of grit and blood crisscrossing my skin, the scabbed sores. "Are you hurt?"

"My thigh." I gesture to the teeth marks. Blood collects at the wound's edges.

He studies it for a moment, then says, "It will need to be cleaned. My brother might have something for it." As if sensing my distress, he adds, "The hounds are not venomous. I'm more concerned with infection."

I nod, drop my dress, though the ground feels unstable. A small miracle, really, that we both escaped the hounds alive.

"The antidote?" Zephyrus asks.

My eyes snap skyward. There, to the east—a thin line of gold. "Here." I pull it from my pocket and pass it over.

The West Wind studies the clear liquid, twisting the vial this way and that. "This isn't the antidote I gave you."

Grave is his expression. Grave and frightening. "Yes," I reply cautiously, "it is."

Crushing the vial in his grip, he turns away. "Then we have been deceived."

"What do you mean?" When he does not reply, I grab his shoulder. "Zephyrus."

His muscles lock beneath my fingers, wooden and inflexible. "I mean it's a fake!" he roars, hurling the vial into the brush. Glass shatters against the hard corners of the forest.

"Are you sure?" How exactly can he know? "Maybe there's an explanation."

He shrugs off my touch. "I'm certain, Brielle. We need bezoar grounds. This is water, nothing more. I'm not sure if he changed the contents somehow or ..." What follows is the low, tortured sound of the helpless and the broken. "I was so focused on deceiving Yakim I didn't stop to consider whether he would do the same." He's shaking, a fist pressed to his forehead. "*Damn him!*"

Numbness begins to branch through my body, heavy and cold. The journey, the deceit, the charade, yet our actions have made no difference. We are only miles nearer to Zephyrus' total paralysis.

The West Wind limps off a few steps before one knee folds and he's forced to use a tree for support. Seconds later, his other knee buckles. He collapses with a cry of pain.

Rushing to his side, I take his hand in mine. We had days, he and I. In another life, perhaps years. But the venom permeates his body with increasing rapidity. I do not know how much time remains.

"Can we talk about this?" I ask.

Zephyrus pinches the bridge of his nose. "What is there to discuss? The entire mission was pointless."

Gently, I draw Zephyrus' hand to my heart. His palm splays to absorb the throbbing beat.

"Do not give in to despair," I whisper, pressing my cheek to his. "You are alive. We both are. The day is not yet done."

His swallow clicks near my ear. "I appreciate the sentiment, but this is the end for me. I can't escape this fate." A hard breath shudders out of him, and he pulls away, rubbing at the wetness trickling down his cheeks. "I might as well wait for the paralysis to set in. It's what Pierus expected anyway."

Curling my arms around his waist, I draw him deeper into my embrace. He is stiffer than a plank of wood, but our warmth blends, and he eventually sags into me with a small sound of relief.

"Every moment spent in my company is a risk to your life," he argues. "Forget this, Brielle. Let us return to Carterhaugh in the time we have left."

"I'm not giving up." How could I sleep knowing he has used his waning strength to ensure my safety at the detriment of his own life? If he cannot carry himself, then I will carry us both. "We still have a few days before the paralysis takes effect."

"It's not days," he responds, the words flat. "It's hours, and I need rest."

Panic continues to pummel the door. I will not let it in. "Then you will rest." As much as we must push onward, sleep would benefit him greatly, even if it's for an hour. "How much farther until we reach Notus' realm?"

Again, Zephyrus pulls away, but doesn't go far. "Fifteen miles? Forty?" He shakes his head. "Whatever the number, it is too far and too much to ask of you."

"It's not," I reassure him.

"You're not listening to me. I'm telling you it's dangerous. I'm giving you an out. Why won't you take it?"

He reminds me of a captured bird, too fearful to fly when the cage stands open. "What is this truly about, Zephyrus?"

His emerald eyes meet mine. "Why won't you leave me?" he whispers, low and agonized. I grasp his hand again and refuse to let go.

"Because I know how it feels to watch someone you care for walk away from you, and I would spare you that pain if I could." With our hands locked, I squeeze tighter. "And because we're in this together."

His throat dips. "Together?"

I nod. It doesn't sting as it once did. It feels fresh, like newly healed skin.

"Lie down," I say, and help him settle into the grass, his head resting against my thigh. "I'm going to tell you a story from the Book of Fate." My fingers slip through his hair, separating the damp curls, and Zephyrus sighs, leaning fully against me. "The story begins, as all stories do, with a dream."

33

A SHUDDER WRACKS THE MASSIVE SLAB OF STONE WHERE WE'VE made camp, startling me awake. The low rumble of distant thunder follows.

It is dark. Zephyrus sleeps, unaware of the grit shaking free of the rocky overhang to blanket his clothes in pale dust. One tremor bleeds into the next, and the forest groans, straining to keep itself rooted to the mountainside.

Mile after mile, we traveled until reaching the mountain Zephyrus claimed would lead us to his brother's realm. There, we stopped to rest. I promised to take first watch, but shortly after he fell asleep I must have followed, succumbing to the exhaustion of fleeing the Orchid King's hounds. I'm not sure how much time has passed, but we must move.

"Zephyrus." As I shake him awake, the ground lurches, tossing me sideways. Something cracks in the vast darkness beyond sight.

He stirs, props himself up with an elbow. "Brielle?" In the watery light cast by the waning moon, his skin appears sallow, his eyes deep pits.

Another shock rolls through Under. "What's happening?" I whisper.

A gust snaps from Zephyrus' palm to race across the valley, blasting through brush and felled trees. Less than two heartbeats later, the wind returns, dragging a fetid scent with it.

He peers out into the darkness, grim-faced. "Under demands blood," he replies. "It must be given soon if it is to survive another cycle."

I, too, scour the landscape. I do not recognize this part of the realm: rivers and mountains beneath the earth. "What happens if it doesn't receive any?"

"If it fails to receive my blood, the realm will begin to collapse. It did not used to be this way, but once Pierus took control, Under grew dependent on my power. The tithe cannot be delayed for long."

The next quake runs cracks through the stone. When the rumbling quiets, I hear it: the baying of hounds on a hunt.

Zephyrus' breath spikes, and his pupils shrink, twin drops of blood squeezed to nothing. His smell—crisp sunlight—begins to turn, curdling like a bowl of milk that has spoiled.

"But you killed them . . ." My voice trails off. He'd torn those beasts apart with nothing but wind.

Zephyrus scrubs a hand down his face. "Pierus has countless hounds at his disposal. An army, if you will."

Beneath the spreading numbness, I am afraid. I wonder when this journey will end. "How close?"

"The hounds move quickly. They will likely arrive within the hour."

We cannot outrun them. And yet we must.

Zephyrus shudders then, though the ground itself lies still. One hand fists atop his thigh, long fingers contained by the clasp of his hand. "Pierus calls for me."

"You've ignored the call before, right?" I remind him. "When you visited Boreas."

I called for you three months ago, the Orchid King had said, his voice the only evidence of the insidious ritual awaiting Zephyrus in that chambered field of roses.

"Yes." Zephyrus nods with a vague blankness. "Distance eases the strain. If we can reach Notus' realm, I'll be safe."

I'm on my feet, gathering supplies and shoving them into my knapsack. Pivoting, the roselight held high, I take in the cave mouth a stone's throw ahead, tall and narrow, chilled air wafting from the mountain's depths.

"If we keep pace," I say, turning to face Zephyrus, "we should reach your brother in a few hours." That is, after all, what he told me yesterday.

"It won't be a few hours, Brielle."

I understand the journey's difficulties, but I grow weary of his skepticism and negativity. "I know things haven't gone smoothly—"

"I can't move my legs."

It is as though I hear these words from a great distance. They cannot touch me where I stand. "Are you sure?"

"I think I know when I can't move my legs," Zephyrus snaps.

My hands shake, but I shove them under my arms for additional warmth, smothering the panic before it overwhelms. It will do no good to fall apart. "We knew this was going to happen," I say, my gaze steady on the West Wind. "We still have time."

He continues to stare at his unresponsive legs. "Time?" One hand drags through his curls, yanking strands of hair free. "We are out of time. We cannot reach my brother if I cannot walk."

"Then I will carry you."

He shakes his head, and oh, what bitterness that smile has wrought. "You cannot carry me, Brielle."

Normally, I would not take offense, but I am weary, hungry, and short on patience. My reply snaps out. "And why not?"

A momentary brightness revives his gaze. It is nearly as shrewd as I remember. "Perhaps on a sunny day, across flat ground, after we had rested and filled our bellies. But fleeing the Orchid King's hounds in the dark? While Under shakes itself to pieces?" He attempts to push himself upright on quavering arms, then wilts, cursing beneath his breath when he fails to gather the required strength. "These obstacles would be trying for a god," he adds, "much less a mortal woman."

Zephyrus isn't the heaviest thing I have carried, but he has walled himself into an early defeat. He sees how high the walls rise and will remain confined within them until the light is gone, his world naught but damp and cold.

"All I want is to try. We owe it to ourselves to do so."

He shakes his head. "I will not ask you to carry me."

"You do not have to ask." Only now do I rest a hand on his. "I'm offering."

"It's too far," he grinds out.

"Says who?"

A gust snaps through camp. "What will you do, drag me the remaining ten miles? Will you break your spine to ensure I reach Notus before my demise?" Breath by scalding breath, the air crackles around him. "I will not subject you to that burden."

"You are not a burden," I argue. "Not to me."

He slumps lower to the ground. "Return to Carterhaugh and forget about me."

I watch him calmly, hoping to draw his attention back to me, but Zephyrus, Bringer of Spring, is defeated. He is both a god and a boy, beloved and abandoned. His hurt reflects my own.

"Have my actions misguided you?" I whisper, curling my fingers around my trinity knot pendant.

"Your actions have only demonstrated your kindness and compassion, but this is not about me," he growls, a sound more animal than man. "This is about you, the life you must live. There's still time to make this right. You can return to Miles Cross and rejoin your people. You will live a long, happy, healthy life. A *free* life."

"Zephyrus." Reluctantly, his gaze meets mine. "Do you think I would come all this way, go through all this trouble, to turn back?" My mouth quirks. Brielle of *then* would never have taken such a risk.

He appears tentative, unsure of his place. "I would not blame you if that were so."

"It's my choice." My tone will not yield, and neither will I. "I don't care what you *think* you deserve. You have atoned for your actions, and now is the time to forgive yourself." Then I add, as if speaking to a small child, "You can have good things, too, you know."

"What is the point of having good things," he whispers, "if I fail to care for them?"

He blinks, and I'm shocked by the tears slipping down his cheeks. Here, at the end of days, the West Wind falls to pieces. My heart aches at the sight. "Zephyrus."

"I sabotage," he goes on. "I do not know how to do otherwise. I take and I take until nothing remains. It is a sickness in me."

"You are not your past." And then, gently, "You are so much more than your mistakes."

Shame colors his skin a dull pink. "You are perhaps the only good thing in my life, and I treated you no better than a dog called to heel." A hitch in his breath. "I am sorry," he says. "For everything."

Cupping his face in my hands, I brush my mouth across his damp cheek. "Do not cry for me, Zephyrus," I whisper. "Cry for the girl who had yet to meet you, who did not realize how small her world had become."

No matter the ways Zephyrus wronged me, my heart is a cup filled to brimming. I let him purge these hurts. This, I understand.

"I forgive you," I murmur into his cheek. "For all that you have done, I forgive you."

He turns his head, studying the cave opening as the barking nears. Even with a head start, I question whether we will be able to outrun the hounds. "Are you sure you can carry me? I'm a grown man. It will not be easy."

I pull away, give him a dismissive once-over: lean musculature, a distinct lack of fat. "Please," I scoff. "Don't insult me."

Carrying the West Wind, as it turns out, isn't nearly as bad as the long days spent carting barley from the fields. Guided by the roselight pulsing dimly in my hand, we venture through the carved network of tunnels below the mountain. The light grows more feeble with each passing hour, small clots of what looks like blood held suspended inside the glass.

We round a bend into yet more darkness. My back twinges as Zephyrus' weight drags at me, but I heft him higher where he hangs against my side, tightening my arm around his waist. Another step, a slow shuffle against the hard-packed soil. Eventually, the dim begins to recede.

Gasping, I pick up the pace. First mauve, then gray, the pinprick of brightness ahead guiding me onward despite my body's exhaustion. And then I am running, dragging Zephyrus forward, slipping through the narrow vein to emerge, unscathed, into the world above.

The light is a flood, and I recoil from its intensity, the cool darkness driven back by a swell of unbearable heat. In the distance, mounds of sand shimmer like great heaps of gold coins, their gleaming peaks slanting into strips of violet. At my feet, the earth is baked red, cracked like a turtle's shell. After days belowground, the sun—the *real* sun—warms my weary soul.

"Zephyrus," I breathe. "You were right." The world is vast, and what a shame it would be to know only one piece of it.

East to west and beyond, there is the sky. It is sapphire, cerulean, cobalt, azure. At our backs, cliffs of smooth clay interrupted by pale striations act as a soaring wall enclosing the desert realm, their massive shadow stamped onto the fissured ground. Even my lungs prickle from the heat.

There is no sign of Under's twisted roots. Only salt. Only sand.

"Will your brother meet us here?" I ask.

A scorching gust screams over the dunes, and in the ensuing silence, I realize I have not heard my companion speak in some time.

I look down. Zephyrus sags against my side. His face is slack, eyes closed. "Zephyrus." I shake him hard. His head lolls.

I lower him onto the sizzling earth. My hands tremble as I check for a pulse. It is too faint.

A glance around the gold and ruby landscape. What of the South Wind, whom we have need of? Did he receive his brother's message? And what will become of us if he has not?

As I brush the curls from Zephyrus' clammy forehead, a shadow falls over me. Springing to my feet, I whirl, drawing my dagger in a seamless motion to meet a pair of dark, glittering eyes.

34

THE TIP OF THE MAN'S BLADE RESTS LEVEL WITH MY THROAT. Mine points directly between his eyes.

An impressive physique strains against the long, sapphire robe the man wears. Its slitted hem hits knee-high, revealing cream trousers and soft, worn slippers. This man is wide, dense, compact. Zephyrus is practically anemic in comparison.

My attention remains locked on the man's sword. Curved, thinly hammered metal arcs toward the tip—an unusual design, to be certain. My old bladesmithing mentor had one hanging in his forge. A scimitar, I believe it's called.

"Are you the South Wind?" I do not lower my blade. I do not dare.

He only stares. His black eyes, set beneath heavy lids, remind me of small, glinting seeds.

A scouring wind stirs the ochre sands. Even on the hottest days in the highest altitudes, Carterhaugh always offers shady reprieve. With no trees for miles, the heat cooks my flesh. "Do you understand me?"

With a dismissive glance, he sidesteps me and strides toward Zephyrus. I plant myself between them, dagger raised, eyes cold. "Not another step."

The man's gaze narrows above the white scarf concealing the lower portion of his face. A length of equally pale cloth swathes his skull.

"I received a message from my brother." His voice rumbles with the resonance of bass church bells.

"You are the South Wind?" He looks nothing like Zephyrus. His skin is the deep brown of baked bread.

"I am." After a moment, he lowers his weapon, and I follow suit. "Is he dead?"

Days of travel without stopping for rest, and my exhaustion outstrips any intruding fear. "Paralyzed, or nearly so. Will you help him?"

He regards my unsightly appearance, then Zephyrus' disheveled state, evidence of our arduous trek.

"I will not." Turning on his heel, he strides for the dunes.

My mouth parts in surprise. "Wait!" I stumble after him. It's so hot the heat seeps through the soles of my boots. "Where are you going?"

"Home." He keeps walking. For a man of shorter stature, he has an impressive stride.

"But he's your brother." Lifting my shredded emerald skirt, I pick up the pace, knees to chest as the cracked ground transitions to soft sand. I slip sideways, which allows the South Wind to put additional distance between us. "Don't you care for his life?"

His scabbard slaps the outside of his thigh. "You obviously do not know Zephyrus."

"A manipulative, selfish ass?"

His footsteps slow, revealing a trail of shallow indentations leading back to the West Wind. Hours from now, the depressions will smooth, the winds filling what is empty. How many pass through this realm, all evidence of their presence cleansed come morning?

"However he has wronged you," I say, "Zephyrus is changed." Somewhat.

The South Wind cuts me a sidelong glance, then shakes his head. "My brother is many things, but *changed* is not one of them." He begins to climb the nearest dune, veering toward what appears to be a small sailing vessel ahead. The distance between brothers grows, and with it, my own feeling of hopelessness. Though I feel myself shrinking beneath the prospect of confrontation, I am no longer that person.

A burst of speed plants me in his path, palms lifted to halt his progress.

I do not see the man move. A sword point pricks the rise of my cheek. I flinch from the sting of it. "Stand aside, girl."

"Please." Hands clasped, I fall to my knees. Pride means nothing to me. I will beg, I will plead, I will explain my case however many times is necessary. "We came all this way. You wouldn't believe what we have been through, what Zephyrus has endured." What *I* have endured.

The man peers down his nose dispassionately. "That is not my concern."

"Then why did you answer his call for aid?"

He gazes beyond my shoulder. When he speaks, the response is one of fine craftsmanship, each word tucked deliberately in its place. "I did not know whether I would help until I saw him. But when I looked upon him, I remembered his past transgressions. Brother or not, my time will not be wasted on a man who lacks honor."

The South Wind does not bid me goodbye. He simply strides off, a figure swathed in jewel tones, shrinking beneath the wavering heat.

When he vanishes behind a dune, I return to Zephyrus—because it comforts me, and because I will stand by him, even at the unfortunate end. Tomorrow, the paralysis will likely claim him. I must decide what to do next.

I kneel, cracked clay hard against my creaking knees. This realm, strange and alien to me. Dry where Carterhaugh is damp, sandy where the soil is firm, scalding where the forest is cool. "I'm sorry," I whisper, fighting tears. Clutching his hand to my chest, I bow my head. "I tried, but it was not enough."

If I had stayed in Thornbrook, if I had remained where it was safe and familiar, perhaps my heart would have remained unbroken. I'd hoped for a more encouraging outcome, but it was not meant to be. If we cannot go forward, then we must return to Under.

What will occur when we cross back into Pierus' realm? Will I be able to return to Thornbrook content and purposeful after what I have experienced, the West Wind in chains beneath the earth?

"You care for Zephyrus. Why?"

My head snaps up. The South Wind stands over me, sturdy legs braced, one hand clasping the hilt of his sword. That's twice I have not heard his approach. The sun sinks at his back, and what a glorious sight it is to behold.

"Because he is lost," I say. "Because he has made mistakes. Because he is hurting. Because he has embraced the gray areas of himself." And maybe I have, too. "Because he is too clever by half. Because of his infectious smile. Because a lonely life is not easy." Tenderly, I wipe a smudge of dirt from Zephyrus' jaw. "You question your brother's ability to change, but I have seen it. So I ask you again. Will you help him?"

"A god's memory is long," he says in that low, resonant tone. "I cannot forget all the ways in which my brother wronged me."

I pull my dagger from its sheath. "You claim Zephyrus lacks honor." I lift the blade so its dark taper catches the light. "But what of me?" When he does not respond, I press, "A duel. Let me prove my honor in Zephyrus' stead."

The South Wind examines the dagger's iron glint, perhaps more curious than he lets on. "There is an oasis not far from here," he relents. "Its waters have the potential to heal Zephyrus, but there is no guarantee."

I don't need a guarantee. Hope is enough to sustain me.

He steps back, sweeps those black eyes over the West Wind's disheveled form. "I will aid my brother, just this once. And when he awakens, we will duel, and he will watch you die."

My expression remains neutral despite the twist in my gut, but I nod. The South Wind likely underestimates my capabilities. I can use that to my advantage.

"Gather Zephyrus. Meet me at my sailer." He gestures to the contraption in the distance. "Do not delay."

As I watch the South Wind turn to go, I haul Zephyrus into my arms and struggle to my feet. His limbs swing freely, like those of a corpse.

I'm panting by the time I reach the South Wind's strange apparatus. It looks like a sailboat, yet instead of a curved hull, the bottom is flat, cut into the shape of an arrowhead. Two masts jut upward, sails secured to the wooden beams. As the South Wind unties the canvas, he calls over his shoulder, "Sit at the bow. Don't touch anything."

Climbing toward the vessel's tapered nose, I lay Zephyrus near a stack of boxes secured with rope and settle beside him. The sails snap open, wind filling their hollow bellies as the South Wind takes the large rudder in hand.

"Hold on."

The boat jerks forward, lifting clear of the sand. A scream wrenches free of my chest. We are climbing, hurtling, careening. We soar with breakneck speed.

At the dune's apex, we drop, the nose plunging sharply into the trough, my stomach dragged in its wake. A glance at the stern reveals the South Wind shifting the rudder, feet planted firmly despite the swift motion, eyes thin over his face scarf. If Zephyrus is an errant breeze, his brother, Notus, is the most stable of substances—the rigid, unbending earth.

Wind shrieks past my ears, and my fingers clamp the boat's frame as I brace for another ascent. We release our hold on the earth, which sizzles in patches of brown, violet, and gold. The sky is endless, blue in perpetuity brushed by the whiteness of intense sun.

After a time, the terrain flattens, rolling into soft, wet sand. Trees with sword-tipped fronds cast meager shade across a body of water flanked by boulders and sparse greenery. The South Wind curbs the strength of his winds so that the vessel coasts to a halt near the bank.

He leaps from the boat, and I follow, Zephyrus in my arms. The South Wind spares no concern for his brother, merely waves me over to the water.

"Submerge him up to his chin," he instructs.

The water is shockingly cool, and seeps greedily into Zephyrus' filthy clothes. I roll up his sleeves, his trousers. Shallow waves lap against the shore.

"The oasis contains special properties," states the South Wind, staring at the dark veins running up his brother's arms, "but its powers cannot heal everything. If it is successful, you should expect to see a reversion of whatever ails him by sunrise." He then gazes westward. A strip of gold clings to the horizon. The sun, nearly gone. "I'll build a fire."

The night is colder than any I have experienced, but the fire crackles pleasantly, a red-gold ring sitting flush against the surrounding darkness.

Zephyrus lies on the sloped, muddy bank of the oasis, submerged neck-high in the water. The South Wind and I sit higher up the incline, my hair still damp from having bathed earlier. If the oasis fails to reverse the nightshade's paralysis, then I'm not sure what comes next. We have traveled all this way. But life, I've learned, has its own rhythm, one I cannot always foresee.

The moon brightens the darkened dunes, cutting the South Wind's silhouette into defined shadow and light. Following the sun's descent, he'd removed his face scarf, though he has left his head scarf intact. The man appears to be hewn from granite.

"You mentioned Zephyrus wronged you," I say, knees drawn to my chest. Beneath the crusted fabric of my emerald gown, the wound I sustained from the hounds is now freshly bandaged, the oasis waters having cleansed it of infection. "What did he do?"

The South Wind tips back his head to study the dark basin over-head. He appears at home beneath its spread. I, however, am unused to such unfiltered vastness. If I were to lift my hand, the tips of my fingers might stir the stars from their distant nest.

"Early during our banishment," he says, "Zephyrus sent out a call for aid. My brothers and I were to join forces against Pierus, who had crossed into Carterhaugh to oversee Zephyrus' punishment. The plan was to kill him. Unfortunately, I was the only one who showed. I am lucky I was able to escape Pierus alive."

"Zephyrus didn't show?" I murmur.

"He did not."

While I am tempted to defend his behavior, the Zephyrus of *before* did not hold himself to the same level of accountability he does now. "Did you ever ask your brother why he failed to show?"

"I was never granted the opportunity," he says.

"You didn't visit him?"

The South Wind at last shifts position, one hand pressed flat against the sand, perhaps calling back the heat that has leached away in the passing hours. "People fall into their lives, and their world narrows to the walls they've built. The desert is my realm just as Carterhaugh belongs to Zephyrus. There is order in separation."

I wait for him to go on, but he seems content to let the silence stretch. "You don't talk much, do you?"

"My brother talks enough for the both of us."

I smile, mostly because I agree. The West Wind is fond of the spoken word. And I suppose I've become fond of him, too.

The realization sobers me. *Fond*? Or is that too weak a word? Would I have risked everything to help someone I was merely fond of?

The South Wind tosses a stick into the fire. "It has been a long time since we were children, a long time since we first became men. I do not know how my brother has changed."

"Did you know about Hyacinth?" I ask.

"Zephyrus and I were never close," he replies. "He kept to himself when it came to matters of the heart." He turns to me then. "I commend you for helping my brother. Not many would."

"Perhaps he only needed someone to show they cared for him."

"Perhaps." With that, he rises, the hem of his sapphire robe fluttering behind him, his silhouette etched against the expansive desert.

Hopefully he will not go far. We need his sailer to return to Under safely.

I doze for a few hours. It feels as though I've just closed my eyes before I waken, body stiff with cold. Day breaks to the east. Since I have never experienced a desert sunrise, I watch the realm warm to blush, the dunes sparked with gathering light. Carterhaugh, with

354 • ALEXANDRIA WARWICK

its clambering vines and slithering roots, rarely allows for space to breathe.

After brushing sand from my dress, I check on Zephyrus. Pulling open the tunic at his throat, I examine his chest, stomach, and arms with impending dread. The veins remain blacker than ever, a green tinge to the surrounding skin.

Blowing out a breath, I brush the wet curls from Zephyrus' face. He stirs at my touch. "Brielle."

"I'm here." At least he's awake. At least there's that.

"You're sad," he murmurs, eyes still closed. "I can hear it in your voice."

The knot in my throat thickens. It is a deeper sadness, one stitched into my heart. "We reached your brother's realm. He brought you to an oasis last night. Supposedly, it has special healing properties."

"Let me guess." He cracks open his eyes. Fatigue clouds the emerald rings. "It didn't work."

I consider how best to phrase my response, but in the end, the truth is best. "No," I reply. "It didn't."

There are many forms of pain, after all. The pain of heartache. The pain of grief. The pain of unrealized dreams. The pain of regret, wasted time. But I think this might be the worst pain of all: the pain of what could have been.

"Then I will need to return to Pierus," he says.

Did I expect this? Was my attempt at saving his life always a fool's errand, a mortal woman battling powers too strong, too strange, to comprehend?

As soon as the West Wind steps foot into Under, the hounds will descend. The Orchid King will drag him back to that cavity in the ground, his lifeblood consumed by nightshade. I do not want Zephyrus to suffer. It frightens me how far I would go to prevent that. "Can you move your limbs at all?"

He lifts his arms, his legs. Even if the oasis wasn't able to nullify the venom, it seems to have temporarily reversed its effects. There's no telling how long the reprieve will last.

Quietly, I ask, "You truly wish to return?"

"Wish? No." He gazes upward and sighs. "Pierus will enjoy his punishments, but after a few centuries, he will grow bored and lift the chains again."

I believe what he says, despite the precarious lies he has built his life upon. "You deserve more than a cage."

Zephyrus sits up, and water streams from his shoulders. His soaked tunic molds like a second skin to his frame. I can't help but notice the fine carving of his torso.

"There are many things I deserve, Brielle. I'm not saying this to attract pity. I'm saying this because the world may work in mysterious ways, but debts are never truly forgotten. People like me?" A cold smile curls his mouth. "We do not deserve happiness."

I sit beside him on the shore. "What is the point of an immortal life if you spend eternity in misery?"

"Easy to say when one is mortal." When our eyes meet, I recognize his resolve, the acceptance of the hand he has been dealt. "As much as I yearn for another life," he says, "I will return to Under, and I will accept Pierus' punishment. Such is my fate."

I cannot accept that. I won't.

The sound of approaching footsteps draws my attention. The South Wind has returned, face scarf back in place. A hot, dry wind blows, turning my mouth to dust.

The West Wind peers upward at his brother, expression guarded. From this position, the South Wind appears massive, a giant among the sands. "Notus." Zephyrus then notices the curved sword his brother carries. "I hope you're not here to use that on me." He offers his most charming smile.

The South Wind tosses me a small bundle stuffed with fresh fruit, and a waterskin. "It is time, mortal." He gestures to an area of cracked earth located between two palm trees. "I will await you," he says, and strides off.

As Zephyrus watches his brother depart, his suspicion deepens. "What was that about?"

I palm the dagger tucked against my back. "Your brother's assistance came at a price," I admit, watching the West Wind's eyes narrow. "A duel."

Blood drains from his face, whitening it to a ghostly hue. "Tell me you speak in jest."

The South Wind completes a pattern of exercises in my peripheral vision, sword a blur in the patchy shade. For a man so bulky, he moves with understated grace.

"He wouldn't have agreed to help you otherwise." My thumb passes over the blade's smooth base, its lack of a touchmark stamp despite the metal having been fired, cooled, and hammered by my own hand. It feels dishonest that I would not claim this work as my own with pride.

"The only reason Notus agreed to the duel," Zephyrus argues, "was so he could have his revenge on me for leaving him to fight Pierus alone all those centuries ago." His mouth pinches. "I urge you to reconsider. Think of the risk. Think of all there is to lose."

I stand, brush the sand from my gown, and take a deep, satisfying swallow from the waterskin. "I weighed the risk days ago. And anyway, it's not your decision to make."

"His strength will overpower yours tenfold."

I do not think it will. I'm stronger than I look.

Zephyrus closes his eyes and murmurs, "I would not see him hurt you."

Something inside me softens. "You forget that I have trained, too."

"He is a god."

"And?" I hold his gaze until he looks away. "I am the Father's servant." It may not be enough to convince Zephyrus, but it's enough for me. The weight of my dagger confirms this decision is right. Blade to blade, I will face the South Wind.

The West Wind tries to catch my hand as I pass. "Brielle, wait."

"This is my life, Zephyrus. It's time I start living it."

35

THE DESERT BURNS GOLD BENEATH THE DAWN. WE GATHER ON the hard, flat ground, the earth baked into a glaze. Beyond the oasis, sand stretches as far as the eye can see. The sun has yet to pull away from the horizon and I'm already sweating.

The South Wind and I stand a few paces apart. He surveys me calmly. Blade—paltry, frail. Attire—inadequate, the dress likely to tangle around my legs. Physique—lacking muscle, or so it appears, my curves unmistakable. Let him think what he will.

He has the advantage. The desert belongs to him just as Thornbrook belongs to me. I know every darkened passage, every creaking stair, every cracked window and loose stone. Here, I am a visitor, ignorant, uninformed.

My opponent sinks into the guard position, the curve of his scimitar so thin it might be shaped from the air itself. The cold blacks of his eyes hold mine in thrall. The South Wind is ageless, but even gods have their shortcomings.

"Make the call, Brother," announces the South Wind.

Zephyrus looks to me from where he sits propped against a tree, mouth tight with unease. No matter his opinion, I understand actions have consequences. I gave the South Wind my word, and here I stand.

"Begin."

The South Wind uncoils, quick as an asp. I lift my dagger in retaliation, for this maneuver is familiar. Metal clangs as the blades collide. I'm out of reach less than a heartbeat later.

He doesn't follow, merely begins to circle, forcing me into motion if I want to protect my back. The first strike was a test, an attempt to measure my strength, reflexes, agility. The next blow rattles my teeth. I hold steady, our blades locked above the hilts, his scimitar overshadowing my much smaller dagger. My muscles strain, unwilling to give ground. His arms flex beneath his robe, and the veins pull taut in his neck.

Down he pushes, forcing pressure into my wrists. They twinge painfully. Though I stand a few inches taller, the South Wind possesses wide, powerful shoulders. Sweat slicks my hand, fusing my glove to the leather-banded hilt. I cannot break.

But I do not anticipate the sun, nor the well-timed angle of his blade. A starburst hits the shining metal of his scimitar, and the reflected light whitens my vision. I leap backward, the sharpened edge nicking me in the arm, a bright sting.

"Careful!" Zephyrus snarls.

The air stirs to my right. I whirl, tracking the crunch of grit over rock, my skin prickled with perspiration. Through slitted eyes, I pursue my opponent's blurred outline until the blindness recedes.

He lunges then, and we collide. The speed of his assault forces my focus to narrow. Block, strike, duck, parry. My opponent is always one step ahead. By the time I aim for his abdomen, he is already gone, flicking the sword tip across my upper arm. I hiss at the bite of metal slicing flesh.

"Enough." Zephyrus climbs to his feet, one hand braced against the curved trunk. "Let this duel be done."

I ignore him. What is a duel without a little blood? I will not make the same mistake twice.

In the next blink, the South Wind slips his blade beneath my guard. I dodge, knocking the sword aside. The time for defense has passed. What is here in this moment? A god and a mortal. My blade and his. The scream of metal, its ringing clarity.

I am a blade.

I move through the exercises fluently, utilizing every piece of knowledge at my disposal. When the South Wind reveals an opening, I lunge. My dagger swipes low, across the heavily muscled thigh, parting cloth and flesh with the ease of a vessel gliding through water.

He withdraws, dark eyes flat with irritation. I draw him in with an opening, force him back with a series of brutal stabs. Now that I'm better acquainted with his fighting style, I adapt to it. Strikes lead to retreat, reevaluation. He favors jabs and unexpected deflections. The man is too quick.

I give it my best, and I give it my all, but who am I to think I can best a god? It is hardly a match. In the next heartbeat, his blade flicks upward, kissing my throat.

The South Wind examines me with cool detachment, the blacks of his eyes brightened by the bout. He has not broken a sweat. Was it even an effort for him?

"In my realm," he murmurs, "he who wins a duel, takes a life."

"Excuse me?" Zephyrus lurches forward. "Since when do our duels end in bloodshed? Or have you learned nothing from our upbringing? The Council of Gods allows for bloodshed only in the event of a serious grievance. Brielle has done nothing. She is innocent."

I swallow, feeling the scrape of the metal tip. I made a promise, and I will not cower. If I am to die, let it be on my feet rather than my knees.

"Zephyrus," Notus says with utter stillness, "we have not inhabited the City of Gods in millennia. This is my realm. Its rules are not the same."

"She is mortal." The words emerge as a snarl.

"I am aware."

His eyes flash with frightening ire. "Touch one hair on her head," Zephyrus spits, "and you will not live beyond your next breath."

The South Wind regards his brother calmly. "You would deny me my prize?"

Zephyrus flinches. "Not her," he whispers. "Please."

"The deal must be upheld."

"What do I have to do in order for you to spare her?" Zephyrus grinds out.

He lowers his blade a hair. "Would you give up your life in her stead?"

"Yes," he says without hesitation.

"No," I snap. Stupid man. What is the point of having gone through all this trouble to seek healing from the venom, only for Zephyrus to give up his life? If I am killed, I lose a few decades of mundane mortal life, but Zephyrus has an eternity ahead of him, and all of Under relying on his blood for its existence. "I accepted the bargain. Let it be fulfilled."

"Brielle." He stumbles forward with a plea. "Don't give up your life for one so undeserving."

The South Wind considers his brother for a moment. He glances between us, then lowers his sword, the grooves around his eyes deepening in puzzlement. "Well fought." The husk of his voice has warmed with what I believe is respect. "I underestimated you."

I do not understand. "You will not kill me?"

"Not today, no. I suppose my brother is right. There is little honor in killing a mortal whose only mistake is caring for a disgraced god."

Zephyrus goggles at Notus, but the South Wind doesn't rescind his offer of mercy. Instead, he heads for the oasis while Zephyrus and I retreat to the shade of the surrounding trees. A rash has begun to spread across my freckled skin. I miss the low-hanging mists of Carterhaugh. I am not built for heat like this.

After sheathing my dagger, I accept the waterskin from Zephyrus.

"You did well," he murmurs.

The water slides down my throat like the sweetest relief. I drain the container of its last drop. "For a novitiate," I say with a pointed look. "Right?"

"For anyone." If I'm not mistaken, he regards me with newfound admiration. "Fighting darkwalkers, taking down Yakim, dueling my brother. It is obvious you know your way around a blade. Who taught you how to fight?"

"The bladesmith I apprenticed with taught me the fundamentals. I studied with him for three years. Sometimes I'd spar with the boys in town." A blade in my hand freed me. It still does. "Mother Mabel took over my training two years ago."

His head cants in curiosity, but he only says, "I'm impressed you held out for so long against Notus. He is a superior swordsman."

"He is." The best I have ever fought.

With the skin empty, I set it aside, tip back my head to the burning wind. The slender trees bend, yet never break. "How long before we must return?"

Zephyrus rests his hand on mine, drawing my attention. I still wear my gloves. "We will go tomorrow."

It is too soon.

I've prayed for a miracle, done everything in my power to save the West Wind. But his curse precedes my arrival and will persist long after I am gone. Better to return to Under while he is still of able body.

"We had a good run, yes?" In the cooling shade, his green eyes brighten like the purest jewels.

The ache in my chest migrates to my throat. He tries to make light of the situation, but it hurts too much. We have fought and fallen and risen again, but Zephyrus is still no nearer to freedom. "It didn't work," I say.

"I'm not so sure," he murmurs, fingers tightening over mine. "I suppose it depends on one's perspective."

"We failed." My voice strains. "*I* failed you."

"My darling novitiate, you could never fail me." At my look of skepticism, he says, "It has been a long time since I've allowed myself to hope, but you have made me feel as though anything is possible. That is something I will never be able to repay. Whatever time we have left, I'm grateful for it."

Why do the people I care for always leave me? "I wish . . ." Yet my longing dies, the thought too tender, a bruise.

Together, we gaze out at the oasis, the water placid, painted blue by the sky's reflection. The South Wind has made himself scarce.

"You once asked me if I had faith in the good forces of the world," Zephyrus says, "and I would not give you a straight answer." He lifts his solemn eyes to mine. "But having spent time in your presence, I'm convinced there must be some unexplainable phenomenon of all-encompassing good in this world. You helped me see that."

I have never been good with words, so I cup the West Wind's cheek, his bristly facial hair scraping my glove. "Can I ask why your face continues to change?"

"Because you have begun to see the decency inside me," he says, "instead of only the foul parts."

"I do not understand."

"My brother, Boreas, cursed me to wear that hideous face. Only when someone recognized a change in me would I begin to change myself."

I sweep my touch along his jaw. He tips his head into my hand, an expression of quiet agony passing over his features.

"I see you," I whisper. It has taken months, but I see the West Wind for who he is: deeply flawed, a man amidst transition.

Zephyrus exhales a shuddering breath. "Wait." He pushes my hand aside. "Ask me why Boreas cursed me. Ask me why I crossed into his realm, knowing Pierus' wrath awaited when I returned."

I have wondered this. And now I ask.

His features contort, and then: "I planned to kill my brother."

There is no mistaking the confession. I do not know what I expected. Certainly not this.

Thou shalt not kill.

Deep beneath the blanketing shock, I am saddened. I didn't realize how immoral Zephyrus was in the years before we met. Family must mean little to him.

"Many months ago," he begins, the words thick, caked in long-buried regrets, "Boreas' power had begun to spread beyond the Deadlands. Pierus was not happy, and for good reason. Whatever affects Carter-haugh, affects Under. Thus, the realm began to wither, its strength sapped by cold. I thought, if I could fix this one thing, if I could stop

THE WEST WIND ◆ 363

my brother's power from infiltrating, maybe Pierus would reward me. Maybe he would shorten my sentence."

I do recall a strange chill settling over Carterhaugh last winter. "So your solution was to kill Boreas," I state flatly.

He drops his eyes. "Not at first." Grabbing a fistful of sand, he lets the grains sprinkle into a small pile. "I arrived in the Deadlands at his doorstep, hoping to reason with him. When that didn't work, I planned to steal Boreas' spear, use it to kill him, thus ceasing his power's infiltration. I could have used my bow, but by that time I had already gifted it to Wren as a means to win her trust."

Wren—Boreas' wife, if I recall correctly. "Why wouldn't Boreas listen to your reasoning?"

"I was not welcome in his home." His gaze skips to the water, the distant dunes—everywhere but me. "You see, it was not my first visit to the Deadlands."

I shiver with foreboding, for I cannot see what lies beyond this moment. Change, to be certain. "Go on."

"I had visited Boreas several centuries earlier. He was married then to a different woman, with a son. I beseeched him to fight Pierus for my freedom, as I had beseeched all my brothers, but Boreas, understandably, said no. He had a family to protect. He was content and wasn't interested in conflict."

There is a pause. "The plan was already in place. Notus had agreed to help and was prepared to meet me in Under. I did not hear from our youngest brother, Eurus, but I expected that. Boreas was the last piece of the puzzle. I couldn't take no for an answer."

The Bringer of Spring: devious and self-absorbed, yet in this moment, shame-faced, wracked by guilt. My apprehension grows fangs.

"His wife was easier to sway," he says, too quiet. "I convinced her she would be happier in Carterhaugh, she and her son, though I harbored no romantic feelings toward her. She was merely a tool."

"Stop." I lift my hand, fighting for breath in the heat. "I don't want to hear anymore." The thought of anyone coming between a man and his wife, voluntarily tainting that relationship, makes me ill. The Third Decree: thou shalt not covet.

"Please, Brielle. I need to say this."

The moment I begin to accept Zephyrus for who he is, he reveals yet another sharp corner, and I retreat, unwilling to prick myself against it. I think about trust, vulnerability, the terror of being seen. I promised I would stay. He trusts me not to abandon him. Willing or not, I must see this through.

I nod, the motion stilted. Zephyrus swallows and goes on.

"When I offered Boreas' wife the opportunity to visit Carterhaugh, she accepted. It was my hope Boreas would follow. Once there, I thought that I could convince him to journey to Under and fight Pierus for my freedom. Only, we never reached Carterhaugh."

He stares at the ground so intently I'm surprised holes do not form in the sand. I do not like the direction this story has taken. "Why—"

"Bandits attacked us mid-journey, killing Boreas' wife and son."

I turn away, eyes closed. A god's loss must be unending, every day a bruise flushed anew.

Zephyrus speaks in a rush, a great outpouring of emotion. "When Boreas discovered what had happened, he spiraled into rage and grief. I fled, fearing his wrath, and stayed away for centuries."

"But you returned," I grind out. Zephyrus flinches beneath my disparaging gaze.

"I did return," he whispers. "But I had not learned my lesson. In the centuries following the death of his late wife and son, Boreas had remarried. I felt feral. Overcome with jealousy, guilt, self-loathing. I am not proud to say I tried to convince his wife, Wren, to kill him. If I did not deserve happiness, then neither did he. But I underestimated his dedication to Wren, her developing feelings for Boreas. I failed. Again."

What was it the Orchid King had said to Zephyrus?

I'm surprised your brother let you stay at all.

"I'm lucky he did not kill me, though I wonder if that would have been preferable. Boreas is clever. He knew the curse would prolong my suffering."

I don't know what to say. I'm sickened, tormented, melancholy. But mostly, I'm confused. I wonder what kind of person would go to such lengths to hurt his own brother. I can only conclude it must be someone who believes himself beyond redemption.

"Is that what you think?" I demand. "That if you don't deserve happiness, no one does?"

His eyes shine, and he blinks rapidly to clear them. "I am not a good man, Brielle. I fear my past transgressions will always burden me."

"Why would they burden you?"

"Because I am the same as I have always been."

"I do not believe that." Even in the short time I have known Zephyrus, I recognize a change in him. "You are more than the man you were. Of that, I am certain."

He shakes his head. "I am not so sure."

I consider his tale with newfound perspective. A tragic series of mistakes? Maybe. I will not know until I ask the only question able to alleviate my doubt.

"Are you sorry for what you did? Do you regret treating your brother so poorly?"

"Every day," Zephyrus says. "Every gods-forsaken day. There is a rot within me. It cannot be changed, nor can it be purged. It stays with me, always."

The horror of his past softens in me, and fades. We are all made of separate parts. Zephyrus might always carry this rot with him, but who is to say it cannot be burned away to some degree, or lessened? The West Wind is the grower of green things. He is relief in the cold. I choose to see him as a collection of parts, some undesirable, others shaped by curiosity, playfulness, wonder.

"Maybe you're not the most likeable person," I admit, to which Zephyrus laughs, a noise strained to breaking, "but I like you well enough. I'm not perfect either. You erred, as we all do. What matters is how we learn from our missteps. That is how we grow." Briefly, I touch his arm. "Tell me what you have learned."

"That I am the cause of my misfortune. My selfish, self-centered, sabotaging nature." He speaks harshly toward himself. "An immortal who is careless with his own life. Imagine that." Yet eventually his voice gentles. The lines smooth from his skin, as though warmed by a touch of compassion.

"But life, I've learned, is fragile, even mine," he continues. "It must be cherished, nurtured, embraced. I must not be careless with others' emotions, for it will lead to my own isolation. I must hold myself accountable for my actions, for how else am I to understand the harm I inflict on others? And you, Brielle . . ." He regards me with an openness I have yearned to witness since our first meeting. "You have been the wisest of all my teachers. You are a teacher of faith, of how to live an unselfish life, of patience and empathic humility. You are," he says haltingly, "too good."

"I am Brielle. Nothing less, nothing more."

One of his hands lifts, strong fingers encircling my wrist. "We do not have much time."

Indeed, the sun has begun its descent. I look to Zephyrus' hand, pondering all I have been through. I wonder what tomorrow will bring. I ask myself what I will regret. I think of what could have been.

Pulling my wrist free, I begin to tug off my gloves. Zephyrus watches, marveling at the sight of my pale, freckled hands, their hardened calluses.

As his gaze locks with mine, my belly quivers. If he were to close the distance, I might again experience the sweet pressure of his mouth, the wet slide of his tongue.

"You once asked me if I wondered what a man's touch felt like," I say, and those piercing eyes flicker. "I didn't then. I do now."

He watches me with grave understanding. I have removed my gloves, this inviolable barrier cast aside at last.

"I want to know what it feels like to lie with a man."

"Brielle." Zephyrus shifts closer, though he does not touch me. "We don't have to do this. It is enough to be in your presence. There's nothing you need to prove, not to me, nor to anyone else."

"I know I have nothing to prove," I state. "I want to know how it feels, just once."

"Only a virgin may become an acolyte. You said so yourself."

"I know."

There is a change, and it is a change in him, and in me: two contraries falling into harmony with one another. "Are you sure?"

"Zephyrus." I cup his face in my hands, and oh, how his skin sings to mine. "I am sure."

Leaning forward, I press my mouth to his. Curved and smooth, his lips part, slotting briefly into mine. Warmth blooms in my chest as I ease back. "Though I do not know what to do."

Wrapping his fingers around my wrists, he anchors me in place with the delicious heat of his skin. "Do you trust me?"

"Yes," I whisper, allowing him to pull me closer. "I trust you." That which had been broken is finally mended. It is worth more to me now. "Are you feeling strong enough?"

The tightness in his face eases, and his hands loosen, skimming up my arms, across my shoulders, down my back. "The oasis gifted me a reprieve, but we will not have long. What about pregnancy? Is there . . . that is, you're not taking anything to protect against it, are you?"

"I took a vow of celibacy, Zephyrus. There was never a need to protect against it."

He nods in acknowledgment. "Here." Growing from his open palm, a small shoot spreads its leaves. "Chewing on these leaves will prevent pregnancy. You might feel a bit nauseated tomorrow, but the effects will wear off in a few days."

The leaves taste bitter, but I dutifully swallow them. I appreciate Zephyrus' foresight.

His expression softens as he takes me in, and my cheeks flame. "I am remembering that kiss in the glade," he whispers.

A flutter stirs my heart, for I, too, recall the hushed darkness, how distant I felt in that moment, completely removed from reality. Some bold, entirely fearless part of me dares to ask, "What do you remember about it?"

Reaching out, he presses a fingertip to the pliant center of my lower lip. "I remember your smell. I remember the small, breathless sounds you made. I remember the shape of your body in my hands. But mostly," he says, low with yearning, "I remember you left me wanting. I have been wanting ever since."

Clasping my jaw, Zephyrus coaxes my mouth to part, his lips capturing mine. Together, we sink. Peace in drowning.

His breath is elixir. The air is but particles between us, our faces so near I can count the pores on his nose, the silver striations in the dark green irises. Our noses brush, and my eyelids sink closed as the heat of his tongue plunges past my teeth.

I gasp, hands clamping his shoulders, spearing upward into his silken curls. So many textures await exploration. The edge of his jaw, coarse with facial hair. The delicate shell of one ear. The smooth skin of his neck. I touch them all with unabashed curiosity.

"I love your freckles," he murmurs. "Like small grains of sand." Then his mouth returns to mine, and he eats at me hungrily. My lips move with equal fervor.

I push to my knees. The West Wind grunts and hauls me closer, the gold sand beneath the trees scattering like a thousand flaming stars. The kiss does not break; it only deepens. I am unraveling. Consumed. Body and mind reshape themselves, for I am pious, yet desired. A novitiate, yet still a woman. What do I wish? To climb beneath his skin. To tuck my heart alongside his. To know, truly know, that I am loved—mind, body, soul.

As the sun begins to set, the warm tones give way to cooling hues, and still we are kissing, reaching, tangling into one being. His fingers twist in my snarling hair, tightening near the scalp, and a moan breaks free.

After two failed attempts, I clumsily manage to straddle him. Something long and stiff juts into my inner thigh, and I whimper.

Zephyrus breaks the kiss, panting. His eyes flicker, pupils like dark pools within.

"I adore you like this," he whispers. "With your legs spread and your weight on my lap."

The gravel in his voice intensifies the flush in my face. "You are pleased?"

Gripping my waist, he shifts me back and forth across his erection. My breath catches as the pressure begins to sharpen. "Do you not feel this?" He grinds upward, and the delicious friction sends a hot pulse through my legs.

"I do," I stammer. Strands of damp hair stick to his temples, his skin warmed by the sinking sun. "Can I touch you?"

The question slips out with all the awkwardness of inexperience. I want to know what Zephyrus feels like in my hand, but it is difficult navigating a road untraveled.

Down his hands slide, stroking the tops of my thighs. "Brielle." Bright, glancing heat marks the curve of my neck—a swipe of his ravenous tongue. "I would love nothing more than for you to explore my body."

"What if I do something wrong?"

"Darling." The slow spread of his smile is my undoing. "You can do nothing wrong as long as you are touching me." His palms coast around my waist, up to the heavy curves of my breasts. The dress is so torn the neckline hangs in strips, exposing the generous flesh of my cleavage, which twitches with each shortened breath.

With some effort, I manage to detach myself, sliding free of his lap onto the sand. His stiffened groin pushes against the cotton of his trousers.

He widens his legs suggestively, and my throat tightens, desire and shame warring within me. In the violet-edged dusk, I am bold. Reaching out, I clasp my hand around his length through the fabric of his trousers.

The West Wind expels a deep, shuddering groan. He studies my efforts through slitted eyes. "How does it feel?"

I laugh nervously. "Strange." Neither hard nor soft, it pulses as I run my thumb beneath the lip of the head, tracing its fleshy rim through the cotton. I give it an experimental squeeze.

He curses, and I snatch my hand away, cheeks hot. "Did I hurt you?"

"On the contrary, it felt too good." He grits his teeth, one hand clamped around his bent knee. "Here." He angles my hand, places it over his bulge. "Try again."

As my fingers clasp his thickness, he guides me in a steady rhythm, his larger hand enveloping mine. Tucked inside his trousers, his length pulses against my palm, then hardens, the wide head oozing dampness into the fabric.

My mouth parts in surprise. "You reached completion?"

The West Wind snorts. "No, though I admit I'm close." The strokes are firmer, long and unbroken, root to crown and back. His hips twitch, rising to meet my touch.

Mother Mabel never educated us on sex. I was forced to acquire any pertinent information from books or town gossip, so my understanding is rudimentary at best. It is pleasurable. It hurts. It is messy. It is brief. It is prolonged. It is uneventful. It is life-altering. I wonder which is true.

"That's good," he breathes, head falling forward. He watches my hand work him over.

I, Brielle of Thornbrook, will bring the West Wind to his brink. It does not seem entirely real.

Up my fingers skate, circling the head, squeezing in curiosity, and the wet spot enlarges, a spreading blemish in the fabric. I continue to pleasure Zephyrus until he removes my hand.

"Lean back," he coaxes.

I follow his guidance, nestling into the cooling sand while he hovers over me. One hand drifts under my gown, tugging the hem suggestively. His burning gaze meets mine. "May I?"

The oasis drifts in the darkness of desertion. The South Wind has disappeared, and we are alone. I trust Zephyrus. I will not be afraid. "Yes."

Carefully, his hands slip beneath the fabric, coasting up my calves, behind my knees, across the paler insides of my thighs. A gentle push widens my legs, and he kneels between them. The West Wind is faithless, I remind myself, but tonight, I might be his altar, my flesh and blood an offering, his head bowed as though in prayer.

Higher my dress creeps, gathered in folds around my waist. My feet dig into the sand, and I stare upward through the fronds of the trees swaying overhead, beyond which lie the Eternal Lands. Warmth gathers in my pelvis.

"I once asked if you had ever touched yourself," Zephyrus murmurs. Long, deft fingers drift nearer to the apex of my thighs. "You did not give me an answer then."

It was too embarrassing a thought. My own flesh, forbidden to me. Now? Legs bared and spread, my breasts so sensitized they ache against my corset, my heart racing beyond my control. This moment feels inevitable, as if it had been set in motion all those months before.

After my return from Under, I grew curious. My attempts at shuttering those licentious thoughts failed. I locked my bedroom door and explored my body. I touched my breasts, between my legs. Come morning, I knelt before the altar, head bent in repentance.

"I have," I confess, breathy and low.

His gaze snaps to mine, stunned. The West Wind's smile grows, a decidedly hungry thing. "How did it feel?"

It is too humiliating for words, so I mutter, "Fine," and say nothing more.

"You already have an idea of what you like. We can work with that." He massages shallow circles into my thighs. When his fingertips brush the edge of my chemise, I stiffen.

Zephyrus retreats as if nothing is amiss, moving back down my legs to my knees, calves, ankles. Eventually, he moves upward once more. A broken sound rises in me as he skims the top of my pubic bone. My core clenches reflexively.

Without looking at me, Zephyrus asks, "How did you touch yourself?"

The thought of him watching an incredibly private act . . . I do not know if I am brave enough for that.

"Close your eyes," he croons. "Pretend you are alone in your room at the abbey." He peels the skirt away from my legs. "I want to see how you pleasure yourself. I want to imagine my hands on your skin, the breathless sounds you'll make."

Settling deeper into the soft, whispering sand, I close my eyes. Dipping one hand beneath the hem of my chemise, I brush the top of my seam with two fingers, a bright, tender touch. I remember sliding my hand between my legs, evening veiled beyond the window, all those lightless pockets of Carterhaugh hidden until morning. I'd felt maddened, compelled, free.

As I did then, I slip my fingers between my thighs, lightly brushing the bud nestled below the thatch of mahogany hair. The sweetest agony darts through me, and I bite the inside of my cheek, hips lifting nearer to the touch.

Here is something I never told Zephyrus: when I first touched myself, I imagined his hands cupping my breasts, his muscled torso bent between my legs. Wetness trickles through my folds, which I catch and use to ease the passing of my fingers across my flesh. Slowly, I circle around my entrance. Pleasure gathers to a point.

A hand grabs my wrist, and my eyes fly open. Zephyrus kneels above me. His eyes glitter like cut gems.

"I have a confession," he says.

My thighs clamp together, and I nod, licking salt from my lips.

"The thoughts I have about you are not meant for mortal ears."

It is cruel, his beauty. I'm caught, dragged in by the enchantment that is the West Wind. "Tell me."

"My mind is twisted," he whispers. "I want you filthy, unclean. I want you breaking apart beneath me. I want to fuck you like an animal, to claim you as mine." He palms my breast, his thumb brushing over the boned corset above my hardening nipple. "I want everything you can give me. I want it all."

His fervor frightens me even as it comforts me. To know the wanting is soul-deep, that is here and he will stay. That, too, frightens me, comforts me.

"Zephyrus," I say. "I want that more than you know."

Pushing my hand aside, he hooks his fingers in the hem of my chemise, yet pauses, looking to me for permission. I nod and lift my hips, allowing him to push the folds of the undergarment toward my stomach.

A shiver of cold air slinks across my naked legs. I'm afraid Zephyrus notices the size of my thighs, their unsightly pallor, the lack of defined muscle. But his lips part, and his eyes darken with unmistakable hunger.

His hand replaces mine at the juncture of my thighs and begins to move, drifting across the wet folds, lower, before dragging upward again, brushing the nub there. Over and over, his touch draws the pleasure to higher peaks. Sand scrunches in my sweaty palms as the trembling worsens and the ache between my legs throbs so intensely I fear I might pass out.

Leaning forward, Zephyrus catches my mouth. "Let the pleasure come."

One of his hands lifts, cupping the back of my head while the other slicks upward in a hot glide. Two fingers brush the top of my sex where the nerves pinch, quivering. Faster and faster, he circles. My legs widen, heels digging into the sand, hips lifting for prolonged contact. The burn is unbearable. When he returns to the throbbing bud, he flicks there, and the heat ruptures.

A hoarse, broken moan peals out of me. My body splinters and heals in turn. My hips shudder as they rise and fall, his fingers plunging inside me, and the pleasure explodes with glittering intensity. I cry out, clamping my legs around his arm as a second wave of pleasure barrels into me, sweeping me asunder.

All at once, the tension inside me drains, and I slump onto the sand. As Zephyrus pulls away, I grab his arm, my eyes searching his.

"Do you need space?" he asks carefully.

"No." I try to catch my breath. "Do *you* need space?"

He laughs, and I laugh, because it's the most infectious sound. "No, Brielle," he chuckles. "I need the opposite of space, if I'm being honest."

My smile widens, for I, too, desire the closeness of two bodies aligned.

"You're sure this is what you want?" he probes. "It cannot be undone."

I reach for his hand, seeking the connection that has been built, strengthened, broken, and reforged since we first met. "I'm certain."

"We'll go slow," he assures me. "All right?"

My eyes drop to his groin. I swallow to draw moisture to my mouth. "Yes."

A few deft movements, and Zephyrus disposes of his trousers. His pubic hair is much darker than what lies on his head. The length of his sex protrudes, veins ridged down the shaft.

The sight is . . . well. Again, I've seen nakedness before, but never a man fully erect.

As if sensing my trepidation, Zephyrus brings a hand softly to my face. A breeze disturbs the moonlit oasis. "If at any point it feels uncomfortable, tell me. I'll stop."

He will. If nothing else, I trust him to honor my boundaries.

Settling back, I focus on slowing my breathing. When the head of his erection brushes my entrance, I tense, yet force another exhalation from my lungs. I feel no apprehension, only fear of pain. I've heard the first time can hurt. It stings as he pushes inside.

Knees braced, Zephyrus leans forward, gripping my outer thighs as he slides deeper. I flinch, hissing softly.

He stops, head bowed. "No." He shakes his head and pulls out. "We'll do it another way."

I prop myself on my elbows, thoroughly confused. "I want to continue." I see no blood. Not yet, anyway.

"Not like this. Your first time should be handled with care."

Emotion swells as a lump in my throat. I appreciate his consideration, though admittedly, I'm distracted. His erection glistens, the head ruddy with color. My fingertips brush the flared crown. It twitches beneath my exploration, a clear substance beading at the slit, sticky to the touch.

"Lie back," Zephyrus orders, and I relent, his gaze warm, bright with adoration. He massages my upper thighs, thumbs indenting the soft skin. His mouth drifts upward, skimming the top of my sex. Zephyrus pauses there, inhales, eyes shut. When they open, the emerald glimmers with vibrancy.

"I want to taste you."

I blink at him. "You mean—" I cringe at the thought. "But it's unclean."

"Is it?" He drops his nose to the slope of my pubic bone. I try to close my legs, but his shoulders prevent me from doing so.

"Zephyrus."

"Do you want me to stop?"

I bite the inside of my cheek. "If you're sure." I can't imagine I would taste good.

He sinks his weight into my hips, pinning me as his tongue darts out, swiping the divot at the top of my seam. Another slow, lingering swipe of his tongue, the end curled, dragging upward through the wiry hair. Sparks fly behind my closed eyelids, and I gasp as a wave of heat rolls through me.

He devours me with increased enthusiasm. When the heat of his mouth latches over me, his tongue flutters, bending the tension through my core. A low moan snags in my chest.

"That's it," he whispers. "You're doing so well, Brielle. I love how your body opens at my touch."

The praise lights me up. I want to please him. I want to know him as he knows me, two hearts colliding, bodies connected in harmony. I do not think of who I was before this moment. I cannot regret following my heart, no matter how filthy the act may seem.

I spread my legs wider, groaning. His first finger slides in easier than the second, but once he begins to work me open, the pain lessens, my muscles relaxing to accommodate the intrusion. He curls his fingers, pushing against the walls until they give. The pleasure crests, warm and slow and drenched in heat.

"Zephyrus." A whimper shudders out of me.

"Am I hurting you?"

"No." On the contrary, I've never felt so relaxed, so attuned to another, so unashamed in my nakedness.

He pulls away then. "Get on your hands and knees."

I do as he commands. He lifts my dress, tossing it over my back. My exposed backside tingles in the cool night air.

The shame does not come. I have broken every vow, snapped them as easily as twigs. But I feel crazed by the West Wind's smell, like sun warming the wet earth, the delicious abrasion of his touch. My senses snap and sharpen, and I am awake.

One palm coasts over the curve of my rear. A crack rings out, and I whimper, jerking forward as the sting of his slap erupts across my naked cheek.

His palm returns, rubbing the irritated skin until the hurt abates. My nipples catch the inside of my corset, peaked and aching.

"Too much?" he asks.

I'm panting as though I've run miles, but I shake my head.

"Brielle," the West Wind murmurs. "You've been an obedient girl, but I see what desires lie in your heart." He leans forward to suck my earlobe into his mouth. "Such thoughts are sinful and must be punished."

I glance over my shoulder. Zephyrus continues to rub my backside with a look of sharp greed. "Will you do it again?" I ask, surprising myself.

"As your Text states: ask and you shall receive."

My head drops forward, scarlet curls curtaining my face. I bite my lip as the smack rings out.

Abruptly, he grasps my hair, drawing my neck backward until it strains. His teeth hook into my shoulder, and a moan floods out of me. My body tightens as the West Wind, curled over my back, begins to slap my rear with increasing force, the hot wind stirring the sting into permanent irritation.

I am neither obedient, nor devout, nor pure. I am simply Brielle, a woman, desired.

Shoving two fingers into me, Zephyrus hammers them against my inner walls. Tension spirals as choked moans fall from my open mouth. Then release rips and roars through me.

My body contracts on a wave of heat. I'm so far gone I don't realize Zephyrus has removed his fingers until the head of his sex nudges my entrance.

"Slow," he reassures me, and sinks in.

My loosened muscles allow him deeper penetration compared to our previous attempt. A continuous push and retreat, a wonderful, breathless stretch. When he's fully sheathed, he murmurs, "All right?" One of his hands clasps the back of my neck. The other grips my hip.

My head hangs. "Yes." There is no pain, only a feeling of fullness.

His slow, deliberate thrust sends warmth blooming through my lower belly. My fingers curl into the sand. As his thighs slap against my bottom, I choke for breath, arms trembling. At the next thrust, my vision slides out of focus.

Faster, harder, wickedly deep, Zephyrus finds his rhythm as the heat builds. What am I? A vessel for the West Wind's pleasure. He squeezes my breasts, bites my shoulder, teeth hooked into my skin. I take it all. I release myself from shame. I become my bones and skin, heart and breath. I simply *become*.

"You feel so good, Brielle. So damn good." He hits a spot that makes my nerve endings sing. "I'm close."

"Zephyrus." Drenched in the heat of lovemaking, I remember only his name.

My core clenches around him as a second wave hits unexpectedly. I moan through the pleasure, as does he, riding it out until my arms can no longer bear my weight. Together, we collapse onto the sand, reality returning in fragments of color and light.

Unbidden, a sob wrenches itself free of my mouth.

Zephyrus freezes, his eyes snapping to mine. "Did I hurt you?"

I grab fistfuls of his tunic. "It's not that." I know only this: I am changed. I have seen the world. I have felt another's heart beating in time with mine. To think I might have missed the feeling of being held close by a man I have grown to care for deeply. "Sorry."

He soothes me with long strokes up my back, his concern plain. "You have nothing to apologize for." He kisses my cheek. "You need not hide from me."

In time, my emotional high returns to rest, and our bodies cool. It doesn't take long before the West Wind's breathing evens out. Sleep, however, eludes me. I have traveled far. I have fought and overcome.

I have fallen and risen again. I have pushed myself to the extremity of what I believed I could sustain, and now, lying beneath the stars, I can't help but wonder.

What if I have seen my god in another?

36

TIME IS NOT MY FRIEND. STARS WHEEL OVERHEAD IN THE LENGTH-ening hours, yet despite Zephyrus' presence, I'm unable to sleep. I know how this night will end. Eventually, moon will give way to sun. The star-dusted sky will brighten to a rosy hue, and my time with the West Wind will begin to reach its end.

Dawn, however, is still an hour off. Moving quietly, I retreat to the damp bank of the oasis, where I kneel, my journal resting beside me. The water sleeps.

The distance between who I was then and who I am now is vast. I am Brielle, changed. Brielle, transformed. The prayers I'd once spoken do not sit comfortably in my mouth. They pile up like sharpened rocks, cutting into my tongue.

"Hello, Father. It has been some time since we last spoke. I hope you will forgive me for the oversight."

Eyes closed, palms pressed to the moist sand, I retreat inside myself. My heart is full of tiny, snarling knots. It *hurts*. That is something no one tells you. Faith is not separate from your life. It touches upon every aspect. When you begin to question how it fits, small tears form in its fabric, and the slightest pull threatens to unravel the painstaking weave.

"I returned to Under, Father, but not for the reason you might think. While the Daughters of Thornbrook awaited the tithe in Miles Cross, I stole away. My duty was to Zephyrus. But I fear I have come too late."

Tears collect along my eyelashes, and I gaze upward, soothed by the sky's paling hue. "His body fades. Today, the paralysis will likely reach completion. We have no choice but to return to the Orchid King."

If I hadn't killed off the nightshade . . . but how was I to anticipate the consequences of removing Zephyrus prior to the ritual's completion? All I saw was a man in need.

"I have failed you, Father. You, who have never turned from me, even in my darkest hours. You see, I have given my heart to another."

The night's stillness claps upon my ears, yet I go on. I cannot stop a flood in motion.

"It was not my intention," I murmur, staring into the glassy water, "but in opening my heart, I realized I have grown beyond Thornbrook's walls. I ask, can I not keep the faith without giving all of myself to it? Can I not be your Daughter *and* Brielle?"

I am no singular entity. I have spread beyond my bounds. But I am not afraid. For that is an even greater strength, to look at something you once valued and decide, *That is not for me.*

A subtle breeze skates across the water, stirring the surface into shallow waves. It smells of the incense used during service. It settles over my shoulders, the warmest, thickest cloak. I do not know what this day will bring, but I've learned the difference between what one should be and what someone is. I will only ever be Brielle. It's time I embraced that.

I end the prayer with a softly uttered, "Amen."

To the east, a sleek object arrows over the dunes, shadows rapidly evaporating in light of the rising sun. Quill and journal in hand, I inscribe my thoughts about last night. Silence does not necessarily mean peace. I have learned the distinction over the years. Silence lacks, yet peace is full.

There is no peace within the desert.

With a heavy heart, I return to find Zephyrus sitting upright, knees drawn to his chest, peering across the oasis in contemplation. "How are you?" I whisper, kneeling beside him.

"As well as one can be when returning to captivity." He looks me over as I slide my journal into my pack, and his expression softens. "I do not regret this time spent with you." His hand rests on mine, no gloves between us. His fingers tremble. "Whatever awaits me back in Under, I will face it without fear. I have you to thank for that."

He will not face it alone. Not if I have anything to do with it.

Zephyrus clears his throat. "How do you feel after last night?"

The memory of his hands marking my skin draws heat to my cheeks. "I feel somewhat nauseated from the herb," I admit, dropping my eyes. And yet, I do not regret what we shared. How could I when my heart beat alongside the West Wind's, peaceful at long last?

"What will happen when you return to Carterhaugh?" he asks. His fingers tighten over mine. "Where will you go?"

I stare at our intertwined fingers, their pattern of wheat and cream. "Once Mother Mabel learns I am no longer a virgin," I say, "I will be dismissed from service, my title stripped. I may never again serve as a Daughter of Thornbrook."

"Brielle—"

My smile strains. "It's all right, Zephyrus. I'm at peace with the choice I made." When I imagine myself departing Thornbrook's pale stone walls, I do not despair. My skill as a bladesmith will allow me to begin again elsewhere. Kilkare, perhaps.

"And if I am not at peace with it?"

I appreciate his willingness to shield me from the consequences of my actions, even if his efforts are wasted. "What's done is done," I say. "There's no use dwelling on the past."

"But—"

The hiss of sand draws my attention. Twin canvas sails snap with fury as the South Wind speeds toward us. The arrow-shaped sailer hits a peak, soaring an incredible distance before skimming across the cracked ground. He leaps from his vessel mid-slide.

"We must go." He is breathless, dark eyes bright above his white scarf. "I'm needed back at the palace."

"The palace?" Zephyrus scans his brother's face, intrigued. "Whatever for?"

As the South Wind glances between Zephyrus and I, my hand lifts to my burning cheek. He can probably infer what occurred last night, if the wild state of my hair is any indication.

Notus climbs aboard his sailer without answering Zephyrus' question. He may have agreed to help his brother, but that doesn't mean he has forgiven him, or even likes him.

"Well." Zephyrus sighs. "Let's get this over with, shall we?"

Even if I wanted to move, I cannot. A part of me recoils at the idea of leaving the desert haven. I do not know if I can handle another loss.

"Brielle," he murmurs. "It's time."

So it is.

Slipping an arm around his lower back, I help Zephyrus hobble onto the vessel. Once settled, the sails bow with wind, and we're off.

The return journey passes too quickly. Sitting mute beside me, Zephyrus observes the passing dunes with faraway eyes. Mother Mabel always claimed prayer did not hold the world's answers. It couldn't make water into wine. It couldn't change what had been done. Turns out she was right.

We sail until the sand recedes and the earth splinters into fine cracks. Ahead, the cliffs climb to impressive heights, beneath which lies the cave entrance—the boundary between realms.

We disembark, lurching from the boat as Zephyrus' right knee gives out. I pull him tight against my side, absorbing the tremors running up his legs. He regards the South Wind for a moment, head bent in rare humility.

"Thank you, Notus, for your help. I will not forget this." Weak and disheveled he may be, but he attempts to straighten, to stand tall despite what it costs him.

The South Wind dips his chin. "Be well, Zephyrus."

He springs onto his vessel. Moments later, he vanishes beyond the shimmering lines of heat.

Zephyrus turns to me. Resignation sharpens his somber expression.

"Once we cross back into Under, it will not take the hounds long to pick up my scent, if they are not already waiting for me."

I slip my hand into his, palm to palm, flesh to flesh. "Whatever happens," I whisper, "never forget that you are good."

It is not enough, but it is all I can offer.

We cross into Under with heavy hearts. An uprising of grass springs beneath my boots, and scarlet-tinged light blurs the gloom of the underground. Tucked against my side, the West Wind limps forward, panting, curls askew. The sweet aroma of rotting flowers drifts from the passage, along with a sound I know well.

Zephyrus braces a hand against the wall where a roselight flickers. "The hounds."

The baying is close. The air shudders with their thunderous approach. It hits me then—what I have gained, what I will lose.

"Zephyrus." I grab him by the shoulders. "Were you lying when you said there wasn't another way to break the curse?" When he does not respond, I give him a shake. "Were you?"

Fingers clasping my wrists, he lowers my hands, perhaps the last touch we will share with one another. "It would make no difference, for it will never come to pass."

I search his green eyes. How dear this color has become to me. "Why not?"

He smiles sadly. "Because I broke your trust, and that was an unforgiveable offense."

What was broken has now been mended. The heart endures. This I know. "I forgive you, Zephyrus. I do."

"Brielle," he whispers. "It's too late."

A tear slips from the corner of my eye. He catches it with his thumb, the watery track wiped away as if it had never been.

Clutching the front of his tunic, I draw him forward, hips notched, legs aligned. My mind is a sieve. There is much I desire to say. *I adore you. I understand you. I see you. I need you.* Loving someone is no imprisonment, as I had once believed. It is the cool, bracing relief of clean air within the lungs. It is, at its heart, a choice.

But as the yelps magnify to a crashing uproar, my confidence flags, and I yank him forward, crushing my mouth to his. All that I cannot say, I tell him with lips and tongue and teeth. I kiss him for the *maybes* and *could have beens*. I kiss him because his taste is the only one I have ever known, and I do not want to forget it.

Zephyrus breaks away first. "There's not much time."

He is not yet gone, and already, I miss him. "I promised I wouldn't leave you," I choke. "I promised."

"I know." Beneath the wailing of the hounds, the clop of hooves echoes sharply. Horses—many of them. "But I would have you live, Brielle. I would see you happy, free of this wretched place."

"Zephyrus." I caress his cheek with one hand. "I am happy. I *am* free."

He kisses me then, hard and swift, barely a taste before he pulls back. "Forget this," he says. "Forget me and do not return."

Does the sun not sink to the west? Do rivers not flow downhill? These are truths, and here is one more: I cannot forget the West Wind. I would always remember him.

As his head whips toward the darkness, he shoves me toward an opening in the wall. "Shelter there until it's safe," he says. "The grassy path will lead you back to Thornbrook." When I regain my balance, he has vanished from sight.

If he expects me to watch him martyr himself, he is sadly mistaken. Dagger in hand, I lunge through the opening.

Pain shatters through my face, and I recoil with a sharp cry. Something trickles from my nostrils. I swipe at my nose in bewilderment. Blood. By the Father ... I press my palm against the smooth, transparent partition erected at the niche's opening. Zephyrus has constructed a wall fashioned of air, a barrier to keep me out of sight until the immediate danger passes.

Crouching down, I seek out a crack or seam that might collapse beneath the right pressure. Nothing. I stand and pace in the narrow space, wondering if the hounds have arrived, if Zephyrus has collapsed, if Mother Mabel has been searching for me. Sooner or later, the barrier must fall.

The click of claws on stone reaches me, followed by the sound of gnashing teeth. Zephyrus lurches into sight, thudding into the rock as the hounds surround him, their emaciated bodies hanging in tatters of old skin. A shudder wracks his body, and he curses, sliding to the ground as the paralysis claims him.

"Zephyrus." I pound the barrier, my voice muted. "Zephyrus!"

Either he cannot hear me, or he ignores my call. I pace again, the iron blade hanging between my useless fingers, for it's all I can do. Am I to watch his demise? He went to enormous lengths to protect me from the hounds, yet I cannot do the same for him. I must sit here, bound by this cage.

A sharp whistle draws the beasts to heel. As one, they arrange themselves in a tidy line, awaiting whatever lurks in the shadows.

A handful of roots slither into sight, their paleness reminiscent of bloated flesh. They coast over the stone with an awful hiss, dragging the Orchid King into the shining red glow. Beneath the curled fronds of his eyelashes, a set of pitiless blue eyes examines Zephyrus where he has collapsed, head lolling, face drawn with fatigue.

"Zephyrus." He tsks in disappointment. "I'd hoped you would have learned by now you cannot escape justice."

My palm connects with the barrier. "Pierus!"

The Orchid King gives no indication that he's heard me. While I can see him, hear him, I might as well be locked in an airless box.

"To be honest, I am not surprised by this foolhardy attempt to evade me, though I do not appreciate the tithe being delayed."

Zephyrus regards his captor blankly.

"You are aware of the contract. The Daughters of Thornbrook are only required to give their blood on the promise that you provide the majority of Under's power. Should you fail to sacrifice yourself, the contract between Under and Thornbrook is null."

I wasn't aware of this loophole. I assume Mother Mabel isn't either. She loathes the tithe.

"Due to your insolence"—Pierus smiles thinly—"I was forced to extend Thornbrook's lease of Carterhaugh to assuage Mother Mabel.

Why, you might wonder? Because you were not there, Zephyrus. And without the West Wind, the tithe remains unfulfilled. But we will rectify that situation soon enough."

From the blackness beyond, a small herd of white horses emerges, fair folk with goatlike faces perched in fine leather saddles upon the horses' pristine backs. Each newcomer wears a jewel-toned cloak: emerald, ruby, sapphire, amethyst, citrine. I recognize Pierus' council immediately. The large, ornamental rings hanging from their snouts glint in the low light.

Pierus shifts closer to his captive, his bulk engulfing the much smaller West Wind. "You smell of the desert sand. A visit to Notus, then?" When Zephyrus fails to reply, Pierus frowns. "Ah. Allow me."

The flowers on his shoulders unwind, suctioning themselves to the West Wind's face and neck. His green eyes brighten in the harsh glare. Even the stutter of his breath smooths. After a time, the night-shade flowers detach, slithering back to their nests across Pierus' muscled torso. When I fumble for the roselight in my pocket, I find all signs of hemorrhaging gone, its hue having returned to a clear, pale blush.

"Better?" asks the Orchid King. "That must have been uncomfortable for you."

Zephyrus pushes himself off the ground, quiet with defeat.

"By the way, how *did* you escape the cleansing ritual?" He gives a bird-like cant of his head. "Where, might I ask, is your sweet, red-headed friend?"

I shrink, make myself as small as possible, though I am well shielded. When Zephyrus does not reply, a smile crawls across the Orchid King's mouth. "Your silence is telling. But no matter. Come," he says. "Under is expecting you."

By the time the barrier vanishes, Zephyrus and the Orchid King are long gone.

The air hangs stagnant, any trace of Zephyrus' scent—loam, fresh roses—crushed beneath Under's rot. Standing alone in the darkened passage, I weigh my options. The grassy path twists to my right. According to Zephyrus, it will lead me safely back to Thornbrook. But that is not where my heart lies.

I'm no god, but I'm overcome by the desperation that sends mothers into burning buildings to save their children. What would I do to spare Zephyrus from his fate?

Anything.

As I follow the tunnel at a run, the strangest thing occurs. Grass erupts beneath my boots, carpeting the ground ahead, guiding me in the opposite direction to Thornbrook. Under must sense my intention, the urgency to reach Miles Cross in time.

The cave empties onto a grassy knoll, which perches above a wide green field. Gasping, I survey my surroundings. I've been here before. There is the bridge my peers and I crossed days earlier, the spread of the River Mur beneath. Tucked amongst the woods edging the opposite bank lies the cave leading to Miles Cross.

Movement draws my eye to the distant shore. Five white steeds surge forward like snow rolling down a mountainside. The Orchid King sits at the head of the party. His gruesome load of roots dwarfs the poor beast forced to carry him. I spot the West Wind at the very back, tied to a man wearing a ruby cloak.

Palming my dagger, I take a running start downhill. Cutting them off before they reach Miles Cross is the only way to save Zephyrus.

The horses are still a mile away when I cross the bridge and reach the wall of trees. There I crouch, awaiting their arrival. With Zephyrus seated atop the last horse in the group, I should be able to drag him down without being trampled. I have my blade and my conviction. It's all anyone really needs.

But I have overlooked the West Wind's inherent inquisitiveness. Despite his weakened state, he continues to ponder; he questions why. Even the slightest disturbance draws his focus, for as I push aside the ferns and prepare to leap, his keen eyes find mine with startling ease, and widen with unmistakable terror.

Zephyrus manages to yank the reins, steering the horse *away* from me, toward the river. I cannot reach him now, not unless I wish to be trampled by the herd. The cloaked man snarls, regaining control of his mount and cuffing Zephyrus into submission. By the time I realize what he's done, the party has already galloped past, five white steeds disappearing into the darkness of Miles Cross.

37

AN ALTAR HAS BEEN ERECTED IN THE CENTER OF MILES CROSS.
Lush grass cushions the slab of pure white marble. Surrounding
the field, the amphitheater rises in three tiers where the fair folk have
gathered, partially shielded by shadows where the moonlight pouring
through the ceiling cannot reach. The third tier is so high it hangs
behind wisps of fog.

Vines cling to the archway of an abandoned side entrance. It is there
I crouch, having navigated the network of tunnels in near darkness. I do
not see Zephyrus, nor Mother Mabel. Only the altar, the glen, tendrils
of thickening night.

A set of massive wooden doors heaves open in the back of the cavern.

First come the roots. Their white, waxy coating, the small, bristly
hairs. Soil sprays the air as the Orchid King slides his bulk over the
threshold.

It is so quiet I can hear the spit of candle flame. Breath held, I
watch Pierus slither toward the altar. His muscled abdomen flexes with
each sinuous movement. Upon reaching the altar, he turns to face the
audience.

A bell chimes. Again, the doors open. I bite the inside of my cheek
so hard blood marks my tongue.

The five members of Pierus' council drag Zephyrus into the cavern,
jewel-toned cloaks hissing in their wake. His head hangs. Rusted

chains bind his wrists at his back. A roar of approval shudders through the cave walls.

Fury is a hard, pointed star inside my chest. His garb hangs off his frame in precarious threads, and filth coats him from head to toe. He's tossed at the base of the altar, a crumple of limbs, while Pierus' council departs. After a moment, Zephyrus manages to prop himself upright using his knees. Livid green eyes glare through the dirt-caked curls hanging in his face. It eases the tightness in my throat. He is not defeated. Not yet, anyway.

"You remember this altar, do you not?" The Orchid King runs a hand across the gleaming marble surface. "You will be reacquainted soon enough."

The West Wind regards the structure coolly. Meanwhile, the crowd's eagerness continues to climb, tearing free of the earth's restraint.

"Look alive, Zephyrus," drawls the Orchid King. "You have a visitor."

A disembodied voice drifts through the heavy fog. "All rise for the Abbess of Thornbrook."

The doors at the rear of the cave groan as they're pushed open a third time, allowing a small procession to enter: twenty cloaked acolytes and novitiates, and lastly, the face of one I know well.

She glides forth, the sleeves of her alb swathing her delicate wrists, hands clasped solemnly at her front. The sleeveless gold chasuble envelops her body like loving hands.

A hush seeps into the cavern. The Daughters of Thornbrook position themselves against the far wall in a half-moon at Mother Mabel's back. I spot Harper at the rear, hunched beneath my white cloak. What have they done over the last few days? Did they return to Thornbrook, or sleep in Under's vast belly? Did anyone notice my absence, or care?

As if scenting iron, the fair folk retreat deeper into the shadows, stony eyes wary. The sight of my peers passes like stillness through me, this troubling pairing of faith and blood: all these women, shepherds of the Father, blades seated comfortably in their palms.

With soundless footsteps, Mother Mabel approaches Zephyrus where he kneels, head bowed, back bent, hands bound. She lifts a hand, and the silence deepens.

"Bringer of Spring." Here, the sound of her voice is peculiar. It lacks resonance, hitting as abruptly as a rock chucked at the ground. "For centuries, you have been bound to Under, the realm fed by the power of your lifeblood. Tonight, we celebrate another tithe and call in your debt."

Zephyrus lifts his head to study the abbess. "Only the truly conniving twist faith to their own advantage."

The fair folk stir like a nest of worms, their interest piqued by the unanticipated malevolence. Nausea continues to churn in my belly, for I am familiar with Mother Mabel's expression, the polish coating the surface of her flat, ebony gaze. She is far from pleased. "I do not take advantage of the Father," she says. "It is because of His mercy that I am alive to this day, standing before you."

Zephyrus chuffs a laugh. A trickle of blood oozes from his split lip. "Then you deny the corruption of your faith?"

"I'm not sure I understand." She surveys him as one would a stain upon a pristine robe. Meirlach shimmers star-bright at her waist.

He bares his teeth. "What of your vows, your Seven Decrees? Or do you only abide by them when it is convenient?" A few of my peers gasp at the implication. "Your willingness to participate in this violent ritual reveals how debased you truly are."

A fine, bloodless line shapes her mouth. As Mother Mabel begins to circle him, she says, "Thornbrook's preservation depends on Under's health. That is why your blood is necessary, why my charges' blood is necessary."

"It is cruel." His gaze cuts to Pierus. "I am not who I was centuries ago."

One of the Orchid King's vines reaches out to stroke Zephyrus' hair, tugging on a wheaten curl until it springs back into its tight coil. "How precious that you believe such things," Pierus drawls.

Mother Mabel continues to survey the West Wind. "All gods are unchanging, eternal. It is a truth of the world you know well."

"I disagree," Zephyrus says quietly.

"This does not have to be difficult," she says. "You know the law. Another cycle has reached its close, and your curse remains unbroken. An unfortunate occurrence, but according to the Orchid King, unsurprising."

So there *is* a way to break his curse. What must Zephyrus do? Is it as impossible as he suggested, or merely improbable?

"The time has come," she announces. "Kneel, and let your power empty into Under."

A smile stretches wide across the West Wind's mouth. "I will not bow to a false god."

Mother Mabel bristles. "Considering your current position," she snaps, "I would suggest you mind your tongue."

"Look at you. Look at these women at your back. They have offered their lives in service, placed their trust in you, and you've led them into a viper's nest."

"Do not speak of my charges," she warns.

From where I crouch, I observe the women exchanging worried glances amongst themselves.

He goes on, pressing his advantage. "What is it that bothers you, Mother Mabel? That I speak the truth, or that you are not strong enough to weather it?"

She halts her circling. My peers hold tight to dark iron at her back. Had I understood what purpose the blades served in perpetuating this bloodletting, I would have set down my hammer long ago. "I will not tell you again."

"Punish me as you see fit." He shrugs. "My life is forfeit anyway."

Her eyebrows crawl all the way to her hairline. Then the abbess smiles, face contorting into punishing angles. "You want your life?" She draws her sword. "Then fight for it."

The Orchid King lurches forward with a scowl. "That is not in your power to decide, Mother Mabel. Zephyrus is mine."

Mother Mabel maintains her focus on the man bent before her as she says, "You have seen me spar before. Do you doubt my ability to win this bout?" With his silence, she indicates the audience overhead. "Your subjects came all this way. Why not give them a tithe to remember?"

Jeers cut the air, and shadows flex in the darkest corners. The Orchid King considers the abbess, then the West Wind, blue eyes watchful.

"Very well," he relents. "I suppose there is little harm in it."

My fingers curl into the grass, hooking me in place so I will not intervene. Aside from our weekly training, I've witnessed Mother Mabel duel a handful of times during my apprenticeship. She handled the blade with remarkable mastery.

"Well?" She peers down at the West Wind.

He stands. How can he not? Many centuries he has run, but today, Zephyrus, Bringer of Spring, will fight.

"You have a blade," he states evenly, "but you will not grace me with one?"

Mother Mabel swings Meirlach overhead, testing its response to a new master after centuries gathering dust. It unsettles me. A blade is a tool, a method of defense, yet Mother Mabel, a woman of station in the faith, intends to shed blood for sport.

"You are a god," she replies. "You have your winds, your wit. Let that be enough." Hilt enveloped snugly in her grip, she nods to the Orchid King. "Break his bonds."

Tonight, I understand fear is personal. It manifests in twenty iron daggers held in the hands of the pious, the clank of chains clattering onto softened grass, a heart ceasing its beat. Meirlach is god-touched. If he falls beneath this blade, he will not rise.

Once free, Zephyrus rotates his wrists, massaging away the stiffness with a bland expression. An air-carved sword materializes in hand, its silvery curve haloed in milky light.

Shadows stretch and bend around the fair folk as they grow unruly, electrified by the promise of blood. The altar, an eruption of white stone, smolders at Zephyrus' back. But as Mother Mabel lifts her sword, black eyes remote, she whirls toward the Orchid King instead.

Pierus has anticipated it. That is abundantly clear as his own sword appears, driving upward to catch Meirlach with a startling clash. My peers scramble backward, press into a huddle, their backs to the wall. The fair folk howl and shriek and collapse into squeals of delight.

Between the cross of their blades, Pierus gifts Mother Mabel a close-lipped smile. "All these decades I've wondered when you would make your move. I'm relieved the time has come at last."

Strands of blond hair hang around her reddened face. I've seen disappointment disturb that cool serenity, exasperation, even moments of outrage, rare though they are. Never true abhorrence as I witness now. "I have indeed bided my time." Despite the Orchid King's over-whelming height, her stance remains unbending. "I have endured your horrendous nature and repulsive proclivity for violence, your parasitic bloodletting, the disrespect you show toward my charges. I have endured it all for this moment: an end to an era."

The Orchid King's eyebrows wing upward. "You seem confident of this end."

"Seven years you kept me captive." Mother Mabel speaks no louder than is required for intimate conversation, yet in the silence that has fallen, every word rings clearly. "No matter how I pleaded—*begged*—for mercy, you refused to listen."

"You knew the consequences of a broken contract. You failed to show up for the tithe with the required twenty-one donors. It was well within my right to steal away a few of your women."

Teeth bared, she leans into the stance. "I approached you multiple times concerning the tithe. I wanted change. You agreed it was a barbaric ritual, to force *my* charges to give blood, only to grow *your* power. We agreed Thornbrook's participation in the tithe would be no more."

"You chose to endure the punishment in your charges' stead," he argues. "I did not make the decision for you."

"I do not regret taking the place of my charges all those decades ago. They would not have survived the abuse." Her arms begin to shake, yet she pushes against him so he's forced to give ground. "But I did."

"You did," the Orchid King concedes. "You were strong for a mortal woman. No matter what cruelties you endured, your faith never wavered." Two pale vines curl around her ankles, slinking toward her stomach, up to her breasts. "I admire conviction."

"Don't touch me," Mother Mabel hisses.

"May I remind you, Abbess, that you entered *my* realm? What did you think to accomplish by revealing your hand?"

She sneers. I've never seen such outright revulsion. "Once you're gone, my charges, and all of Thornbrook, will be free of you. Your death will burden me less than your life."

From my position in the tunnel entryway, I look over at Zephyrus, who lounges against the wall, arms crossed, calmly observing the fortuitous turn of events. I've half a mind to drag him away from this place, but I stay put. As silly as it sounds, I fear Mother Mabel's wrath. Tonight is about more than the tithe. Tonight is for cleansing, for vengeance.

"You wish to end my reign?" Pierus considers her with an insulting lack of concern. "I welcome the challenge."

Mother Mabel breaks away with startling litheness. He blocks one, two, three blows before hacking at her stomach. She pivots sideways and slashes low, lopping off a vine at its base and darting out of reach.

A high-pitched cry shivers from the severed appendage. Dark fluid oozes from the flowers, which whiten, then crumble to fine powder.

The Orchid King stretches taller, using his tangled roots to draw himself up. "You may carry a god-touched blade," he says, "but so do I." The steel in question protrudes from a wire and leather hilt. "The necklace you stole from the Stallion may prolong your years indefinitely, but it cannot protect you from a sword in your gut."

Until this moment, I've acquired information only in pieces. Together, they forge something whole: clarity at long last. What do I know? Mother Mabel was held captive by the Orchid King after taking the place of three novitiates decades ago. For seven long years—an entire cycle—she was imprisoned, until the day she managed to escape.

But she did not return to Thornbrook immediately. She sought out the Stallion, stole the serpent necklace now resting against her collarbone. Not a piece of pretty jewelry, but an artifact, a gift of ever-lasting life.

She must have then returned to Thornbrook, carrying the trauma of her enslavement with her, whetting it, oh so slowly, until it bore a sharpened point. For years it must have eaten at her, carved out all the joy until it turned to rot. If she was going to one day enact revenge on the Orchid King, she must live long enough to do so.

And Meirlach? How long had she planned to acquire it? Did she hone me as a blade so I might one day duel the Stallion and win?

The Orchid King lunges, slicing a line through her chasuble. Mother Mabel meets the next strike, parries nimbly and returns. A few vines lash out toward her legs, but she skips aside, far more agile than the Orchid King, whose nest of bramble weighs him down. By the time she slips around his front, quick as an asp, her blade rests at the base of his throat.

"Tell me where you go when you die," she demands, "so I may ensure you never return."

His jaw clenches, and a vein pulses at his temple. Pierus would likely chew off his own tongue before caving in to the abbess' command. But Meirlach demands the truth, and eventually the compulsion to speak overtakes him, the words emerging as a snarl.

"Your people call it Hell. Where I come from, we call it the Chasm."

He winces as she sinks the tip into his neck. A bloody droplet trickles down his skin.

"The thought of your death," she says, "is the only thing that got me through the days. Today, I begin anew—"

A vine slams into the backs of her knees. The sword flies from her hand as she hits the ground.

I fail to muffle my horrified scream as both opponents dive for Meirlach. Blessedly, Mother Mabel reaches the sword first. A blink, and she's back on her feet, slicing through vines, lopping off the vicious flowers. Pierus bellows in pain, attempting to deflect as he scurries from her reach. Her next swipe goes wide, hacking through a pillar that drags the ceiling into partial collapse. Though I have read about the blade's extraordinary power, it is still a strange thing to see it cut through solid stone.

"You tire, Pierus," she pants coarsely, spinning to avoid a slash to the thigh. "Such is the lot of a man fatted on power."

A wall of vines erupts in a wave of deadly points. The abbess severs two. A third clips her on the shoulder, spinning her toward the altar. She hits the corner with shattering impact, crumpling to her knees.

Terror locks me in place as the Orchid King descends. She's not moving. Face slack, eyes closed. Pierus is within striking distance, arms lifted, as she lies motionless. The women gasp. His sword falls, a precise crescent toward Mother Mabel's neck.

Her eyes fly open. Snapping upright, she thrusts Meirlach through his heart.

The long, steel blade protrudes from the Orchid King's back. Blood patters onto the grass like soft rain. With a twist, she yanks the sword free. Pierus sags forward with a groan, collapsing at the altar's base.

Shock ripples through Miles Cross.

I look to my peers. Their pale faces glow beneath their shadowed cowls. Someone faints near the back, toppling the nearby women into a heap.

The fair folk are oddly mute, their movements stiff with uncertainty. Do they mourn the Orchid King? Or do they, too, feel free? But through the unholy quiet, a new realization emerges, one of breath and a life not yet lived. My heart lightens in the most profound relief. For with the Orchid King's death, the Bringer of Spring walks free.

Without the slightest unease, Mother Mabel promptly wipes the sword clean with the hem of her alb. She then mops her clammy face before turning to Zephyrus, her expression as cold and closed as ever. "If I am correct, the debt between you and Pierus is now void, is it not?"

The West Wind pushes off the wall he leans against, yet keeps a healthy distance between them. Flowers spring from the press of his heels against the grass, and his green eyes possess an immortal glow, flush with unleashed power.

"It is." He stares a touch too long at Meirlach, which she still holds. "I thank you for the favor."

Mother Mabel studies him with icy disinterest. At some point during the duel, her bun must have loosened, for now her hair hangs freely—the first I have ever seen it unbound. "I did not do it for you, Bringer of Spring."

"I'm aware." One of his hands slides into the pocket of his filthy trousers. "Nonetheless, I benefited, as did you."

She glances down at the mythical blade. Zephyrus' attention returns to the sword as well. "Yet I find myself in a curious predicament," she clips. "My duty is to Thornbrook and my charges. It has always been so."

"I understand."

"I'm not sure you do." Meirlach cuts through the air with a high whine as the abbess tests her swing. "Unfortunately, your presence complicates matters."

He quirks a brow, at ease to all outward appearances, but I have spent enough time in his company to recognize the subtleties of mounting concern. My feet bid me to go to him. I would stand at his side as I promised to do, yet I'm reluctant to show myself. "Enlighten me, please," Zephyrus says.

"Your life is a hazard to all I have built. I cannot allow you to further tempt the women under my protection." She holds the gleaming steel steady. "It's nothing personal."

I am still. This is something I had not foreseen.

Zephyrus angles toward her, for she has begun to approach. "I have no need to tempt anyone now that I am free."

"Really. Then tell me where my bladesmith is. Brielle," she snaps. "Where is she?"

"I do not follow." Yet his eyes flicker.

Another step forward. "She was accounted for when we arrived," Mother Mabel says, voice low with rage. "Now she is missing. Am I to believe you had nothing to do with her disappearance? You, who lured her into Under to begin with?" She halts a stone's throw away.

"Perhaps," he says with a glance in Harper's direction, "you should ask your other charges where she is."

"Do not place blame on these women. They are innocent. But you, Zephyrus of the West? You are a god, and gods do not change."

She leaps, hacking toward his neck with brutal ferocity. He springs sideways, aided by a rush of air beneath his boots, and touches down on the other side of the pond. Grass rushes upward around his thighs, long stalks looping into multiple braids, which lash out at Mother Mabel's legs.

She cuts them down. But Zephyrus' reign over all things green tears up walls of roots, individual blades of grass arrowing toward her exposed skin. Small, weeping cuts color Mother Mabel's face and neck. I flinch as another wound peels open her cheek.

A sphere of air punches out from Meirlach's tip, barreling toward the West Wind, who diverts its path with a gust of his own. The sphere slams into the wall, spraying grit.

Enlivened by the entertainment, the audience cackles and screams. I had completely forgotten about Meirlach's ability to command the wind. It gives Mother Mabel an advantage.

The duel intensifies before my eyes. Both hurl wind at each other with increasing force. I'm not sure what I fear more: Zephyrus' death, or Mother Mabel's. At one point, they veer frighteningly close to the Daughters of Thornbrook. Harper shoves the younger girls behind her, iron dagger held aloft. I force myself to remain in place as the fight progresses toward my position.

Blow by blow, the cavern crumbles to dust. Deflected gusts pummel the ceiling and walls. The West Wind rams Mother Mabel into a pillar, which cracks, the rock groaning. A massive chunk plummets from overhead, missing the abbess by a foot.

She struggles to stand, seething. Sweat drips from her face. No matter how much effort she exerts, Zephyrus is always one step ahead. She will never be able to reach him on foot. He is simply too powerful.

As Mother Mabel lifts Meirlach, wind explodes from the blade, sending Zephyrus soaring across the room. Moments before he lands, she takes aim, readying herself to throw.

In hindsight, it was all meticulously planned. For I understand that, with Mother Mabel already in motion, it is too late for him.

Her wrist snaps forward. And as the sword's gold-plated hilt leaves her hand, I spring from the corner, hurling myself into the path between god and blade.

The sword hits my left breast, sinking deep. Blood pours from the opening as I stumble, then fall, hands scrabbling at the protruding hilt, Zephyrus lurching forward with a roar.

And just like that, I have come undone.

38

MY BODY HITS THE GROUND WITH A DISTANT THUMP. IMMEDI-ately, my senses dull and darken, as though I observe the world through a film of murky water. Mother Mabel's face drains of color, and she sways where she stands. "Brielle?"

The West Wind falls to his knees beside me. All-powerful Meirlach, whose steel can master any foe, protrudes from my left breast. "No," he whispers. "No, no, no, no, no—" It is a mantra, the holiest of chants.

Mother Mabel stares at the spreading pool of blood. She lifts a trembling hand, presses two fingers to her quavering mouth as she scans the novitiates clumped together in their white cloaks, Harper among them. Her hood has fallen back, revealing lustrous ebony hair, blue eyes swimming with tears.

Gently, Zephyrus lifts me across his thighs. "Stay with me." He cradles the side of my slackened jaw, and his voice cracks as he searches my face. I try to focus on him amidst the looming shadows, but I am floundering, dragged farther beneath the surface of the murk. The deeper I sink, the less agony I experience. I do not fight the pull.

"Look at me." He shakes me desperately. My head lolls. "Damn it all, look at me!"

As Mother Mabel reaches my side, a wall of air catapults her across the room. She hits the wall with a violent crack, and there are screams, terrible screams. She slides onto her backside, dazed. Blood trickles from her hairline.

"Someone get me a gods-damned healer!" Zephyrus roars.

Yet all is silent. All is still.

"We'll fix this." He fumbles for the hilt protruding from my chest. "We'll ..." Blood-soaked hands slip over the gold plating. No matter how hard he yanks, the sword does not pull free.

With a hoarse cry, he releases the weapon. He shakes, fighting to maintain control, and then, as if having succumbed, deflates.

It is an effort to move my hand. Its weight is unbearable. Yet my fingers twitch, brushing Zephyrus' thigh in whatever comfort I can offer him.

His head snaps up. "Brielle." Leaning over me, he peers into my eyes.

I swallow around the blood flooding my mouth and throat. "I tried."

"Shh. Don't say that." He pulls me against his sweaty chest. The pulse of his heart beneath my ear begins to fade, as all things do. "Help is coming for you. Just hold on. You have to hold on."

Deeper and deeper I sink. My words, when they emerge, are naught but breath. "I wish ..." A shudder wracks my body, and the blackness spreads, veiling him momentarily from sight. "I would have told you—"

"Told me what?"

I cannot remember.

"Brielle." The word is too sharp. "What did you want to tell me?" He shakes me again. "Brielle."

My fingers slacken, fall loose upon the ground. I am dissolving. My thoughts erode, and I begin to forget.

The West Wind dips his head to mine. Even in my blood-saturated haze, I can smell his breath, sweet as honeysuckle. "You can't leave me," he murmurs. "Not like this."

I do not have the words to inform him that I am already gone.

Peeling itself from my body, my soul floats higher in the cavern, far above the gathered spectators, the lush field of grass. I never gave much thought as to how I would die. All I know is what follows: the Eternal Lands. There, I would want for nothing. My belly full. My heart whole. My body restful, rid of aches and pains.

But—Zephyrus. Dear, complicated Zephyrus, who smooths the red, tangled curls from my face with his filth-encrusted hands. A rough, broken sound falls unchecked from his mouth. "Why?" He lifts his head, that emerald gaze piercing Mother Mabel across the field as two acolytes help her to stand. "Why would you send Brielle on that fool's errand into Under? Why demand she collect the sword? I thought you cared for her."

The Abbess of Thornbrook is many things. Austere. Rigid. Never bent, as she is now. "I care for each of my charges. Brielle was . . ." Her expression falters. "She was special. No one else was more dutiful or willing to please. How could I have predicted she would stray?"

He sneers. "You claim to care for Brielle, yet it is clear you barely know her."

"And you do?" Her eyes narrow. "I have looked after Brielle for a decade. You have known her for a handful of months."

"It takes more than time to know another's heart. She is a curious, willful woman. She questions the world in which she lives."

"Let me be clear, Bringer of Spring." Mother Mabel's voice quavers despite the steel beneath. "It is because of *you* that Brielle is dead."

A snarl rips through the cavern.

The West Wind leaps to his feet, wind-carved blade in hand. "Take accountability for your actions, Abbess," he spits. "It was your hand that threw the blade. Do not deny it."

The fair folk, drawn by the whiff of spilled blood, have crept forward in their tiers, but one quelling look from Mother Mabel herds them back into the gloom.

"Do not doubt my care," she goes on. "I loved Brielle like a daughter. I tried to guide her to the best of my abilities, but you were selfish. You wanted her for yourself. Now here she lies, a corpse."

Indeed, my freckles appear as broken scabs against my colorless skin. My blank eyes resemble muddy pools.

"If you truly cared for her well-being," Zephyrus hisses, lifting the sword with blood in his teeth and grief in his heart, "you would have nurtured her. You would have built her up, infused her with the confidence required to face the world. Instead, she floundered, torn down by the cruelty of her peers." Another tear courses down his cheek. "The true mark of a coward is choosing to do nothing."

I peer at Harper from above, my soul grasping onto the last frail tether binding me to my physical self. She bows her head, shamefaced. Isobel appears equally remorseful.

"Better a coward," Mother Mabel replies with cold scorn, "than a disgraced god. It is not my job to nurture and protect. That is the Father's duty. My job is to instruct my charges of their faith." Her upper lip curls. "But what would you know of faith? You have avoided duty your entire life. Why cling to something that does not belong to you and never will?"

She steps forward, skirting Pierus' body, the oozing roots. Her gaze falls to my blood-drenched form before darting away, pain tightening her features. "Brielle belongs with her people. We will take her back to Thornbrook, where she will be buried. I will not allow her to rot in this place."

"You would take her from me?"

Mother Mabel peers carefully at Zephyrus. "If you cared for her at all," she says quietly, "you would wish her a peaceful rest."

I've never seen his features so anguished. "I told Brielle to return to Thornbrook. I did not want Pierus to harm her. But she did not listen to me."

"Do you not see the pattern of your actions?" A few more strides bring Mother Mabel nearer to my side. "The death of one lover, and now the death of another. When will enough be enough? When will you learn?"

The devastation, when it hits, is total. I watch Zephyrus' expression fracture, its slow, shameful crush beneath remembrance.

"Live your life, Zephyrus. Leave this place, if you wish. You're free." Mother Mabel reaches out a beseeching hand. "Just return Brielle to us."

Indeed, freedom is something he has long desired. I'm only disappointed I cannot share this joyous moment with him.

Curled over my corpse, Zephyrus weeps in earnest. Great, heaving sobs that would break the back of a weaker man. His sadness is so potent it tinges the air, feathering the edges of my waning soul. Something tugs at my gut as I float higher. The Father calls. I'm not ready to go.

"I don't care for my freedom," Zephyrus grinds out. "All I want is for this woman in my arms to be alive, unbroken, whole." He touches the corner of my mouth where the blood has begun to harden. "What must I do to bring her back?"

"It cannot be done." The long column of Mother Mabel's neck is a pillar of palest marble as she lifts her chin. "That is the unfortunate reality of a mortal life."

"I will not accept that." He snarls it, his face a mess of snot and tears. "Under holds the well of my power, and I, dear Abbess, am a god unchained. We shape the world as we see fit. Nothing is stronger."

She stands uncowed. "It is the law."

"Laws can be rewritten."

"Not this law," she says. "Not death."

Brow scrunched, Zephyrus stares into my pallid face. His palm cups my cheek tenderly, and I see the man he could have been, unburdened, free to choose. He is not like his brothers. He is neither bleak winter nor the scouring air to the south. Spring is gentle at heart. It shatters the earth's icy, hardened skin.

"Do you believe in miracles, Mother Mabel?"

Her black eyes narrow to slits. Fine facial lines tell the tale of restless nights.

"It seems exactly the sort of question one who knows nothing of our faith would ask," she responds with a bone-deep weariness. "If you had bothered to read our Text, you would know that in the Book of Grief—"

"Aiden the Blessed healed a drowned woman after she lay dead for three days?" Mother Mabel stares. "Or perhaps in the Book of Fate, when Ian the Just regained sight after a lifetime of blindness?" He smiles a hard sort of smile. "I am well acquainted with your Text, Abbess. But I did not ask what is written in its pages. I asked if you believe in miracles."

The question clearly makes her uncomfortable. Another moment passes before she states, "I do."

"Then take me instead. My life in exchange for Brielle's."

Mother Mabel blinks at him, dumbfounded. A hush dampens the gloom of Miles Cross. "You, a god, offer your life for a mortal woman?"

He dips his chin in a rare display of subservience. "I am kneeling before you, willing to do whatever it takes to bring the woman I love back to life. If you believe nothing else, believe this."

She frowns, crosses her arms over her stomach, a shield to protect the soft, vulnerable parts of her body. "I do not know if it can be done."

"You are a vessel of your god, are you not?" When she nods, Zephyrus says, "Then tonight, you will act as my vessel. We will use the combined power of our blood to reverse Brielle's death. Mine, yours, the Daughters of Thornbrook."

She contemplates the West Wind as one might a particularly frustrating enigma. The fair folk are so quiet they have faded into the background. "You loved Brielle, and I believe she loved you, too. Why else would she sacrifice her life for yours? Perhaps what you speak of is still possible."

Mother Mabel peers down at me. How tall she stands when no longer cloaked in Pierus' shadow. "It is time Brielle returns to Thornbrook and takes up her mantle as acolyte. Once her death is reversed, I will ensure that she remembers nothing of this night, or any that came after your first encounter. I cannot risk losing her to you again. It will be as though you had never met."

"If that is the price of her life," he whispers, "then I will gladly pay it."

Pressing a kiss to my chilled cheek, he sets me aside, careful not to disturb the sword jutting from my chest. He then stands before the altar, dagger in hand. He does not flinch as he drags the blade through the center of his palm. Blood drips onto the white stone.

He turns, motions to my peers with grief-hardened features. "They will each gift their blood. You will go last, Abbess."

The Daughters of Thornbrook calmly approach the altar. They readily pierce their fingers, squeezing the skin until blood wells, then patters onto the snowy slab. Harper slices her palm with a quiet sob. The remaining women add their blood to the mix without complaint, even capricious Isobel.

Mother Mabel is the last to approach, appearing small and bent in the vast space. "Heavenly Father," she says. "For you, our hearts are open."

As her blood joins the small pool, a wind snaps through the cavern, stirring shadows into dust.

"Let it be done," intones the West Wind, and the world ruptures in the white light of a newborn star.

PART 3

THE GRACED

39

"SHOULDN'T SHE HAVE WOKEN UP BY NOW?"

"Hush." A pointed demand. "Healing takes time."

I feel myself sloughing off the dense, dream-thick sleep, rising nearer toward the surface, toward sun.

"And you care why?" Isobel's nasal voice. I would recognize it anywhere.

"Brielle almost *died*," Harper responds with a low hiss. "Of course I would care."

"Since when? You hate Brielle."

"I don't hate Brielle." But she does not sound entirely convinced.

The silence, though brief, snaps against my skin with rising tension.

"I don't know what's happened to you of late," Isobel sneers, "but I would rethink your allegiance here. The higher you climb, the harder you fall. Who you befriend matters. Remember that."

Boots stomp across the room. A door opens, then slams shut.

A sharp pain pulses through my chest. My eyes fly open on a gasp, palm lifting to cover the hurt when my hand is caught by another's— long-fingered, porcelain smooth. My bleary gaze lifts to Harper.

"Don't touch," she says, "or you risk reopening the wound."

That fine-boned face, the midnight hair falling in sheets over her shoulders, her skin a startling purity against the soft gray cotton of her dress. It feels like an age since I have seen her.

Briefly, I scan my surroundings. The infirmary is a rectangular room lined with cots, crisp white sheets stretched tautly over the thin mattresses. Salves, tinctures, and balms clutter the shelves built into the far wall. Curtains mask the windows. We are the only ones occupying the space.

I snatch my hand away. "What are you doing?" My throat grates, the words hoarse and weak. Why is Harper sitting at my bedside? "Where's Mother Mabel?"

Calmly, she reaches for the glass of water on my nightstand. Candles brighten the dim room with pockets of wavering light. "Thirsty?" She shoves the drink into my hand.

I stare at it. Plain water. Poisoned? Maybe.

A small sip coats my parched tongue. I take a larger swallow before returning the glass, which Harper sets on the bedside table with the agreeable nature of a small puppy. "That doesn't answer the question. What are you doing?"

"Helping you."

I can see that. "Why?"

Those lake-water eyes meet mine. "Why not?"

This has become too strange for words. "Because my very existence offends you?"

She's on her feet between one second and the next. Puzzlement twists her expression, yet she retorts, "You're covered in bandages, so I would strongly suggest you restrain yourself, otherwise you'll bleed out and cause more work for the rest of us." Pivoting, she strides for the door.

The sight of her retreating back sparks panic in me. "Wait." I attempt to sit up, yet cry out as my flesh tugs beneath the bandages. "What happened? Why am I injured?" The inside of my head holds only darkness.

She turns, blue gaze narrowed over her perfect nose. "You don't remember?"

"Obviously not."

Her confusion resurfaces far too readily. I am used to Harper's cruelty. Rarely her uncertainty. "Fiona and Isobel found you in the vineyards. You were . . ." Then she stops. Swallows. "Mother Mabel says you were attacked by a bear."

My jaw slackens. "A bear?"

She moves toward the shuttered windows, hauls back the heavy drapes to reveal the mountain's crown edged in warm sunlight, the River Twee a distant silver band nestled in the hillside. "Apparently, they found you just in time."

Stunned, I rest my fingers against my chest where the ache unfolds. The wound feels raw, as though the skin has been recently sutured.

"You're certain it was a bear?" They're scarcely found on the mountain, likely avoiding the strange power flowing through its heart. "Could it have been one of the fair folk?"

"It was a bear. Isobel saw it run off." She sniffs, leans against the windowsill. "You're lucky they found you in time. You could be a tad more grateful."

A bear attack? It doesn't sound plausible. Stranger things have happened, I suppose.

A thought suddenly comes to mind. "What day is it?"

"The Holy Day." Harper fiddles with her cincture, tracing the three knots secured at her waist. I blink in shock. When did Harper become an acolyte? "They brought you in mid-week."

Either she misspoke, or I've yet to cast off the fog dampening my thoughts. "Why would I have been in the vineyards?" I say. "I don't work the vineyards in the spring." My forge burns for the majority of the day and well into the night once the cold season passes.

Harper goes still. "Brielle," she says. "It's the harvest season."

"What?" It cannot be. It is most certainly the growing season, when the foothills burst into riotous color beneath the frost. "I don't appreciate the deception." It's bad enough I've awoken in the infirmary without any recollection of how I got here. But this is a new low, even for Harper.

She sighs. "Why would I lie?" There was a time when any minor slight against her might cause a furious outburst, yet the tranquility Harper exudes takes me aback. I do not recognize this unruffled woman.

"I don't know. Because that's what you do? Lie and scheme?"

Obvious hurt darkens her eyes. "Look closer." She gestures to the open window—Carterhaugh's leaves tipped in red, the edges browning. Autumn in glorious luster.

My heart thuds sickeningly. Any attempt at recollection sends me ramming into a mental block I cannot breach. "Was there. head trauma?" It would explain the memory loss.

"Not that I'm aware of, but you were out for a few days. The injury was contained to your chest."

"I don't remember." My voice catches. "Why don't I remember?"

Arms crossed over her stomach, Harper studies me from where she loiters near the window. "Unfortunately, I don't have an answer for you."

Someone must have answers. If not Harper, then Mother Mabel. If not Mother Mabel, then Isobel, or Fiona, or one of the other women working the vineyards that day. "Don't you think it's strange I was attacked? Or that I can't remember what happened?"

She plucks a sprig of barley from the windowsill, twirls its stem between her fingertips, then releases it to the wind. "It is odd, admittedly. I'm sure there's an explanation." She can't quite meet my eyes. "Hopefully it isn't permanent," she adds. "The memory loss."

I stare at Harper until the silence grows uncomfortable. She seems to care for my well-being, though we both know that's not possible. Then there is the strange lack of anxiety I experience in her presence. I do not understand it.

Harper clears her throat, pushes off the windowsill. "If that's all, I will inform Mother Mabel you're awake." She departs, closing the door behind her.

Alone, I take stock of my faculties. I retain all my limbs, every finger and toe, yet no matter how deeply I search my memory, I hit a wall. There is only darkness. A massive, sucking pit. Nothing lives within it.

Who are we if not our memories?

My hands tremble, but that cannot be helped. Sleep will restore what is missing. It will patch the holes, exhume old pathways. Come morning, the world will right itself, and all will make sense.

Pushing aside the blanket covering my lap, I carefully draw the soft white gown upward, revealing legs mottled with bruises, skin covered in abrasions. I need to see how severe the wound is, how close I came to embracing death. A large bandage wraps my stomach and chest.

Despite the pain, I manage to untie the bandage, peeling back the cloth to reveal the injury, its neat sutures. I freeze as a lick of cold moves through me. Indeed, it is severe. But that is not what prompts my unease, for I have seen such a wound before.

Harper is wrong. I was not attacked by a bear. Someone ran me through with a sword.

40

MOTHER MABEL DOES NOT VISIT THE INFIRMARY UNTIL SUNSET, when the bell signaling supper's end tolls. She does not knock. As abbess, Thornbrook is hers to shape, hers to bend. Though this has never bothered me before, something bristles within me as she enters unannounced.

"Brielle. How are you feeling?" The hem of her alb hisses against the floor. For whatever reason, she does not wear her gold stole, only the white cord around her waist.

My arms quiver with weakness as I push upright against the pillows. "Tired," I whisper.

"I can imagine," she soothes. "You have experienced an ordeal, and recovery takes time." She crosses to the window, where the last of the sun's rays vanish behind the ridge of maple trees clumped at the wall's perimeter. Catching the heavy curtains, she pulls them closed, a gloomy pall shuttering the space.

"Maria has informed me that you are healing exceptionally well. By the end of the week, you should be able to return to your daily tasks. No smithing, however." As she approaches my bedside, she spots the untouched plate of food on my nightstand. "You were not hungry?"

I should be hungry, considering I can't remember when I last ate, but the craving isn't there. "I've had much on my mind."

"Oh?" Her voice is gentle. And I remember then that it was she who raised me and placed the heavily bound manuscript that is the Text into my hands. Obedience, purity, devotion. Mother Mabel knows me like no other.

The pit in my stomach, which has steadily amassed throughout the day, yawns deep and wide. Yes, she knows me, or a single version of me, but do I know her? I'm not sure that I do. "Harper informed me of what happened," I say, fingers hooking into the blanket. It is soft, heavy enough to ground me. "I have questions."

Sinking onto the edge of my cot, she smooths the blanket around my legs, adjusts the pillows at my back. "What are your questions, Brielle?"

"According to Harper, it is the harvest season. How can that be? I don't recall any passing time. Not the attack, nor what came before. I don't remember *anything*."

She nods, eyes soft with understanding. "It is a valid concern. After we carried you back to the abbey, we immediately sent for the physician. Your wounds were severe. Twice, we nearly lost you." Her right hand trembles, and she curls her gloved fingers tight into a ball. "Due to the traumatic nature of the attack, Maria mentioned the possibility of temporary memory loss. It is your mind's way of protecting you from reliving the experience."

It makes sense, I suppose. "So my memory will eventually return?"

The straw-filled mattress crinkles beneath her shifting weight. She does not look at me. I dread the reason why.

"It could be some time before your memory returns," she admits. "But there is the possibility it might not return at all."

"I see."

I have lost the summer—an entire season of my life. It's not right.

My last recollection does not sit like a leaf upon a crystal pool, something I might easily pluck free. No, I must submerge my hand and sift through the mucky riverbed until I find it: a head of gold-tipped curls, a laughing mouth and crinkling green eyes. I've never seen a face so compelling.

Mother Mabel pats my hand, and I snap free of my stupefaction. "Try not to worry," she says. "In time, you will begin to feel like your old self. I am certain."

"It's not that." My hand drifts across my sternum, the bandages crusted in blood. They will need to be changed soon. "Harper claimed I was attacked by a bear, but the wound I sustained came from a sword."

"What makes you think that?"

Her terse inquiry doesn't sit well. She has never doubted me before. I must be imagining it. "The stitches reveal a clean line. A bear would have torn the skin, left multiple puncture wounds." And I would likely be dead.

"Brielle." My name, a word infused with compassion. I'm helpless to resist its pull. "I know this is upsetting, but Isobel saw the bear flee across the fields." She searches my gaze. "Are you suggesting she lies?"

"No," I rush to say. For whatever reason, the implication leaves me breathless. "That's not what I mean." And yet, the concession only serves to heighten my turmoil. I want to believe her. The Abbess of Thornbrook is, above all else, forthright. But what she claims does not align with what I have seen. "Mother Mabel—"

"They killed the bear, you know." Her icy declaration halts my tongue. "Kilkare sent out a group of huntsmen to search the woods. An attack is incredibly rare, but this bear was ill, foam rimming its mouth. Who knows what could have happened had it not been brought down."

It makes perfect sense. So why this sustained unease? "That is . . . good." I attempt a smile.

"You have experienced a traumatic event. You are likely trying to reframe the attack through a familiar lens. Bladesmithing is what you know best. Of course you would make that connection."

Is it true? Has my own mind manipulated my perception of the experience in order to cope with the trauma of an attack I can't even remember? If it truly is the harvest season, then the tithe has already come and gone. Twice I have missed the opportunity to participate. I'm reminded of Harper's cincture, the three knots proudly displayed at her waist.

"Can I ask, Mother Mabel, when Harper became an acolyte?" It stings. I'd never considered the possibility she would ascend to that station before me. She must have taken her final vows during the summer, her appointment shrouded in the vague pool containing my lost memories.

"It was recent, only within the last few months." She frowns, suddenly concerned. "Are you upset? I know you've had your heart set on it, but be patient. Your time will come."

The possibility sparks no joy inside me, which only deepens my confoundment. It's what I've worked toward for the last ten years.

Mother Mabel sighs, then stands. "Do not strain yourself. Rest for a few more days. Returning to your routine will help center you, I'm sure." On her way out the door, she asks, "Would you like me to bring your Text for the nightly readings?"

Only now do I realize how tightly my hands clamp the blanket. With some effort, I pry my fingers loose, let them relax in my lap. Candlelight wanes, eating down the wick until the flame succumbs to the pool of melted wax. The thought of praying feels strange, but I nod anyway. "Thank you."

She returns with the leatherbound manuscript, placing it on my bedside table. After a brief farewell, I am again alone, awash in dying light. Though the gleam of the oiled leather draws my attention, I do not speak my prayers aloud. Nor do I pray the next day. Nor the next.

41

FOUR WEEKS FOLLOWING MY ATTACK, I RETURN TO MY DAILY routine. Mornings bring prayer, breakfast, crisp dew on blades of grass. Then chores: weeding the gardens, scrubbing pots, fixing the carts, chopping vegetables for the midday meal. When the tenebrous air cools with approaching dusk, I retreat to the forge for a moment of stolen peace among the clutter of tools and half-baked metal. Another fortnight, and I can return to smithing. Physician's orders.

Late evenings bring fractured sleep in my thin, narrow cot. I dream of an emerald gown, a set of hands bracing my waist. Sometimes, I light a lamp and hang it in my window, though I do not know why.

Waking or dreaming, I feel neither peace nor clarity. Thornbrook has dulled, and steeps in a perpetual, lackluster gloom. My memories have not returned. When I address Mother Mabel about my concerns, she merely says, "Give it time, Brielle. You're still recovering."

One morning, when the bell tolls for breakfast, I trail my peers in their rush through the corridors, eager as puppies at play. As I turn into the cloister, the hair at the back of my neck stands on end, and against my better judgment, I slow. It is not the first time I have sensed another's presence beyond my line of sight.

No, the first instance occurred two days following my release from the infirmary. On my walk to the forge, something shifted in the corner of my eye. I turned, and watched a figure leap over the stone wall. Later that evening, I wondered if I had imagined it.

Three days passed before I again spotted movement: long, stream-lined legs and threads of curling brown hair. No one seems to have noticed anything unusual, so I've told not a soul of my suspicion. I fear the madness will deepen.

I'm the last to arrive at breakfast. Harper sits separately from Isobel, I notice. This is the third week she has eaten alone. Without Isobel to warm her side, no one will bear her company. At least my solitude is chosen.

Breakfast ends as quickly as it began. According to the schedule, I'm harvesting vegetables this morning. I look forward to spending time outdoors, reacquainting myself with the earth. The day is warm and sunlit, with puffy white clouds strung across the blue sky, the air plucking lightly at my cotton dress.

Unfortunately, I'm paired with Harper for the day's work. She observes me from her perch on a slatted bench beneath one of the maple trees shading the enclosed herbarium. It's strange to see her seated as opposed to standing, feet planted decisively, aggressively. To watch her eyes catch mine before flitting away.

Normally, my unease stirs in Harper's presence, but now my heart thumps with the placid rhythm of the undisturbed. Perhaps that is why I decide to acknowledge her. "Good morning." I still question her presence in the infirmary when I woke. She was my only visitor during my recovery.

"Morning," she murmurs.

After gathering a basket, spade, and gloves, I crouch at one of the larger vegetable beds and begin yanking carrots free by their scraggly green tops, tossing them into my basket. For whatever reason, I have abandoned my gloves of late. The need to pull them on is strangely absent. Admittedly, I've enjoyed the varied textures against my skin. I delight in each one.

I finish one row, begin another. Harper's attention feels hotter than the sun on my back. Still, I focus on my task. If she wants to speak with me, she'll need to take that step herself.

Soil darkens my nails and sprinkles the tops of my thighs. With the first bed complete, I move on to the next. Maybe I do not remember much, but I remember this: the give of the earth beneath my fingers, the wrench of roots being pulled free.

"How are you recovering?"

I startle, dropping a fistful of carrots. Harper harvests a neighboring bed, hair restrained in a braid, sweat dotting her face. For once, she appears unconcerned by her rumpled state.

I gather the carrots I dropped. "Some lingering pain, but otherwise, I am well." They fall into my basket with a solid thump.

"Did Mother Mabel inform you that the bear was killed?"

"She did."

Harper shares in my relief, nodding far too enthusiastically for comfort. "I'm glad no one else got hurt."

It was no bear, I nearly say, but what if I am wrong? Now that my wound has healed, I wonder: was it from a sword, as I believe, or has my perception altered as Mother Mabel claimed it would? I am no nearer to answers than I was weeks ago.

I assume that will be the extent of our conversation, but Harper surprises me by adding, "If you're feeling tired, I can finish the harvest. It's not an issue."

I do not trust her intentions. A mouse does not willingly venture into the nest of a snake. "Why do you pretend to care for me?" I ask, unable to contain my frustration.

"It is no lie. I swear it."

I stare at Harper. First the infirmary, and now this. "So you claim. You have always treated me with contempt."

"I know." At least she has the decency to appear remorseful.

"Then why?"

"According to the Text—"

"Oh, please." Now she mocks me. "As if you care about that." I return to ripping up carrots, soil flying.

Harper falls quiet.

When my basket overflows with vegetables, I grab another from the shed. Harper kneels in place, staring at her gloved hands, her small frame swallowed by her gray dress. If I'm not mistaken, she has recently lost weight. I sigh, toss another carrot onto my pile, and demand, "Have I offended you?"

She frowns, brushes the dark soil from her palms. "I guess I never realized how small I made others feel."

Does she expect an apology? "Guilt is a terrible thing." I regard her with limited patience.

A dull flush colors her sweaty cheeks as she drops her attention to the ground. "I've had to face"—deep breath—"uncomfortable truths about myself. Namely, that my behavior has been harmful to the abbey, our peers."

"You don't say."

Her mouth parts, then clamps shut. "I don't remember you being this spirited," she says, blue eyes narrowed.

I shrug. I wasted so much of my life obsessing over Harper's opinion of me, but her insults have lost their sting. I'd like to think I've evolved.

There does, however, remain one mystery I'd like settled. "Why aren't you and Isobel friends anymore?" They had been attached at the hip since I arrived at Thornbrook. It is a difficult thing, navigating the world friendless.

"To tell you the truth, I'm not sure. I think we became different people." Her brow furrows. "I've asked Isobel what happened between us. She said I had changed."

I don't recall this change. Perhaps it dwells in the hole of my mind. "Do you think you've changed?" There is, undeniably, a softness to Harper that was not previously present, a new and welcome vulnerability.

She drops her spade into the bucket with a clatter. "It is hard to see change from within, is it not?"

Wise words from a woman I believed possessed not even a shred of self-awareness.

She taps a finger against her leg with obvious hesitation, then: "Has your memory returned?"

"No." Daily, I scour my mind for any flicker of recognition, an anchor I might use to ground myself. But—nothing.

Harper nods, as if that was to be expected. But something in her expression snags my attention and refuses to let go.

Dropping her voice so it will not carry over the moss-eaten walls, Harper says, "The truth is, I have blank spots in my memory, too."

Carefully, I set my basket aside. I glance around the herbarium, but we are alone in the walled garden with its neat rows of vegetable beds. "You're certain?" I've told no one my suspicion about the sword wound. I don't want that getting back to Mother Mabel.

"Yes."

"Did you participate in the tithe?" That would explain it—those who participate have their memories of the experience wiped.

"I think so?" Harper abandons her post to kneel at my side. She holds out her hand, pointing to the scar across her palm, evidence of her contribution. "The problem is, I remember nothing of the tithe, nor of the months preceding it. I don't even remember when I became an acolyte." She gestures to her cincture, twisted into its trio of knots. "Wouldn't I remember my ceremony, or at the very least, whatever task I was given to prove myself worthy of the station?"

She makes a good point. "What else have you forgotten?"

"My friendship with Isobel." As she speaks, she begins to snap matured broccoli crowns from their stalks. "Looking back, I can't remember any specific moment when we fought. It seems like one day I woke up and decided she wasn't someone whose company I cared for anymore. I mean, we've been friends for years. Why would I suddenly change my mind without cause?"

Another valid point.

"But mostly, it's how I feel in here." Harper presses a hand to her heart. "I look at Thornbrook, and I feel changed. Do you understand?"

I understand more than anyone. And since she has admitted her apprehensions, I feel comfortable sharing my own experience. "I think someone's watching me."

Harper goes still, a head of broccoli clamped in one fist. "Really? Who?"

At least she isn't claiming I've slipped into insanity, though that's a definite concern I have for myself. "I don't know. I believe it's a man." The breadth of the shoulders, the height and narrow hips. "I can't make out his features. He's never close enough."

"You've seen him inside the abbey?"

"Twice on my walk to the forge." Then this morning, on my way to breakfast, though I'd only sensed his presence.

A man watches me. What does he want? I haven't informed Mother Mabel of my concerns. My trust in her is no longer absolute.

Harper appears deeply disturbed, for men are forbidden to enter the grounds. "What are you going to do?"

"I don't know." I feel stuck. Stagnant. I am not sure of my path forward.

She frowns, then says, "I will pray for your memories to return— and my own."

It is not her prayers I need, only that elusive truth. But I nod, and gather up my basket, and harvest carrots until the noon bell tolls.

42

KILKARE BEGINS TO STIR AS WE ARRIVE AT THE MARKET TO SET UP shop. Soon, the scents of burned sugar and roasted meat saturate the air, and color brightens the wide thoroughfare, the stalls overwhelmed with abundance.

Within the first hour, I sell four knives. By noon, three more daggers have disappeared from my collection.

What's surprising is how many people ask after me. Though I do not remember, it's been months since I attended Market Day. They ask how I have been, if I am well. They inquire about my studies and ask if I will one day offer private commissions: knives, axes, swords. I've considered it. Thornbrook, however, comes first.

"I understand," the local baker, Gabe, says with a smile. "But if you ever change your mind, consider me your first client." He passes a small pastry box to me. Inside, four raspberry tarts sit like sweetened fruits, ripe for plucking.

A few stalls down, Isobel eyes my gift, her long coiled braids secured in a low tail. I select a tart, its cool white icing smearing my fingertips, and shove it into my mouth, all without breaking eye contact. She sneers, then returns to her bartering.

"Are you the abbey bladesmith?"

A short, cloaked figure approaches my table. I peer down at the visitor, frowning. "I am."

Pushing back her hood, the patron reveals herself. I gasp and stumble back. She is short and rotund, with twiggy legs and long, knobby fingers. A shabby waistcoat hangs over a gauzy white dress. Dull, stony eyes swallow the brightness of midday. An ancient gaze, cunning despite her childlike appearance.

Fair folk. I thought they couldn't pass through Kilkare's iron gates, but I wouldn't put it past them to carry enchantments that protect against iron, even salt.

My frown returns as she continues to stare. The weight of my dagger reminds me I am not without a means of defense. "Is there something I can help you with?" Surely, she would not attack me in broad daylight, though little is known about the fair folk and their motives.

The girl-woman's lower lip pokes outward. "You do not remember me, sweet?"

"I'm sorry, but you must have me confused with someone else." From the corner of my eye, I search for Mother Mabel. I haven't seen her since our arrival, hours ago.

"Then it is true what they are saying," she whispers. A lock of snowy hair brushes her chin. "You have forgotten us."

I straighten and take a long look at the unwanted visitor who claims to know me. I think of the months I've lost, the knowledge drowned. "Who have I forgotten?"

"The fair folk, of course."

One of the textile merchants across the lane crows in delight as she makes a sale. Still, I do not move. "We have met before?"

"We have. You were such a treat." She drinks me in, head to toe, lingering on my red hair. "Are you eating properly? You look wan." Reaching over the table, she touches my chin with a bony finger. "Who must I kill to avenge this?"

My heart thumps hard against my rib cage. She addresses me with too much familiarity for this meeting to have unfolded by happenstance. "That won't be necessary," I croak, easing out of range. A few patrons give the creature a wide berth, but most people are too focused on their shopping to notice. "When did we meet?" I press. "I was in an accident and don't remember much. Were we ... I mean, are we friends?"

"Not friends, but we were friendly in the months leading up to the tithe." Then she smiles, showcasing rotting gums. "You were so innocent then. It was the most irresistible allure."

A chill pricks my body despite the heat. The fair folk cannot tell a lie. What have I forgotten? What, exactly, did I lose?

"Were you there?" I demand, low and urgent. "Did you witness the tithe take place?" Mother Mabel has claimed I didn't participate, but I wonder if that is true.

She has opened her mouth to respond when Mother Mabel suddenly materializes, jostling the curious creature aside. "If you aren't buying," she snaps, "move along."

The girl-woman—I don't even know her name—glares at the abbess. Her long, crooked fingers pet the fabric of her dress, black eyes dull with suspicion. "As a matter of fact, I was inquiring about this blade." She points to a recent design. It took me weeks to complete.

"That dagger is pure iron," Mother Mabel states. "How do you expect to wield it?" When the girl-woman does not respond, Mother Mabel inclines her head. "As I suspected. Move along." A not-so-gentle nudge sends the creature out onto the road.

I'm frowning as Mother Mabel whirls toward me. "Brielle." Her waspish tone carries over the crowded lane. "You must be careful with the fair folk. I do not want to see you fall to one of their scams."

My attention shifts to where the girl-woman vanished into the crowd. "That girl—"

"You cannot trust every traveler you meet." Grabbing my upper arm, she steers me through the bustle of the market, dodging carts with expertise. "People will say anything to gain your trust." When we reach a less congested area, she slows, turning to me. "I am only looking out for you. The world is not safe."

A strange sensation passes through me. I do not believe her. Neither do I trust her.

Pulling my arm free, I respond, "I appreciate your concern." The words taste unpleasant. Bitter, even. "Next time I will be more vigilant."

The skin around Mother Mabel's lips tightens. "Very good. We will return soon, so I suggest you begin packing up. Meet me at the gates within the hour. Do not be late."

As she wanders off, I think, *When am I ever?*

The queasy feeling has not abated by the time we reach Thornbrook. I think of that girl-woman, a creature from the depths of Under. It is my belief that Mother Mabel knows of my connection with her and purposefully sent her away. The only question is why.

I head to my room to change for dinner. As I gather clean clothes for my bath, I spot my journal tucked alongside my garments. I haven't written in it since ... Actually, I cannot remember. There was a time when I wrote daily. This journal was my mother, my father, my friend. Unwrapping the twine holding the cover closed, I crack the spine to my latest entry.

I suppose there's not much to say. I've tried to fight this feeling, but I cannot deny my heart. The truth is this: I love him. I do not know what to do.

The entry is dated five months ago.

My heart pounds so forcefully I fear it will crack a rib. This cannot be right. Me, fall in love with a man? I can count on one hand the number of interactions I've shared with men, and they were always in the presence of Mother Mabel. I promised my heart to the Father, yet these words suggest otherwise.

I trace the messy scrawl marking the rough parchment. If this is true, where is the man now? What is his name and what qualities did he possess that would make me rescind my vows? Weeks I have searched for answers, yet here lies a clue. I'm ready to learn what happened, though I wonder how high the cost will be.

Girding myself for what will come, I flip back to the last point in time I remember—early spring—and begin to read.

I do not know where this man has come from. I am not sure of my way forward.

I frown in puzzlement. Sparse information—too sparse. Perhaps I met him during one of our visits to Kilkare? I flip the page.

His eyes are inhumanly green, like light shining through colored glass. There is a darkness beneath the surface I sometimes glimpse. I wonder what pains him.

And the next page.

After visiting Under, I cannot trust the West Wind's intentions. Unfortunately, I do not have a choice. Not if I want to become the next acolyte.

A breeze stirs the leaves beyond my open window. Then there is my heart, twinging with a combination of fear and inexplicable longing. The West Wind. Could this be the man I claimed to love?

Lowering myself onto the edge of my cot, I read ahead, breath held.

I am very ill. I do not know if I will survive the night.

The scrawl betrays a jittery hand. This Brielle was afraid. Desperate. I return to the previous entry. *Not if I want to become the next acolyte.*

As I read the rest of my journal, information begins to patch the holes of this forgotten summer season. If I'm inferring correctly, I was eligible to prove myself as an acolyte. But if Harper earned the honor instead, she must have journeyed into Under with me, whatever quest we'd been granted forcing us into the realm beneath Carterhaugh. If Harper can't remember becoming an acolyte, what really happened in Under all those months ago?

My fingers tremble with rare fury. Slowly, I close my journal and set it on my desk.

This has Mother Mabel's name written all over it. Only she decides what task a novitiate must fulfill to ascend, which means she knows what I do not. As for me? I have been too trusting. I have drifted through time, idle and drowsy, awaiting change. But change comes from within. I cannot expect another to whet my blade. Enough is enough.

Twilight softens the curves of the long arcade as I depart the dormitory and turn right down the cloister. I push inside the abbess' house before courage deserts me.

Candlelight streams beneath her office door. I do not knock. It feels good to barge in and reclaim that power for myself.

Mother Mabel glances up from her desk in shock. "Brielle." She appraises me with a critical eye: the clench of my hands, the steel in my spine, the directness of my gaze. "Did you forget something in town?"

"That's not why I have come, Mother Mabel." I shut the door behind me and cross the room, ignoring the empty seat I would normally occupy to receive council. Today, I stand.

Deliberately, she sets down her quill, straightens in her high-backed chair. Curtains shutter the window at her back, veiling the evening landscape. "I'm listening."

"I want to ask you about that girl in the market, the one you sent away."

Her bland expression doesn't falter. "We have been over this. You cannot trust the fair folk. I am only looking out for you."

"I'm not interested in more of your lies."

She stiffens. "Excuse me?"

It frightens me how quickly the demands surge forth. I am obedient Brielle, agreeable Brielle, soft Brielle, demure Brielle. Mother Mabel fashioned the mold I was poured into, but I do not have to retain this shape.

"Do you deny that you lied to me?" It takes every scrap of valor not to quail before the woman who has filled so many roles in my life. Mentor, mother, teacher, guide. I trusted her implicitly. I thought she could do no wrong.

"You are going to have to be a little more specific," she clips. "After all, I cannot read minds."

Fair enough. "I want to know what happened during the tithe. I know I have visited Under. I—" This, too, must be said. "I had relations with a man and gifted him my virginity." According to my journal, I had no regrets.

Her dark eyes flare, and my fingers twitch toward the dagger at my waist. A beautiful sword hangs on the wall behind her desk. Its blade draws the warmth of candlelight inward until it seems as if the light is absorbed. I've never seen this sword before. I can barely tear my eyes away.

With a strained smile, she nudges her documents aside. "You must understand. Everything I do for you girls, and for Thornbrook, is to ensure there remains a refuge for those who need it. What kind of abbess would I be if I did not do everything in my power to spread His goodness, His kindness, to all?"

I've heard this before. Traps nestled in traps, one of distraction, another of evasion, to imbue my own thoughts with doubt.

"I wish things had gone differently, Brielle. I really do—"

"Enough." My hand cuts the air. "You evade the issue. Do you deny that you lied to me?"

And Mother Mabel says, "I do not."

My heart sinks, stone-like, and I retreat a step. The Abbess of Thornbrook preaches morality, truth, but she has not lived that life herself. Can I trust no maternal figures in my life?

"I want to know what happened during the summer months," I say. "I deserve that much."

She considers me for a long moment. I'm afraid she will deny me. It is well within her rights. "Very well." Her hands come to rest atop the desk, fingers interlaced. "To put it simply, you entered Under without my permission. Obedience—the first of your broken vows."

I fight the urge—the necessity—to fold forward, bowing my spine beneath her disapproval. The force of Mother Mabel's gaze is strong, but I will not bend. "According to my journal entries, I was selected to vie for the position of acolyte, and I'm assuming your quest sent me into Under. How could I break my vows if I entered under your instruction?"

"That was not the first time you entered Under, Brielle."

I go quiet. *Under.* It is a memory I can neither see nor hear nor taste, its identity obstructed behind the veil of forgetfulness.

"You were tempted by Under. I could see it in your eyes. You nearly died during the tithe. You would have, under different circumstances."

Then it is true I was present during the tithe, though I do not remember. "How?"

"A sword." The words tremble. "You were very lucky. It could have been so much worse."

My attention shifts to the blade hanging from the wall, its ruby-inlaid pommel. "Who cut me down?" I was not aware that I had enemies.

A slow hiss seethes from between Mother Mabel's thinned lips. It is another moment before she speaks. "The task I gave you and Harper was a difficult one. I asked you to seek out the fabled sword called Meirlach, which I then used to kill Pierus, the Orchid King."

Light and shade take shape around that name—Orchid King. A ghost in my mind's eye.

"Is that it?" I point to the sword. "Meirlach?"

"Yes. I was dueling the West Wind when you intervened. I did not see you, and by the time I realized what had happened, it was too late." Her dark eyes meet mine. "I did," she whispers. "I cut you down."

She admits to maiming me, yet I feel nothing. No betrayal, no heartache. I touch the scar resting directly over my heart. "I should be dead."

"As I said before, we nearly lost you."

Mother Mabel continues to withhold information as she has always done, but for now, I let it pass. I've other matters to discuss. "Who is the West Wind?"

Again, I've caught her off guard. Shifting in her chair, she peers out the window, only to find the heavy drapes masking her view. Her fingers drum against the desk. "A man I believe you loved," she says, turning back to face me. "Though it hardly matters. He is gone."

Gone as in dead? My palm presses against my chest where the ache spreads. "What of Harper?" Because if she struggles to place her memories, were they, too, taken? "She was assigned the quest as well, but doesn't remember."

Her mouth twitches in suppressed distaste. "Harper must focus on her duties as a newly appointed acolyte. I thought it better that she not be weighed down by her past transgressions. Those who participate in the tithe remember nothing from that night, as you are aware. I do not wish my charges to recall the horrors I myself witnessed for seven long years. But Maria managed to acquire a special tonic that *cleanses the mind*, as she says. Harper was equally tangled in the West Wind's web. In removing both your memories, I had hoped to give each of you a fresh start."

"You had no right," I snap.

"I am sorry, Brielle. I truly am." She smooths her palms down the front of her gold stole. One end bears a long line of stitching, as though from a recent tear. "Your experiences changed you, and I would not see you return to that confused, conflicted woman."

"What do you mean?"

"You turned your back on the Father."

The blow lands exactly as she intended it to. But I do not flinch.

Mother Mabel is wrong. I did not turn my back on the Father. It was she who turned her back on me.

In a cool, detached manner, she goes on, "You claim to have had relations with a man, but purity, both of mind and body, is required to become an acolyte. I cannot in good conscience allow you to ascend."

Then that door is officially shut.

I expected grief, its sundering wave, but my feet remain on solid ground. She has barred me from the opportunity of taking my final vows, but the truth is I no longer desire to give myself fully to the Father. Pieces of me, and of my life, yes, but a world awaits me beyond Thornbrook's walls, and I can't wait to explore it.

"I understand," I reply calmly. "For what it's worth, I believe you're doing what you feel is right, even if it is misguided. I regret to inform you that I will not be joining you for evening Mass."

She pauses with her hand on the Text. Even before she speaks, I sense her disapproval, like a whiff of rot sweeping into the room. "I do not follow. Are you feeling poorly?"

"No, Mother Mabel." It is easy to feel small in her presence, this woman who sits nearest to our god, but I do not cave beneath her will as I once did. "I must pack, for I am leaving Thornbrook."

She opens her mouth, closes it after a moment of indecision. "Is there a reason why you feel the need to leave us? Is your connection to the Father not what it once was?" She does not give me the opportunity to defend myself. "Even though you are no longer a Daughter of Thornbrook, I understand this is your home. I will make an exception and allow you to remain at the abbey, should you continue your duty as the bladesmith."

Someone needs to continue forging blades, is that it? Mother Mabel has lied to me, but that is neither the whole of it, nor the root. "Truth be told, I feel I have outgrown the abbey."

Her hand curls atop the tome. "In what way?"

I have wounded her pride, as I knew I would. "Mother Mabel—"

"Have I done something to offend you, Brielle?"

The unease I've tried to stymie revives at full force. I knew informing the abbess of my decision would not be easy, but I underestimated how powerful an influence she has been in my life. A small part of me still craves her approval.

"No, Mother Mabel. I've only realized that my views of the faith no longer align with those of Thornbrook."

Her eyebrows snap together over her hawkish nose. "I see." She takes me in, seeking out any crack or fault or doubt. "When did you decide this?"

I do not make this decision lightly. Since my recovery, I have questioned my place at Thornbrook. I've asked myself those trying questions. Who am I? What, above all else, do I want? Learning of the abbess' betrayal solidifies this choice.

"When I decided does not matter," I say. "My mind will not change."

"What will you do out there? Where will you go?" Tension pulls her voice taut, and the skin around her mouth whitens. "The world is not kind to women."

Does she think so little of me and my accomplishments? "It will take time to get my bearings," I say, the words edged, "but I'm not without a plan."

The journey to Kilkare will take the day. I'll then contact my old swordsmithing mentor. I've no doubt he will hire me. After a year or two, hopefully my wages will enable me to open my own shop.

"Do you hear yourself?" she argues. "You have no money, no means to build a life. Once you leave Thornbrook, I will no longer be able to protect you."

I lift my chin. "Is it my protection you care for, or control?"

Her nostrils flare. Her spine straightens. It is answer enough.

Blowing out a breath, I unclench my fists at my side. Perhaps that was unfair. I believe Mother Mabel cares for her charges. I was given a home and a purpose when I had none. "You do not need to worry about me."

"Brielle—"

"Thank you," I say, "for putting a sword into my hand. That is something I will never be able to repay you for."

"You can repay me," she grinds out, "by remaining here, where I can keep you safe."

Keep me safe. Keep me small. There is no difference in my eyes.

"I am going out into the world, Mother Mabel," I state, heading for the door. "It's past time that my life begins."

43

"You're sure of this?" Harper asks, watching as I store the last of my belongings.

It's not much. A handful of clothes and two pairs of shoes—slippers for service, boots for work. My journal, my most beloved possession, every word of heartbreak, self-consciousness, fear. The small woven basket containing my mother's poultices. Lastly, the Text, its pages worn thin. There is still much I can learn from its teachings.

"I am sure." My pack, which sits at the foot of my cot, is only half full. The sight saddens me. Ten years I've lived here, yet there is so little that is truly mine.

"Aren't you afraid?"

I turn to Harper. Arms crossed, she perches on the windowsill, the green wellspring of Carterhaugh framed at her back. I have misunderstood her. I recognize that now.

"Yes, I'm afraid." The thought of stepping beyond Thornbrook's gates, never to return, kicks my pulse into a mad dash. "But the fear reminds me I still have miles to go on this journey."

"To Kilkare?"

My mouth quirks, and I rest a palm over my sternum. "In here." Perhaps this journey will help me come to terms with my abandonment. The pain of losing my mother might always linger, but that doesn't mean I cannot grow from it. It doesn't mean I am in any way at fault.

Harper frowns dubiously—an expression I know well. "I always knew there was something strange about you."

I bite back a smile. It wouldn't be a proper farewell without Harper's uninvited snark.

"I'll write you," I say, securing my bag once the Text is nestled safely inside. "And you're always welcome to stay with me once I find permanent housing."

She hesitates, then seems to come to a decision. "It will not be the same with you gone."

"Harper," I tease, seeking to lighten the mood. "Are you implying you'll miss me?"

The woman sniffs. "I am saying no such thing."

Through the open window, I catch sight of Mother Mabel crossing the outer grounds toward the church. With her hands tucked into the voluminous sleeves of her robe, she glides ghostlike across the grass. Harper, who notices where my attention has gone, asks, "What does Mother Mabel think of your departure?"

My heart has not healed from her betrayal. It rests in pieces, the shards grinding painfully between breaths. It hurts. All those lies. All those dreams that never came true.

I've considered telling Harper the truth about Mother Mabel, but despite the abbess' questionable behavior, she dearly loves Thornbrook. She cares for her charges. She sacrifices for our faith. She bleeds. Thornbrook needs Mother Mabel the way a plant needs sunlight.

"She is disappointed," I admit. "She had high hopes for me."

Wide blue eyes search mine. "Did you break your vows?"

Did I? Or was I merely following my heart?

Sorrow weighs upon my back, but I clear my throat, take a steadying breath. I haven't even walked out the door and I already want to dive beneath my blanket, curl into a ball, and await the next sunrise. The Harper I know now is not the Harper I knew then. Whatever I confess will not pass beyond these walls. "I did."

She nods, her expression solemn. I would like to think I see understanding there.

Grabbing my pack, I swing it over my shoulder and face Harper. Somehow, despite living as enemies for a decade, we are parting as friends. "I suppose this is goodbye."

We stare at each other awkwardly, Harper in her white alb and diaconal red stole, me in my plain gray dress. It feels odd without the cincture at my waist, but I will grow used to it, in time.

I'm not sure who moves first, but we embrace. She feels small in my arms. Not weak. Never weak.

"Take care of yourself," she whispers.

I remember Harper's first words to me: *Move, cow.* But it is our last exchange I intend to carry with me.

As I reach the threshold, Harper asks, "Don't you want your lantern?"

Against my better judgment, I glance at the lantern hanging in my window. The sight unnerves me. I've lit it nightly these past weeks, unable to temper the urge. I do not know why.

"Keep it," I say, and quickly depart.

After stopping by the kitchen for bread and cheese, I head for the herbarium. A few apples, a handful of carrots, and I'll be on my way. As I yank carrots from the soil, however, the back of my neck prickles. My hand, wrapped around the tufted greens, twitches for my dagger.

I'm up, spinning toward the shed, when I spot a figure hopping over the wall, vanishing from view.

Abandoning my pack, I dash through the raised beds and crash through the side gate leading to the outer grounds. Long, desperate strides carry me to the gatehouse. The porter opens the gate, and I dive through, catching sight of a man's emerald cloak before Carterhaugh swallows his retreating form.

He will not escape me this time.

Dirt and pebbles fling from my bootheels as I navigate the winding trail downhill, racing over treacherous roots and moistened ground. He is a phantom, a flicker of light and shade. His long-legged stride sends him vaulting through the bottlebrush ferns.

"Wait!" Another leap over a fallen tree. I must see his face. I must learn his name. I must ask him why.

Yet he is simply too fast. Feet like quicksilver, a gait buoyed by the wind itself. My leaden legs pound the earth, and my chest burns, and still the distance between us grows.

But I do not stop running. Carterhaugh splits open before me, its canopy punched through by sunlight splashing the moss-eaten ground. I burst into a small clearing, chest heaving, sweat fusing the fabric of my dress to my skin. And there the man stands, aglow in dew and sun, hands in his trouser pockets as he watches me stumble, then slow.

My tired heart begins to thunder with renewed energy. Beneath his knee-length cloak, the stranger wears a gray tunic and simple brown trousers. He is the loveliest man I have ever laid eyes on. An impossible beauty, warm as flushed spring.

His eyes are green.

I'm staring. It's rude, I know, but I can't help myself. I remember my journal entries. I remember the sleepless nights, a gaze like cut gemstones flashing behind my eyes.

Today, I am bold.

"You've been following me," I say, chin lifted. "Why?"

Something passes behind his expression, vanishing between one breath and the next. "Do you know who I am?" he asks. The man's voice possesses a timbre I was not expecting. Its smooth, melodious resonance reminds me of birdsong. "No." I step closer, afraid he'll bolt like a buck through the brush. "Should I?"

His throat dips. Sadness, or guilt? "I suppose not."

There's something about him. I can't put my finger on it. Is it possible I recognize him from the market? Kilkare is Carterhaugh's largest town, and many travel from their small settlements to acquire goods.

"Have we met before?" I blurt.

He studies me for an uncomfortably long moment. I may as well stand naked before him, cloth and skin stripped away, unable to withstand the intensity of his scrutiny. "You remind me of a woman I once knew."

My stomach sinks. Then he isn't the green-eyed man from my journal. The foolishness I feel is nearly as acute as the disappointment, but I am intrigued by him regardless. "What was she like?" Another step nearer. It's not my business. He is a stranger and I am a woman alone in the woods.

That pretty mouth quirks, and his eyes momentarily catch the light. "Marvelous."

"How so?"

The man rocks back on his heels. His curling hair shifts with the motion. "Where to begin? She taught me about forgiveness. She taught me to listen when I would rather speak. She understood, perhaps better than anyone, that life is a journey. But mostly, she taught me to open my heart and embrace a depth of love I had not experienced in centuries."

I blink at the unexpected statement. "Centuries?" A bit of laughter slips out. "Surely you mean years. Unless you are somehow immortal?"

For whatever reason, he appears ridiculously pleased by my question. Then his face alters, and all those bright points dim. "You share the same laugh."

The man's voice is nice, I decide. Not too rough or deep. "Is that why you're following me?" I whisper. "Because I remind you of this woman?"

"I apologize if I frightened you. It was not my intention."

"You didn't frighten me." That he would think so saddens me for reasons I cannot name.

His gaze falls to my empty hands, and he says, "I noticed you carried a pack before. Are you traveling?"

"Moving, actually."

He blinks in puzzlement. "I do not understand. The abbey is moving elsewhere?"

"Not the abbey. Me. *I* am leaving Thornbrook."

Beneath the dappled light, the man shifts nearer, partial shade muddying his eyes. "Do you turn from your faith?"

The notion seizes me like a physical ailment. "No." The Father is a permanent fixture in my life. Always will be. But faith is not a mold

I must pour myself into. It takes the shape of one's heart. "I'm interested in exploring what faith looks like beyond the walls of an abbey." Mother Mabel claims I'm making a small-minded mistake. It turns out she knows little of me and my capabilities.

"Are you frightened?"

Odd, that this stranger would ask me a question so personal, but I respond to him the same way I replied to Harper. "Very much so."

His expression softens. "It takes courage to walk a new path. Should you continue on this road, I think you will find yourself in a better place."

His confidence grounds me, oddly enough. I offer him a small smile as silence takes root. I'm not sure what to say. I cannot explain this pull to shift nearer to him.

"Well then," says the man. "I don't want to keep you." Our eyes lock and hold.

My pulse spikes, for I do not want to leave. I know him. I must. For what other reason would I feel this compulsion to remain in his presence? But the truth is I know nothing about him. We are just two people crossing paths, our journeys having briefly converged.

"Right." I force myself to retreat a step, nearer to the clearing's edge, though it pains me to do so. "Good luck to you."

He swallows, appearing as if he might speak, yet eventually nods in farewell. I feel nauseated turning my back on him, but I must return to Thornbrook for my supplies.

"Brielle."

I pause mid-turn. The man stares at me with tears in his eyes, and an answering lump wells in my throat. I do not understand this sadness, this profound grief. "How do you know my name?"

"It doesn't matter." The words are choked, frail things. "Here." Reaching into his pocket, he pulls out a crystal sphere, a perfectly encapsulated dawn. "For those dark nights when you need it."

As though caught in a trance, I take the orb in hand.

I know this object. I know its contrasting sensations—cool glass, warm heartbeat—and how the curve perfectly fits the well of my palm.

THE WEST WIND • 443

I know its unspoiled rosy kiss. I know the chime it makes upon hitting rock, like a nail flicked against a windowpane. I know its reassuring weight in my pocket. And I know that, until this moment, I did not realize I had missed its presence.

My eyes lift to the man standing before me. He is beautiful. The curve of his cheek splays into the sharp, stubbled jaw, then dips to the darker skin of his neck where the sun has baked it. That crinkling gaze and laughing mouth.

"Zephyrus," I whisper, for it could be no one else.

Tears pour unhindered down his face. "You remember."

How could I not? For there is our first encounter in Carterhaugh, the West Wind unconscious. His unwanted presence in my bedroom. My visit to Willow. Our kiss in the glen. With every unearthed recollection, heat gathers to a point inside me, and climbs up my throat, and collects behind my eyes. I let it come. There is relief in surrender, relief in knowing that I was not mad, that I have found him. Bringer of Spring.

"I missed you," Zephyrus whispers.

I fall to my knees.

I'm crying so hard it cuts my breath. My hands lift, shielding my face. Things had gone so horribly wrong. The tithe. How could I have forgotten? That final battle. The Orchid King's death. And fabled Meirlach, puncturing my chest like a bright, silver star.

The heel of my palm digs into my chest. Fresh anguish courses through me. It is both now and then, here and there. I am a body strewn across the ground. I am a woman bent double, on her knees. I am drenched in blood, and still.

Kneeling at my side, Zephyrus envelops me in his embrace. Even after all this time, he still smells of damp earth, sprigs of clover, honeysuckle. My tears are boundless. For long moments, we do not speak.

"How?" I whisper. "How is this possible? How are you here, alive? My soul rose from my body, and I s-saw the bargain. Your life in exchange for mine."

"But the bargain *was* satisfied," Zephyrus explains. "The tithe stripped me of my immortality. I am a god no longer."

Shock hits, bleeding into a well of deep sadness. He could have been free. Now he is mortal, and powerless. "Tell me that's not true."

Quietly, he says, "I cannot."

"Zephyrus—"

"Why, Brielle?" he murmurs. "Why would you sacrifice yourself for me?"

As if he doesn't know.

"I didn't have a choice." A sharp cry cracks against my teeth, and I choke, hot tears blurring his form.

"You did have a choice! The sword was meant for me."

"No!" I weep harder, folding into deeper blackness. "She would have killed you." By the Father, I never want to experience that helplessness again.

"Brielle." Leaning back, Zephyrus captures my hands, brings them to his tear-dampened mouth. "When I saw you step in front of that sword—" He breaks off, and the rough, tearing sounds of his grief shatter something in me.

"I would do it all over again," I say. "I have no regrets." Bringer of Spring, who so loved his winds. I squeeze his fingers tighter. "I know what power means to you."

He appears slightly bemused. I realize I've only known Zephyrus as he was: a captive. But here kneels a free man, and I have never seen his shoulders so unburdened. "And what does it mean to me, darling?" he asks.

A warm breeze lifts the fine hairs falling around my face and coaxes Carterhaugh from its doze. Control, freedom—he'd clung to both for all he was worth. "It means everything."

"Brielle." Gentle is my name in his mouth. "I was an incredibly powerful immortal. I was a *god*. And I was alone."

Fresh emotion rises as a knot in my throat. His wound is my wound, and if I could relieve him of it, I would. I understand, I *do*, but—"Better alone than dead."

"I confess I do not share the sentiment."

My mouth parts, and I stare at him, wide-eyed.

"When I saw you step in front of that sword," Zephyrus says lowly, "my heart stopped. And I knew then what I had denied for weeks: that my search for freedom had become secondary to the search for home, and that home was you."

It is the most profound relief to know our hearts are aligned. I haven't the words to combat his claim, for he, too, is my home. "Why do you say the nicest things?" I wail. "It's not right."

I have never heard anything more devastating than his laughter, its warmth and adoration weakening my knees. "Would you prefer I lie?"

"Are you certain this is what you want?" I hiccup. "Your power—"

His mouth brushes mine, effectively silencing my protests. "Power means nothing to me. You, the woman I love with my whole heart, mean everything."

Fresh tears stream down my face. "But—" He would not lie to me. This I know. "You're sure?"

"I have never been more certain." He cups my face, the pads of his thumbs catching the salted droplets. "I was alone in this world, and faithless, but you, with your stubborn belief and maddening conviction, drew light into my gray existence. The strength of your heart, the resilience of your spirit . . . My darling Brielle, I have never met another like you."

I had not realized that Zephyrus saw me as strong. Nor had I realized how badly I wanted him to view me in such a manner. How can I stand against a man who makes me weak in the knees? How can I fight the pull of my heart? I cannot.

"Zephyrus," I whisper. "I love you, too."

I'm not certain who moves first. My arms twine around his neck. His band across my lower back, hauling me against him. His mouth, and mine. The deep, overwhelming kiss of the reunited. Our tongues flirt, and he draws mine past his teeth, licking deep. A groan rushes down my throat, rough with hunger.

In the end, I break away first, lifting a hand to his sun-warmed cheek. All my life, I have wondered what was missing. This, here, now.

My heart is a bird, and look how readily it spreads its wings. "I choose you, Zephyrus of the West. I choose you every day."

He presses his forehead to mine. "And I choose you, Brielle of Thornbrook, for as long as there is breath in my lungs."

Carterhaugh is bright on this day. The West Wind is just a man, a wonderful, mortal man with a lifespan equal to mine. We have today, and tomorrow, and the next day, and the next.

Imagine all that we will see.

EPILOGUE

In which the West Wind
Attempts to Plan a Proposal

ZEPHYRUS HAD IT ALL PLANNED: THE WHITE DAISIES, THE raspberry tarts, the sunlit river, the vows. With each piece of the puzzle artfully arranged, the plan would unfold without a hitch. After all, asking the woman he loved for her hand in marriage was no small thing.

As Zephyrus pondered how the day would progress, he departed the small cottage he shared with Brielle and began his walk into town. He had dressed in his tailored trousers, green cloak tossed over a fresh white tunic—unfortunately, with his powers stripped and the new weight of his mortal skin, he was sweating by the time he reached Kilkare's town square. Shortly after sunrise, and the line to the florist already extended out the door.

He waited impatiently to make his order. When he reached the counter, he asked Lionel to set aside a bouquet of daisies, which he would collect at the end of the day.

The gruff man nodded, jotting down the order on a piece of parchment. "Been busy, but it shouldn't be a problem."

That gave Zephyrus pause.

"The flowers are for a special occasion," he explained. "If you can't guarantee supply at the end of the day, I'll take them now." Better to carry the bouquet than not obtain it at all.

"It won't be an issue," Lionel assured him. "If it were roses, on the other hand . . ." A graceless shrug. "I'll set them aside for later. You can pay upon collection."

Zephyrus managed to exit the shop with dignity, instead of tripping across the threshold. His legs shook from the rising pressure of this day, the need for its impossible perfection.

His next stop was the weaver. After dodging rickety carts and unleashed dogs wandering the main thoroughfare, he arrived at the storefront, only to find it locked, the windows secured. A piece of parchment had been nailed to the front door.

Out of town. Will return next week.

He stared at the dark, looping scrawl. "Shit."

No blanket, then. It wasn't the worst misfortune, but he hadn't anticipated the setback. Nervously, he referred to his list. There was still much to be done. He would spend the day traveling from shop to cart to stall to acquire the necessary supplies.

Candles, next. The merchant, however, was sold out.

He had managed to procure a bottle of fine wine, yet it had shattered when a stray dog barreled into him in the town square.

Fine. That was fine. Next on the list: a new leather journal. Brielle, however, was picky. She favored brown leather, and the salesman only had black leather in stock. He left the shop empty-handed.

With the majority of the day gone, Zephyrus headed back to the florist to pick up his order. Along the way, he passed the church, its curved, oaken doors open to reveal a pew-lined interior, vast windows of stained glass.

Moving to Kilkare had been a difficult transition for Brielle. The first few months, she had cried nearly every night. She collected journals as though they were coin, filling the pages with her innermost musings, the struggles of redefining her faith. Zephyrus felt helpless in those moments, but he stayed by her side, offering what comfort he could, because how could he not? They belonged together.

Eventually, they'd settled in to village life, attending service every Holy Day. Word had spread of her arrival—this bladesmith with a talent for daggers, knives—and after six months of working for her old mentor, Brielle was able to open her own shop. The gray cloud of sadness dissipated. Even Harper visited on occasion.

Though Brielle's relationship with the abbess might never be as it once was, the woman had gone to great lengths to ensure that the abbey would outlive the Orchid King. Since his death, the fair folk had collectively gifted Thornbrook's land to the abbey, to begin mending the relationship between peoples and realms. Zephyrus, who often acted as a mediator between Under and Thornbrook, had enjoyed witnessing Under's recovery, its well of power gradually restored now that there was no one left to consume it. The tithe was thus made redundant.

By the time he reached the florist, the day was fast waning. He strode up to the counter without delay.

"I'm here to pick up the daisies I ordered this morning, Lionel."

"Good day to you, Zephyrus." The man cleared his throat. "The daisies ... yes." Looking over his shoulder, he cast his eyes over his meager stock. "Unfortunately, it seems they've been sold."

That word—*sold*—struck his skin like a sharp stone. "You can't be serious." Empty hands and unfulfilled promises. Is that all he was good for? "You said you'd set a bouquet aside," he whispered, voice dropping to a hiss. "You assured me."

The florist's mouth pulled with strain. "I apologize. Business was unusually demanding, and there was no guarantee you would return."

"I told you I would." And anyway, he was a routine customer. He and Brielle bought flowers from Lionel every few weeks.

"They are sold, as I said. Perhaps you should try again next week?"

Zephyrus gritted his teeth. "The proposal is *today*," he growled, then turned on his heel and shoved out the door, blinking rapidly in the afternoon sun.

Panic thrummed at his temples. He could fix this. He could fashion flowers out of snow, ferns out of rain. Or he used to be able to, rather. With his powers gone, he was just a man. *Mundane.*

He stood by his decision. He would choose this life with Brielle ten times over, but there existed a hollow where his power had once resided.

With a sigh, he scrubbed his hands down his face, needing a moment to gather the scattered fragments of his plan. No blanket, no flowers. Fine. That left the tarts. Hopefully they weren't sold out.

As luck would have it, they weren't. One dozen raspberry tarts—Brielle's favorite dessert. They lined a small box, flaky dough resting beneath cool white icing. The day was looking up.

Brielle's workshop perched along the curve of the broad River Twee. It was a solitary, one-roomed structure, thick black smoke erupting from the brick chimney. Zephyrus had hoped to draw her down to the river, but really, the proposal should take place within these four walls, for it represented the forging of two lives.

The back door lay open, a hot, ghastly mouth ringed in fiery teeth. The peal of a hammer impacting metal rang through the forge.

Inside, the darkness belched flame. From his position near the doorway, he watched Brielle work. She'd tied back her red hair, though a few curls had escaped. A sheen of sweat coated her bare arms, the prominent muscles bulging beneath the straps of her thick canvas apron.

He waited until she lowered the hammer before stepping inside. Heat immediately engulfed him, drawing sweat to his skin. "Hungry?"

Brielle whirled around, beaming. "Hello, my love."

The endearment never failed to make his heart stumble. Soil-dark eyes, rounded cheeks, those scarlet tresses, the bow of her soft pink mouth. He had never met someone more beautiful, either in body or in soul.

"What?" She touched the side of her soot-stained neck self-consciously. "Why are you looking at me like that?"

Sensing her desire to retreat, Zephyrus pressed a hand to the curve of her spine, sliding it low until he cupped her rear in his palm.

Her eyes popped wide. "Zephyrus!" She swatted at him, and he laughed. "That's inappropriate."

Gods, he adored her. "Is it?" A gentle squeeze to her backside, and she flushed.

The distance between them was officially too much. Dragging her close, he crushed his mouth against hers and slid his tongue inside. Fire and salt—the taste of his bladesmith.

Brielle pulled away first. "You look nice," she said, plucking the collar of his tunic. "What's the occasion?"

"You."

Her mouth parted, and she swallowed, red-faced and sniffling. "You always say the nicest things."

His nerves tangled tighter with each successive heartbeat. "That's because they're true." No flowers, no candles, no wine, but—

"Here," he said, and thrust the box of pastries at Brielle. It was perhaps the least refined thing he had done in his life—ever.

She glanced down, a groove notched between her eyebrows. "Um . . ."

His attention dropped to the container clasped between his sweaty hands. The chilled desserts sat wilting in the intolerable heat, pools of white icing having collected in unappealing lumps.

"I guess I didn't realize they needed to remain cool," he said woodenly, staring at the sad, soggy mess.

It was going to shit. It was all going to absolute shit.

"I'm sure they taste delicious," she reassured, plucking a melted tart from the box and popping it between her teeth. Icing dripped down her fingers, which she licked clean. "It's very good!"

With a heavy sigh, Zephyrus set the pastries onto the worktable. "Never mind those." He lifted a shaky hand to his damp curls.

"Are you ill?" Brielle reached for him. "You're sweating quite profusely."

Indeed, his tunic stuck to his clammy back, and his underarms stung with pooling sweat.

Damn it all. He was going to faint.

452 • ALEXANDRIA WARWICK

Brielle's eyes widened, and she lunged, catching him by the arm before his knees buckled. "Here. Sit." She directed him toward a chair. "Was it something you ate? Should I fetch a healer?"

"I'm all right," he managed to say. Though if he vomited whilst professing his love, he would never forgive himself. "I need to tell you something."

The lines on her face deepened. "It sounds serious."

"It is."

Brielle pulled up a chair across from him and sat, her concern plain. "Then we will discuss." She spoke simply. They were, in all ways, a team.

Rubbing his sweaty palms on his trousers, Zephyrus groped for clarity of mind. Why was it suddenly so difficult to grasp? His head felt waterlogged.

"I love you." The rush of emotion broke the words into unintelligible noise. He felt green as an untried soldier, ungainly, graceless. "I wanted—I need—to tell you that. I love you. Only you." By the gods, he was sweating like a pig. "I love this life we've built. I love our home. I love going to service with you and . . . and our home." He'd already said that, hadn't he? "And when I say *home*, I don't mean the cottage itself—though I love that too, of course. I just mean you."

In those early months, Zephyrus had questioned his worth, for paired with the certainty of knowing you were loved was always the possibility that you were not. But after a year and a day, he felt secure in their relationship. He had given Brielle his heart, and she had sheltered it ever since.

A smile softened her features. "And I love you." Framing his face with her sooty hands, she pressed her lips to his, gently. Zephyrus blanked, and his mind frayed. Grasping the back of her neck, he slanted his mouth against hers, rough with hunger. By the time they broke apart, strands of Brielle's hair had escaped her braid, and her porcelain skin had pinkened to the color of sunrise.

It must be here, and it must be now. "Brielle—"

"Will you marry me?"

This boiling heat was melting his mind. He hadn't spoken those words aloud yet, had he?

He cleared his throat. "Would you mind repeating that?"

Her teeth sank into her lower lip. "Will you marry me, Zephyrus, and continue to build a life with me?"

He blinked, shook his head, dazed. But it could not be stopped. Hoarse laughter hollowed out his chest, wrung every drop of apprehension from his body until he slumped back into the chair. Brielle's mouth quirked. Oh, she knew, had likely known the whole time. Fiendish woman.

"How?" he said. "How did you know I was going to ask you?"

"You've been acting rather secretive of late." She tapped a finger against the battered worktable, clearly fighting a smile. "And you may have accidentally revealed your intentions last week while you slept. You muttered something about *the grandest proposal of all time*." At last, her smile broke free.

He groaned into his hands good-naturedly. Sleep-talking. He'd sabotaged himself without even being aware of it.

"Well?" Brielle asked tentatively.

"Well, what?"

Her eyes flicked to his with a shyness he had grown to appreciate. "You didn't answer the question."

As if there was ever a doubt.

"Yes, Brielle. I'll marry you, and love you, and do everything in my power to bring you happiness for the rest of our lives." Pushing to his feet, Zephyrus enfolded her into his embrace—the woman who had stolen his corrupted heart, who he wanted nothing more than to grow old with, day after passing day, until they were bones in the earth. "That's a promise I intend to keep."

ACKNOWLEDGMENTS

This book was a finicky beast, but I would expect nothing less for Zephyrus' story. I want to thank those who helped pave the way for the final product, because I couldn't have done it alone.

A huge and gratifying thank you to Anthea, Charlotte, and Lizzie for your incredible editorial guidance in helping shape this story into the brightest emerald. I am so thrilled to work with such wonderful editors who see the vision of this story and help me polish it into what it is today.

To the brilliant minds behind publicity and marketing at Simon & Schuster UK and Simon & Schuster Australia: you are amazing in so many ways, and I appreciate all your work! A big shout-out to Laurie, Sarah, and Kelly. To Amy and Ben, thank you for bringing the book and series to territories and languages throughout the world. To the production team, especially Kiara, and everyone who has helped place the Four Winds series on the map—my deepest thanks.

My sincerest gratitude to the entire Saga Press team for all their work in bringing this story to North America. Thank you to Jéla, Karintha, Shauneice, and Savannah for your incredible efforts!

Thank you to Lisa and Kaycee for beta reading early drafts and offering some fantastic feedback. And to Kourtney, the first of my editors! Your insight was so valuable in helping me shape this story. I appreciate every suggestion, whether big or small. Love to my family for their support.

For the most beautiful cover, thank you so much to K.D. Ritchie. I think I may even love this one more than *The North Wind*!

As always, to Jon. Thank you for allowing me to live a true fairytale romance. I am so grateful I get to write stories every day, but even more grateful that I get to share my wins with you. I love you.

Lastly, to my readers. I cannot express the depth of my appreciation that you have championed the Four Winds series. It is because of you I get to live my dream every day. From the bottom of my heart, thank you for being on this journey with me.

ABOUT THE AUTHOR

Alexandria Warwick is the author of the Four Winds series and the North series. A classically trained violinist, she spends much of her time performing in orchestras. She lives in Florida.

For Wren and Boreas' story, read *The North Wind*,
book one in the Four Winds series.

Available now.